PIECES OF EIGHT

BOOK TWO OF THE GUARDIAN OF EMPIRE CITY SERIES

PETER HARTOG

To Universicon 1989, and the beginning of many glorious adventures

1

I stared down the barrel of a shotgun held in the grubby paws of a very smelly, and extremely ugly, Thing.

Covered in short, matted fur from oblong head to clawed toe, the creature stood half my nearly six-foot height. Oh, and there were three of them. Each glowered at me with orange eyes which were slitted like a cat's, except inverted.

To be fair, "Thing" really was the best I could come up with on short notice, given I'd only been with the Empire City Special Crimes Unit for four months. Sanctioned by the Mayor's office and tasked with investigating the strange and unusual "by any means necessary", I'd already had close encounters with a pack of bio-engineered vampires, some parasitic inter-dimensional shadow monsters that fed off your soul, and an android masquerading as one of those same vampires. And that was just from my first case.

I was chosen for SCU because I possess an ability I've nicknamed the Insight, something I picked up when I tried to kill myself at rehab eight years ago. It's a magical lens through which my eyes sometimes perceived people, objects and places, revealing whatever veil masked them. But it was also fickle and wouldn't necessarily work even when I needed it. Empathy was a part of it, too. I sensed emotions, hidden plans, even witnessed events that had occurred in the past.

The things I'd seen over the years ran the gamut of brilliant and beautiful to mind-bendingly awful. Yet they all remained with me, indelibly imprinted on my soul. The jury was out as to whether the Insight was worth the price it exacted. Regardless, I'd decided to use the Insight to uphold the law and protect the citizens of Empire City because it was the right thing to do.

I thanked my deceased mother and grandfather for instilling in me a strong, moral fiber.

And my dad for everything else.

Besides, the intense pressure of having my life threatened by this Thing hadn't done much for my clever nomenclature skills. I'd have to figure out a better name later, presuming I survived. And judging by the sharp-toothed scowls on their rat-like faces, they weren't happy to see me, either.

Then again, I'd be unhappy too had I been caught in the middle of a jewelry heist, their sixth such robbery in the span of two months.

"Snergle balugey!" Mr. Shotgun threatened.

There, that was better.

Diamonds lay in a glittering pool at their feet. The fuzzy bastards' escape route bubbled behind me—a dark hole in the wall large enough to accommodate one of them outlined by a clear, viscous goo. I'd collected similar sticky ectoplasmic samples from jewelers in the East Village, Westchester Square, and now Queens.

ECPD's Central Robbery Division had been working the

heists for weeks with no leads until a small patch of the gunk was discovered by one Theodore Nathaniel, a store owner who lived in the adjoining apartment and was awakened by noise coming from his store. In his statement, Mr. Nathaniel had claimed "furry gremlins" had robbed him. That was enough for Robbery to make a call to Captain William "Bill" Mahoney, aka my Boss, and the head of Special Crimes, who then handed the case over to me.

I figured I was dealing with a professional crew. They had somehow entered the store, bypassed or disabled the alarm and security cameras, then exited the premises by means unknown. It didn't take my team long to work out that the mucilaginous shit these creatures excreted allowed them to pass through solid surfaces. The fluid created a null space between the molecules of the air, wood and concrete establishing a "gap" in the fabric of reality. The temporary rift closed quickly, restoring the surface to its original condition, minus the mucus. No fuss, no muss, and no mess to clean up.

It was magic, so I didn't ask too many questions. What mattered now was I stood in their way, which meant shooting me was a good idea.

Thankfully, I also came prepared. Armed with the Superior Military Armament Retaliatory Tool, or SMART gun, the weapon was a mini bazooka that could blow man-sized holes through tanks, depending upon the round in the chamber. Mine was currently trained on Mr. Shotgun. A little red dot glowed at the center of its forehead. However, I wasn't entirely convinced the gun could hurt any of them.

Fortunately, I knew something, or, more to the point, someone, that could.

"Holliday, we ain't got time for this," an irritated voice grated in my ear. "Just shoot the fuckers."

Oh, right, the introductions. Where are my manners? I'm homicide detective Thomas Henry Holliday. What few friends I have call me "Doc," not because I'm a dead shot with a gun, like that Old West gunslinger from those holo-histories you might've watched at school, but because I hold a PhD in English Literature from Empire City University.

The jerk on the other line was Deacon Kole, a former Protector from the Confederate States of Birmingham. They're a bunch of religious fanatical fruitcakes who shot first and never asked questions. Fortunately, Deacon no longer worked for them, but as an independent contractor with Special Crimes, his predilection to kill things indiscriminately hadn't changed much in the four months I'd known him.

I rolled my eyes and said, "It would help if I knew what they were saying."

"They're called 'kobolds,' Doc," a young woman's voice explained through my earpiece. "According to my source, they travel in packs of four. Oh, and they're supposed to understand English."

That's my other partner, Leyla, and one of the best holo-tech hackers I know. She can also wield magic to remarkable and, at times, frightening effect. Deacon had once called her a witch, but I was glad she was on my side all the same.

"Is that right?" I directed my reply at the kobolds. "So, where's the fourth musketeer?"

Their combined glares grew hotter.

I sighed. "This doesn't need to get messy, boys. You're under arrest for breaking and entering, and attempted burglary. Please drop the gun and keep your, um, paws where I can see them."

The kobolds convened, although Mr. Shotgun kept a wary eye on me. From the sound of their exchange, Mr. Shotgun wanted messy over easy, but his cohorts weren't on board.

"You not the One," Mr. Shotgun growled at me. "We want, we take! You go. Shinies ours!"

"Last chance, fellas," I warned.

"GO!"

"Your funeral," I said, stowing the gun slowly. I held up both empty hands in a non-threatening manner and edged toward the front door.

A wintry blast welcomed me as I stepped into the frigid February night. The cold and snow had kept most reasonable folks indoors. You know, the ones that worked reasonable jobs, with reasonable hours and reasonable pay? Thankfully, the good citizens of Empire City had unreasonable me to keep an eye out for shotgun-toting extra-dimensional jewel thieves.

At least, that's what I keep telling myself.

I stood beneath a streetlamp, limned by its pale glow while wispy white flakes swirled around me, and regarded the storefront. Strachman Jeweler's occupied the first floor of a squat, two-story faded brick building. Its neighbors included Manny's Hair Salon and Madame Ruth's Psychic Parlor. The sidewalk had been cleared, although treacherous pockets of black ice were like landmines for the unwary.

My fingers grew numb, and I realized belatedly that I'd left my gloves back in the ECPD pod I had parked a block from here. As I rubbed my hands together for warmth, what looked like a woman's silhouette in Madame Ruth's window drew my attention. I blinked, and the window was empty.

Probably just my sleep-deprived brain playing tricks on me again.

Strachman's interior lights suddenly went dark. Flickering light appeared a moment later, casting chaotic shadows behind the barred and curtained windows. Muffled shouts, crashes and curses erupted from inside. I waited with my arms folded. The steamy ghosts of my breath plumed then disappeared. I scratched one stubbly cheek, wondering how long this was going to take. The noise grew louder as the light flared once, then twice, before darkness and silence reclaimed the store.

"Clear?" I asked, suppressing a yawn.

"Clear," Deacon announced as he sauntered from the store, a ferocious smile on his face. "Showed them fucking rodents who's boss. And don't you worry none about cleanup, Holliday. Ain't nothing left to be worth a damn."

The lean man carried a truncheon in his left hand, reminiscent of the old nightsticks beat cops used to carry back in the day. Cold white fire played along the runic surface of its business end, then winked out, leaving the wood unblemished. The former Protector twirled the truncheon between his fingers before returning it to a leather shoulder rig inside his long coat.

"That's great, but what about the next time?" I groused. "We can't kill every Jumper who breaks the law."

Long before I was born, nukes and the pandemics that followed had devastated Earth. The destructive forces unleashed from that time had weakened the fabric of reality, earning beings from an infinite number of so-called alternate Earths an inadvertent one-way ticket here. They'd "jumped" from their world to ours. As far as I knew, there had never been a portal to appear inside any of the fifty-two worldwide enclaves.

How the kobolds had come to Empire City was anyone's guess, but Leyla had theorized they must've used their translocation ability on the mile-high spell-forged steel perimeter wall surrounding Empire City to infiltrate the enclave. That, or there really was a portal somewhere in the city, and that wasn't something I really wanted to think about.

The nukes had also restored magic, a clean, sustainable energy found in pod-sized sparkling orbs called Nexus nodes. Like most of the world, I had believed our so-called Vellan "friends" were the only civilized inter-dimensional travelers living on Earth. They had taught us how to harness the magic from the nodes in exchange for asylum here. While the average person associated Nexus energy with heating bath water or cooling their ice box, I knew better. Leyla wasn't the only one capable of manipulating magic to do all sorts of crazy shit.

However, since my run-in with the mysterious Orpheus last October, my eyes had been opened to an even deeper, and far more sinister reality.

Your world has changed, doorways have opened, and old things return that have not seen this sun in an age.

My one and only encounter with Orpheus, or M. Fatima, or whatever the fuck she called herself these days, and her psycho-killer hand-bitch of hers Julie DeGrassi had left behind plenty of scars. Despite Leyla's extensive hacker network, and both Deacon's and my own law enforcement contacts, those two remained in the wind, their where-abouts unknown. None of us had found any credible or actionable information on either woman. But I knew I hadn't seen the last of them. I sensed that whatever Game she played with that brother of hers still had plenty of moves left.

I shivered, and not from the cold.

"I don't make the rules, Holliday," Deacon chuckled mirthlessly, breaking me from my troublesome thoughts. "I just finish the job."

"Fair enough," I said. My eyes glazed over. "EVI, please amend the Strachman B&E status to 'resolved.'"

"Affirmative, Detective," the AI's soft response filtered through my brain's audio center. "How can I be of further assistance?"

"That's it for now, sweetie. Thanks."

EVI, or Enhanced Virtual Intellect, organized all of Empire City's law enforcement, social and emergency services, right down to the lunch menu. Every Empire City civil and military employee was chipped, granting us access to the vast cloud of information at EVI's command. The tech nerds gave her a female persona for all the obvious reasons. Thankfully, EVI had survived a brief campaign to mothball her. A major outage had disabled her functionality enclave-wide as part of a diabolical game played by some very nefarious characters, including the former goldjoy kingpin himself, Rumpelstiltskin. I'd put an end to him, and after some significant software and hardware upgrades and protections, EVI was kept in place.

"Jesus, it's cold!" I rubbed my hands together again to restore feeling.

"More snow in the forecast too, Doc," Leyla announced happily in my ear. "Isn't it wonderful?"

"Sure." I stuck my hands in my pant pockets and ambled along the sidewalk. Deacon walked beside me, a lit cigarette in his mouth, its vapor trail rapidly dissolving in his wake. While everything else annoyed him, the cold wasn't one of them.

"Appreciate the assist, Deacon," I said.

The Confederate was athletic and thin, standing a few inches taller than me. Sharp features framed high cheekbones, a thin nose, and grizzled mustache with goatee. A small silver hoop hung from his left ear.

"S'happy to help," he replied easily. "Saranda's been busy, so I had time to kill."

My face clouded at the mention of his employer, Doctor Besim Saranda, the only Vellan with whom I was on a first-name basis, for whatever that's worth. She was also an acclaimed singer, an accomplished biologist, shrewd businesswoman, and SCU's very own consultant, thanks to her close friendship with Captain Mahoney. I hadn't spoken with her since I left her penthouse suite at L'Hotel Internacional last October.

Things hadn't ended well between us.

"She done consulting with pharmaceutical companies?" I asked lightly, dragging my mind from a worn, dark place.

"Fuck yes." Deacon flicked the dead butt to the ground in mild disgust. "She's moved on to other things, none worth mentioning."

We had arrived at our official transport which rested on its Pathway, one of the specially designed spell-forged steel roads that wrapped above and below a large portion of Empire City. The oval-shaped vehicle resembled a centipede segment that had come loose from the swarm. The pod was spacious enough for eight, boasted heavy armor, tactical, a beverage station, and a john. Powered by electro-magnetic propulsion, it could reach a speed of one hundred miles an hour without breaking a sweat.

While both clean-energy and dubious, liquid-powered vehicles continued to roll around on pavement, most mass transit had been converted to accommodate the width and breadth of Empire City. Much of the architecture and layout of old New York City remained, including the names of places that had been around since the eighteenth century. However, Manhattan had grown taller and wider, and that had necessitated both the expansion of the old Metro lines, as well as additional elevated transportation.

Once inside the pod, I hit the beverage station to pour myself a hot mug of liquid brown ambrosia.

"Heya, Doc!" a slim, white-haired girl with dimples waved from one of the two forward cabin command chairs. She wore black leggings, open-toed sandals and a pink t-shirt with a white heart bearing Albert Einstein's face and the caption $E = Me + You^2$ emblazoned on its front.

"Hey yourself," I smiled as I occupied the other seat. The interior was several degrees colder than the outside. "You mind dialing that back?"

"Sorry!" Leyla flushed with embarrassment. Warmth from the pod's heating system flowed in to chase away the chill.

"EVI, please take us to L'Hotel Internacional," I instructed aloud.

The vehicle slid smoothly into motion. While Leyla and Deacon engaged in small-talk, I stared beyond the windshield's reinforced glass at the blaze of chiaroscuro that marked the urban concrete jungle. A half hour later, we dropped Deacon off at the expansive entrance to the massive hotel that resembled a castle, minus the moat. Besim owned the penthouse above, but I had no interest in making a house call.

"Y'all be good." Deacon nodded at us before debarking through the hatchway.

We drove away in silence. I idly reviewed my notes of the kobold bust on the pod's heads-up display while nursing my fourth mug of coffee. Leyla sat quietly next to me, but I felt the crushing weight of her reproachful stare as it centered on me. I ignored her for a solid five minutes before I gave up.

"What?"

"I miss working with them," Leyla sighed. "*Both* of them."

I set my jaw but didn't respond and went back to the kobold report.

"And I know you do, too."

We eventually arrived at a rundown section of Brooklyn's Brighton Beach. Parking the pod at a Metro station festooned with faded graffiti, we exited the transport and took three flights of stairs down to street level.

ECPD municipal services avoided the area known by the locals as "Little Odessa", and it showed. The familiar city block of dingy storefronts and ragged tenements was buried beneath unforgiving ice and dirty snow. No sidewalks had been cleared. Derelict vehicles, no more than white lumps, lay along the otherwise quiet streets as if they'd been tossed like craps dice.

A brisk two block walk brought us to an old bookstore that was flanked by a laundromat and a tattoo parlor. A pale aisle of light spilled out from beneath the black canopy that hung over the entrance.

"You coming?" Leyla asked hopefully. "Abner's got a fresh pot waiting for you."

"Not tonight, kiddo," I replied.

She studied my worn face, concern mirrored in her startlingly blue eyes.

I assumed a reassuring smile and said, "I've got paperwork to finish."

She crossed her arms over her chest, unconvinced.

"I'm fine," I affirmed. "Really. I'll call you later, okay?"

"Sure."

I watched her cross the street until she reached the store's entrance. She turned, gave me a look that screamed "I don't believe you" before entering the store. The light disappeared behind her like a dream.

I studied the darkness, but it held no answers. An empty, hollow ache bled into my heart. I rubbed my hands together and returned to the pod. Once inside, I filled another mug before resuming my seat in the command chair.

Restlessness gnawed at me. Company would've been nice, but I wasn't in the mood. Uncle Mortie's deli wouldn't open for a few more hours, and I didn't relish the prospect of sitting in my one-bedroom bachelor pad in all its spartan glory. Instead, I directed EVI to roam the neighborhood. At some point, I nodded off.

"Incoming call from Captain Mahoney," EVI announced, jerking me awake.

I stared bleary-eyed at the HUD as the image of Bill Mahoney appeared. "Sir? Um, I was just finishing up the Strachman B&E—"

"There's been a homicide," the captain said without preamble. The look in his eyes sent a foreboding shiver down my spine.

So much for rest and the weary guy.

"Copy that, sir." I shuffled to the beverage station to pour a fresh round of brain igniter fluid. "Where to?"

"The Holy Redeemer Church."

The mug fell from my nerveless fingers.

2

The red and blue flare of emergency and law enforcement illuminated the scene as the pod settled to a stop. EVI fed the chatter of the onsite personnel through the internal comm system, but it was background noise to me.

I stared out the window at a massive stone edifice, its tall walls alit with the scurrying shadows from the activity below. The Holy Redeemer Church hunkered along Brighton Beach Avenue within a few blocks of the waterfront. Made of thick wood and solid stone, its origin hearkened back to the late nineteenth century, and held a storied reputation in the surrounding community for its educational, social and religious outreach programs.

I'd grown up several blocks from the church. Despite my mixed religious heritage, the Redeemer had been a safe harbor for me, one of the few places where I'd felt welcome. Back then, my education choices were limited. There were no active synagogues in Brighton Beach, or many other neighborhoods throughout Empire City for that matter. Those had shut down decades ago from rampant anti-semitism and both the half-hearted and futile attempts by local authorities to combat it. Eventually, a lack of funds coupled with disinterest from a dwindling and fearful Jewish population made any brick-and-mortar institution a thing of the past.

But thanks to my grandfather's job as the Redeemer's gardener and custodian, I had attended the church's parochial school. The church was also the home of Father John Davis, a man who had helped shape the paths of hundreds of families over the years, including my own. I'd always known him as Father Jack. To me, he wasn't just a teacher. He was family, something that I'd had in short supply throughout my life.

I shrugged on my blazer and stormed from the hatchway into the brittle morning, making a beeline for the main entrance. Despite the cold and the early hour, several uniformed officers had created a cordon to keep the gawkers and media swarm at bay. EVI registered me with the attendance log, but I flashed my silver SCU badge at one of the officers. The strange, ambient glow it produced shrouded me in an argent nimbus as I passed through the translucent yellow holo-tape ringing the perimeter.

"Captain Mahoney is awaiting you," EVI announced.

She provided me his location as well as a layout of the church, although I didn't need the latter. Heart racing, I crossed the entrance broad steps and through the double doors.

A small command center had been established in the vestibule, but I veered sharply to the right, then moved along a broad pillared aisle past the nave toward a flight of steps leading into the basement. The air down here smelled musty and warm, mingled with the sickly-sweet metallic tang of blood. The sounds of activity above were muted by the dense stone of the church.

Mahoney stood in the hallway conversing with a tall, thin man wearing a heavy winter coat. My heart unclenched at the sight of them.

"Detective," Mahoney said in his gravelly voice. The captain resembled everyone's grandfather everywhere. He was medium height, with close-cropped white hair and deep crow's feet around the eyes. A twin to the badge I carried rode on his breast pocket. I nodded at him, then turned my attention to the other man.

"You okay?" I asked.

Father Jack had a widow's peak at both temples, and salty gray hair. His brown eyes, normally brimming with good-natured humor, were wide and apprehensive.

"No," he replied. "But I am better than poor Gus in there. He—"

"You should go upstairs," I interrupted gently. "I'll be along in a bit."

I wanted to reach out, provide some sign that everything would be all right. But I couldn't. Not in front of the captain. Not while I was on the job.

The old pastor was about to protest, then thought better of it, and excused himself. I watched him go, crushing my roiling emotions in favor of the need to be dispassionate and professional.

"What do we have?" I asked.

"The room's clean," Mahoney began. "Dispatch contacted me after Father Davis made the nine-one-one. The description was, well, you'll see for yourself. I've appropriated it, Tom. I knew you'd want to be here."

Mahoney's voice faded as I moved past him to study the room beyond.

I hadn't noticed the Insight's presence until now. The magic seethed around my eyes, its effect tingeing everything I saw with its silver haze. I'd been told the fickle clairvoyance was a living magic of an ancient order, but I still had no idea where it came from. It also represented a destiny I refused to accept. Because I kept telling myself that I lived in the real world, and not some fairytale where the concepts of good and evil were living, tangible things.

Then I joined SCU, uncovered an ancient magical conspiracy orchestrated by a mysterious woman named Orpheus, and destroyed a shadow parasite with consecrated bullets that had never been consecrated. I tried not to dwell on that, or Besim, the individual who had clued me in on my unwanted destiny in the first place.

Grinding my teeth, I focused on the present. My vision responded to the Insight's magic, sharpening with intensity. Everything around me had slowed to a crawl. Dust motes clung to the air, suspended between time. I saw the current of heated air propelled through the vent high on the far wall opposite me, undulating in rhythmic waves. I knew the thread count on the old sheets of the twin bed just by glancing at them.

The room was simple—bed, footlocker, closet, virtual workstation, chair. One thin window ran horizontally along the upper wall, barred and secured from the outside. Nothing adorned the walls, other than an eggshell coat that had been applied within the past six months.

"Jesus Christ," I swore quietly.

The body slumped in the chair, arms and legs splayed wide. Blood stained the floor, covering the walls, the ceiling, the workstation, behind the open door and the bed. I couldn't get too close without stepping in any of it, although my preternatural senses were already swimming in the stuff.

"Stentstrom's arrived," Mahoney announced, breaking me from my trance.

"Good," I said absently. My eyes shifted from the corpse back to the desk.

The workstation was active. A darkened holo-window floated dormant above it. An open book lay atop the desk, but no holo-picture frames or other personal items.

I needed to get in there.

"Who's our vic?" I asked.

"Gustavo Sanarov," the captain replied. The name meant nothing to me, but something in Mahoney's voice drew my attention. "He was the soup kitchen super for the church. Father Davis said he'd only been staying with them until he could get back on his feet."

I nodded, and as I did so, the Insight evacuated from me in a rush. I staggered against the doorframe. Bill stepped forward, but I waved him away. He watched me with wintry eyes. I was about to ask him a question when a sing-song voice greeted me.

"Ah, Detective Holliday!" gushed Doctor Gilbert Stentstrom, chief medical examiner for Empire City.

The skinny little man was covered head to foot in a bulky white overcoat, gloves and matching *ushanka* with the earflaps down. He carried a steel briefcase. A sticker was affixed at an angle on one side displaying a symbol of two poodle heads back-to-back, one black and the other white, with the tagline "Loud and proud member of the PC of EC".

Stentstrom was the only other person inside ECPD that knew the specifics about Special Crimes. I'd known him years before when I was a cadet at the academy. He was one of the good guys, brilliant with just the right dose of crazy.

I filled him in on what little I knew. His bulbous eyes widened with interest.

"Good," the medical examiner enthused. "With all the garden-variety murders that have come through my office lately, it will be refreshing to work on something with meat on the bone! No pun intended, of course."

"Um, sure," I remarked, my smile faltering.

"Will Mr. Kole and Doctor Saranda be joining us?" he asked, looking around hopefully.

"No," I exchanged a glance with Mahoney, who raised his eyebrows in silent question. "At least, not for the moment," I added hurriedly. "It'll depend on what we find."

Stentstrom set his briefcase on the floor. He removed his coat, folded it neatly, followed by his hat and gloves. He placed them carefully next to the briefcase. Popping the top, he opened the case. Inside lay plastic clothing, shoe covers and gloves, as well as a variety of forensic tools.

"Please help yourselves," he gestured.

Moments later, Stentstrom and I were bedecked in clear plastic from head to toe. We entered the room, stepping lightly around the blood splatter. Mahoney remained behind, an inscrutable look on his worn face.

The Insight returned, simmering on the edge of my senses, present, yet aloof. I sensed its hesitation, as if held back by apprehension, or fear.

That was a new experience, the Insight afraid of something. Because that didn't bother me at all. Nope, not one bit. Now wasn't the time to analyze the Insight's feelings. Or the fact it might have any.

"EVI, calculate the bloodstain pattern following my POV, and share the results with Detective Holliday and Captain Mahoney," Stentstrom stated, making a slow, wide circuit around the body in the chair.

Three-dimensional graphs and figures appeared in my visual center, revealing angles, points and areas of convergence as well as the area of origin. As the images cycled, EVI included expected trajectories, and projected heights and distances.

"Extraordinary," Stentstrom remarked. He shuffled up beside me with a hop to his step. "Do you see it?"

"It looks like our vic was shot by dozens of small-caliber bullets," I replied slowly as I assimilated the data stream. "But I don't see any stippling or powder burns around the wounds. And the angles are all wrong. No shell casings, and no bullet holes or scoring in the wall or ceiling."

"What do you think it means?" Stentstrom asked, his voice quivering with barely suppressed excitement.

"He wasn't shot," I answered, feeling like a trainee back at the Academy attending my first forensic science class. "At least, not in the traditional sense. So, what killed him?"

"An excellent question. Look closer at the blood stains. Notice the lengths, and the direction of travel. Do you see anything now?"

I turned toward the wall near the door to study the stains. The Insight continued to roil behind its self-imposed exile.

"I don't get it," I frowned. "This is all wrong."

"Indeed, Detective Holliday." Stentstrom came up next to me and pointed at several splotches with his plastic finger. "Here, and here. Note how these stains are inverted because of the force which caused them. Now, look at the body. Tell me what you see."

I moved toward the chair to study the corpse.

Sanarov had been in his late sixties or early seventies, judging from his sallow skin, gray hair and liver spots on his hands, neck and head. He was tall, an inch or two over six feet, and his body was muscular despite his age. I caught an old, faded tattoo on the upper bicep of his left arm around the short sleeve. It was a spider web, with the spider climbing out. Three small bell tattoos were arrayed on the back of his left hand, starting at the pinkie finger, one along each consecutive knuckle. However, his body was covered in thumbnail-size wounds. Even his clothes had holes in them, as if he'd been perforated by a high-powered nail gun. As I looked more closely, I realized the fleshy wounds resembled boils that had burst outward, rather than skin that had been punctured or cut.

"He exploded," I said.

The Insight eased into me as if inhaling, like a cup filling with water. My senses swelled, and I was drawn to the open book on the desk. Even at this distance, I recognized the unmistakable structure and style of the Bible. I couldn't see which passage, but the pages were marked with crib notes and other scribblings. When my eyes raked across the desk, the holo-screen flickered. Instinctively, I waved my hand at the screen, expecting nothing since I stood beyond its standard activation radius, and didn't have Sanarov's password to reactivate it.

The screen flared to life. One line of text appeared in big, bold letters. I focused on the text.

"*Why do the righteous suffer?*" I recited. As I uttered the words, the holo-screen shimmered, and the verse changed. "*He repays everyone for what they have done. He brings on them what their conduct deserves.*"

I became dimly aware of Mahoney behind me in the doorway. I smelled his body wash and sharp cologne, and beneath that, stark and painful memories of his past coming back to roost. The Insight gave them life and depth, and a distinct bouquet of frustration and loss. Mahoney knew something about the victim. Their paths had intersected at some point.

"Detective?" Stentstrom asked, his voice quivering. "What is happening?"

Before I could answer, the words faded to be replaced by a new passage.

"*And no creature is hidden from His sight,*" I continued. "*But all are naked and exposed to the eyes of Him to whom we must give account.*"

"How are you doing this?" the medical examiner whispered.

I shook my head and said, "I don't know."

More text appeared. My heartbeat accelerated.

"*For your sins will always find you,*" I read, my eyes captured by the words scrolling across the holo-screen. My breathing quickened. Sweat gathered on my brow. "*Your sins will never forget you. Your sins can never forgive you.*"

The screen went dark.

With the last vestiges of the magic dissipating, I turned to Mahoney, only to face a youthful version of the man wearing a fresh-pressed suit and tie. He stood in a dank, dark room that was not the church basement, but somewhere else. The stench of blood and gore filled my nostrils. A small body lay at Young Mahoney's feet. Whoever this had been, the head and face had been crushed by a tremendous force. The face was a pulpy mess.

Suddenly, an unbridled hatred and despair permeated the room in which I stood, and I nearly choked on its intensity. I tried clearing my throat several times hoping to wash the feeling away without success.

The Insight vanished, enervating me further. My breathing grew shallow. Sweat ran down my face in cold rivulets. The image of the captain and that room dissolved, and with it, the raw emotion I'd just experienced. Something very bad had happened both here, and in that place from Mahoney's past.

But of one thing I was certain: Gustavo Sanarov had been killed in an unnatural manner. Not by a gunshot or stab wound, but by something far more profound, primal, and sinister.

I also realized whoever or whatever had done this didn't just want Sanarov dead. They had wanted him to suffer until the very end.

3

S tentstrom continued his meticulous examination, murmuring commands to EVI who captured all the images for further evaluation. Two of Stentstrom's people wearing plastic gear arrived to perform a thorough scan of the room using an alphabet soup of forensic devices that detected everything from fingerprints, clothing fragments and chemicals to shoe scuff marks and old boogers. They came up with nothing out of the ordinary other than Sanarov's own castoff detritus. Eventually, they carried the stiff from the room in a black body bag. Mahoney and I stood aside to let them pass. Stentstrom removed his gloves and handed them to a third tech. After washing his hands thoroughly from a proto-sanitizer another tech provided for him, he donned his coat, *ushanka* and winter gloves.

"I shall do the cut later today," the medical examiner said quietly, still visibly shaken. "My other appointments can wait."

"Time of death?" I asked.

"At a guess, sometime between ten and two," he answered. "I'll know better once I've had a chance to examine the decedent at my lab. I will let you know what I find as soon as I can."

Stentstrom departed, leaving me with Mahoney in the hallway. I held a plastic bag containing Sanarov's Bible. His remaining effects had been bagged and sent to my pod. Mahoney waved me away before I could say anything. "Not now. Interview Father Davis first. I need to make a few calls."

I hesitated, then nodded and left him, my mood in a dark place. Instinct told me whatever Bill knew needed to play out a bit more first.

It didn't take me long to find Father Jack. He sat in the small breakroom down the hall from the sanctuary. Normally a warm and inviting place, the two windows were covered up to keep the February chill at bay. A coffee maker slept on the counter next to a double-sink and a large holo-frame cycling between hundreds of images of various churchgoers and their families.

"How you holding up?" I settled into the chair by him.

"This isn't my first death, Tom." He cracked a smile. It disappeared quickly. "Death and I have a long history together. I've watched families come and go, generations of Sokolovs and Lebedevas, even the occasional Romano, Jones and Ramirez. Our little cemetery isn't so little anymore."

"But it is your first murder," I said gently. "Tell me what happened."

"Gus and I were supposed to go to the Pantry," he said, but as he spoke, the lines around his eyes deepened, the circles below darkened as if bruised. "That's our soup kitchen over on 5th. We usually arrive around seven to set up for the morning breakfast prayer. I unlocked the front door and went inside to disarm the alarm. I noticed all the lights were off, which isn't unusual, but something felt... wrong. Now, Tommy, before you ask, Gus doesn't...didn't know the code. He was instructed that so long as he didn't open any exterior doors or windows, the alarm wouldn't sound."

I didn't take notes. EVI catalogued everything which freed me up to focus on the interview.

"When was the last time you saw Mr. Sanarov?"

"Last night. We had dinner, then I took him back here around eight. I locked the doors, set the alarm and went home."

"Who else has the alarm code and a key?"

He provided me a list of names and said, "Ever since Mary passed a few years ago, it's just been me in the parsonage."

"I'll need their contact information," I said. "Let them know I'll be reaching out very soon."

"You think one of them could have done this?" Father Jack was shocked.

"I have to cover all the bases. With a limited number of people having keys, any one of them could be involved, even if it's as simple as unlocking the door for the real killer."

The pastor's eyebrows shot up, but then he nodded quickly. "I understand."

"What happened next?" I asked.

"I went downstairs," he said with a pained look. "I called out, but there was no answer. I turned on the lights and found him there. That's when I called the police."

"How long did you know Mr. Sanarov?"

"He went by Gus." The old man stared down at his hands, gnarled from years of hard work in the gardens by the playground. "He grew up about five blocks from here."

"Did he ever have any visitors?"

"None that I saw. Gus enjoyed his privacy. He'd work at the Pantry, then return here and help out where he could."

"What about family?"

"He never talked about a family, loved ones, or much of anything really." Father Jack paused, then lowered his voice. "Did you know he was an ex-convict?"

I nodded and said, "I haven't reviewed his background yet, but I saw his tattoos. I'm guessing New Rikers, or maybe EC Correctional. The bells on his knuckles, one for each decade spent in the joint. Three bells, so at least thirty years. He was a lifer. The spider web's a new one for me, though. I've seen the one where the spider sits in the web, but not trying to get out."

"Gus told me it meant he was reformed," Father Jack said quietly. "He moved along a righteous path, with the Lord as his guide."

"You gave him the job at the Pantry?" I kicked my legs out to stretch them. Both knees popped.

"Gus came here eight months ago," the pastor replied with a sad smile. "He said a friend recommended us to him. We talked for several hours. He needed to find his place again, so I offered him the job. Gus was a diligent worker, showed up on time, never complained, but kept to himself most days. I offered him the room here once I learned that he didn't have a place to stay. He'd help around the grounds and the garden. Gus was also very good with his hands. He repaired the old swing set, among other things. Whenever he prayed, he sat alone, near the back. I don't think he wanted anyone to notice he was there."

"You didn't do a reference check, background, nothing?"

"No, Tom, I did not." He met my eyes with an indignant defiance I'd never seen from him before. "Someone needed help. *My* help. He had no one. I took him at his word."

"Well, he had a friend to recommend him here," I pointed out.

"He came here."

"You ever get the friend's name?"

"He came *here*."

"Right." I changed tactics, not wishing to antagonize Father Jack further. "Did he talk about doing time? Mention why he was there? Why he came back to the old neighborhood?"

"We explored the Bible together," he replied, the defiance melting into sorrow. "We spent hours in the sanctuary, or in one of the classrooms, reading passages from both the Old and New Testament to discuss their meanings. Gus was a man possessed of very old, and very deep wounds. He quoted Scripture, drawing strength and purpose from it. Other than the tattoos, he never talked about serving time in prison, and I never asked. Would we have gotten to it eventually? Perhaps, but building trust is a delicate process, something I don't need to explain to you."

My eyes wandered around the kitchen. How many times had I sat with Father Jack in this very room discussing the struggles of puberty, of finding my way in the world, and growing up without a mother?

"Fair enough," I said, then remembered something, and placed the evidence bag with the Bible on the table. "Were the two of you studying anything in particular?"

Father Jack's open hand hovered above the bag without touching it, as if contact would somehow spoil its contents.

"Job," he replied, and a tremor passed through his hand. "*If I sin, what do I do to you, you watcher of humanity? Why have you made me your target?*"

"Gus had already sinned," I pointed out. "He went to prison because of it."

"Yes, he did," Father Jack sighed. He coughed suddenly, a harsh racking sound. "But his penance wasn't enough for someone, was it?"

"It's not your fault." I reached across the table to grasp his hand. His skin was clammy to the touch, the bones thin. Despite his composure, he seemed nervous, almost feverish. "You gave him a home, a job, and a safe place to be, something Gus hadn't had in over thirty years."

"I know." The pastor gripped my hand tighter as he regarded me with melancholy. "But I can't help feeling as if I had let him down somehow. That even in the house of the Lord Gus could not be saved."

"Not everyone can be." I released his hand, then stood up.

"On that we will always disagree," he said with a sad smile, but it slipped as he regarded me. "Am I a suspect?"

"Of course not," I reassured him. "If you'd done it, they'd never find the body. It's just not your style."

The pastor didn't laugh. "I'm serious. Am I a suspect?"

"No," I replied solemnly, locking eyes with him. "I need to talk with my captain, and then I'll be back. I want to go over Gus' room another time and see if I can find anything that might help me figure out who could've done this."

"Don't you have a team of specialists that handles this sort of thing?" he asked curiously.

"Not exactly," I said with a sour grimace. SCU didn't have much of anything. Our tight budget was one of several drawbacks working for Mahoney's paranormal unit. But I still got paid somehow, which was nice. "I'm going to call in a couple of consultants."

"I hope it won't be that Tribulation Protector you mentioned the last time you were here," the pastor chided with mild distaste. "Having one of those lunatics wandering around my church, well, I don't need to tell you how antithetical their beliefs are."

"Deacon's harmless," I said with more confidence than I felt. "And he's a professional."

I didn't mention Leyla. If he wasn't keen on Deacon, I could only imagine how the pastor would feel about her roaming the Redeemer's hallowed halls.

"I'm sure he is." Father Jack gave me one of those "You damn well better be right" looks. "You're not going to ask me to bless any bullets again, are you?"

"I don't handle your garden-variety murders these days," I chuckled ruefully. "And no, I won't need you to do that. At least, I hope not."

"What about your other friend? The Vellan?"

"She's not my friend," I stated coldly, but cooled my tone and added quickly, "Doctor Saranda is too busy these days. She doesn't have time to slum with the hired help. You going to be okay with the media and ECPD crawling around here for a while?"

"We live in Little Odessa," he said with a heavy sigh. "I can handle them. Besides, what choice do I have?"

"Fair enough," I relented. "How about I bring you some chicken and matzoh ball soup for that cough of yours?"

"It's just a cold," He said, waving me away with a tired smile. "I'll be fine, Tommy."

I patted him on the shoulder and left.

Mahoney was waiting for me in the pod. He occupied one of the command chairs, a cup of coffee untouched before him. I filled my mug and took the other chair. We both stared out the windshield at the glow of early morning. A light dusting covered the mounds of compacted ice and snow that had been mashed to the side by shovels and autoplows. The street outside the church as well as the parking lot glistened with white fringed with scarlet and gold from the rising sun. Like fire on water, it was a heat that never quenched the icy heart beneath it.

"It was on a day like this one," Mahoney began. "February. Snow. Icy cold. I'd been working the homicide table for a few years back then. The Flynn kidnapping. Calvin Flynn. Eight years old, from a very wealthy family. The mayor specifically picked me to handle it because of the high profile. Really pissed off Bob Rogers and his Ransom Squad."

Bill smiled at the memory, his eyes distant.

"It was the usual. Kidnapper demands lots of credits, no cops, no media. We couldn't trace the calls. The kidnapper used burners. Then we get an anonymous tip from the hotline. The caller said Calvin and the kidnapper were holed up in a warehouse down by the waterfront in Midland Beach. It checked out."

He paused. I didn't interrupt.

"I followed SOP, despite the kidnapper's demands," he continued. "Went in with SWAT and found Gustavo Sanarov along with Calvin. The boy's head and face had been crushed. Sanarov was unarmed and gave himself up. Said he didn't kill the boy, that he had found him like that. Forensics went over the scene. No DNA on Sanarov, no murder weapon, nothing. No evidence to support what I knew had to have happened. Yet there he was, dead to rights. Sanarov admitted to the kidnapping, the ransom calls, all of it. But not the murder. Never that. He avoided the death penalty, but the D.A.'s Office still had enough evidence to put him away for life."

The captain picked up his coffee and took a sip. "You saw the tattoos?"

I didn't answer.

"Released from New Rikers last year as part of Mayor Samson's Pieces of Eight program, an enclave-wide initiative to assist ex-cons' return to society. Get them back on track, provide education, jobs, counseling, and help them manage the pressure and anxiety of post-prison life. Eight steps toward re-entry and rehabilitation. Apparently, Sanarov had become a role model in prison. Found Jesus, established a school for inmates to teach them reading, writing, even led regular prayer groups and workshops. He was granted clemency from the life sentence, and that was that."

I'd heard of the mayor's drive to reduce the prison populations in Empire City. Despite its success, the other precincts had dubbed the program "Pieces of Shit". I never paid much attention to it, as most of the scumbags I'd busted back when I was a big-time homicide detective got the death penalty. There was no rehabbing from that.

The captain's voice lowered to an angry whisper. "It's been over thirty years, Tom. I can still see Calvin Flynn's body and what had been done to it. That poor boy. Goddamn Sanarov got off fucking easy."

"Sir, I'm going to need to see your old case file on the Flynn kidnapping and murder," I said.

"I've already taken care of that," he replied, gathering himself. "I doubt there are many people from that investigation still around, though. It was a long time ago. The obvious suspect would be Donald Flynn, the boy's father. He still lives in Empire City. CEO of a bank, I think. Runs a foundation called Brave New Beginnings which does a lot of philanthropic work for underprivileged kids. I'd check him first."

"I'll do that once I'm finished with the crime scene."

"You saw something down there." Bill turned to me, his jaw set. "What was it?"

"I'm not sure," I hesitated. Dread washed over me again, along with the overpowering hatred that had saturated Sanarov's room. "I'll need Deacon, though. Leyla, too."

"Do what you have to do, Tom," he said. Bill straightened his back, his old authority reasserting itself. "I'll ask Besim to—"

"With all due respect, sir, but she, um, won't be needed," I said. "Besides, Deacon mentioned she's already engaged in some other projects. She probably doesn't have time to get involved."

"All right." Mahoney appraised me a moment, his lips pursed. He stood up, leaving the coffee behind. "Keep me informed, Detective. Regular updates. Even murderers of convicted felons need to be caught."

The captain left the pod. I nursed my coffee, immune to the warmth of the mug, and cocooned within my own troubled thoughts.

4

Once EVI verified my access to Mahoney's files, I returned to the church. The media circus had dispersed. They had their own research to do. Rena Macsomethingorother (I always forgot her last name), a reporter for the online sensationalist rag *The Daily Dose,* skulked by the front doors, unobtrusive in her heavy gray winter parka and knitted pink hat. Rena had spent years stalking spooky stories, the kind that most passed off as bullshit. Right now, she eyed me like Sunday dinner. I gave her my patented detective's "Fuck off, I'm busy" glare.

It didn't work.

"Detective Holliday," Rena said, sidling toward me with one of those we're-friends-but-not-really smiles plastered on her face. The reporter shoved her holo-phone under my nose. "Care to dish to the *Dose?*"

"No," I snapped, resisting the urge to step upwind and away from the stale stench of white zinfandel and moth balls. "Just a crime scene, a stiff, and lots of questions with no answers. How about you call me in a month?"

"Come on, Holliday," she wheedled. Our images were

reflected in shiny miniature above her phone's screen, recording everything. "Just a little something-something for me? I promise not to use your name this time."

"Wow, you're such a giver. Talk to Media Relations. I'm working."

"Oh, I'm sure you are," Rena purred. "I heard about the jewelry heist at Strachman's last night. Reports of little furry creatures, and a white fire that didn't burn the place down. You worked that one, no doubt about it. And now, here you are, inside a church where an ex-con from New Rikers was murdered. Whispers of the boogeyman and dark magic. Will the Confederate show up soon? I'd *love* to get an exclusive with him."

"Rena, I don't know where you get your information. And right now, I don't care. You're impeding an official investigation. Please vacate the premises, before I ask one of those nice officers over there to escort you somewhere very unpleasant. Am I clear?"

Rena's predatory smile widened as she sized me up. Her teeth were crooked, yellowed from coffee, proto-candy and a lot of bad choices. It took all my willpower not to cringe away from her.

"Here's my number if you change your mind," she said and handed me her holo-card before waving me an airy goodbye.

I pocketed the card, then went inside to instruct the remaining officers and emergency services that SCU was handling the case going forward. Since Mahoney had already cleared it through channels, I played cleanup. I got several looks from some of the veteran cops, but no one questioned me or the silver SCU badge I carried. The command center was stowed, and everyone left in an orderly fashion.

A quiet calm descended on the church, broken only by the soft echoes of its mechanicals, as the building settled into its natural state. I returned to the kitchen, but Father Jack wasn't there. The brick parsonage where he lived was adjacent to the church connected by an old cemetery. The pastor had retired there to take a breather from the media maelstrom. I decided not to bother him. And I wasn't ready to call on the list of names he'd given me. The coffee pot was warm, so I filled one of the mugs on the counter and sat down at the table.

"EVI, please feed me everything you have on Gustavo Sanarov and the Flynn kidnapping," I instructed aloud.

Instantly, the archived documents on Sanarov appeared in the visual center of my brain. I used my eye movement to sift through the various documents and images. The reports were short since the man had spent more than three quarters of his life in prison. Born in Brighton Beach, from an early age he had run around with the wrong crowd. Career drop out, odd jobs here and there. I recognized several of the places where he'd been employed. Most were either boarded up or occupied by different businesses. Busted twice for B&E, once for burglary, then the big one for kidnapping the Flynn boy. Married, but no kids.

Sanarov had been working for a landscaping company that serviced high-end homes along Long Island. The Flynn family owned a massive estate in the Hamptons on four acres overlooking the water. Mahoney had presumed Sanarov coveted the extreme wealth surrounding him, and the kidnapping plan was formed. Classic motive and opportunity.

There was also a prominent write-up in the *EC Times* about Sanarov dated five years ago outlining his involvement in the establishment of educational and religious programming for the inmates at New Rikers, and co-sponsored by the Empire City Correctional Services, and Donald Flynn's Brave New Beginnings. One image showcased Mayor Harold Samson and D.A. Franklin Fassendale standing outside the entrance to the prison, as well as a tall, handsome older man in a three-piece power suit who I took to be Flynn, and an assortment of other enclave administrators. A follow-up to that piece dated last April, also in the *Times*, detailed Sanarov's program's continued success, and its implementation at East State, EC Correctional and Attica. Sanarov was fast-tracked to the Pieces of Eight initiative and released a few months later.

I paused my review to take a pull from my mug. As the warm rush of liquid delight tumbled down my happy throat, I fingered aside the window covering to regard the old snowbound swing-set and slide. The double-paned glass frosted from the proximity of the coffee's heat.

Mahoney had mentioned Flynn's involvement with Brave New Beginnings. Why would Flynn want to help Sanarov, the man who had kidnapped then allegedly murdered his son?

"But mercy is above this sceptered sway," I said softly, drawing on the Bard for inspiration. *"It is enthroned in the heart of kings. It is an attribute to God himself. And earthly power doth then show likest God's when mercy seasons justice."*

I shivered as my mind went back to the words that had appeared on Sanarov's holo-screen. There had been no mercy in that message.

I moved to Mahoney's archived case files. These were more complete: interviews with Sanarov's family, known associates, financial statements, forensics, toxicology and psychiatric profiler reports, the works. Mahoney's notes were crisp and concise, and included the medical examiner's report.

The images were gruesome.

Multiple shots from different angles heightened the brutality. Repeated blunt force trauma had turned the boy's head and face into paste. I forced myself to examine each one despite the bile in my throat, but I couldn't remain dispassionate. Anger filled me, and I had to will my hands to unclench before I crushed the coffee mug.

Positive ID confirmation had been made using the fingerprints on record but couldn't be corroborated via dental records because the boy's teeth had been smashed or were missing, nor did he have any unusual features documented for comparison purposes. Forensics also concluded that there had been no trace of Sanarov's DNA, clothing fibers or any other environmental samples at the crime scene linking the kidnapper to the murder.

Sanarov had confessed to the kidnapping, but the murder weapon had never been found. Mahoney had requested a remote drone scuba team to search the water the following day, but they'd come up with nothing. Beyond that, the scene had been clean.

Too clean, in my opinion, which was also echoed in Mahoney's report. The captain's crime scene techs didn't have the luxury of today's P-Scanners or any other leading-edge forensic equipment ECPD now had at our disposal. Unless Sanarov had had a partner, the physical evidence pointed Bill and his team in only one direction.

I frowned. No obvious *bratva* connections, either. Apparently, Sanarov's graduation from two-bit criminal to the big time was all on his own. I'd had plenty of run-ins with the *bratva* over the years to warrant my suspicions despite Mahoney's report to the contrary.

The Russian mob was like irritable bowel syndrome. They never went away.

My eyes lingered on Sanarov's background. Judging from the ages of the other family members and known associates Bill and his team had interviewed, they'd all be dead by now. EVI confirmed that, along with the passing of the medical examiner, prosecuting DA, Sanarov's court-appointed attorney, the officers assisting Mahoney with the case, and a slew of other individuals. Only Bill, Sanarov's wife and Donald Flynn remained.

Yet Father Jack had mentioned an old friend had recommended Sanarov to the Holy Redeemer. Mahoney must've missed somebody. But who? Despite his insistence Sanarov had come to the church for help, instinct told me Father Jack knew who it was, too.

Why hide that from me?

"EVI, I'll need everything New Rikers has on our victim. Medical reports, behavior and psych evals. If they're reluctant to provide it, let the captain know and I'm sure he'll get it pushed through."

"Detective, Captain Mahoney has already requested the information," she replied in my ear.

I nodded, not surprised. Bill had a hard-on for this case, so making everything available to me was the obvious play.

I stared at the timeline Mahoney had put together leading up to Sanarov's eventual capture. According to the tip-line call center, the voice had been digitally altered to prevent ID'ing it as male or female. Interesting that Bill had never chased down the caller with Cyber, although even a talented holo-hacker like Leyla would've had a hard time ID'ing it. Maybe he'd decided it wasn't worth his time?

I finished the coffee, poured myself another cup, and downed it in a few gulps. I used the sink and cleaned out the mug and pot, then added new grounds and water. The morning had dragged on during my review of the reports, but no one was allowed inside the church without my say-so other than Father Jack until I'd finished with the crime scene.

It was time to get the band back together. After I reached out to Deacon and Leyla to meet me here, I took a stroll around the church.

The place was enormous, boasting a massive nave and sanctuary, several alcoves with fonts and statuary, as well as separate wings for outreach programs, Bible study and the parochial school. The stained-glass windows high above were intricate and beautiful, reflecting the light of the morning sun in glittering red, white, blue and gold.

I knew the church well. My grandfather had worked here for decades, even before Father Jack's arrival. The two had made quite the friendship—the Minsk enclave immigrant Jew and the young, enthusiastic Catholic. Father Jack knew my parents before my mother had been murdered in a home invasion. He'd grown up with my dad in the neighborhood, two mixed-up Irish kids surrounded by mostly black, Russian, Italian and Hispanic families.

To say I had history here was an understatement.

I found myself inside the nave, studying the sanctuary. Countless people had congregated within these walls, seeking wisdom or solace, hope and redemption. Many had found guidance and inspiration, as they continued their lifelong search for the divine. I'd seen Father Jack help so many people over the years, his devotion a gentle hand propping up the downtrodden. And while I'd never subscribed to his faith, I still held it with respect.

But right now, everything it represented gave me a profound sense of unease. Gustavo Sanarov had been murdered beneath the watchful eye of the Holy Redeemer, and all I tasted was ash.

I recalled a conversation I'd had with Besim in this very building.

"That is why you came here," she'd said to me. "You chose a place whose faith is steeped in the very bedrock of its foundation, whose identity is unquestioned, and whose compassion is endless."

At the time, it had made sense.

However, Sanarov's killer hadn't cared.

"*There are more things in heaven and earth, Horatio,*" I murmured. "*Than are dreamt of in your philosophy.*"

I went back to the vestibule, troubled and on edge.

Leyla arrived first. Her portable holo-rig slept in a faded leather satchel slung at her side. She wore a blue and yellow flower-patterned tank top, a short black skirt and leggings, and no jacket. I smiled and shook my head, then gave her a quick hug. Despite the brief contact, I shivered as intense cold permeated my bones.

Deacon showed up shortly thereafter. He stank of cigarettes and engine exhaust. By the look of him, he hadn't slept much since our encounter with the kobolds. He still wore the same clothes. His eyes were sunken and shadowy, the circles below them weighed down by enough luggage to support a family of four.

"You rode your bike here?" Leyla asked, incredulous.

"Yeah," he replied laconically, admiring the church interior like a six-year old eyed cough medicine.

"Through the snow."

"Yep."

"And ice."

"That's right."

Deacon produced a cigarette and lighter from an inner

pocket of his leather biker jacket and fired one up. Smoking wasn't allowed inside the church. However, asking Deacon to put it out would be like telling the wind not to blow. I yielded to the immovable object.

"You okay?" I asked.

"Fine."

"Need a moment?"

"I said I'm fucking fine, Holliday." He took a long drag from his cigarette, then exhaled slowly. "Just show me the goddamn scene."

I exchanged a meaningful glance with Leyla, who offered a slight shrug, then headed to Sanarov's room.

As soon as the Confederate stepped across the threshold, he reeled backward as if he'd been punched in the face.

"Jesus fucking Christ, Holliday!" Deacon's eyes widened in shock and pain. The truncheon appeared in his hand, but no fire burned along its business end. "What the fuck happened in there?"

"You tell me." I filled them in on what I'd learned. "The sense of weird saturating this room was almost too much for the Insight to handle. I've never encountered anything like it before."

Leyla hesitated before leaning forward. Nothing happened. Whatever had repelled Deacon didn't affect the young hacker. She tip-toed inside, her black and white flats clad in the plastic covers I'd given her. At my request, a narrow aisle had been cleared of Sanarov's blood by Stentstrom's techs allowing access to the workstation. The blood-stained chair sat in its original position. Stentstrom's techs had been careful not to disturb it too much when they retrieved the body.

"I'm okay to work this, right?" she asked over her shoulder. Her pale features had grown lighter.

"Yeah, just wear the gloves I gave you," I replied.

Leyla donned her gloves but paused while her worried eyes scanned the room again.

"It's okay kiddo," I reassured her.

She nodded, then placed her rig on top of a clean portion of the workstation and went to work.

Leyla collected gobs of information as she plundered Sanarov's workstation. It didn't take her long. I watched, fascinated, while dozens of holo-windows appeared or were pushed to the side as Leyla tore the workstation a new one.

"Your vic got waxed by something awful, Holliday," Deacon said. He glared at the room as if daring it to disagree with him.

"You think someone hocus-pocused him?" I wiggled my fingers while waggling my eyebrows.

The Confederate rolled his eyes and shook his head in disgust. "You're a fucking infant, Holliday. But, yeah, I think someone did. It's more than that, though. There's a powerful sense of retribution here, and something else. Something darker, more primal. Like two different intents workin' simultaneously. It ain't just hatred. Revenant, maybe."

"Reva-what?" I frowned.

"Specters," he supplied, rolling his hand suggestively. "Wraiths, vengeful spirits, that sort of shit."

"Please tell me we're not dealing with another *fetch*," I lamented, my stomach sinking to the floor. "I thought I took care of that."

Deacon scowled. "This ain't one of them. Like I said, it just don't feel the same. For starters, a *fetch* ain't the undead. But a revenant? That's somebody that did some very bad shit when they were living and came back from the dead to do more of it to the people who had done some very bad shit to them before they died."

"Revenant," I mused, rubbing my jaw while giving the Confederate a skeptical look.

"Remember when you didn't believe in vampires, Holliday?" Deacon countered with a sly grin.

"Crain and his goons were biogenetically-engineered humans, Deacon. Not the undead. Big difference."

"They were still goddamn blood-suckers."

I threw up my hands in defeat. "Fine, have it your way. So how are we supposed to stop a revenant?"

"Not sure," Deacon replied sourly. "But I reckon we damn well better find out before it kills again."

5

"You're thinking Sanarov was the start of something."

"Like I said, vengeful spirit," the Confederate nodded. "The dark shit in that room is strong, and it's got unfinished business."

He paused to study the room's interior again.

"*And no creature is hidden from His sight,*" Deacon spoke quietly. "*But all are naked and exposed to the eyes of Him to whom we must give account.* Hebrews 4:13."

"The Bible isn't my strong suit," I said. "But even I'm not blind to that message. I had EVI compile the verses from Sanarov's workstation."

"Our killer's got themselves a strong sense of righteous irony, Holliday," Deacon growled with disgust. "They think their goddamn cause is just, that by taking out Sanarov they did the world a fucking favor! And maybe they did. But then there's our vic, some ex-con who'd found Jesus while doing time and believed the word of the Lord might protect him from his past sins. Just another fucking hypocrite in a world full of them."

"Sounds like you've encountered this kind of situation before," I said.

Deacon lit another cigarette. "Not in a long time," he answered after a few thoughtful puffs. "Back in Birmingham, I'd investigated plenty of boogeyman stories. Then I spent a turn as an adjunct with New Scotland Yard. This was back before I hooked up with Saranda. The Euro-Bloc has a lot of ancient shit, and an ass-ton of restless dead. Those cases remain unsolved for a reason."

"You've actually seen a ghost?" I was intrigued. There was still so much about Deacon that I didn't know.

"Nothing substantial, more like poltergeists and apparitions, and definitely not this," Deacon admitted. "It's all feelings and emotions. Like stepping into a room that's always cold, even when the heat's on. Or flickering lights where there ain't nothin' there or knowing somebody's watching you even though you know you're alone. I ain't never seen one, but that don't mean they don't exist."

"If a revenant killed Sanarov," I said slowly, the idea settling in my stomach like a half-cooked meal. "Then it's a spirit we can't see, but only sense might be there?"

Deacon crushed the half-smoked butt into his palm before replying, "There's got to be a lot of hatred involved, enough that whoever died ain't happy about being part of the dearly departed. Their hatred acts like an anchor, makes their will strong enough to keep 'em here instead of moving on."

I shook my head, forgoing questions about what Deacon's charming version of an afterlife might be. I was about to move into the room when another thought hit me.

"If we're dealing with a spirit, then an anchor implies that spirit is stationary. Which means it should still be in there?"

"That's right," Deacon said, a grim gleam in his eye. "So long as whatever happened to it in the past, happened in that room. At least, that's the theory."

Calvin Flynn had been found in a warehouse. Had there been foul play at the Redeemer? And what would that have to do with Gustavo Sanarov?

"I've never heard of anything like that occurring at this church," I said. "But it's been around a few centuries. I'll check with Father Jack."

"Even if the anchor ain't here, the thing that did this probably left something of itself behind," Deacon said. "Like an echo. You think that Insight of yours can see it?"

"I don't know," I replied in frustration. "The crime scene somehow chased the Insight away. I can't feel it at all, and that's never happened before."

"That's a fucked-up ability you got there, Holliday," the former Protector chuckled. "Comes and goes when it wants, and you ain't got no control over it. Like the fucking weather."

"Yeah," I smiled ruefully. "Well, it's better than nothing." I paused as the image of a shadowy silhouette by Madame Ruth's Psychic Parlor window tickled my memory. An idea began percolating in my empty head. "In the meantime, I need to schedule interviews with all the church employees, and anyone associated with the Pantry. I'll ask Mahoney if he can assign some uniforms to canvass the neighborhood. Maybe someone saw something."

"You do that," Deacon said. "I'm checking in with Saranda and see if she needs me for anything."

"You're not sticking around?"

"Fuck no." He gave me a disgusted look. "This whole place is a goddamn mess. Besides, I know I ain't welcome here. Call me if something comes up and tries to eat you."

"All right," I said as the Confederate moved past me and out of sight.

"Just about done, Doc," Leyla announced.

"You can explain it to me on the way," I replied. I stared after the former Protector, wondering if the man would always remain a mystery to me.

"Where are we going?" she asked.

"To see Donald Flynn. He's the one with the most motive."

I stopped by the parsonage briefly to let Father Jack know we'd be leaving, but to expect me tomorrow morning because I wanted to conduct the church and Pantry interviews here. The pastor's answers were short and clipped, his worn demeanor that of a man who didn't want to be disturbed. It was obvious he had a lot on his plate. I wished him well, then caught up to Leyla who was basking in the morning cold air by the front door. We walked back to the pod, exchanging loose thoughts regarding the crime scene and Deacon's revenant theory.

Once we were underway, I contacted Donald Flynn's office, while Leyla jacked her holo-rig remotely into the transport's onboard systems. My conversation with his executive assistant was brief. She had a lovely accent and confirmed our meeting for this afternoon. I hung up, then called Mahoney to give him an update as well as request some officers to do a canvass. He said he would take care of it, but he didn't ask me any other questions. I could tell by his tone that he was still stewing in the past, so I let him go.

Holo-windows from Sanarov's workstation flocked around the pod windshield's interior HUD like a gaggle of geese waiting for a Metro pod.

"That's it?" I frowned, studying the limited information.

"That's it," Leyla answered, shifting in her seat for a

more comfortable position. "It's an older model, probably something Father Davis kept in his basement for rainy days. The data and cache were limited, and Gus didn't have access to the church's cloud either."

"So where did those messages come from?" I asked.

"I don't know."

The hesitation in her voice made me turn to regard the young hacker.

"Doc, I don't know who killed Gus, or how it was done," Leyla said, "but I can tell you no hacker remotely programmed or projected those messages. You know I'm sensitive to that kind of thing. It's just a feeling. Like knowing when somebody's been in your house while you weren't home. Everything is in its place, but you know that somebody's walked around the room looking at all your stuff."

"You sound like Deacon," I said. "You both possess an acuity for the supernatural. Different flavors, I suppose. I assume his is a result of his affiliation with the Tribulation Church, but I think the premise is the same. What's your excuse?"

Leyla considered my question before answering. "Ever since I survived the Nexus node explosion in Reykjavik that killed my parents, my life's been one messed up ride. When I want to use my powers, they're just there. It's like I'm tapping into some vast ocean of energy that also feels like it's a living thing. Scientifically, I understand how breathing and oxygen and my lungs work. I need it all to survive. With my abilities, well, it's sort of like that. It's a part of me just as much as my heart and brain are. I know what I want to do, I visualize it, and then I just do it."

"Well, mine only shows up when it wants to," I grumbled.

"That's because the Insight is like having a girlfriend," Leyla laughed while she manipulated more holo-windows. Several new floating bubbles appeared on the HUD. "It's not about what you want. It's what she wants."

"Cute," I smiled. "What're those?"

"I don't think Gus had a holo-phone. He used his box, instead. Here's a list of all the incoming and outgoing calls. Father Davis, the Pantry, his parole officer Jim Stantz, and a couple of messages to a Stacey Schrodinger. Hers is a residential address. As for the rest, Gus got a lot of junk mail and engaged in very little online activity. He wasn't linked to any sites. No subscriptions, no porn sites, message boards or much of a digital presence anywhere, at least, not from that workstation. If he had a portable rig, that's a different story."

"Judging from the small number of personal effects he had in his room, I doubt he had one," I said.

"Well, I'll keep looking for Gus online, but I don't think he's there. I've put all the correspondence up on the HUD, but I didn't see anything out of the ordinary with those. I've also tacked on transcripts of his phone conversations—"

"You can do that?" I asked, swiveling the chair to face her.

"Doc, my phishing-fu is very strong," Leyla said with pride. "If I can evade the ECBI, accessing holo-phone imagery and transcripts from his phone carrier is child's play. Besides, the EC FCC can kiss my ass. And after everything that went down last October, I thought it was a good idea I learned how to do it myself."

"I don't want to know." I raised both hands in defeat. "I'm going to officially request them through the proper channels anyway. You know, in case we catch the killer and then someone from the D.A.'s Office asks me about the chain-of-evidence and how I magically obtained Sanarov's phone records during that whole legal process thing that they do."

"You do you, Doc."

I had EVI request a warrant from the D.A.'s Office for Sanarov's phone records. Despite SCU's "by any means" directive, I tried to follow standard ECPD procedure, regardless of how abnormal our small sample size of cases had been since we started. I didn't want any blowback from our investigations should something bad happen that would plant us as the root cause for a civil case. Mahoney had said he'd handle any bureaucratic bullshit we might encounter, but I hedged my bets anyway.

Still, since I had them handy, I studied the transcripts while the pod hurtled toward Midtown. The conversations with his parole officer were as expected. Sanarov checked in regularly, answered the usual questions, and that was that. I put in a call to Stantz, explained who I was, and asked him about Sanarov. He didn't provide us anything we didn't already know.

"Yeah, Gus was like clockwork," Stantz's holo-image finished. He was around my age, with a full beard flecked with gray, and blood-shot eyes. "Always called me on time. No complaints, and no trouble. Wish all my ex-cons were like him. Sucks he's dead. Seemed like a reformed guy, all things considered."

"Appreciate the information," I said, and killed the call.

I got up to refill my mug of pure java delight.

"Figure Schrodinger is the ex?" Leyla asked.

"She is." I took a long sip, filled the mug again, then returned to my chair. The transcripts for those calls were short. It was clear Schrodinger didn't want to talk to Sanarov. "She divorced him while he did time. I'll give her a call after we visit Flynn."

I waved my hand and relegated the windows from the main viewer to the background. What remained were Stentstrom's images of Sanarov in situ. I stared at them for a while, lost in thought.

"EVI, please bring up a list of all the inmates who had participated in any of Sanarov's workshops during his time of incarceration, as well as any visitors he had."

A new window appeared filled with the names of the workshop attendees. None of them stood out to me. Other than his court-appointed lawyer, Sanarov hadn't had any visitors during his time there, either.

"Cross-reference any of those names with inmates who were released as part of the Pieces of Eight program."

Once the list appeared, I started at the top and had EVI provide me updated bios and current whereabouts. I rubbed my stubbly chin and frowned. This was going to take a while.

"Why haven't you talked to Besim?" Leyla asked suddenly.

"Huh?" I replied absently.

"Besim," she repeated. "You haven't been by to see her."

"Been busy. Haven't had time."

"Look, Doc, I'm not happy with how everything went down with Patricia Sullinger, either, but I got over it. She's still in Vellas, and from what Deacon's told me, she's fine. Whatever the Vellan doctors did worked."

"That's great."

"So?"

"So, what?" I replied irritably. I flicked some of the transcript windows back to review them again. "Besim has her life, and I have mine. And right now, I don't need her on this investigation."

An awkward silence followed.

"You know it couldn't hurt to call her."

"Are you done?"

"Doc, it's just one call."

"Seriously? We're still talking about this?"

"I miss her," Leyla sighed wistfully. "Wouldn't it be great to have everyone working together again?"

"No, kiddo, it would not."

"But—"

"No."

"But—"

"No means no."

"But it would be fun!"

"Murder investigations aren't supposed to be fun."

"But they could be."

"No."

"Well, you're no fun."

We rode the rest of the way in silence.

6

Titan Banking and Life was another in a long line of one hundred-plus story monstrosities decorating Park Avenue in Midtown. As the pod skimmed up and along the 'way that curved around the building's mammoth girth, garish live-action holo-ads smothered the walls of the skyscrapers we passed, peddling all manner of products and services. Blue, red and gold vied with white, green, orange and purple to see which advertisement was the most ostentatious. It was a reminder of the disparity between the haves and the have-nots in Empire City. An elite one percent held a majority stake in the real estate holdings throughout the enclave, trading billions of credits on the Azyrim-Dow and Nikkei exchanges daily, gaining and losing, buying and selling, and possessed of a voracious need to drive the market up and down based on whimsy, luck, fear and greed.

"I guess Nick was right," I muttered darkly as I shook my head.

"What's that, Doc?" Leyla asked. Her feet were propped

on the command console while she idly sifted through her holo-phone.

"This." I swept my hand wide as we passed another holo-ad depicting a well-endowed, scantily clad woman offering the latest in protoplast-organic surgery. Everything about her was perfect, right down to her manicured eyebrows. "When does it end?"

She shrugged. "It's the world we live in. If you don't like what someone's selling, then don't buy it."

I stared out the windshield at another holo-ad, this one for beauty and health supplements. The three-story tagline read "Beautiful is better."

"Gatsby believed in the green light, the orgiastic future that year by year recedes before us," I quoted as the holo-ad lights covered me with their false promises. *"It eluded us then, but that's no matter—tomorrow we will run faster, stretch out our arms farther...And one fine morning—So we beat on, boats against the current, borne back ceaselessly into the past."*

"That Shakespeare?"

"No, kiddo," I responded forlornly. "It's from an old, but great book. It means that if you keep on chasing the future, you're just chasing your own death."

"A metaphor?"

"Something like that."

"Doc, you're too stuck in the past, you know that?" Leyla placed her phone on the console and crossed her arms, giving me a critical look. "You need to get out more. Work isn't everything."

"You're saying I work too much? I'm a homicide detective. My work *is* everything."

Leyla pursed her lips and frowned.

"You know I love you to the moon and back, Doc, so please don't take this the wrong way." She sucked in a deep breath, then let it out in a rush. "I know how much Kate meant to you. I really do. You needed time to heal. I get that, too. But I think you need a girlfriend. Or at least someone you can have a drink with and talk about something that doesn't involve autopsies and ballistic reports. Kate's been gone eight years. Haven't you mourned her death long enough?"

I stared unblinking at the young hacker, the color draining from my face. Different emotions vied for control as they swirled through me. Outrage at Leyla for having the audacity to say what she said. Guilt and shame for myself as I replayed in my mind everything that went down with Kate Foster that fateful night at Wallingbrooke as if it were only yesterday. Melancholia for the time that had passed since her death, and the weeping hole it had left in my broken heart. I'd wandered the world with my head in a fog for so long, I'd forgotten what it was like to not be stuck in a daily funk.

Kate had been everything to me, despite our short time together. But as I stood before Leyla, the realization hit me that I'd held a death grip on all that emotional baggage out of fear. That if I let the past go, Kate would be gone forever. As if anything less would be a betrayal of her memory.

Could I do it? Could I finally put Kate to rest?

Something had changed inside of me since last October. Whether it was joining SCU and meeting Deacon and Besim, coming to grips that I lived in a much stranger and more fantastic world than one I had ever known, or merely trusting the Insight more, I had changed. I'd gained a clarity I hadn't had before. My heart had grown stronger. I now had purpose, something I thought I'd lost after my life and career had spiraled out of control. The pod-wreck that had been homicide detective third grade Tom Holliday was gone, replaced by this new guy.

I was different now. Stronger. Stable. More in control.

Or at least not as fucked-up as I had been.

"Maybe you're right, kiddo," I sighed heavily. "It's just hard, you know?"

Leyla reached out and gripped my shoulder. Her eyes glistened with compassion. "I know, and I'm here for you. So is Abner. And Deacon. And even Besim if you'd let her. We're your family now, Doc. Let us help you."

I stared out the windshield, then nodded and said, "I wouldn't even know where to start."

"Yay!" Leyla clapped with delight. "Well, I've already put together a quick starter profile on one of the dating sites I know, and—"

Leyla grabbed her phone and began manipulating its small holo-windows faster than I could keep up.

"Back up a second." I blinked in confusion. "Profile? What profile?"

"I mean, it wasn't like you were going to do it anytime soon."

"How long have you been planning this?"

"That's not important right now."

"But I don't want to go out on a blind date!"

"It's not a blind date, silly." She showed me the phone's display where a dating site called *Smoulder* figured prominently. "These women all have profiles with images. See? I'll just input your details here and—"

Bubbles appeared, each one displaying a woman around my age. A few were in risqué poses, and one was naked, although her interesting parts had been redacted. I caught myself staring, then shook my head.

"Now I'll put in your preferences and—"

"My what?" I spluttered.

"The type of woman you'd like to meet, if you own pets, you're a smoker, any hobbies and interests, although that's a pretty short list." She frowned, studying me with a critical eye. "You really don't like much, do you. Right, well, I'll just add a bunch of images I have of you and—"

"What images?"

"These." Leyla threw up several holo-windows on the windshield HUD containing candid pictures of me at Abner's, as well as a few that could only be described as "action shots" collected from the kobold case.

"Are you out of your mind?" I roared. "That's official ECPD footage! Where did you get that?"

"Remember when you gave me access to EVI when I was tracking down the surveillance signals last October?" she asked innocently.

"I'm revoking that. Effective now."

"But, Doc, I'm almost finished!"

"Oh, you're finished all right. I'm—"

"Detective Holliday," EVI interrupted. "We have arrived. Exterior temperature is twenty-three degrees Fahrenheit with winds out of—"

"That'll be all, EVI," I said.

Leyla had disentangled herself from the command chair and was already at the main hatch. She flicked a window away before stowing the phone in her skirt pocket.

"We'll discuss this later," I stated.

"Sure, Doc, whatever you say." She flashed me a winning smile.

I sighed, opened the hatch, and gestured for Leyla to precede me out.

The Titan Bank Metro station was packed. Dozens of people jostled each other as they moved along the enclosed concrete and glass walkway toward the bank entrance. Space heaters had been installed at regular intervals to glare down at the throngs passing beneath them. Despite the season, the hustle and bustle of movement coupled with the heaters kept the chill largely away.

As we passed through the tall entrance to the bank, an attractive woman with short, raven-black hair stepped up to meet us. She wore a smart navy business skirt-suit and powdered white blouse, which contrasted well with her dusky complexion.

"Good morning, Detective Holliday," she said with a friendly smile. I returned it with a broad one of my own, recognizing her accented voice as the young woman I'd spoken with earlier. Her eyes were a deep brown with a hint of hazel, and a spark of mischief. A translucent monocle covered her left eye. Information streamed along its surface, but the text was too small for me to read.

"I am Charlotte, Mr. Flynn's executive assistant. He is awaiting you in his office. Unfortunately, Mr. Flynn has several meetings scheduled for today, and won't be available for long. If you would follow me, please?"

I watched her go. Leyla's bony elbow jabbed me in the ribs.

"Hey!" I cried.

"Quit staring. You're supposed to be the professional."

"What does that make you?"

"The professional's babysitter."

Charlotte led us through the broad highway that was Titan's lobby. Gold-filigreed marble and smooth stone polished to a fine sheen spoke of the elegance and majesty the bank proffered to its corporate clientele. A genuine high relief sculpture filled an interior wall depicting dragons with a snake-like head and tail, and the scaled body of a lion, as well as beasts that resembled large horned bison. The vivid blue, gold and brown glazing of the individual bricks and the black, white and gold borders was striking.

I gawked at the work of art. "Is that...?"

"The Ishtar Gate," Charlotte provided with a bored nod as if she were describing the weather. "It was transported here from the Mutter Berlin enclave over twenty years ago. Mr. Flynn personally oversaw its installation."

"That's not a replica?" I asked. "It's the real McCoy?"

"It most certainly is," she replied. "You will find there are many priceless artistic pieces within, and upon the walls, of this bank. Titan is one of the most secure buildings in Empire City. Our security plays a significant role in our continued global success."

"Then I guess we shouldn't try to rob the place," Leyla whispered to me. "Although I'd love to take a crack at it."

"Hush. Babysitter. Remember?"

"You really are no fun."

"We must pass through the security check-in," Charlotte continued, ignoring our exchange. "This will include a full body scan. Detective, if you or your assistant are carrying any metal, you will need to declare it before you pass."

The security gate was the archway set at the center of the sculpture. Three aisles had been established, each separated by ropes connected to stanchions, and ending at two pairs of uniformed security guards wearing stony faces and carrying stun batons. Two of the lines were backed up with people, but the third was empty. I spied eight elevator bays beyond the queue.

A burly guard, sporting round eyeglasses and wearing a holo-nametag designating him as "P. J. Martin" met us at the third aisle. He gestured for me to step forward. A pair of shoe prints were embedded into the floor across from a translucent holo-screen that was twice my height. The moment I settled into position a stream of blue-white light covered me from head to toe and back up again. My scalp tingled from the sensors. Martin studied my badge and the SMART gun on the large screen before consulting a razor-thin holo-pad he carried.

"Problem?" I asked.

"Not at all, Detective," Charlotte replied smoothly, moving beside me to regard the main screen.

I inhaled. She smelled like summer and fresh laundry. I stole a quick glance at her. She caught me looking and smiled in response. I waited for the fire department's arrival to put out my burning cheeks.

"He's good," Martin grunted, breaking the moment. "Next."

After Leyla was scanned, we moved toward the first elevator in the row. It opened at our approach. The interior was spacious, complete with a voice-activated holo-directory, and a holo-vision showing three talking heads babbling on about high-yield investments. The elevator car rose swiftly. My ears popped in response. I dug a finger in one to help clear it. Both women regarded me with arched eyebrows.

"Sorry," I mumbled in embarrassment.

We arrived on the one hundred and second floor a short time later. The quiet felt proprietary, as if speech was allowed by invitation only. A comfortable lobby was decorated with more lavish art. Soft music circulated the area from hidden speakers. Leyla admired the pieces while Charlotte spoke in soft tones with a young man who occupied a half-moon shaped desk. The rest of the office was hidden behind thick, dark paneling. Given the opulence I'd witnessed so far, I expected the oak was real.

"Detective?" Charlotte gestured for us to follow.

As we passed along a short hallway, I became aware of the sound of running water ahead of us. I exchanged an intrigued glance with Leyla. We caught up to Charlotte who graced us with glimmering eyes as a secret smile played across her lips.

"Mr. Flynn will see you now," she said, then stepped into the room beyond.

Donald Flynn's office was enormous—a two-story space separated horizontally by air. The illusion created by the translucent glass floor sent a wave of vertigo through me, and I nearly fell flat on my face had Leyla not grabbed me in time. The area was abuzz with dozens of holo-screens above and below, and a natural lighting whose source I couldn't determine. A reflecting pond lay to our right, although how it was attached to the floor was a mystery of both art and architecture. Fresh water cascaded into it through cunningly concealed piping. I caught the flash of a fin as a submerged fish crested the surface. Two short marble benches were arranged on opposite sides of the pool.

Charlotte crossed the room, a wingless corporate angel without strings heedless of the emptiness below her. Leyla pointed at the grid of smaller workstations that had been set up on the lower floor. Each contained employees who manipulated virtual control over the vast collection of holo-windows. Voices and music droned around us colliding in a dissonance of disparate echoes.

Flynn's virtual workstation occupied the top floor. Before it lay a sitting area with plush carpet and very expensive furniture. He had more active holo-windows than the entire 98th Precinct, and these filled one glass wall with images and information. News feeds competed with live sports and leisure programs, while a steady stream of trading data curved and flowed through the screens like the historical images I'd seen highlighting the Amazon River before it became a dried out husk. As I stared at the information clusterfuck, I was amazed that anyone could digest a small portion of it, let alone all of it.

Tall, tinted windows surrounded the perimeter, normally providing a commanding view of Lower Manhattan. However, today's army of thick, gray clouds cloaked the city in wintry shadow. At this rarified height, we were head and shoulders above many of the skyscrapers that peaked through the cloud cover. In the distance, one tower was taller still—Azyrim Technologies, the largest building in Empire City. As I considered the distant edifice, a sense of dread overcame me. I ran a hand over my eyes, but the Insight wasn't present, and nothing revealed itself to me.

"*When Alexander saw the breadth of his domain, he wept for there were no more worlds to conquer,*" I muttered under my breath as we crossed the floor to meet Donald Flynn.

7

Leyla and I occupied one of the chic couches. I ran my hand along its sleek covering and wasn't surprised to discover it had the smell and feel of real leather. A smoky, emerald-colored marble sculpture fashioned into some obscure shape was the centerpiece atop the glass coffee table that separated the furniture. Holo-controls had been installed on the armrests of the chairs and couches so that visitors could summon Titan Bank's cloud of information at the flick of a finger. From the look of it, you could even order pizza delivery.

Donald Flynn sat in a comfortable chair opposite the couch. Dressed in a sharp charcoal suit, Flynn was athletic, with white hair, matching mustache and goatee, and intelligent brown eyes. I advised Flynn that he would be recorded, then made with the formal introductions, indicating both the date and time, and explained the purpose of our visit.

"Detective Holliday, I'm shocked and appalled by this horrible turn of events," Flynn said. His mannerisms were relaxed, the kind powerful men possessed who were accustomed to getting what they wanted with little fuss. "Gustavo

Sanarov had been an ideal candidate for the Pieces of Eight program. He'd only been released, what, eight or nine months ago? I'm sure you're aware of the tremendous work he did with the inmates at New Rikers, as well as the other penitentiaries throughout Empire City. I hear plans have moved forward to institute his programs in New Hollywood and Gateway City. Such a tragedy that he won't witness his vision come to life."

"You consider an ex-con's murder to be tragic, Mr. Flynn?" I asked curiously, shifting positions on the couch cushions. No matter how I sat, the stupid things kept moving beneath me.

"I'm not as jaded about such things as you seem to be, Detective Holliday," Flynn answered urbanely. "The loss of life, or any life for that matter, isn't some small thing to be taken lightly. From everything I'd read about him, Gustavo was a reformed man."

"Well, someone didn't think he deserved a second chance," I stated. "Which is why we're here today."

"Yes, I've heard about your ballyhooed Special Crimes Unit," Flynn remarked with a quirk to his lips. It was an oily smile, the expression reserved for bad advice and expensive hookers. "Harold mentioned it to me when we had dinner at the mayoral estate back in December. Or was it November? Solving the strange and unusual, isn't that right, Detective?

"I really couldn't say," I answered in a neutral tone.

Asshole, I added in my head. Suits like Flynn got on my last nerve, especially when they name-dropped important people like the mayor, but I kept my cool.

"Harold seemed genuinely engaged by your success solving that awful goldjoy and alleged vampire-killing mess. I dare say he nearly popped open a case of Dom for the occasion. Did you know Wrigley-Boes was put up for auction two weeks ago? Other than the real estate, the remaining assets were worthless, but I heard the parent had lost interest and took a bath just to be rid of it. Some kind of European interest, if I recall. Named after a Greek myth."

"Have you ever spoken with Mr. Sanarov?" I asked, trying to stay on task.

Charlotte returned with refreshments and offered me a mug bearing the Titan logo. The delightful aroma of an amaretto blend distracted me. I looked up at her. She smiled, and my cheeks flushed again. Taking a quick sip to hide my embarrassment, I choked on the coffee and nearly spat it up.

"Are you all right, Detective?" she asked solicitously.

"Oh, Detective Holliday will be just fine," Leyla said while patting my back. Hard. "He sometimes has trouble thinking and drinking at the same time."

Charlotte suppressed a laugh. I glared daggers at the young hacker.

"As I was about to say," Flynn resumed with a hint of annoyance, "twelve of us interviewed Gustavo during the program's review process. District Attorney Fassendale was among them. I didn't speak with Gustavo other than to ask him questions pertinent to the program. He appeared to be genuinely contrite. I was moved by his devotion to his faith, which had become an integral part of his rehabilitation process. The anecdotes Gustavo recounted regarding several inmates who were scheduled to be released for good behavior as a direct result of his guidance were truly inspiring to me."

Charlotte placed a glass of water before Leyla, and another steaming mug for Flynn, then moved a modest distance from the sitting area to give us the semblance of privacy.

"How did you become involved with the Pieces of Eight program?" I asked.

"My work with Brave New Beginnings," he replied easily. "Harold asked me to help establish the program, develop its criteria, and leverage my extensive enclave connections to bring about a positive change to those men and women who had paid for their time in prison. Detective, I don't need to remind you that Empire City has a serious overpopulation problem within our penitentiary system. Privatization of maximum-security facilities has helped to some degree. Populations at New Rikers and the other local prisons, on the other hand, have swelled by more than ten percent year-over-year. They are at capacity, or worse. Something had to be done to ameliorate the problem. Thus, the Pieces of Eight program was born."

What Flynn described wasn't anything new to me. Although I'd never visited one, I knew all about Empire City's supermax prisons beyond the spell-forged steel walls. They were black pits from which no inmate ever returned. Back when I'd been working the homicide table downtown, the convicted killers who somehow didn't get the death penalty had been sent there. I'd never bothered to check in on any of them. Considering what they'd done to their victims, those bastards deserved whatever they got.

"So, you've had no contact with Mr. Sanarov, other than the interview?"

The corners of Flynn's eyes crinkled as a deprecating smile played across his face.

"Have you ever lost anyone close to you, Detective?" he asked.

"I have," I replied, shifting uneasily.

"Wife? Partner?"

"Something like that."

"Do you have children?"

"I do not."

"I see." Flynn steepled his fingers and pressed them against his lips and nose as he studied me. "While you might be able to appreciate the loss of a loved one, the loss of a child is unlike anything you've ever experienced. The pain is truly unbearable. As if someone took a knife and tore out your heart while you watched. Each waking moment is agony, and everything you do, or see, or say is a constant reminder of what might have been had tragedy not struck."

He paused, then folded his hands across his lap.

"Detective, I recognize that I'm the obvious choice for your lead suspect, but I'm not your killer. I have far too much invested in both my reputation and my business interests. Why jeopardize my position for the sake of something as prosaic as revenge?"

"Mr. Flynn, I've been a cop for more than fifteen years," I replied. "I've worked some mean streets, and I've seen a lot of bodies. And murderers are people, just like you and me. Maybe they killed because it was a crime of passion. Maybe they were paid to do it. Or maybe it's something that goes deeper, something beyond society's concepts of good or bad, or right and wrong. In the end it doesn't really matter, but that's who murdered Gustavo Sanarov, and it's my job to stop them so they don't kill again."

Flynn waved away my comments as if rejecting a bottle of three-hundred credit wine.

"I respect your experience, and certainly admire your service to the citizens of Empire City, so please, spare me the criminology lecture, Detective," Flynn said. "That may work for the juveniles and drunks at your local precinct, but I'm well-aware of how the real world operates. To answer your original question, no, I've never spoken to, or had contact with, Gustavo other than the interview. I've had more than thirty years to think about what happened to my son. In that time, I've lost a wife, and raised another son who has given me three wonderful grandchildren. I've been married two more times, helped grow a regional bank into an international financial juggernaut, and built one of the most successful non-profit youth outreach, healthcare and education programs in Empire City. My life is full, and I am content. I have everything I've ever wanted, and then some. Why would I wait all this time just to murder that poor man?"

"You tell me."

"Oh, it certainly crossed my mind," Flynn chuckled mirthlessly. "I wouldn't be a parent if I hadn't. Hell, I wouldn't be human! The man had kidnapped and murdered my son! I didn't care that the investigators couldn't prove the murder. It was him. What was I going to do? Show up to the courthouse steps with a gun and shoot him? Of course not. Then I'd be no better than him."

He paused, studying the drinks on the table.

"I lost Angelina soon after," he continued quietly. "My first wife. Too much wine and sleeping pills from the stress of losing Calvin. One night after a dinner out with friends, she disabled the autopilot to her car and drove it into a tree. So, yes, I know hardship, Detective Holliday. I understand anger and despair all too well."

He met my eyes with a hard stare.

"But I didn't let it consume me. After Angelina died in the crash, well, I realized I needed to do more than just line my bank account with credits or push the Azyrim-Dow higher. I wanted to do something more, something with purpose, something that would honor the memories of both my wife and my son. That's why I established Brave New

Beginnings, to help the less fortunate children of Empire City overcome the adversity facing their lives. To make a difference in theirs. I'd like to think I've accomplished that, and with interest."

Flynn picked up his mug and sipped at it. He regarded me with calculating eyes.

"You ever live with regret, Detective?"

"All my life."

"Well, I don't." Flynn gestured dismissively with one hand, then leaned back in the chair. "It's a waste of valuable time and energy. Instead of regretting the mistakes I've made, I've learned from them, and moved on. And that's what I did with Gustavo Sanarov. The man went to prison. Justice was served. He paid for what he did to Calvin, and I moved on."

My holo-phone buzzed in my blazer pocket, but I ignored it. Out of the corner of my eye, I caught Charlotte raising two fingers at her boss.

"Unless there's anything else, I'm afraid I have another appointment," Flynn announced perfunctorily, and stood up. He didn't offer his hand.

"I appreciate your time, Mr. Flynn," I said, also standing.

The Insight remained quiescent. I saw nothing in his eyes. No sign of guilt or remorse. Just the dead stare of a man who had already dismissed us so that he could return to his rightful place above the clouds. I left the rest of the coffee unfinished.

"If you will excuse me, I have a merger to oversee," Flynn said as he returned to his workstation. "Charlotte, cycle the prep treatment for Pearson and Matthews, then let everyone know I'll be on in five. Good day to you, Detective."

I looked at Leyla who shrugged her shoulders. She

walked with Charlotte to the hallway. I made a move to follow, then turned back to observe Flynn as he manipulated several holo-windows above his workstation. As I watched, a thick book with a dark cover caught my attention. It lay unopened next to a holo-frame that cycled between images of what appeared to be moments of time spent with extended family. I focused on the book, and silently asked EVI to magnify and enhance her recording to make certain she captured it.

"Image registered, Detective," she said in my ear.

"Mr. Flynn," I called out. The bank executive was surrounded by glowing holo-windows at the center of a virtual maelstrom. "Do you go to church?"

"Excuse me?"

"Do you go to church?"

"On occasion," he replied with an irritated frown. "Easter Sunday, weddings, funerals. Why?"

"No reason," I answered, and left his office.

We rode in silence down the elevator. I stared at the floor, lost in thought. The business broadcast playing on one window had been interrupted by a news bulletin about a recent theft of Spanish silver coins and other priceless art from three different art exhibits, one in Lower Manhattan, and the other two in Astoria and SoHo. Apparently, more than two million credits' worth of coins had been stolen. My thoughts strayed to the fourth kobold that we never saw. My phone buzzed again, but I ignored it.

After the doors opened, Charlotte escorted us past security. As we approached the Ishtar Gate, it had lost its luster, resembling more a wall decorated by some poor man's faded graffiti rather than one of the most resplendent art pieces in the world. I made a sour face, pulled one of my holo-cards from my brown blazer's inside pocket, and handed it to Charlotte.

"Please give this to Mr. Flynn in case he has anything else he'd like to add," I said.

Charlotte took the card but didn't read it.

"And what if I have anything I'd like to add?" she asked suggestively with an arched eyebrow.

"Um, excuse me?"

All the blood suddenly rushed to my head. The world spun a little. My palms were sweaty, and my breathing became short and shallow.

"Perhaps over a cocktail or two?" she continued. "I'm off work at nine."

"Um—"

"He'd be delighted," Leyla interrupted with a grin. "You have the number. Just give him a call."

The young hacker linked her arm with mine and steered me like a dolly toward the building's exit.

8

I don't remember the walk back to the pod. Well, I did, but then I didn't. Light pressure on my body confirmed the pod's acceleration as we sped from Titan Bank.

"This. Is. Great!" Leyla raised her arms above her head in triumph.

"What just happened?" Confusion warred with shock as to which had current jurisdiction over my brain.

"Charlotte asked you out on a date, silly." Leyla appraised me with a critical frown while wiggling her index finger in my general direction. "And you are absolutely not meeting her wearing any of *that*."

"Wearing what?"

"EVI, please take us to Macy's," she pronounced, ignoring me. "We're going shopping."

"Shopping?"

"That's right," she sniffed primly. "And after that, we're going to Mortie's because you're buying me an early dinner."

Two hours, four dress shirts, three pairs of slacks, and a new brown blazer later, Leyla and I sat at one of the booths inside Mortie's Kosher Delicatessen and Family Restaurant. The homely smells of Uncle Mortie's Old World recipes drifted throughout the diner, hearkening its customers back to simpler times before enclaves, pandemics, nukes and magic. The late lunch crowd had thinned out, leaving the two of us nursing coffee and sandwich debris.

"You think Flynn was telling the truth?" Leyla asked as she sopped up brisket gravy with a bagel.

"Huh?" I held a piece of Uncle Mortie's world famous chocolate rugelach inches from my mouth as I stared blankly out the long window.

Charlotte and our whirlwind shopping spree had scrambled my thoughts. I bit into the pastry, idly savoring the fresh blend of baked chocolate, nut and cinnamon. A thickset older woman wearing a blue apron and carrying a coffee pot in one hand and a water pitcher in the other swooped in to refill my empty mug.

"You okay, *bubbalah*?" she asked me with a frown. "You look *far'misht*!"

"He's fine, Myrna," Leyla replied cheerfully, then her eyes narrowed with mischief. "Doc here has a date tonight!"

"A date? Wid a real girl?" Uncle Mortie's wife crowed with delight. "Happy days! You hear dis, Mortie! Tommy has a date!"

A loud crash of metal and crockery from behind the open window of the kitchen were hallmarked by angry cursing.

"Mortie is happy for you, too," Myrna chuckled, then her expression grew serious. "So. Tell me. Who is she? Is she nice? Pretty? Jewish?"

"Slow down." I held both hands up to shield myself from the motherly barrage. "I just met her today. She works for one of the suspects in an ongoing murder investigation, which makes it very complicated. And, besides, it's just drinks. I think. Anyway, yes to everything except the Jewish part. At least, I don't think she is. Okay?"

Myrna clucked with indignation. She was about to grill me further when another crash from the kitchen drew her attention.

"Is fine." She set the coffee pot on the table, then stroked my hair in the same gentle and familiar manner she'd been doing since I was old enough to walk. "You tell me about it later, yes?"

"Yes, ma'am," I responded dutifully.

"*Gut eyngl*," Myrna said before grabbing the pot. She topped us off with a flourish and a fond smile before waddling off toward the kitchen, berating Uncle Mortie in unintelligible Yiddish.

"I am *so* excited!" Leyla enthused.

"That makes one of us."

"Lighten up, Doc." The young hacker folded her hands on the table and adopted a business-like posture. "Are you going to bring her flowers?"

"She hasn't called yet," I grumbled. "And she probably won't. Can you just give it a rest?"

"Charlotte's going to call. She was giving you the 'look' in the elevator. And I watched her while you interviewed Flynn. She's definitely interested."

My body surged with excitement, but I tried not to let it show. These were uncomfortable feelings, emotions I hadn't explored in a long time. With the Sanarov investigation, and the fact Charlotte's boss was a suspect, I couldn't afford the luxury of experiencing them. I sipped at my coffee, marshaling my thoughts as I focused on the case.

"We need to get back on point," I said. "To answer your original question, the interview with Flynn went as I expected. Both his attitude and demeanor reflected a man who had nothing to fear from anyone, let alone ECPD or SCU. While I don't believe he's directly responsible for Sanarov's murder, he's not innocent either."

"Yeah, well he seemed pretty happy to smother us with all that moralizing bullshit," Leyla said. "Like he was daring us to accuse him of something. Did the Insight reveal anything?"

I shook my head and said, "If there was something for me to see, the Insight should've picked up on it. No, I think whatever game Flynn is playing, it's something that'll require some good ole-fashioned detective work to figure out. And, speaking of that, Flynn had a Bible at his workstation. I went through EVI's recording and had her crosscheck the image against the one we found at the crime scene, but both printing and editions are different. My gut's telling me Flynn is somehow connected to Sanarov beyond what happened in that warehouse thirty years ago. We just need to figure out what."

The bell above the diner's entrance jingled. A heartbeat later, Deacon slid into the booth next to Leyla. Steam wafted from his head and shoulders as the outdoor chill evaporated from the deli's warm interior.

"Is Flynn the killer?" he asked without preamble.

"Deacon." Myrna wandered over to us and gave the Confederate a fond smile. "Tea?"

"Sure," he replied, sparing her half a glance before turning back to us.

"Und bagel," she added.

"Thanks. So, Holliday is—"

"Toasted, und wid honey butter, yes?" Myrna finished in a tone that brooked no argument.

Deacon's face pinched with annoyance. He looked at

Myrna, who met his glare with a stony one of her own. The moment crystallized, and I thought Mortie's was about to erupt in brimstone and fire.

Surprisingly, Deacon broke first.

"Yes ma'am," the former Protector mumbled. "Thank you."

The world had officially ended.

"*Gut.* I get you tea now."

With a satisfied smile, Myrna bustled to the kitchen.

"What are you two lookin' at?" Deacon scowled.

After Myrna returned with his food, I recapped our meeting with Flynn.

"Then there's anyone from New Rikers that might've known Sanarov, including everyone on the inside that participated in his workshops who were subsequently released via the Pieces of Eight program," I concluded.

"That's a shitload of suspects, Holliday," Deacon remarked in-between munching on a toasted sesame bagel. "Thirty-plus years in lockup is a long time."

"I've made notes on several of them already, which cut the list in half," I said. "But I need someone to run the rest of them down which is why I'm so glad to have the two of you here to help me." I turned to Leyla. "I want you to ID any standouts with violent pasts or similar tendencies. That'll pretty much be all of them, but we've got to start some-where. Find out where they went, what they're doing, check in with their parole officers, and if any of them haven't kept their noses clean since their release."

"Got it," Leyla said.

"Deacon, I need you to visit Stentstrom at the morgue," I continued. "He left me a message while we were with Flynn. He's done the cut, and it didn't sound like he found anything worthwhile, but I want you to examine the body all the same. Maybe he missed something."

"Or maybe there ain't nothin' to see," the Confederate stated grimly. "A revenant ain't leavin' fingerprints, Holliday. What'll you be doing?"

Myrna swung by to refill our cups.

"Thanks." I took a healthy gulp. "I'll call Father Jack to schedule sit-downs with all the church officers and staff, and the Pantry volunteers between later today and tomorrow. If something comes up, I'll contact you."

"Not burning the midnight oil this time, Holliday?" Deacon raised an eyebrow. "You sick or something?"

"He can't," Leyla chimed in, unable to contain herself.

"Can't?" he squawked. "What's that supposed to mean? And why're you grinnin' like some fucking ghoul, girlie?"

I sighed, bowed my head and rolled my hand for Leyla to continue.

"Doc has a date!" Leyla burst triumphantly.

"S'that right?" Deacon eyed me with amusement. "How much you payin'? 'Cause she sure as shit ain't payin' you."

"Very funny," I said. "No, his executive assistant asked me out for drinks tonight. I figure she might know something that could help the case."

"Bullshit," Deacon was skeptical. "*She* asked *you*?"

"What?" I glanced between the two of them. "You don't think it's unreasonable that someone would ask me out?"

Deacon snorted but didn't reply.

"Doc, what about the revenant-thingy that Deacon mentioned earlier?" Leyla asked. "Shouldn't we look into that, too?"

A chill wandered the length of my spine at the dark turn in the conversation.

"If that's what did in Gus, its imprint should still be in

that room," the former Protector said. "Although, I reckon it won't be around too much longer. You want to take another crack at it with the Insight?"

"I'm still working on something," I said. "Let's get the interviews and fact-finding done first. We've got a lot of work ahead of us."

"And you've got a date!" Leyla crooned.

"She hasn't called yet."

"She will."

"Whatever."

I left the booth with the two of them discussing strategy and returned to the pod. During the ride back to the Redeemer, I reached out to Father Jack to let him know I was headed there. He informed me he had already contacted everyone on the list and scheduled meetings with them in an hour. The Pantry volunteers would arrive at the church tomorrow morning around ten. I thanked him, and we disconnected.

Jack had sounded business-like on the call, which was understandable, yet made me sad. I had few people I could call friends. I didn't want to lose the old pastor over this investigation. But I was also tasked with finding Sanarov's killer. If that meant breaking a few proto-eggs, then tomorrow I'd be eating omelets for breakfast.

Outside the Redeemer, brisk February winds blazed through the church's parking lot, now filled with a variety of automobiles. However, none of them stood out to me as ostentatious or out-of-place. I crossed the lot quickly to escape the wind and cold.

Inside, I walked down the long west wing of the church to one of the parochial school classrooms where I'd conduct the interviews. More than a dozen people awaited me huddled together in small knots and speaking in hushed voices. Fruit, snacks, and coffee had been arranged on a cloth-covered table along one wall.

Leave it to Father Jack to try and alleviate some of the anxiety of having a homicide detective in their midst. The arrangement felt more like a meet-and-greet rather than a murder investigation.

The pastor greeted me courteously, made with introductions, then left me to the interviews. His handshake had been formal, and his smile seemed forced, but his relief at not seeing Deacon accompanying me was genuine enough.

I sat at the teacher's desk, arranged my holo-phone on its surface, and had EVI project directly to my retina the names in alphabetical order. Once set up, I directed all but the first person on the list to exit the classroom. I shut the door, then gestured politely for a woman in her late sixties to take a seat.

I then spent the next five hours on a fruitless search for a needle in a haystack.

The door closed with an audible thump as the last interviewee left for the night. Alone in the classroom, I stared at the ceiling, its surface chipped in several places. I heaved a heavy sigh. None of these people had set off either the Insight, or my bullshit meter. While it was necessary to eliminate every possibility, the tedium of conducting these kinds of interviews sucked the life from me. Still, as my grandfather Harry used to say, the Devil always hid in the details, and I hated letting that pointy-tailed bastard get the best of me.

I gathered my things, shut the lights, and wandered back to the sanctuary. Jack was at the center of a small group of people I'd interviewed. I waved from a distance, and he nodded. There was no sense interrupting him now. We'd chat tomorrow.

I heard the splash of water as something wet hit the floor outside the sanctuary.

"Been a long day," remarked Orlando Denning, the church's sexton, and the second person that I'd interviewed today. He was a stocky man in his sixties, clean-shaven with thick arms and pepper gray in his crewcut. The older man maneuvered the mop along the floor with stuttered swipes.

"Too long," I agreed.

"Thanks for checking into all this," Denning said. "Father Jack, he's a good soul. Doesn't deserve none of this. You back tomorrow?"

"Yes," I nodded. "The Pantry volunteers are next. Will you be here?"

"No, it's my day off." The sexton paused in his work and leaned on the mop. "I pray you catch whoever murdered Gus, Detective Holliday. God bless and have a good night."

"You, too."

Bracing myself against the deep cold, I pushed through the heavy door and jogged quickly back to the pod. Once inside, I directed EVI to take us to Central Dispatch where I'd drop off the transport, then head home.

My phone had buzzed twice during the interviews. Mahoney had called again asking for an update. I finally returned his call, offering what few details I'd gathered so far, and informed him I'd have the results of the New Rikers group as soon as I could. Bill asked very few questions. He sounded weary, his words slurring enough that he'd probably been drinking. He ordered me to call him by lunchtime tomorrow for another update.

The other message was from Deacon. He'd met with Stentstrom, but neither of them had discovered anything unusual about the body. Stentstrom confirmed small nodules of pressure had built up throughout the victim's organs, then exploded at the same time. He surmised the amount of agony Sanarov had suffered was off the scale. Deacon said the medical examiner hadn't heard of or read about any drug or medical condition capable of doing that. None of Sanarov's prison medical history indicated he had had health problems, either. The former Protector also provided a systematic breakdown of the scant forensic evidence found in Sanarov's room. None of it stood out to either Deacon or Stentstrom. Whoever had killed Sanarov hadn't left any physical breadcrumbs behind. The Confederate ended by saying he'd check in on Leyla to give her a hand if she needed it.

"Oh, and good luck tonight, Holliday," Deacon chuckled. "Hopefully, you ain't forgotten how to show a lady a good time."

I rolled my eyes. The little fantasy I'd held that someone who looked like Charlotte would be interested in a poor *schmo* like me had set sail right after I left the diner. For now, it was time to go home and settle in with some quality classic rock-and-roll while I did the initial write-up on the investigation. Uncle Mortie's special grounds percolated happily from inside the onboard beverage dispenser. I filled my mug before crashing in a chair.

"Detective Holliday," EVI said via the pod's comm speakers. "Would you like for me to replay your private messages?"

I sat upright, spilling the hot coffee on my shirt and hand. I hadn't bothered checking those.

"How many are there?" I shook my wet hand in irritation.

"One," she replied. "From Charlotte Sloane. Shall I play it for you now?"

"Uh, yeah. Go ahead."

"I hope the day finds you well, Detective Holliday." Charlotte's warm, accented voice played over the speaker like slow jazz.

A stupid grin plastered my face.

Leyla was right.

I had a date.

9

I met Charlotte at Fernand's, an upscale watering hole on the ground floor of a ninety-story office building catering to Park and Madison Avenue's shameless and beautiful. I immediately hated the place. Not because I couldn't afford any of their so-called "organic-infused" appetizers. Or because the place required a jacket and tie.

No, I hated Fernand's because their coffee tasted like shit.

You'd think an upper-crusty establishment like this would serve java that didn't pour like syrup and taste like day-old puke, but it did. Not nearly as bad were the snotty looks I got the moment I sat down across from Charlotte, as if I had paid her to be my date.

Our table-for-two, located in the middle of a designer-shoe scarred floor, was bookended by other Wall Street types who were all engaged in boisterous conversations, each louder than the next. Theirs was a healthy blend of hormones and arrogance. They touted their latest financial conquests, as if they'd just invented the cure for taxes. The noise was like standing in the middle of Grand Central during rush hour while the rest of humanity thundered by to who knew where.

Fortunately, my lovely companion more than made up for everything else.

Charlotte had an exotic quality about her that I found captivating. She wore the same outfit from earlier, but she had freshened her makeup which complimented the delicate curves of her face. Her wavy hair bucked the latest scythe-cut rainbow hued hairstyles the women of Empire City had been adopting since last November. It hinted at an unconventional personality lurking behind her otherwise corporate conformity.

I caught myself staring and coughed in embarrassment. Charlotte's eyes danced with amusement as she observed my discomfort.

"We could go somewhere else, Detective," she offered politely. "Perhaps some place less crowded? I know of several within half-a-block which offer less noise and more room."

"No, this is fine," I said, feigning indifference. "And, please, call me Tom. I'm off the clock. So, um, tell me about yourself. Where are you from?"

Charlotte chuckled. She sipped at her wine, some pricey cabernet from the Bordeaux Regime. I drank water after the disastrous first cup of coffee and hoped the coffee gods would smite Fernand's soon. Other than my goldjoy misadventure at the nightclub Kraze last October, I hadn't touched alcohol since I left Wallingbrooke eight years ago. Falling off the wagon again wasn't something I could afford.

"New London," she replied with a smile. "I moved to Empire City over a year ago."

"By yourself?" I asked, then realized how sophomoric that sounded. "I mean, you just picked up and moved here?"

I should've stayed home with my head in the oven.

"Yes," Charlotte laughed again. "I was actually born in Romford, about an hour outside of the city. I had visited here previously with my parents when we were on holiday, and immediately fell in love with the enclave. Empire City is so full of diversity! There is a vibrancy to it unlike anywhere else that I have traveled. And there is so much to see! What about you, Tom?"

"I'm from Brighton Beach, east across the river," I pointed in the direction I thought was east, then added quickly, "It's not that, um, vibrant. The old neighborhood can be, well, rough."

"I see," she said, then smiled mischievously. "Perhaps you could escort me around sometime? I've seen the shinier side of Empire City. I'd love to get to know its dirtier parts as well."

I blushed and rubbed the back of my neck. Charlotte took a long sip of wine. I couldn't meet her gaze and stared down at my empty plate.

"I'm sure you've been to all sorts of wicked places, hunting down killers," she remarked casually. "How long have you worked in law enforcement?"

I looked up, relieved she had changed the subject. Charlotte held her glass in her right hand. I noticed her knuckles had old white scars on them. They reminded me of Deacon for some reason.

"Almost sixteen years," I said, failing to get comfortable in the narrow chair. Whoever had designed the chair had someone with more rear cushion than me in mind. "I was a beat cop, then got promoted to homicide. Eventually, I ended up with Special Crimes."

We spent the next two hours talking, the time melting away with pleasant stories and anecdotes about friends and family. I told her about being raised in the Jewish faith yet attending the Redeemer's parochial school. Charlotte mentioned her father had been an officer for London's Perimeter Defense Force, before retiring after forty years of decorated service. Her mother was also retired, an ER nurse who had spent time abroad helping several of the less fortunate enclaves down in war-torn Nouveau Afrikaans.

Charlotte possessed a quick wit I found endearing. Her sardonic sense of humor reminded me of Kate, and to my surprise, I wasn't bothered by it. I had been worried meeting with Charlotte would be a betrayal of Kate's memory, but that wasn't the case. Sitting here with her only reinforced how emotionally remote I'd become since Wallingbrooke. I'd refrained from anything more than cursory day-to-day contact with most everyone else in my life. I had stopped attending my mandatory weekly checkups with a psychiatrist years ago. And other than Abner and Leyla, I didn't want the complications that came with more intimate relationships. All I had to do was look at my dad and what little relationship we had for affirmation.

Life stayed simpler that way.

But Charlotte was bright, a breath of fresh air I hadn't realized I needed. Our conversation flowed easily. Soon enough, cracks appeared in my armor of apathy. At some point during the evening, a strange tingling had formed at the base of my skull, yet my eyes didn't burn with the Insight. My skin felt warm, almost feverish, but I chalked it up to my strong attraction to Charlotte.

"Have you ever been shot?" she asked at one point.

The two tables of Wall Street blowhards had been replaced by an equal gaggle of twenty-something debutantes wearing much less than the winter weather required.

Charlotte's quiet elegance and proper hauteur put them all to shame.

"It's an occupational hazard," I smiled deprecatingly, spreading my hands wide. "But, yes, I've been shot. One time, there was this implant junkie who was squatting on the first floor of a condemned building in Little Odessa. That's what us locals call Brighton Beach. Anyway, I took him out, but not before my shoulder was hit. I have to admit, I am a bleeder."

"You killed him?" Charlotte asked, her eyes wide.

"Oh, no," I said in alarm, dismayed at how it must've sounded to her. "Beat cops carry stun batons as well as guns. He shot me, but I subdued him."

"Thank goodness!" she breathed, then gave me a shy look. "But, have you?"

"Have I what?"

"Killed anyone?"

The question hung in the air, a silent divide more than the eighteen inches of table that separated us. I ignored the animated conversations and general clamor of the restaurant and focused my attention on Charlotte. There was something about the question that compelled me to answer. The tingling had grown stronger. This moment was important, as if it was more than two people having a conversation over dinner.

It felt like a test.

"Yes," I answered slowly, choosing my words with care. "I swore an oath to protect Empire City and her citizenry. And while I may not be perfect, I do my best. But it goes beyond simply 'to serve and protect'. The average person needs me out there, busting my ass to keep them safe. But they also want me to stay out of their business. It's a fine line all cops walk every day."

I paused and held her gaze with a bleak one of my own.

"Nothing is ever truly black and white though, is it," I said with a wry smile, then pulled out the silver SCU badge from around my neck and placed it on the table. Light seemed to be drawn into it. "I wear that badge with both respect and pride. It's my duty to enforce the law in a manner commensurate with that trust. But, sometimes, I'm not given much of a choice. Investigations are fluid. I never know when I'll have to make the hard choices, only that they happen. And when that time comes, my response must be commensurate with what I truly believe as, and what my constant training has prepared me for, the right thing to do. Otherwise, I'm no better than the monsters I chase."

I scooped up the badge and returned it around my neck, its weight somehow heavier.

"I recognize the people I investigate don't have the same moral compass as me. They can't. Like I told your boss earlier, people kill because they like it, because they get off on it, or they're paid to do it. In the end, though, it doesn't matter. They're on the other side, the *wrong* side, and it's my job to stop them."

The moment ended. Charlotte watched me with rapt attention. The server had refilled her wine, yet Charlotte hadn't touched her glass while I spoke.

"How remarkable," she murmured.

"Oh, I don't know about that," I said. Both the tingling and warmth had vanished.

Charlotte appraised me with a slight curl to her lip, tracing a finger along the top of the wine glass. It was then that I realized I couldn't read her at all, that her personality, her laughter, the way she carried herself, even the way she spoke seemed more of an affectation, a role she was playing than what was really, truly her.

The server returned with our dinner—fresh soy-glazed salmon and actual soil-grown asparagus for the lady, and well-done meat and cheese potatoes for the barbarian. Our conversation was light yet substance-less, as we both avoided whatever weight had been brought to the table following my answer to her question. We both declined coffee and dessert, although to my credit I did politely ask Charlotte if she wanted a cup. Thankfully, Charlotte said she was full, and that was that. With dinner finished, we walked over to the *maitre d'* to retrieve Charlotte's coat, then went outside.

It was nearing midnight. The temperature had plummeted to well below freezing. Several Nexus-powered yellow auto-cabs waited along the curb. Their engines purred softly like a collection of caged cats. The closest one to us had its door open expectantly. Charlotte moved toward it, and I followed a few hesitant steps behind, uncertain what to do, then stopped. I dug my hands into my pockets and blinked at the colorful holo-ads flashing above me.

"Thank you for dinner," Charlotte said, turning toward me.

I looked back at her and was about to respond when she stepped up and kissed me full on the mouth.

Her tongue tasted like a cabernet had married a proto-cinnamon bar, then had babies.

I melted.

THE DREAM WAS UNFAMILIAR.

I was alone. My breath streamed before me in whispery smoke, but I wasn't cold.

The room I was in contained a central aisle separating

two rows of beds. Each bed was properly made, a tight blanket even with the covers, capped by a white pillow. Light glimmered faintly from somewhere, dousing the room in shadowy gray. Heavy beige drapes covered the windows along one wall. A single closed door was set at the far end.

I heard crying, muted and faint, but couldn't pinpoint its source. The sobs were laced with despair, anger and loss. Moving to the windows, I pulled the drapes aside to reveal brick walls with no glass. Behind the door was another brick wall. There was nothing under the beds, not even a speck of dust. I stared at my hands. They were smaller, the flesh newer, unblemished by hard work and time. I wore a blue hospital gown with white puffy clouds on the front. I ran my hand over my head and found it shaven and smooth.

And when they have finished their testimony, the beast that rises from the bottomless pit will make war on them and conquer them and kill them.

The voice came from everywhere and nowhere, filling me with an awful dread. The crying had disappeared.

"Who are you?" I asked, but my voice was younger and bereft of its rough edge. "What do you want?"

The righteous will rejoice when he sees the vengeance. He will bathe his feet in the blood of the wicked.

"I don't understand."

I moved around the room. The voice, neither loud or soft, was forceful, and dripped with an agony that clawed at my senses.

It began here. And it will end here.

"Where am I?"

You cannot stop me, Guardian of Empire City. Stand against me and fail.

"I don't understand!"

You have been warned.

I awoke with a start, bathed in sweat.

"Detective Holliday, you have a priority message from Captain Mahoney," EVI announced in my ear.

"Give me a minute," I mumbled.

Charlotte snored softly next to me. The sheets of her bed were wrapped around the curves of her body. My skin rippled with goose flesh, and a powerful need for her gripped me. I suppressed my desire, although one part of me had other ideas. Light from her bathroom spilled into the bedroom, cloaking our discarded clothing in soft shadows. I stared at Charlotte as my brain registered what EVI was trying to tell me. Work was the last thing on my mind, but I couldn't keep Mahoney waiting. As quietly as I could, I got out of bed and dressed. Charlotte didn't stir.

"Put it through," I thought via the implant as I moved into the adjoining living room.

"Tom, get down to Eddie's in Brighton Beach, ASAP." The captain's voice was tired. "We've got three new bodies."

10

E ddie's took up the corner of Coney Island Boulevard and Brighton 10th Street like a skulking drug dealer selling low-grade shit in a high-class neighborhood. The dilapidated dive filled one end of a rundown city block, sharing space with a laundromat, two hookah lounges and a burned-out husk. The few working streetlamps were interspersed sparingly, spilling small circles of faded light that seemed to conceal more than they revealed.

Across the way was a five-story tenement called Rhona's whose transient clientele ranged from low-brow to desperate. I'd spent plenty of nights in its one-bedroom efficiencies with my head buried in a toilet. The fact that I had never contracted anything more than a head-cold back then was a testament to the amount of bad shit coursing through my bloodstream.

I glanced at Rhona's. Twin pinpoint cigarette flares lit up the shadows to reveal two figures lurking inside the doorway, one leaning against a wall. My eyes lingered on them before I hefted the heavy metal box containing the portable

P-Scanner and shouldered through the front entrance into Eddie's.

There had been no flashing lights or media presence when the pod had pulled up a block from the dive bar. The streets were quiet thanks in part to the snow dusting the world, the intense cold, and the early morning hour. Mahoney had sent a text informing me that he'd kept the situation off air. But with three more bodies, it wouldn't stay that way for long.

Before debarking the pod, I had called and left a holo-recording on Charlotte's phone apologizing for my sudden departure, and my fervent hope we could get together again later today. Remnants of her perfume still lingered on my clothes and skin, lusty intimations from our night of passion. What had happened between us still resonated with me, and my heart skipped a beat at the prospect of seeing her again.

However, as I crossed the threshold into Eddie's taproom, the Insight had other ideas.

The fickle magic took hold of me in the covetous embrace of a jealous lover. It rippled along my spine, its light current of vibrant energy causing the hair on my arms to stand on end. Silver fire flecked the fringes of my vision, and with it, a bright clarity sharpened my senses. Thoughts of Charlotte were replaced by the sight of three broken bodies lying in a bloody heap.

"*Hell is empty,*" I whispered. "*And all the devils are here.*"

The Insight exacerbated the charnel-house smell, but I managed to keep last night's dinner down. A wisp of silver fire tickled my eyes, drawing me to the dark-paneled wall closest to me. Random patterns and streaks of blood soaked its surface. As I watched, the crimson runnels resolved into letters, a dire message meant for anyone with the power to see it.

And when they have finished their testimony, the beast that rises from the bottomless pit will make war on them and conquer them and kill them.

The words scrawled in blood had run down its length and pooled on the floor.

I turned away to study the bar's interior before the sight overwhelmed me. Eddie's was narrow, windowless, and drenched in shadows. At the curve of the short bar to my right stood Mahoney, Stentstrom and a stocky woman drying her hands on a dirty towel. She was half my height with short, spiky colorful hair and dozens of face and ear piercings. Mahoney was speaking to her, but she only had frightened eyes for the awful tableau before her.

Without acknowledging anyone, I donned the plastic outerwear Stentstrom had left for me on the bar, then stepped forward and placed the P-Scanner on the floor. After flipping open the box top, I withdrew the sensor, a cordless flashlight tube which collected the raw data and transmitted its findings back to both EVI and the main unit. The P-Scanner detected and measured a wide variety of compounds and substances, both organic and synthetic, as well as an array of energy signatures. It was no replacement for a proper forensics team, but it was a solid second.

I waved the sensor slowly around the area containing the bodies, as well as the bloody wall and the nearby high-top. Soft violet light emanated in a cone from its business end. Above the metal box hovered a wheel of five small holo-windows, each containing the results collected from my sweep.

I glanced at the readings and frowned. One window included a detailed list of all the foreign elements that had been discovered by the scan. Amidst the detritus the three corpses had tracked in before they got waxed, along with whatever shit that had accumulated on the floor since its last cleaning, the scanner had picked up water containing 3.5% salinity from the rubber soles of their shoes. These guys had spent some time either on the boardwalk, at the beach, or near the waterfront.

Once I finished my circuit of the kill zone, I knelt on the sticky floor to study the three mutilated bodies. I made out faded tattoos along the necks of two of them, familiar etchings that conveyed more than their lack of aesthetic appeal. These were ceremonial markings denoting whatever long and illustrious criminal careers they'd enjoyed before they died. However, the tattoos were all marred by dozens of small wounds, far too many perforations for anyone to endure and survive.

Just like Sanarov.

Judging from the position of the four chairs surrounding the high-top, the three dead men were in mid-motion when they were struck down. Three empty glasses and a bottle of some cheap vodka had been left undisturbed, but a fourth glass was full.

I worked around the blood on the floor to gain a better vantage point to examine the table. A clear aisle by the fourth chair gave me the access I needed allowing me to scan the high-top. I had EVI lock onto the images to register any fingerprints. Then I stowed the sensor in my belt and withdrew two large evidence bags from my pocket. I placed the three empty glasses and the bottle in one, and the fourth, including the vodka, in the other.

"Detective Holliday," Stentstrom called out tremulously, breaking the silence. I released my breath, unaware of how long I'd been holding it. "EVI confirmed the elliptical spatter pattern. It's the same as Mr. Sanarov. Multiple, sharp force exit injuries resulting from severe, penetrating bursts of the torso, extremities, head, and face. The exit wounds are throughout the body, with no apparent single location as the principal cause of death. Massive trauma and organ failure were immediate. And I predict there will be no indication of any foreign substances in the body, either, beyond the obvious, that is."

I nodded but didn't respond.

Low music warbled from speakers throughout the taproom, some slow, dirge-like number that mirrored the drab interior. The heavy paneled walls hadn't seen lacquer or a good paint job in decades. The tables and chairs were chipped and uneven, and the metallic tang of blood, cigarette, cigar, vape and other, less savory aromas stuck to the room like a cancer. The bar ran the length of one side, behind which was arrayed a who's who of bottled spirits. Ten tables were strewn throughout, with the high-tops up front, and the lower tables near the back. The kitchen was hidden behind a gray curtain at the bar's far end, while a darkened hallway led to the bathroom and the rear exit.

I returned to the bodies and began my careful search of their clothes. The first man's face was unrecognizable, a viscous map of torn flesh, blood, bone and brain matter. An old, but well-kept MP-446 Viking was shoved inside his belt buckle. Whatever had hit him took the man out before he could draw his weapon. I also knew the handgun had a magazine capacity of eighteen rounds, unlike the civilian market version. Black Sea Conglomerate make with no serial number.

"Time of death?" I asked, withdrawing his holo-ID, although I had already made him once I saw the gun.

Pyotr Ushakov.

"Shit," I muttered under my breath. Things had just gotten messier.

"Just after midnight," the woman spoke up. Her accent was thick and heavy, a hallmark to her Black Sea Conglomerate upbringing. "I went in back to get something. Then I hear screaming. When I come back, they like this. So, I call police."

I folded my arms and nodded. Bill must've been monitoring the feed and picked it up before Dispatch could redirect the call to the local precinct.

"Who was the fourth?" I asked her. "Where'd they go?"

"They wanted four glasses," Eddie replied. "But no other was here before I go in back."

"You were ordered to leave?"

Eddie fixed me with a gimlet stare and said, "You knew these men, yes?"

"Yeah, Eddie," I replied with a heavy sigh. "Yeah, I knew them."

Edwina Rastakovich had owned this gin joint for as long as I could remember. I used to be a regular here, back when I didn't care what I had put in my body or how it got there. The place was considered neutral ground for the locals, where business was brokered and settled, usually without bloodshed. And it was a favorite haunt for Ushakov, Vlad Borovich and Stan Staszlov, three members of the Kiev Brotherhood.

Little Odessa's very own *bratva*.

"Not anymore," I murmured.

Anyone who grew up in Brighton Beach knew about these guys. They'd been terrorizing neighborhoods since before I was born. The former Ukrainian mafia from the late twenty-first century had changed leaders and faces since the nukes happened, but their penchant for organized crime never wavered.

The Kiev Brotherhood was led by a mysterious *Pakhan*, or "boss", who controlled four criminal cells through an intermediary called a "brigadier". One of the presiding principles for their criminal model was to minimize contact with the other cells to prevent identification of the entire organization. ECPD's Organized Crime Taskforce had spent years accumulating information on the Kiev Brotherhood, but they were as slippery as shit on hot pavement. The number of untraceable credits burning holes in the cloud accounts of cops, lawyers and ECPD admins on the take was enough to run a few of the smaller enclaves.

The three stiffs at Eddie's had started out as low-level enforcers, local punks who zealously pursued the time-honored tradition of extreme violence. Whether it was murder-for-hire, shaking down local businesses for protection, or selling and distributing drugs, when these three showed up, it was wise to leave before things got nasty.

Unless, of course, they happened to run into something nastier than them.

I returned the sensor to the box, deactivated the P-Scanner and instructed EVI to analogize the rest of the data. If I was lucky, she could determine some commonality between the raw data sets that would help link what happened here to the killer.

Of course, I'm never that lucky.

I pulled the IDs from the other two, gave them a cursory glance, and placed all three in another plastic bag. They were all similar in age with Sanarov. That wasn't a coincidence, either. I didn't believe in them.

"You know they come soon," Eddie warned.

"They're already here," I answered. "There's two across the street, and I'd bet a couple more out back."

"Why they no come in?" she asked.

"Because they've been told not to interfere," Mahoney answered.

I grimaced. This case was ugly with a capital F.

I stood up to regard Mahoney and the others. The captain's face was drawn, his eyes dark and haunted. Even without the Insight, I knew the man hadn't slept since I last saw him. Mahoney's conscience was wracked by something, a deeply rooted guilt that had everything to do with this case.

With that fresh in my mind, the taproom wrinkled in time, a compression of reality bending light and space. Gone were the bodies, the blood, the stench, all of it. I found myself in a small office somewhere else, but the details were unclear, cloudy, like the half-baked pieces of someone's cracked memory.

Young Mahoney stood before me, wearing a brown suit and a gold shield hanging from a chain around his neck. There was a susurration of voices, but I couldn't make out what was being said. Young Mahoney grimaced, then gave a begrudging nod to someone not readily visible. The defeated expression on his face was something I never thought I'd ever see. Emotions rolled off him in waves—frustration, anger, anxiety, and shame.

My ears popped suddenly as if I had stepped from a vacuum.

"But it's wrong," Young Mahoney said. "We can't do this. It's tampering with an investigation that you know—"

"If you want things to work, you have to make sacrifices," a man's stern voice interrupted, but I couldn't place it. "Commitments and concessions, remember? For the greater good."

"What the hell do you know about the 'greater good,'" Young Mahoney shot back. "You're just a goddamn politician wearing a fucking uniform."

"That's enough, Detective," the voice snapped with authority. "You'll do this, because you know it's the right call, and because both of our careers are riding on it. Am I clear?"

Young Mahoney was silent, the disgust plain on his face. I could almost hear the gears turning in his head.

"Good," the voice said in a more pleasant tone. "Now, get out of my office and clean that shit up."

My world spiraled as if flushed down a toilet. Eddie's reappeared, along with a healthy dose of vertigo, thanks to the wrenching sensation of being yanked from one point in time back to the present.

"Are you all right, Detective?" Bill asked. The captain was beside me, frowning with concern. Stentstrom and Eddie hadn't moved.

"I'm, ah, fine," I replied. I removed a plastic glove, then rubbed a finger in one ear, while moving my lower jaw in circles. Both ears popped again before clearing. "Just got caught up in the smell, that's all. Give me a minute."

Bill nodded, although he wasn't convinced.

My mind raced as I gathered up my time-addled marbles. The pieces of the puzzle were still disjointed. Sanarov had been convicted for kidnapping Calvin Flynn, but not for the boy's murder. With what I'd just seen through the Insight, some of that began to make a little more sense. The connections were there, but remained vague shapes, too faint to see. It was like collecting breadcrumbs in the middle of the woods.

At midnight.

And I was blindfolded.

Which wasn't anything new.

"Captain, why are we the only ones here?" I asked. "Why didn't you call it in this time?"

"Because, Detective Holliday," an accented voice answered from behind me, "I asked William not to."

11

Besim Saranda loomed in the doorway, an enigmatic shadow shrouded in secrets I had no interest in uncovering. The Vellan was slight of build, but at six and a half feet tall, her presence bore a weight that dampened my already darkened mood.

"What the hell are you doing here?" I demanded, angry heat etching each word.

"I wished to accompany William," she replied coolly.

She gave the room a cursory glance, a detached and clinical expression, unaffected by the bloody spectacle covering the walls and floor. The SCU consultant wore a heavy longshoreman's overcoat, unbuttoned to reveal a green and orange-patterned peasant top and a matching loose-fitting skirt that reached her ankles. Open-toed sandals with mismatching blue, green and yellow painted toes completed the ensemble. She and Leyla must've shopped at the same shoe store.

Besim's oval face was caked in fresh makeup, the style almost reminiscent of an old PT Barnum circus clown. Her short-cropped hair was dyed a dark brown and tied with a flower-patterned bandana. On the surface, it was Besim's attempt to blend in with the people of Empire City, an affectation to appear as a native, and thereby less alien to her human counterparts.

But I knew the truth.

Beneath the layers of foundation and eyeliner, her skin was etched with an intricate series of tattoos that ran along her forehead and temple, and down the sides of her face and swan-like neck. Those same tattoos acted as a cultural fingerprint, identifying a Vellan's house and familial history. The markings were also linked to a Vellan's hair color, both of which acted as a demarcation of their unique standing within their caste-system hierarchy. I knew that to conceal either was an affront to Vellan society.

To conceal both, though, was tantamount to exile.

But what was most striking about Besim were her eyes. Almond-shaped, gray and wider than a human's, they registered everything she saw, missing nothing. And right now, she studied me with a curious intensity.

"Where's Deacon?" I glared at the captain, ignoring her for the moment. Besim rarely went anywhere without him by her side.

"Deacon Kole is indisposed," the consultant answered.

"Unlike Patricia Sullinger, this doesn't involve the Vellan government," I stated coldly, then turned back to Besim. "Or am I missing something?"

Besim returned my stare with a placid one of her own.

"No, Tom, you're right," Mahoney said. "But given the unusual circumstances surrounding these murders, I thought you could use Besim's unique perspective."

"With all due respect, sir," I said evenly, trying to keep my temper from boiling over, "I already told you I don't need her help. Besides, the investigation began yesterday!

Give me some time to analyze the evidence and formulate a few theories first."

Besim began a slow, deliberate circuit of the three corpses, then stopped to study the bloodied wall. She reached out with a hand, her long, tapered fingers hovering over the crimson lines that streaked the paneling.

"Don't. Touch. Anything," I warned her.

She didn't respond. Instead, she closed her eyes and stood still.

"It's not that, Tom." The captain held up a placating hand, then lowered his voice. "There's some pressure on SCU from Mayor Samson to handle this one with kid gloves. Donald Flynn called the mayor today to let him know you came by to question him. Apparently, Flynn complimented your efficiency and professionalism."

"Lucky me," I grumbled. Flynn flaunting his close relationship with Empire City's royalty really frosted my ass. "He's the most likely suspect, given his history with Sanarov. Off the record, I don't trust him. He gave me all the right answers, but my gut's telling me there's more behind that three-hundred credit face-lift of his. I need time to take a deeper dive into him."

I kept an eye on Besim. Her lips moved, but I heard no sound. The hairs on the back of my neck stood on end.

What the fuck was she doing?

"I understand that Detective but hear me out," Mahoney said, the stress wrinkling the corners of his eyes. "Flynn is one of the enclave's biggest philanthropists, behind Doctor Roberto Montalbas and Alan Azyrim. Between Titan Bank and Brave New Beginnings, Flynn carries a lot of weight, commercially, socially and politically."

"Making Flynn one of the mayor's biggest financial supporters," I guessed.

"That's right," Bill nodded. "With the upcoming election in November, the mayor wants to make sure there are no complications."

"Complications?" I scoffed. "This would be Samson's fifth term! He rebuilt half of Queens with his own campaign funds after the Proto-Orgo-Food plant fires twenty years ago. The man's an institution! Didn't he win the last election by over two million votes?"

Empire City, like many of the enclaves within the former United States, was governed by a modified Constitution. After the nukes, the survivors living in what was left of New York City and parts of New Jersey and Connecticut had banded together to form what would eventually become the enclave. They had decided the old way of governing was still the right way, and wanted to honor the sanctity and memory of the original Founding Fathers, but with a few key changes. While Empire City was a metropolitan municipality with a mayor-council form of government, some genius came up with the idea that elected officials should be allowed to remain in their seats for five four-year consecutive terms, presuming they won. And for some inexplicable reason, it stuck.

To my mind, every vote counted, but politics remained an incurable venereal disease.

"He did," Mahoney said. "But that doesn't mean the mayor isn't paranoid, or stupid. Tom, SCU is under the microscope again. This investigation needs to remain above board at all times."

I was about to let the captain know exactly how I felt about the election in relation to how I investigated cases but thought better of it. Between the DA's office and the mayor's backing, SCU wouldn't exist today, and I'd still be filing everyone else's e-reports back at the 98th Precinct. I owed

Mayor Samson that much, at least. The question was, what did Mahoney owe him?

"Copy that," I relented. "So, what is she really doing here?"

"She insisted," Mahoney explained. "And, after careful consideration, I agreed. Given her experience as a consultant, and your success with the previous case, I felt having her along would benefit the investigation."

I gave up. Bill wouldn't make it an order, but I saw the truth in his eyes. Once again, I was on babysitting duty.

"Fine, but the same rules apply. Everything goes through me." I paused as a thought hit me. "Let me handle whoever shows up to claim the bodies. Telling them to stay away gives me time, but the shit will hit the fan soon and that shouldn't involve you, at least not at this level. I'll need you to play more interference, but not with them."

Mahoney's blue eyes sharpened.

"I'll keep my ears on the OC Taskforce," the captain said.

"I may need you to play more interference," I pointed out. "It's not just our own guys I'm worried about."

"Understood, Detective."

"One more thing, sir," I said, placing my hand on his shoulder. Mahoney stiffened at my touch. I knew the familiar gesture overstepped protocol, but Bill looked like he needed a hug, and five gallons of the hardest liquor credits could buy. "Go home. Get some rest. There's not much more you can do right now."

I recognized his reaction as a stubbornness born from years of being on the job, working cases and burning the candle at both ends to catch killers. But the intervening years since he'd left Empire City had been hard on him. His family had been murdered by a serial killer years ago. It had taken a long sabbatical to the Euro-Bloc and a not-so-chance meeting with Besim to get him back on track. Although how he was able to get up in the morning after suffering through that kind of tragedy was beyond me. His will to fight, his unwavering belief in what ECPD did, and what SCU was trying to do, was one of the many things I admired about the man.

Bill stared at me a moment. "EVI, pull my car around."

The captain walked over to Eddie and Stentstrom, said something I couldn't hear, then headed to the exit.

"Detective," he called over to me. His shoulders were slumped with exhaustion. "I expect regular updates."

I still had questions for him, but those would have to wait a bit longer. The three bodies demanded my attention. Whatever their connection was to Sanarov, it wasn't in Bill's old case files. And the interlude from Mahoney's past the Insight had provided for me just now was further evidence of old ties. But to whom, and why? I didn't expect Stentstrom's autopsy to reveal anything new. If Deacon was right, and we were dealing with some vengeful spirit, maybe having Besim along wasn't such a bad idea.

At the very least, she could pay for breakfast.

"Detective Holliday," Stentstrom announced. "My team will be arriving shortly. I have also requested Doctor Cohen to handle this morning's examination docket which will free me up to perform the autopsies. I will update EVI with all my findings, of course. However, I need to make a few calls. If you will excuse me?"

"Thank you, Doctor," I said, then regarded Eddie. "We're not done here. I've still got questions for you. But more importantly, do those cameras I had installed still work?"

"Could not Leyla pull feed from cloud?" Eddie asked.

I shook my head. "I'd rather have the micro-drive in-hand. If any of Ushakov's 'friends' figured out it's there, they may have their own watchdogs sitting on it in case someone tries to download it."

"I get feed for you," Eddie said, and moved toward the back.

The bar might be neutral ground, but Eddie was no fool. Its neutrality was held together because of the unspoken understanding between any criminal element that agreed to meet here. The crime syndicates from the surrounding neighborhoods hated each other enough to kill every last one of their opposite number, but they still followed a code of conduct.

Honor amongst thieves, right?

Funny thing was the worst-kept secret in Little Odessa was that Empire City's very own Organized Crime Taskforce had set up surveillance cameras inside Eddie's. Everyone knew that none of the outside neighborhood cameras worked for various (and very deliberate) reasons, so trying to capture anyone on them was a waste of time and resources. OCT had been tipped off about the meetings and hoped they could snag a few bad guys by catching their group therapy sessions. Unfortunately for them, the feeds had been altered by hired hackers to make certain OCT never caught a good look at what really happened here.

However, what no one else but Eddie knew was I had access to the unadulterated feeds so I could keep tabs on things, too. I'd check the recordings periodically, although I hadn't done so in over a year. Given what had gone down here tonight, that would have to change.

I suppose I could've handed it all over to OCT, but after being everyone's punching bag at ECPD for the last eight years, I didn't feel like sharing. Besides, most of what was recorded didn't contain real, prosecutable value anyway.

The real shady deals were struck in other places.

Suddenly, the memory of Vanessa Mallery and the micro-cameras hidden throughout her brownstone came rushing back to me. The former goldjoy drug kingpin Rumpelstiltskin had stripped the murdered girl of everything, even her identity. That bastard had invaded her life in hundreds of ways, each one equally intimate, and deeply personal. If Besim hadn't heard those cameras when we'd investigated the dead girl's home, we would never have been put on the path to discovering the awful truth behind her murder and taken down Rumplestiltskin.

As if she could read my thoughts (something I hadn't entirely ruled out after the last investigation), Besim opened her eyes and sighed.

"Looks like I'm stuck with you again," I said while trying a smile, but it was more a grimace than anything friendly.

"Detective, if I might ask," Besim began, her strange, almond-shaped eyes centering on me. "Where were you before you arrived here?"

I blinked. "Excuse me?"

"There is a residual bouquet which clings to you."

"So?"

"I am curious as to your activities prior to receiving the priority call from William. Were you with someone?"

"I was out."

Besim stepped up to me. Having the Vellan so close reminded me of her sheer physicality. I was forced to look up. The clean scent of sea breezes and the ocean filled my nostrils, clearing away the fetid funk of blood and death. The Insight responded, purring like a cat behind my eyes. The strange sensation was unnerving. There was a camaraderie to it, as if the clairvoyance was greeting a friend.

She raised her hand to place it on my head.

"What the fuck are you doing?" I recoiled from her.

"I would like to understand this further." She raised her hand again.

"The hell you will!"

"Detective, I believe someone has—"

"Don't touch me. Don't *ever* touch me."

The consultant regarded me before lowering her hand.

"As you wish."

"What I do on my personal time is my business," I stated, then knelt by Ushakov again. "EVI, disable recording."

"Confirmed, Detective," she replied in my ear.

"You have not slept?" Besim asked.

"No."

I glanced toward the back exit. Eddie hadn't returned, and I hoped that she'd disabled the cameras while she was putting the recording together. Using my body as cover, I made another quick search of Ushakov. I retrieved his holophone, deactivated it and slipped the small device inside my blazer inner pocket.

"Is that not evidence?" Besim asked with arched eyebrows.

I looked over the bodies again and didn't respond.

Even though I expected Ushakov's "friends" would be here soon, I wanted to be long gone before they arrived. Regardless of what I had told Mahoney, I wasn't ready to have a chat with whoever showed up here. At least, not until after I'd had a chance to review the footage and the phone.

"Should you not—"

"You know, you ask a shitload of questions for someone who hasn't answered any of mine," I glared, standing up.

"As I stated previously, I had accompanied William here."

"Yeah, you said that already. So where were you two before you arrived?"

"With William," Besim replied without blinking. "He needed me to—"

She paused.

"Needed you for what, exactly?" I asked.

Despite the mountain of makeup plastering her cheeks, I could've sworn she blushed.

"William needed me to offer him clarity," she finished with a firm nod.

"Is that what they call it nowadays?"

"I fail to ascertain your meaning, Detective," Besim said, cocking her head to one side.

"Forget about it."

I looked around a final time before retrieving the P-Scanner. Eddie returned and hurried over to me. Her hand trembled as I took the micro-drive. Stentstrom was still on his holo-phone.

"You never saw the other person?" I asked.

"I was gone a few minutes before I heard screams," Eddie replied. "Only three before I leave. No one else. You think other one is killer?"

My eyes shifted to the bloody wall.

"No," I said. My mouth compressed to a thin line. "But definitely someone I'd like to meet."

Besim stared at me expectantly. I ignored her.

"Eddie, you know the drill," I instructed. "Doctor Stentstrom's people will remove the bodies. And I'll help pay for the clean-up. If anyone else shows up, especially the media, just refer questions back to me, okay?"

"This I no like, Thomas." She was pale, her eyes round as she took in Besim and the bodies. "*Neyestestvennyye veshchi.*"

Unnatural things.

I knew enough Russian to be dangerous.

"I'm going to catch who did this," I assured her, offering Eddie a smile that held more confidence than I felt.

"*Dah*, Thomas, but..." Eddie paused, a pensive frown scribbling her brow.

"What is it?"

"These were bad men," she said quietly. "You know better than anyone. Deserved what they got."

"Murder is still murder," I replied. "And it's my job to catch whoever did this. What would you have me do?"

Eddie fixed me with a melancholy smile.

"Let them lie."

12

Once Stentstrom's people arrived, we said our goodbyes and left.

The outdoor air was brittle and sharp, penetrating to the bone. Raw cold bit into my exposed cheeks, numbing them and causing my eyes to water. Besim appeared unaffected, her face a serene mask in the glow of her holo-phone. I heard little of her conversation, still caught up by both the images the Insight had shown me, and Eddie's parting words.

Bill was neck-deep in this mess. His past had caught up with him, although instinct told me he was an outsider, some collateral damage that only hinted at the whole story. Whatever part Sanarov, Ushakov and the other dead Russians had played felt more like appetizers before the main course. The killings were more than murders. They'd been a message that said, "I know you. I see you. And I'm coming."

But coming for who? And why?

Donald Flynn had to be connected to all of this, but was he the target, or the perpetrator? My bullshit meter went off the charts during our meeting. Some of that was due to my distaste for any corporate stooge like Flynn who wore their arrogance and wealth like badges of honor. They took pride in how easily they stomped the little guy into goo with a flick of a holo-window. A man who had Mayor Samson on his holo-phone's Friend's List could've had Sanarov killed in prison, and no one would've noticed or cared.

That's why I trusted Deacon's righteous sense of weird. If he believed a revenant, or something akin to it, had done the killings, then maybe I could rule out a techno-killer. Which beget the question: why would Flynn contract with some supernatural being to exact revenge against anyone who had murdered his son?

Wait, did I just think that?

Given what I'd experienced over the past four months, I couldn't discount the possibility.

I recalled the dream. The boy whose body I'd inhabited had to be Calvin Flynn. But where had that taken place? The room contained elements of both a hospital and a boarding school. The short-list of private schools located within the confines of Empire City numbered in the dozens. Of course, Calvin had been murdered over thirty years ago, so the school might no longer exist.

You cannot stop me, Guardian of Empire City.

The sound of that voice scraped across my psyche like a twisted wire brush. Was this Orpheus all over again? No, the voice I'd heard sounded and felt different. There was a menace and hatred to it that spoke of a dark and hungry power. It had been more than a warning to me. It had been a promise.

Besides, that kind of melodramatic bullshit was beneath Orpheus. She'd rather taunt me in person.

While eating my entrails.

Maybe Eddie was right. Maybe I should walk away from this one and let Ushakov and the others lie.

And maybe I should start a nudist colony down in Hoboken.

"EVI, please get me what you can on Brave New Beginnings," I said aloud. "And see if you can find any connection between Donald Flynn and Pyotr Ushakov. Business dealings, lunch dates, greeting cards, whatever you can find. Also, I need you to search the registrars of all the private schools and admission logs for all the hospitals in Empire City dating back to Calvin Flynn's death to verify if Calvin Flynn was enrolled at or admitted to any of them."

"Accessing," EVI said.

I was hoping SCU's unique "carte blanche" status with the mayor's office was the skeleton key I needed to get around Empire City's sticky privacy laws to access the information I'd requested.

I rubbed my arms together for warmth, briefly lamenting my failure to wear an overcoat for my date with Charlotte, then crushed the thought. I'd never been one to dress for the weather under normal circumstances. Regardless of the season, my brown blazer did just fine. Besides, brown was never out of style. I was a simple man, according to Leyla. Although I think our definition of "simple" meant two different things.

"Detective Holliday," the AI said. "I have compiled all applicable data sets regarding Brave New Beginnings. Do you wish to review them?"

"No, sweetie," I replied. "Please set that aside. For now, just get me the results on the other two searches."

EVI paused for half a heartbeat. "My review of the two search requests is complete. I was unable to determine any connection or correlation between the search subjects

'Donald Flynn' and 'Pyotr Ushakov'. In addition, I was unable to locate search subject 'Calvin Flynn' among the two-thousand four hundred and eight private schools and hospitals which met your general search criteria. Would you like me to refine the search parameters?"

"Needles and haystacks," I muttered in irritation. "Why can't anything ever be easy?"

Across the street, Rhona's was dark, the doorway empty. I led Besim quickly back to the pod, aware of hidden eyes upon us the moment we had stepped from the bar. Morning twilight cloaked the neighborhood. The moon peeked between the thick, snow-laden clouds, an aloof white orb spurning the world below. I pulled the SCU badge from beneath my shirt and let it hang on its chain over the front of my blazer. Its silver radiance illuminated the way, a path of pale light to guard against the night. As we moved along the quiet street, dim shapes loomed ahead—abandoned ice-bound vehicles, like derelict castaways from a sunken ship.

With one hand gripping the handle of the P-Scanner carrying case, I kept the other inside my blazer and within easy reach of the SMART gun. My eyes raked both sides of the street. Goose bumps prickled my skin, and not from the cold. Anticipation gnawed at me as my shoulders bunched together.

"Detective," Besim spoke softly. "We are not alone."

The pod was parked at the 'way off-ramp within the bleached sickle of light cast by a battered streetlamp. Three shadows loitered around the transport, making no pretense as to why they were there.

"EVI, activate pod defense protocol," I ordered, projecting my voice loud enough to ensure they heard me. "And keep the engines hot."

"Affirmative, Detective. Should I request assistance?"

"Negative. But keep them on stand-by."

The three resolved themselves into men, rough and hardened by years working the streets. I didn't recognize any of them. They weren't holding weapons, but I wasn't fooled. None of them had stepped within arm's reach of the pod's exterior either, which meant they were familiar with its defenses.

So, smart thugs.

I didn't bother with the niceties. "ECPD. Move aside."

One chuckled and said something very unflattering to his two buddies in Russian about what I could do with myself. They knew who I was, and they didn't care.

"You get one more chance, assholes," I warned. "Move."

Chuckles lit a cigarette, then stepped toward me, while his buddies wandered to either side, pinning us by the boarded windows of a burned-out building.

"What you gonna do, Detective?" Chuckles exhaled smoke from his nostrils. "You gonna shoot me?"

"If I did, nobody would miss you," I replied with a grim smile.

"You a funny guy, Detective, you know that?" Chuckles flicked ash to the pavement. "Still, cops got no business on our street. You trespassin', so you gotta pay the tax."

My hand loosened the SMART gun in its rig as I prepared for a quick draw. "And what would that be?"

"The woman." He jabbed the two fingers scissoring the lit butt at Besim. "She looks like lots of fun. You give us her, and we let you go. Yes?"

"Fuck you and the pod you rode in on. Move your sorry ass. Now."

Anger boiled beneath my skin. Sweat beaded down my back and froze on my brow. I calculated the distances, wondering if I could take them all out without getting us both killed in the process.

Besim placed a calm hand on my shoulder, but I didn't dare shift my eyes from Chuckles.

"Leave," a deep baritone commanded in Russian from behind us.

Chuckles stiffened as his demeanor changed. A look of fear washed over his face. Without another word, the three men fled down the street in the direction of Rhona's.

I turned slowly toward the newcomer, resisting a powerful urge to pull my gun. I'd made hastier decisions in my life, but those had involved ugly strippers. I knew if I drew here, someone would die.

"Hello, Thomas," said a mountain of a man, equal to Besim in height. However, where the consultant was slight, he was broad, filling out his overcoat with muscled girth. He regarded me, a mocking half-smile curling his lips. "Been a while."

"Not long enough, Ivan," I said.

Little Odessa might be under the stewardship of Empire City, but the Kiev Brotherhood ruled here. The *bratva* worked within a pyramid-like structure. The lowest tier were street gangs and goons like Chuckles and his buddies. They reported to a support group that possessed its own security personnel. However, when the Brotherhood needed something done, they called upon Ivan Kruchev.

It was said Ivan had murdered ten people, but I knew the body count was higher. Ten was still a big enough number to scare most people, including me.

The burning of a thousand suns was a candle's flame compared to the hatred I felt for this piece of shit.

"What the hell do you want?" I challenged. "You were told to stay away."

He gestured casually at the empty sidewalk. "Your crime scene is not here. And, so, I honor my agreement with your Captain Mahoney. But I wanted to speak with you, face to face. Like old times."

"I don't make it a habit of sharing my cop crib notes with criminals. Why don't you head home and kick back with some Smirnoff and a nice holo-porn?"

"Come now, Thomas," Ivan said with mild reproach. "Are we not still friends? You and I, we have so much history together. We both care about this neighborhood, no? And we both wish to protect it from outsiders and anyone who would hurt it. We want the same thing, Thomas. To catch a killer of men."

"Don't flatter yourself, Ivan," I shot back. "I'm nothing like you. For starters, I can look at myself in the mirror and know I'm not some fucking murderer-for-hire."

"Thomas, this behavior is beneath you. Where are your loyalties?"

"Not with you, or your goddamn Brotherhood."

"I am being polite." He studied the dark sky with a bored look. "I do not need to be. I merely wish to know what happened at Eddie's."

"Save the pretenses, Ivan," I scoffed. "You're just someone's oversized errand boy."

"Now, now, Thomas," Ivan said, directing his attention back at me. "Your Special Crimes Unit is handling this case, yes? Investigating the strange and unusual? Like that vampire business from last October? Imagine my surprise when I learned my old friend Thomas Holliday was the lead detective. The half-Jew boy who used to follow me around the neighborhood like a lost puppy and get himself into so much trouble with his mouth. Do you not see the value in speaking with me?"

"And here I thought Captain Mahoney was calling the shots," I said. "I didn't know SCU now took orders from assholes."

"Things change, Thomas. And change is good, no? You should embrace it."

"Fuck off."

"You were never one to be flexible."

"That's because, unlike you, I was never interested in being one of your Pakhan's sex toys."

"Clever." One of Ivan's eyes twitched, but he managed to maintain a calm demeanor. "I see you haven't lost your sense of humor, either. A shame no one has beaten it out of you, yet."

"Are you threatening me?"

"Of course not. I would never harm a police officer. That would be against the law."

"Look at you, such an upstanding citizen. Mug any old ladies lately, Ivan?"

"I've always liked you, Thomas. Never afraid to mix it up with the bigger kids, eh? How often have I had to teach you to stay out of other people's business?"

"Not enough, apparently."

This was going nowhere. I suspected Ivan wasn't alone, although he didn't need the backup. If this kept up, we'd be frozen statues by breakfast. Ivan wanted specifics about the case which I wasn't willing to give him, but I also knew we couldn't leave unless he had something concrete that he could take back to his boss. He had to know the raw details by now. Once Stentstrom and his techs transported the bodies to the morgue, Ivan would have unfettered access to Eddie and her bar. Hopefully, Eddie's neutrality would keep her safe. Ivan was just pushing my buttons to see if I'd let something slip. The question was whether he knew anything about Gustavo Sanarov. If he did, then that cemented at least one connection.

I needed to distract him, cause him to slip up somehow and get him off my ass for a little while. I decided to toss him a bone.

Just not the right kind.

"Fine," I heaved a dramatic sigh and let my shoulders slump. "What do you want to know?"

Ivan unfolded his arms and reached into one of his pockets. "Much better."

"Easy there," I warned. The SMART gun was halfway from its holster.

Ivan chuckled. He produced a small metal cigarette case which he paused to display for me. After removing a match and cigarette, the big Russian closed the case with a deliberate snap, hoping to goad me with the sharp sound, but I wouldn't bite. He returned the case to his inner pocket, then lit the smoke, cupping the flame in his massive hand. The brief light glinted from something metallic around his wrist, just beneath his shirt sleeve. Besim's head cocked to one side as her heightened hearing caught a sound. Ivan's arm spasmed, and he nearly burned himself. He glared at it until the arm stabilized as if cowed into submission.

"The three men at Eddie's," he said after a slow smoky exhale. "How did they die?"

I slid the gun back in place and said, "I'm not sure yet."

"But you have a theory?" he asked.

"I have lots of theories," I said. "My current favorite is your boys probably pissed off a rival syndicate, most likely the Albanians. I figure they hired a techno-assassin who used some fancy new nanotech and somehow planted them in their drinks. The nanites slip unnoticed into their bloodstream and detonate, instantly killing Ushakov, Vladdy and

Stan, and probably destroying any evidence the devices were there in the process."

That didn't sound half-baked to me. If this detective gig with SCU didn't work out, maybe I'd become a third-rate science fiction holo-novelist.

Actually, if SCU didn't work out it meant I was dead.

"Why do you think this?" Ivan asked.

"Maybe it was a revenge killing, payback for something Ushakov did on his smoke break when he wasn't fleecing the locals for you?" I shrugged. "Whatever the reason, I'm looking into it, so I'm asking you to stay out of my way. Are we done here?"

Ivan took a long drag from his cigarette, appraising me with a calculating stare.

"And you think the Albanians were involved at the church this morning?" he asked.

"I'm not sure," I hedged, adding just the right level of hesitation to my voice. "How did you—"

"The murdered man there was killed the same, was he not," Ivan said. "Small holes over his entire body, yes?"

Gotcha, asshole.

It was time to go.

"Look, Ivan, it's cold, and we both have things to do," I said. "Why don't you report back to your boss and shove your head up his ass? I'm done talking with you."

Ivan studied me further while he smoked, the cigarette barely a lit nub. It was clear he needed something more. The manner of his men's death bothered him. Ivan wasn't the brightest lamp on the street, but he was far from stupid. After several tense seconds, he discarded the expired cigarette to the pavement and crushed it under the heel of his size eighteen wingtip.

He stepped aside and said, "As you wish."

I remotely activated the hatchway as I led Besim toward the pod.

"I will make a few inquiries of my own, Thomas," Ivan called out to me. "We will speak again soon."

Once aboard, I instructed EVI to get us the hell out of there. I opened one of the insulated compartments and dumped Ushakov's phone inside.

"Destination?" the AI asked over the internal comm.

"L'Hotel Internacional," I sighed, then sank into a command chair.

"Are you all right, Detective?" Besim asked, her brow furrowed with concern. She settled into the other command chair.

I waved her question away with a shaking hand.

This was going to be a very long day.

13

"I would advise against further consumption, Detective," Besim warned. "Your pallor and agitation suggest a high level of dopamine and norepinephrine are present in your bloodstream. With your elevated heart rate, cardiac arrest could be imminent."

I gulped down the third cup of coffee in two swallows. Before the scalding liquid settled in my stomach, I poured a fourth from the pod's beverage dispenser with trembling hands.

"I'm fine," I muttered. "Just give me a minute."

The consultant frowned.

"Detective Holliday, the surveillance footage from the micro-drive you uploaded earlier was corrupted," EVI announced over the comm. "I will inform you once the repair is complete."

"Well, that's damn inconvenient," I grumbled, returning unsteadily to the front.

I set the coffee on the dashboard thankful my hands no longer shook. Besim sat beside me, her hands folded neatly in her lap. The weight of her unblinking stare threatened to crush the life from me.

And Leyla misses this?

I closed my eyes, lowered my forehead to the console's cold surface, and exhaled a long-suffering breath.

"What?" I groaned.

"Detective, please forgive my intrusion, but where were you prior to receiving the call from William?" Besim asked.

"You see I'm busy, right?" I raised my head and gestured at everything. "Murder investigation? Four bodies? No witnesses?"

Besim remained still as a statue, waiting expectantly.

"You really are a pain in the ass, you know that?"

Those almond-shaped eyes of hers never blinked.

"Fine." I threw up my hands in exasperation. "I was out, okay? I wasn't home. Satisfied?"

"You were with a human female?" the consultant asked.

"Yeah," I answered slowly, wondering where this was headed. "What's it to you?"

"The two of you engaged in sexual intercourse," she stated in a matter-of-fact tone.

"Excuse me?" I spluttered. "First of all, that's none of your goddamn business! Besides, how do you even know that?"

"At what point did you discover she had ensorcelled you?"

I stared at her as if she'd sprouted three heads.

"The aura of enchantment still clings to you, Detective," Besim explained patiently. "It is a bouquet akin to what Orpheus had employed to ensnare you, yet far weaker. I would posit it is not the same blend of enchantment, although that does not preclude any relationship to Orpheus. It is reminiscent of truth and persuasion charms members of certain Euro-Bloc criminal and law enforcement organizations favor. Who accompanied you last night, Detective?"

I shrank back in the command chair, the investigation momentarily forgotten, and ran a hand over my stricken face. The strange sensation I had experienced during dinner now made more sense. Anger and embarrassment battled for control of my heart. I wasn't fond of Besim, but I'd seen enough of what she could do that I would never doubt her acute senses.

Most of my life had been disappointment and loss. You'd think I'd be used to it by now, but I wasn't. I was a sucker just like everyone else. Broken glass filled my gut at the thought I'd been played.

"*The fool doth think he is wise, but the wise man knows himself to be a fool,*" I whispered, my voice quivering with despair.

I described Charlotte and recounted our dinner together. Besim's eyes narrowed.

"The Insight attempted to warn you," she explained. "Yet, the charm Charlotte wove was both cunning and delicate. She used her physical allure along with your personal demons to lull you while her magic worked. It is unsurprising the efficacy of the charm was so complete. You are a man whose depth of anguish, memory, and former addiction is great, Detective. Such charms feed upon the most intimate of emotions, weaving a bewitching web to captivate and enthrall. You were easy prey."

I could only nod as I fought to control my burning emotions.

"However, you are no longer beneath its sway," the consultant continued. "And now that you have been made aware of it, I do not feel you could be subjected to its influence again. At least, not so easily."

Cold anger slipped in to replace my initial shock. Charlotte had tricked me into revealing information about my past. But why? We never discussed Special Crimes, Sanarov or the investigation. I hadn't revealed anything I'd consider critical. What had she wanted to know? And if her charm was meant to get me talking, why had we ended up in bed?

"You said Euro-Bloc criminals and law enforcement use this charm," I said while I sorted through the memories of the previous night. "What else do you know about magic?"

"On our home world of Avenir, magic usage was as prevalent as breathing air," Besim replied. "While you humans exploit energy from the Nexus nodes to power your buildings and machines, our relationship is far more intimate. Your Earth has only begun to remember what it was like to experience magic. In your infancy, very few humans can command magic's intricacies, let alone fathom its purpose. Leyla, for example, is a true exception. But there have been others, something I do not need to explain to you."

"And we're back to that, aren't we," I growled. "I told you, I'm no Guardian of Empire City."

"You cannot deny magic's influence upon you and your world, Detective," she said. "Nor can you deny how Special Crimes is needed to stop those who would destroy your enclave for their personal gain."

"Can we table this discussion for another time?" I demanded. "We've got more important business. Like, who is Charlotte, what does she have to do with Sanarov, and how the hell am I going to keep the *bratva* off my ass?"

"They are all intertwined, Detective Holliday," Besim said. "One is not independent of the other. To wit, I have instructed Deacon Kole to meet us at my apartments. I trust you are agreeable to this?"

I nodded.

"Excellent," she said. "There is still the matter of William."

"What do you mean?"

"His involvement in your investigation is obvious."

"Did he say anything to you on the ride over to Eddie's?"

"Only that he had made choices that he regretted. But he would not elaborate further."

"We need to talk with him." I picked up the mug, took a long sip, and added, "He might open up more if you're there."

"A distinct possibility," Besim nodded. "William is also a man of deep feelings, something you both share in common. I will contact Mamika to expect our arrival. If you will excuse me?"

I waved my assent, then had EVI pull up all the evidence and data we'd collected since the investigation began. For the next twenty minutes, I shoved my feelings of Charlotte's betrayal aside and focused on the case. I tried cobbling together any connections or leads between Ushakov, Flynn and Sanarov, but came up empty. And everything on Brave New Beginnings indicated a robust and reputable charitable organization that had helped Empire City's needy children for decades. At one point, EVI provided me with the results of the church neighborhood canvass. I found nothing useful, other than the usual run of neighbors complaining about everyone else.

Leyla called my holo-phone, awake despite the early hour. She and Deacon had returned to L'Hotel Internacional to finish their research from the night before.

"Those Rikers guys were all clean," she concluded, her

ghostly image floating above my phone. "The only direct relationship Deacon and I could find was through the convict education program. Beyond that, nothing."

"It was worth a try," I said. "I appreciate the leg-work, kiddo."

"Anytime," she replied, but then her eyes narrowed with concern. "What's wrong, Doc?"

"Nothing's wrong," I said, forcing a smile.

"I can always tell when something's up with you. What happened? It's Charlotte, isn't it."

I sighed, then recapped my discussion with Besim.

"She *charmed* you?" Leyla roared. "She actually charmed you. What the fuck does she want?"

"I don't know," I replied.

"I am kicking her ass sideways," Leyla declared.

"I didn't know you cared."

"Of course I care, Doc!" she cried. "Nobody messes with my family! Besides, I keep you around in case I ever need you to bust me out of jail."

"See you soon," I laughed and cut the call, my heart swelling with much-needed warmth.

We arrived at L'Hotel Internacional as night brightened to a somber morning. I parked the pod beneath the massive canopy covering the front entrance. Several guests gawked openly as Besim and I hustled toward the lobby. Giles the Pompous Bellman, decked out in his hat, gloves and white and gold uniform, made a beeline to intercept us, but one cold glance from Besim wilted him like erectile dysfunction.

As we walked, Besim assumed the hauteur of a Euro-Bloc businesswoman who owned half the world and leased out the rest to the unwashed masses beneath her. Several well-groomed men and women hailed her as we passed, but she barely spared them a moment. To her, the elegance and opulence of the hotel's lobby was merely a nuisance, decorative aesthetics pleasing to everyone else's eye but her own. My mind still struggled to take in what Charlotte had done to me, but even I wasn't immune to the grandeur of the hotel.

Cinnamon mixed with honey permeated the air as we crossed the broad hall and around the massive fountain that filled its center. Water poured from spigots embedded in the centerpiece statuary and around its base, tinkling merrily to splash in a clear pool.

Despite the early hour, dozens of people milled about or sat on the comfortable furniture. Hotel employees, visitors and guests spoke in knots or moved about their business. Music filtered above the hubbub of activity, stringed and wind instruments working through Mozart's great G-minor symphony. Dozens of holo-tapestries hanging on the walls cycled between panoramic vistas of mountains, deep green valleys, and sun-kissed beaches, few of which existed in today's broken brave new world.

The far end of the lobby held two banks of glass elevators. I watched two cars lifted upward on a current of air, their occupants indifferent to the technological miracle that gave them flight. We rounded the corner beyond the elevators and nearly ran into a dozen elderly women wearing red hats and gabbling about the delicious breakfast prepared for them in the mammoth dining room to our left. Ignoring them, we made a second turn into an alcove guarded by two women wearing matching gray pant suits. Each bore an earpiece and bland expressions that didn't change when Besim and I walked between them and into the open elevator awaiting us.

Slight pressure in my legs and a popping in my ears indicated upward movement after the doors closed. We traveled to the penthouse, a large collection of private rooms dedicated to Besim and her staff. From there, we went to the sitting room, if you want to call an area five times the size of my shitty one room efficiency a room. Creature comfort melded with sublime elegance and tasteful art. Genuine Oriental and Arabian fabrics covered the polished tile, although their patterns were different from the last time I'd visited. A roaring fireplace shed brightness and warmth. I tasted the soft scent of lilac and chamomile mingled with the ashy bouquet from the fire. Four short genuine leather couches had been arrayed before it, with a polished dark oak coffee table in-between bearing a silver tea set. Heavy dark gold drapes hugged the far wall, insulating the room from the outside chill. A darkened holo-vision hovered before another wall.

A tall, handsome woman with short-cropped brown hair streaked with gray met us as the elevator door opened. She wore black slacks, a navy top and held out an active holo-phone to Besim.

She wasn't smiling. I'm not sure if she could.

"Morning, Mamika," I said.

She inclined her head politely, but her eyes never left Besim. "Detective Holliday."

The consultant removed her coat and handed it to her major domo, then accepted the holo-phone and strode purposefully across the spacious living room that spilled out past the elevator entrance. Leyla waved to me from a padded lounging chair, still wearing the same clothes from yesterday. Her hair was tied in a ponytail, and the dark circles beneath her eyes informed me of her lack of sleep. A sad smile played across her lips as I took the chair next to her.

"I'm so sorry, Doc." She placed a cold hand on my shoulder. "It's all my fault."

"You had no idea," I said with a wry smile. "Neither of us did."

"I sure as shit would've sniffed that bitch out," Deacon stated as he marched into the living room. He wore dark jeans and an untucked red and white-checked flannel shirt.

"Well, you weren't there," Leyla countered with a frown. "How were we supposed to know Flynn had some witch working for him?"

"My give-a-damn just broke, girlie," Deacon scowled. "We ain't dealin' with normal no more, remember? Down in Birmingham, we're taught to expect the unexpected."

"He's right," I said, forestalling further argument. "But we'll be better prepared next time."

"If there is a next time," he grunted. The former Protector lit a cigarette from a metal lighter and sat on the couch opposite us. "I just looked into your date, Holliday. Checked the World Pop Database, Interpol, New Scotland Yard, the works. Ain't nobody seen or heard of her before. Her image came up empty. Whoever this Charlotte is, she's a ghost, but I've still got a few inquiries pending. If something comes up, I'll let you know."

"Thanks," I sighed, then stood up and moved to the bar.

A coffee pot rested on a warmer. The delightful aroma of freshly ground goodness tickled my fancy. After a bracing gulp of black deliciousness, I poured a second cup and returned with it to my chair. I outlined my review of the crime scene at Eddie's, what the Insight and P-Scanner had shown me, as well as our encounter with Ivan.

"Fucking *bratva*," Deacon spat. "So Sanarov was wrapped up with them?"

"Maybe," I replied, "but there was no mention of it in Mahoney's files, other than he had that angle checked and it didn't pan out."

"Bullshit," he scoffed. "Sounds to me like Bill's got some explaining to do. He must've covered that shit up. Maybe he was on the take?"

"I honestly don't know," I said. "The Insight gave me that snippet for a reason. Bill was butting heads with someone, although it was clear he wasn't going to win. We need to find out who that was."

"Yeah, but what does any of that have to do with our killer?" Leyla asked, chewing on her lower lip.

"My credits are on the kid," Deacon stated. "Murdered boy's spirit lingers and wants revenge. Simple as that. He's taking out his hatred on the people that did him."

"I don't disagree, but where does the Brotherhood fit in?" I asked.

After another sip of coffee, I looked over my shoulder at Besim. She stood by the dark gold drapes cloaking the long glass window wall, speaking in hushed tones. I couldn't see the image on her phone.

"Maybe they were contracted to kidnap the kid, and they fingered Sanarov for the kill as his way of advancing in the organization?" Deacon mused after a long drag from his cigarette.

"There was no evidence he murdered Calvin Flynn," I said. "He was indicted solely for the kidnapping."

"Who would want to murder an innocent boy?" Leyla asked. "Why go through the trouble of having Sanarov kidnap Calvin in the first place?"

Their questions hung in the air between us, as elusive as catching smoke with a net.

"Donald Flynn may think he's immune because of his relationship with Mayor Samson and his charitable work," I said, "but he's hiding something. I need a second crack at him. And Charlotte will be there. I doubt she's aware that I know what she did to me. Hopefully, I can use that to my advantage."

"So, what's the play?" Deacon dashed the cigarette in an ashtray filled with seven of its dead siblings. "We go back to Titan, kick down the door, and hold Flynn by the ankles out a window until he squeals?"

I chuckled and said, "While that sounds like loads of fun, I think we need to take a subtler approach. Let's pay a visit to Brave New Beginnings. It won't take long for word to reach Flynn that we're snooping around there. Maybe that'll rattle his cage a little bit."

"I concur, Detective," Besim said from behind me, the deactivated holo-phone clutched in her hand. "A more offensive approach would be the wisest course of action."

"I'm glad you agree," I said, surprised, then indicated the phone with my chin. "Who were you speaking with?"

"Donald Flynn," she replied coolly. "He has agreed to provide me a personal tour of Brave New Beginnings later this afternoon."

14

"You did what?" I exclaimed, sloshing hot coffee on my hands. "Ow! Goddammit!"

"I contacted Donald Flynn's office and made intimations of offering a significant charitable donation on behalf of Aurik Enterprises," Besim replied, unfazed by my injury. "Naturally, Mr. Flynn returned my call immediately."

"And you didn't think it was a good idea to consult with, oh I don't know, the veteran homicide detective who might consider it a really bad idea, first?" I glared at her while drying my hands on a cloth napkin. "That maybe your call might tip off our lead suspect in the process? Someone we know to be dinner buddies with Mayor Samson. You don't think he isn't aware you helped me last October?"

Besim frowned and said, "While it was a consideration, I felt my ploy conducted under the pretense of Aurik as cover would provide sufficient disassociation from Special Crimes as to alleviate any of your potential concerns, as well as allay any of Mr. Flynn's suspicions regarding the murder investigation. Would you not agree, Detective?"

"You're a goddamn consultant, Besim!" I balled the

napkin and hurled it to the carpet in disgust. "What the hell were you—"

"What is Aurik Enterprises?" Leyla asked curiously, interrupting what should have been a tirade of epic proportions.

"Aurik is the parent corporation that oversees my business interests around the world," Besim explained. She gestured at the living area with an offhand wave. "These apartments, for example, are owned by Aurik, as well as several other holdings throughout Empire City, the Euro-Bloc and all of the civilized enclaves in the western hemisphere."

"Is there anything you don't own?" I asked after taking a fortifying breath to calm my frazzled nerves.

Besim offered me a secret smile but didn't respond.

"Saranda here dumps a shit ton of credits investing in, or donating to, dozens of companies and philanthropic organizations," Deacon said. "Banks, manufacturers, tech companies, and, of course, big pharma, not to mention hospitals, research foundations, think-tanks and irradiated land reclamation operations. She's got her fingers in a lot of pies. It's a damn good way to keep tabs on what the competition's doing. Maybe even collect a favor or two if we're lucky."

"Wow, with all that corporate circle-jerking, when do you have time for your music career?" I grumbled, then held up a hand to forestall her response. "Don't answer that. I don't really care."

"I have attended many galas and fundraisers since my arrival in Empire City, to maintain appearances and insert myself within the private social sector," Besim said, unperturbed. "I have garnered numerous business opportunities as a result. Of course, the organizations to which Aurik donates are vetted thoroughly to ensure the credits are allocated appropriately, which, at times, has included a personal, onsite evaluation. Judging from his eager tone and shortness of breath, Mr. Flynn salivated at the number that I hinted could be in play and was quick to agree to this 'behind-the-scenes' excursion, as he called it. We are to meet later this afternoon."

"The plan was to hit Brave New Beginnings without Flynn being there!" I threw up my hands in the air. "How the hell is a guided tour supposed to help?"

"You will not accompany me, Detective," Besim replied patiently. "However, I would provide a suitable distraction, thereby allowing you to survey the facility unencumbered by Donald Flynn. His security will ensure that he is aware of your presence, but I will make certain he, and his presumed sorcerous assistant, are unable to extricate themselves from me."

I gaped at her. The consultant folded her hands before her waist, returning my glare with a serene expression.

That's when the subtlety of her ploy dawned on me. Because I'm slow like that.

Like a boulder rolling uphill.

"Which will get further under his skin," I said with grudging respect.

"And when he is in a state of greatest agitation, then you will question him a second time to ascertain anything further in the event he, as you say, 'does something stupid,'" the Vellan concluded, her strange almond-shaped eyes aglow with satisfaction. "Given your suppositions, I felt it would be beneficial to the investigation for me to meet with Mr. Flynn in person. I would hear his voice to take his measure, and that of Charlotte."

"Nicely done, Besim!" Leyla laughed. "You'll use your super hearing to pick out the timbre and intonations to his voice and breathing, and maybe catch him in a lie, right?"

"Correct," Besim nodded.

"I can't believe I'm agreeing to this," I muttered, then turned my head skyward to beseech the proto-eggshell white ceiling, and anyone else up there dumb enough to listen to me. "Why am I agreeing to this?"

"Lighten up, Holliday," Deacon chuckled. "This might work."

"Oh, you mean like when we agreed to send these two alone into Kraze?" I countered.

Deacon stabbed an accusatory finger at me. "First off, you're the lead detective, so that was *your* decision. And second, we kicked the shit out of Crain and his boys, shut down that goddamn goldjoy operation and eventually bagged Rumpelstiltskin, didn't we?"

"Whatever," I mumbled, staring down at my hands, surprised at how they weren't shaking.

"The plan is sound, Detective," Besim said primly. "And I suspect there will be no vampires involved this time."

"We can only hope," I said, giving her a sour look.

"I must prepare for my meeting," Besim declared. "I trust you will stay out of trouble whilst I am out. Please inform Mamika of your needs, and she will expedite them. If you will excuse me?"

I watched her go, wondering if preparing for her meeting meant lying naked in a sarcophagus filled with the skulls of her victims as female Vellans danced for her pleasure.

I shook my head in bemusement. Yeah, there were lots of things wrong with me. I just hadn't bothered fixing any of them yet.

"Detective, you have an incoming call from Charlotte

Sloane," EVI announced in my ear, interrupting my wayward thoughts.

"Send it to voice mail," I grumbled darkly.

"You say something, Doc?" Leyla asked.

"It's nothing, kiddo."

I sipped at my coffee to hide my disappointment. Speaking with Charlotte now could jeopardize Besim's plan, not to mention send me into a tailspin of emotional distress from which no amount of coffee could alleviate. I needed to understand what Charlotte's part was in Sanarov's murder. My wounded heart would have to take a backseat for now.

But that didn't make it hurt any less.

"Well, now that Mother Superior has left us, the mice can play," I said, draining the last of my drink. More of the black ambrosia beckoned me, and I obeyed its seductive siren's summons by moving from my seat to pour another cup. "We still have plenty of leads to run down. I'm contacting Sanarov's wife to set up an interview. EVI, please dig into Stacey Schrodinger's financials back to before the kidnapping. Maybe Sanarov received payoffs leading up to it?"

"Affirmative, Detective," the AI said in my ear.

"I'll tag along for that interview, Holliday," Deacon said. "I hate being cooped up in this fucking place."

"What do you want me to do while you're out?" Leyla asked.

I reached into my blazer's outer pocket, withdrew the plastic bag containing Ushakov's holo-phone and handed it to her. The young hacker's eyes gleamed with intrigue.

"Break into this," I said. "Ushakov was *bratva*, and you know how tricky their tech can be. Try not to blow up half the hotel, okay?"

"The fuck?" Deacon gave me an alarmed look.

"No problem," Leyla answered. She took the bag and offered the former Protector a sly grin. "The Brotherhood doctors their phones with a variety of destruct protocols, even if you pull out the SIM card, the battery, or somehow get around the authentication sequence. You know, corrupt all the data on the phone's drive and even insert micro acid canisters to destroy the circuitry. Doc, how come this one hasn't been slagged yet?"

"Because I kept it in the insulated compartment of the pod on the ride over," I replied. "That blocked any remote destruct signal."

"And L'Hotel Internacional is guarded by Aurik's cyber-defense network," Deacon finished with a nod. "The moment you arrived you were under our virtual protection. Ain't nothing coming through that I don't know about. Nice work, Holliday."

"Unless they have eyes on the inside," I pointed out.

"My people are positioned near every access on the first three floors," he stated flatly. "Those *bratva* fuckers ain't doing shit. Let 'em try."

"Don't underestimate Ivan," I said. "By now he knows I have the phone. He's going to want it back."

"Well, then I won't break it too badly," Leyla snickered, then studied the holo-phone as a frown creased her forehead. "Doc, I can't do the job here. I'll need my tools for this."

"We got ourselves a swanky high-tech clean room on the other side of the elevator, next to Saranda's lab," Deacon offered. "It's got all the toys. Everything you'd ever want is in there, girlie."

"You're cute, Deacon, but I doubt it," the young hacker said, gracing him with a patronizing smile, the kind meant for misbehaving children, or men with big egos and small packages. "Nope, you'll have to drop me off at Abner's."

"The bookstore?" the Confederate blinked. "Why the fuck would you keep your tools there?"

"Because nobody would think twice about the place," she replied with an impish smile. "Unlike some posh penthouse overlooking Central Park."

"Whatever," Deacon muttered. "I'm grabbing a few things. Meet you down at the pod."

He stomped from the room.

"We'll drop you off on the way to Schrodinger's place," I said, suppressing a laugh as I watched him leave. "How long do you think it'll take to crack Ushakov's phone?"

Leyla's round face pinched as she considered my question.

"Depends on how involved their sentry programs are," she said. "Their setup is meant to keep everyone out, unless you know the pass code, which, of course, is encrypted *and* in Russian. I'll have to wiggle through their defensive subroutines and hunter protocols, which could take a while. Then there's the circuitry and physical traps. Did you bring the other phones, just in case?"

"No, just Ushakov's," I replied, finishing my coffee. "His two buddies were the muscle. I doubt low-level schmucks would be entrusted with much. It doesn't matter. Ushakov's phone might have what we need to figure out who's behind the killings."

I stood up and pondered my reflection in the glossy blank holo-vision screen. Real rest would have to wait, although given what I'd already seen over the past day with the Insight, it might be better if I held off on a night's sleep.

"Doc, are you okay?" Leyla asked, her eyes bright with concern.

"I'm fine, kiddo." I gathered the empty coffee cup and saucer and placed them next to the coffee pot.

"I mean, about Charlotte."

"I'll get over it," I sighed wearily. "Right now, I'm more interested in catching a killer than solving my love life. We should go."

Leyla collected her satchel and slung it around her body.

"I'm worried about you," she said, then crushed me in a hug. My body's temperature plummeted despite the layers of clothes I wore.

"I-I-I'll b-b-be f-f-fine," I chattered between shivers. I patted her head and watched silver crystals drift around her hair.

She squeezed me once before letting go.

"The next time I see that bitch, I'm planting an icicle between her eyes," Leyla vowed, full of an icy wrath.

A sense of foreboding washed through me. The Insight seethed, irritating my eyes as it lapped against my senses. For a moment, Leyla's eyes glazed white, the irises nearly disappearing. She grew rigid, her body taut as a live wire. The air around us crackled with violent cold.

I glanced at the floor. Had her shadow grown longer?

I recalled the dreadful moment back at the nightclub Kraze when Leyla had been enshrouded beneath an enormous, ethereal shadow whose wings stretched above and around her. The sense of its raw, pure evil still unnerved me. Since then, its specter had reappeared in my dreams, a harbinger of terrible events to come. It had become yet another vision permanently added to the bevy of other horrible things I'd seen through the Insight that threatened to tear my sanity apart.

Leyla and I had never discussed what had happened that night. I was ashamed to admit I hadn't tried, hoping that the shadow I'd seen had merely been a by-product of the goldjoy seething through me before Besim finally purged it from my bloodstream with her singing. Seeing it now, while awake, rekindled the fear in my heart. Whatever that shadow was, it wasn't going away anytime soon.

"Easy there," I said, trying to quell my sudden fear. "Let me handle Charlotte, okay? Right now, I need you to focus on Ushakov's holo-phone."

"But she—"

"No 'but's,'" I added firmly. The Insight became more insistent, responding to whatever roiled within the young hacker. "We've got a job to do, Leyla. I need my people sharp, especially my favorite little sister."

She appeared ready to explode but exhaled a breath of white and darkness that dissipated against the warmth of the living room, as if rebuked.

"Yeah," Leyla said. Her eyes reverted to their customary blue, and she blinked several times as if waking from a deep sleep. "Yeah, you're right."

I looked at the floor. Her shadow had returned to its normal size.

"Come on," I urged, shepherding her toward the elevator. "Let's get to the pod before Deacon drives off without us."

15

Stacey Schrodinger lived alone in a two-story townhouse with a dusty red brick face along 12th Street, one of the few well-kept neighborhoods in Brighton Beach not overrun by junkies, gangs and dilapidated buildings. The house was within walking distance of a private virtual school where kids spent the day encased in bariatric chambers within honeycombed classrooms jacked into the latest in artificial education and social advancement. The chambers provided a "safe learning environment" where hyperbaric oxygen was pumped in, and kids ate a "robust, foursquare meal" containing all the latest Protoplasmic super vita-foods meant for a clean and healthy life. At least, that's what the holo-ads promised.

What most ignored in favor of little Johnny's improved quality of education and growth over tax-paid public school, was the constant indoctrination that was slipped into these programs by the corporate jerk-offs who had built the schools. They were hellbent on shaping these young, impressionable minds, creating robot children who would eventually become the "great" leaders of tomorrow.

I wasn't a fan.

To be fair, for those fortunate enough to afford sending their kids to these schools also meant freedom from worrying about whether the AI curriculum and teaching protocols were full of bugs, or whether the human instructor had a degree in teaching. Or even a degree in anything.

As Deacon and I approached Schrodinger's home, the first bell rang out, a hollow echo announcing the start of the school's morning session. It was an honest memento from an antiquated time that meant more back then than it did now. I stared down the road at the high walls scrolled with barbed wire protecting the school, their parapets rising above the rooftops of the surrounding homes like some avaricious aristocrat surveying his fiefdom. However, faded graffiti decorated much of the surface, mostly gang signs and pointed suggestions on what the school's owners could do with their credits and soulless, virtual teachers.

"Education is not the filling of a pail, but the lighting of a fire," I muttered, shaking my head in disgust.

"What crawled up your ass, Holliday?" Deacon asked.

"Nothing," I grimaced.

"If you say so." The former Protector lit a cigarette. He eyed the quiet street with suspicion. "How we handlin' this?"

We stood before a waist high wrought-iron fence with a small gate. I surveyed the home and its neighbors, noting the lack of any snowmen, sleds or other signs children lived here. They were all well-kept, suggesting a level of care where the residents paid whatever local "tax" was required to maintain the peace.

"I confirmed with Rikers that she never visited Sanarov while he did time," I answered. A stray white flake wafted lazily upon the breeze. Its frozen siblings followed soon after. Judging by the leaden sky, the extended family wasn't too far behind. "I don't think she knows anything."

"So why the fuck are we here?" Deacon flicked ash away. His cheeks were red, cut by the February draft angling around us. A mantle of light snow curtained his head and shoulders.

"I'm not sure," I admitted. "Something's here, though. I just don't know what."

I climbed the three stone steps leading to her door, then pressed a small button on the white-washed frame. An insistent buzzing issued inside, followed by approaching footsteps that halted behind the door. Deacon crushed his cigarette on the frozen metal railing, then dropped it next to the stairs.

"Good morning, Mrs. Schrodinger," I said. I held my SCU badge before the four digits marking her address. "I'm Detective Tom Holliday, and this is Deacon Kole. We're with Empire City Special Crimes. We spoke on the phone a little while ago."

Secreted behind the numbers was a micro camera and sensor that transmitted data to a centralized alarm monitoring company. They'd run facial recognition and background checks, cross-referencing both the World Population Database, as well as whatever contractual agreements they had with ECPD. That information was then sent back to the resident's holo-phone, holo-vision or a standalone image pad located behind the door.

Several locks clacked open. The door creaked backward, held by a thin woman well past sixty who used the frame as a shield.

"May we come in?" I asked and offered her one of my patented   No-Really-I'm-Actually-A-Friendly-Policeman smiles.

Schrodinger nodded and stepped aside so we could enter, but I noticed how she surreptitiously stole a look up and down the street before shutting the door.

Soothing warmth and the smell of burnt coffee welcomed us as we entered. Schrodinger led us past a small holo-image pad embedded in the wall by the door, and down the narrow hallway into a cramped living space dominated by a thick, blue and green-patterned couch, matching reading chair and a small, rounded coffee table. Behind the chair were built-in bookshelves filled with bric-a-brac, but no books. Dozens of holo-frames in all shapes and sizes lined the walls blinking between hundreds of images. One inert frame leaned against a closed Bible and an empty coffee mug on the table. A long fissure creased the center of the frame's dead screen.

A kitchen separated by an open breakfast bar was to our left, and a short flight of stairs ran up to an open bedroom overlooking the living area. A darkened holo-vision occupied the wall opposite the kitchen. Music filtered from the device, some low melodic ditty my grandfather might have enjoyed. There was no sign of any pets. It appeared Schrodinger lived alone, insulated by the constant rippling virtual memoir of her family.

"Can I offer you anything?" she asked in a querulous voice. "Coffee? Tea?"

"Coffee would be great, thank you," I replied. "Black, please. No sugar. Thank you."

Deacon declined.

"I'll see what I have left," Schrodinger said, and moved to the kitchen.

Moments later, she returned to hand me a colorful butterfly-patterned mug. She avoided looking at me. I nodded my thanks, took a quick sip, and sat on the well-worn couch. The coffee was lukewarm and terrible, but I subscribed to the simple unalterable belief that bad coffee was better than no coffee.

Deacon wandered around the room, peering closely at each holo-frame. Schrodinger tracked his movements before turning her attention to me. I informed her that she would be recorded, formally re-introduced ourselves, and explained the purpose of our visit.

"Mrs. Schrodinger," I began, and placed the mug on the coffee table. "We're sorry for your loss. We won't take too much of your time. But rather than talk about what happened to Gustavo, I want you to tell us what kind of a man he was. Back then, I mean."

The old woman was silent as her eyes strayed hesitantly over to the broken holo-frame.

"Take your time," I added with what I hoped was an unthreatening tone. "We know how hard this must be for you."

The Insight remained quiescent, unaffected by our host or her home. However, my instincts told me something was here. I gazed at the Bible and broken frame but looked up when Schrodinger began speaking.

"This was our place. His and mine." Her voice was soft, layered with melancholy and laden with memory. "He bought it for me. For us. Surprised me on our wedding day. Even carried me over the threshold."

I waited, tasting the coffee from time to time, an attentive listener. Deacon continued his review of the room but maintained a respectful silence.

"I raised two children here," she continued, her voice gathering resolve. "I wasn't going to be one of those women who clung to their men, and I never visited him while he was in prison. I refused to correspond with him, and I never took any of his calls, even after his release. I re-married three years after Gustavo was sent to prison. Joe took good care of me and our boys. Years of Christmas and Easter dinners. Thanksgiving. Happy times, happy memories."

Schrodinger's voice trailed off again as a wry smile trembled across her face. Her fingers traced the cover of the Bible.

"This may sound strange to you, Detective, but Gustavo was a good man, good and proud," she resumed. "At least, I thought he was. He just wanted to take care of me. To take care of us. But we couldn't keep up with the house payments. That's when everything changed for us."

"Mrs. Schrodinger, as part of the investigative process, I reviewed your financials," I said, leaning forward. "I didn't see anything that would indicate you had money problems." Deacon folded his arms, regarding the old woman with flinty eyes.

"No, they wouldn't," she replied with a caustic laugh. "I worked as a waitress at the Red Round Diner over on Brighton Beach Ave by the library. Gustavo eventually got the job working for a landscaping company. Far Scapes, I think it was called. Between the two of us, we barely scraped by. But then he started doing those other...jobs...to keep us afloat. After that, we never missed a payment. I tried working double-shifts to get him out of that life, but it wasn't enough. It was never enough."

"Did Gustavo ever talk about working at the Flynn's home in East Hampton?" I asked.

"Other than they were very rich?" she countered with a bitter laugh.

The landscaping company Sanarov had worked for had

serviced high-end homes along Long Island, and as far east as the Hamptons. The Flynn family lived in East Hampton, a massive estate on four acres overlooking the water. Mahoney had presumed Sanarov coveted the extreme wealth surrounding him, and the kidnapping plan was formed.

Classic motive and opportunity.

But sitting here, listening to Stacey Schrodinger, I wasn't buying it. The problem was, why had Bill? Something else was at play here. I just didn't know what.

"Did you know about Gustavo's other activities before the kidnapping?" I asked. "Is that why he worked the streets?"

"Yes, Detective," Schrodinger said, indignation mixed with disgust on her face. "I warned him about that old neighborhood of his. He'd say, 'Just one more job, Stace. Just one more, and then we'll be golden.' As if that would *ever* happen. I knew how it would all end. Dead in the street, killed after one of those 'jobs' of his. I just didn't think Gustavo was capable of kidnapping a child, let alone murdering one."

"Which old neighborhood would that be?" I asked.

"By that church where Gustavo was found," she replied. "I grew up in Manhattan Beach, over on Oxford Street. Gustavo and I met at a mixer at our church back in our late teens. He had family living there and was invited over for the weekend."

Bitter tears slid down the woman's cheeks from old wounds that, out of necessity, I'd reopened. I felt a momentary pang of guilt but crushed the feeling beneath years of working tough cases like this, knowing that to uncover the dirty little secrets most people hid from the light, I had to be just as invasive. And if that meant making an old lady cry, then that's what I had to do.

But I didn't have to like it.

"Who would want to murder Gustavo?" I asked, deciding to change tacks.

"That poor boy's father," she replied immediately. "And I wouldn't blame him."

"We're considering several suspects, Mrs. Schrodinger," I began.

"Why bother?" Schrodinger leaned back in her chair, each hand clasping the faux wooden arms in a white-knuckled grip. "Had he murdered one of my sons, or one of my grandchildren for that matter, why, I'd probably do the same thing if I were in his shoes! God is watching, and God is merciful to those who deserve His love. Make no mistake, Detective. Gustavo got exactly what he deserved."

Suddenly, all the Scripture messages I'd seen echoed in the dark fringes of my mind. The Insight tingled at the corners of my eyes in response. The hackles on the back of my neck stood at attention.

"Did Gustavo ever talk about the crew he ran with before the kidnapping?" I asked, resisting the urge to rub my eyes. "Maybe mention a name?"

"I never knew their names."

"Did they ever come to the house?"

"No, he kept them far from here. And that was just as well. Gustavo would stay out late, doing God-knew-what. Sometimes, he would come home with bloody knuckles and bruises. He'd never talk about it, and after a while, I never asked. But I knew what he did. Muscle for the Russians. Beating up business owners for protection credits. Hurting people so we could pay our bills, keep the home, and put food on the table."

The implication was plain. Schrodinger couldn't call the cops because then the Russians would know and both she and Sanarov would pay the price. Telling her own family would merely put them in danger, as well. She was trapped.

The irritation in my eyes had grown to a full burn. I grimaced and began shifting in my seat. Deacon noticed my discomfort and raised his eyebrows. I blinked once.

"Ma'am," he said, taking the cue. "I'd appreciate it mightily for a cup of that coffee now, if you wouldn't mind?"

"Excuse me?" she asked absently, distracted by her anger and shame.

"Coffee?" Deacon repeated.

"Of course," the old woman said, dry washing her hands to hide her embarrassment. "How do you take it?"

While Deacon spoke, their voices faded into the background. Once Schrodinger disappeared into the kitchen, I lurched unsteadily to my feet. Deacon made a move to assist, but I staggered forward, head bowed, until I faced the broken holo-frame and the Bible. The tome's lettering glittered, as if lit from beneath the cover. Sounds echoed in my mind, conversations spoken from a vast distance, gathering strength as the words drew closer. I strained my ears to catch bits and shards, but they were meaningless. I needed a focus, something to anchor my preternatural senses. I reached out with trembling fingers and scraped the crack along the holo-frame.

Everything around me changed.

"Now I know this is hard for you," a familiar gravelly voice said. "And I truly appreciate you speaking with us, but is there anything you can recall from the time of the kidnapping, and the events leading up to Gustavo's arrest, that maybe you've forgotten? A small detail, something you might have thought unimportant at the time?"

"No, Detective Mahoney," Stacey Sanarov replied. She occupied the same chair her older incarnation had sat in mere moments before. Gone were the worn care lines, the gray hair and the bitterness and anger, replaced by a frightened, lost young woman seeking answers to a fresh tragedy. "That's all I know."

My eyes were drawn to the unbroken holo-frame sitting beside a new Bible. The frame cycled between images from the Sanarov's on their wedding day, holding hands and wearing smiles filled with the joy of a new life together.

Young Mahoney in his smart dark suit with the golden detective's shield in his breast pocket studied the young woman's distraught and tear-streaked face, his bushy brown eyebrows beetling together in thought. It was clear he wanted to ask more questions, but he held back, relenting to her emotional state. Instead, he handed her a small rectangular plastic card imprinted with his name and contact information.

"Mrs. Sanarov, if you can think of anything that could help me, anything that could help your husband, please let me know."

"Of course, Detective," she sniffled, her red-rimmed eyes brimming with fresh tears.

She rose from her chair to show Young Mahoney out.

As I watched them leave, a flickering of light and shadow drew my attention back to the holo-frame.

The image shifted from the wedding photo to display more images from that day. Group shots of numerous wedding guests arranged around reception tables, everyone dressed in their finest. Couples dancing with the bride and groom celebrating the newly-weds, the cutting of the cake, a bouquet toss and the bright smiles of friends and family.

And as the Insight fled from me, one last image of

Gustavo holding a glass of clear liquor in his hand, along with Pyotr Ushakov and Orlando Denning, the Holy Redeemer's sexton.

16

The Insight had weakened me to the point where a three-year old could've kicked the shit out of me with little effort. Deacon guided me from the living room, citing that I was recovering from a flu, and my meds hadn't kicked in yet. For excuses, it wasn't terrible. Schrodinger didn't question him, given my pallor had turned whiter than curdled proto-milk. Deacon thanked her for the hospitality and shuffled me out the door without turning back. I tried to apologize, but my neck had lost control of my head somewhere between the living room and the welcome mat.

The walk back to the pod consisted of Deacon cursing at me while I mumbled incoherent nonsense.

So, business as usual.

Deacon dumped my carcass in one of the command chairs, had EVI close the hatch, and we departed. EVI informed me that I had two messages—one from Leyla saying she'd cracked the first three layers of encryption on Ushakov's phone, and the other from Charlotte, which I had the AI delete without listening to it. I would've scowled but drool dripped uncontrollably from my numbed lips onto the control console where my face lay. My arms and legs had turned to jelly. This time-walking shit the Insight was doing to me was beginning to suck bio-donkey balls.

"Abner's Vintage Books," Deacon authorized.

I barely felt the movement of the pod as it skidded along its 'way.

"Don't you go dyin' on me, Holliday," Deacon chuckled as he offered me a mug full of warmth and sunshine. He kicked back in the opposite chair and lit a cigarette. Gray smoke billowed around us like fog on the Hudson.

The sight of the liquid pirate's treasure perked me up to the point that normal feeling returned soon after. I sat up straighter, handled the mug and drained its contents with a practiced gulp, before wiping the drool from my face.

Priorities, people.

"Better," I slurred. I stumbled to the beverage station to pour myself a second and third round. Once the fourth cup was filled, I resumed my seat and outlined to Deacon what the Insight had shown me.

"You think Mahoney knew about Sanarov's connection with the sexton?" Deacon exhaled a current of smoke from his nose and mouth.

"His files included all the interviews of Sanarov's known associates," I replied, "which included anyone from the neighborhood, his co-workers at Far Scapes, and even the people at the church both he and Stacey had attended. Neither Ushakov nor Denning were on the list."

"So, now do you think he was on the take, Holliday?" Deacon asked.

I was afraid to answer the question. My fingers fretted with the coffee mug. That sobering thought had been lingering in the back of my mind ever since I had left

Eddie's. I couldn't believe Bill Mahoney, one of the most decorated and venerated policemen in his time could've been owned by the Russian mob. It felt wrong.

"I hope not," I finally answered. "I think it's something else. But what?"

"Beats the shit out of me," he returned. "But that still don't answer the question about who killed Sanarov. And I'm telling you, Holliday, it weren't done by something high-tech, or a rival gangbanger. That death was pure hate."

"I don't disagree," I said. "But I have a hard time believing that Donald Flynn summoned a revenant or had someone work magic to do it for him."

"Well, the echo of that spirit's fading from Sanarov's room," the former Protector said. "And if it wasted those Russians, then it left another echo at that bar, too. Didn't you say you had something in mind?"

"I'm still working that one out," I hedged, not willing to lay my cards on the table just yet.

I grabbed my mug, stood up, and began pacing in the open space behind the chairs. I shunted aside the implication Mahoney might be a flunky to the *bratva*, and instead refocused on the Schrodinger interview. Her admission that she had worked at the diner jarred something loose in my Swiss-cheesed brain.

"EVI, please use Stacey Schrodinger's audio confirmation from her interview as permission to request access to her financial and tax records for the timeframe I'm indicating," I ordered.

The HUD lit up with data as it cascaded across the screen like a leaky faucet. I stopped and stared at the names and figures arranged in neat rows and columns.

That's when I saw it.

"EVI, please enhance only the monthly mortgage payments. I want all of them."

My eyes raked over the information as my pulse quickened. The Confederate finished his cigarette and crushed it on the metal dashboard. After lighting a second, he squinted up at the screen.

"EVI, pull an enhanced due diligence report for the lenders that I'm indicating," I instructed, using my eye-blink to deliberately mark each name for EVI to register. "Now, cross reference Titan Bank, Stacey Sanarov, aka Stacey Schrodinger, and Donald Flynn. Determine any correlation between them."

Seconds passed before EVI responded.

"Detective Holliday, the mortgage companies you have selected that have provided lending services to search subject Stacey Sanarov, also known as Stacey Schrodinger, have been owned, and subsequently sold, by search subject Titan Bank. During this same time, search subject Donald Flynn was also an employee of Titan Bank."

"There it is!" I crowed with triumph, then turned to Deacon. "I kept asking myself, how did Schrodinger manage to keep up with the house payments after Sanarov went to jail, and before she remarried? Her double shifts at the diner couldn't be enough to afford that house. The mortgage was sold and purchased three times in the months before Sanarov's sentencing. Not uncommon, given how home lenders make their money, but the timing is awfully convenient. Notice how each lender lowered Schrodinger's payment or offered favorable interest rates? Maybe they cited good payment history as a reward for the reduced cost. Again, not uncommon."

I pointed at the holo-window containing Titan's affiliations.

"Each of those mortgage companies was owned by Titan Bank. At some point, the loan was sold to a new company, the old company is sold off, but the trail always leads back to Titan. I bet after Stacey married Joe, the rebates and reductions continued as each lender was replaced by a new one. Remember, she told us she raised both kids she had with Joe in that house, which means he moved in with her, and not the other way around."

"Why would Flynn help the family of the man who had just been convicted of kidnapping his son?" Deacon asked.

"I don't know," I replied. "But I think we can infer from this information that Flynn used his position at the bank to acquire the loans. With the case cleared, Mahoney would have had no reason to take a second look at Sanarov's financials. And he certainly wouldn't have looked at Schrodinger's mortgage records afterward, either. Maybe Bill was searching for this connection that we found, only he didn't know where to look?"

"Or was called off the search," the Confederate said.

"Or was called off the search," I repeated soberly.

"At least this case ain't boring," Deacon drawled. He leaned back in the chair and threaded both hands behind his head. "'Course, nobody's tryin' to kill us yet, neither. Just a matter of time."

"That's what I like about you, Deacon," I said. "You're always a glass half-full kind of guy."

"Beats the fucking alternative," he grumbled. "Back in the States, my investigations involved hearsay, libel, blame, convictions and executions. People told on other people that was doing shit that was against the law. Word gets back to the Church of the Tribulation. They send out Inquisitors who put the Accused to the Question, and the Accused usually lied. Then the Retribution squad showed up, knocked the shit out of the Accused, dragged them before the Holy Tribunal, they're forced to tell the truth, and then they'd burn, literally. Oh, a few became redeemed, but I ain't seen that happen in a long time."

"The Question?" I asked with raised eyebrows. "What's that?"

Deacon lit another cigarette and took a long drag before answering.

"Protectors got themselves a few abilities most normal folk don't. Anyways, some feel the call to become Inquisitors. Their job is exactly what it sounds like. They're trained to pick out the lies from the truth. But when they ask the Question, well, that's when shit gets real. Then there's the other ranks, like the Righteous, who mete out justice, the Confessors who work undercover to root out corruption within the Church, and the Hallowed, who cleanse dark sites and can even heal the sick, sometimes. Power of God and all that happy horseshit."

"Which one are you?" I asked. "Before you left Birmingham."

"There ain't no rank for fuck-ups like me, Holliday," he answered bitterly, staring out the windshield at the gray and black cityscape as it streaked past.

"You told me once that you had a falling out with the church," I said. "But I've seen your truncheon in action. The white fire that melted Crain was unlike anything I'd ever encountered. You can take the man out of the Protector, but you can't take the Protector out of the man. It has to mean something, right?"

"Yeah, it means you should mind your own fucking business," he retorted. "We're wasting time here. We should be focusing on the goddamn case, not walking down Memory Fucking Lane."

"You channeled your faith through a consecrated weapon of your own making," I pursued, undaunted by his growing ire. "That white fire had to come from somewhere. It's why I wanted Father Jack to bless the bullets I used against Rumpelstiltskin. Instead, I dipped them in the holy water font at the church. I've witnessed firsthand how real your power is and thought the holy water would help me against the *fetch*."

"Did it?" Deacon turned to regard me with haunted eyes. "Did the water's blessing work?"

"It did," I answered, although the lie hurt on so many levels I nearly winced. I didn't want to admit that the bullets I'd used to kill the *fetch* hadn't been blessed by anything. Because if I admitted that, then I was accepting a belief I didn't entirely share.

"You're a bad liar, Holliday," the former Protector growled, as if reading my guilty thoughts. "But if you don't want to tell me the truth, that's on you."

"What's that supposed to mean?" I demanded.

"I know all about you and the 'Guardian of Empire City,'" he stated flatly. "Known about it since I told Saranda you were our guy back before I met you. She filled me in on the rest, about the Insight, and what really happened with you and that fucker Blakely at Wrigley-Boes. You want to deny your part in all this, fine by me. But something's got you pegged as bein' worth a damn, which is why you possess that goddamn magic. The further you run from it, the harder you'll fall once the truth finally hits you. The Insight ain't come from nowhere. Shit like that is bequeathed, Holliday, and for a goddamn good reason. And don't get me started on your near-death experience in that bathtub. You committed *suicide*, Holliday, but you weren't allowed to move on.

Somethin' brought you back. And that same somethin' left Kate to die."

I turned away from him. The medical staff at Wallingbrooke had kept me alive long enough for the EMTs to cart me off to EC General. There had been nothing they could do for Kate. She'd already lost too much blood before I came upon her in the bathroom. What bits and pieces I remembered from that experience were sketchy at best, other than a dull yet excruciating pain, and the acceptance that my time had come. After everything I'd been through, the corruption probe at ECPD, my addictions, and all the bad shit that came with it, seeing Kate floating in the tub's bloody water had finally broken me.

I thought I'd reconciled the events from that night with myself, but that didn't mean it wouldn't affect me. My vision kindled an incandescent red. Dredging up Kate and that night was low, even for Deacon. I stared at the white puckered scars on my wrist as my heartbeat pounded in my ears. I started to respond, but Deacon cut me off.

"I ain't seen nothing in this enclave to give me hope that kind of purity even exists," he said. "And any blessing coming from that fake fucking priest of yours running the Redeemer is about as worthless as tits on a bull."

My face flushed with fury. "Excuse me? I get you've got issues with God and the church, Deacon, but don't you dare talk shit about Father Jack! That man has saved more lives without using guns or handcuffs than both you and me combined! He's the most honest, upright man I know. Who the hell do you think you are?"

"Oh, for Christ's sake!" Deacon violently crushed the expired cigarette in his palm, then stood up to confront me. "Quit being so fucking blind, Holliday. Open your eyes! You're so caught up in your goddamn emotions you can't see what's happenin' around you! You just found the image of a murdered ex-con, a dead Russian mobster, and the sexton from the fucking Holy Redeemer! Why would the Insight show you that?"

I stared at the former Protector, a harsh rejoinder on my lips, but swallowed it as his question burned in my mind.

"C'mon Holliday, pull your head out of your ass," Deacon continued, although his voice had softened. "There's more going on with that church than meets the eye. I ain't said nothing 'cause I was hoping you'd figure it out for yourself. But that place stinks worse than a goddamn chicken house in August. Father Jack claims he don't know shit about Sanarov or who sent him to the church, and none of that seems odd to you? There's a reason Sanarov was given sanctuary, and it ain't 'cause he'd found God."

The anger I'd felt moments before was replaced by the bleak realization Deacon was right.

"Think, Holliday," the Confederate urged. "*Think*. There were three men in that image, two of who are dead. Sanarov, Ushakov, and Denning. Why those three? What's their connection? What's really going on?"

Suddenly, I recalled the high-top table back at Eddie's, the vodka bottle next to four glasses, three of them empty. I moved to the evidence table which held the plastic bags containing everything else I'd taken from the crime scene. The fourth glass stared at me, its secrets concealed behind a crystal-clear face. Apprehension settled into my bones.

"I don't know," I frowned, willing the evidence to reveal the answers I so desperately wanted.

"Detective Holliday," EVI announced. "I have completed the repairs on the corrupted surveillance footage."

I came back to the command chair. "All right. Please

show the fingerprint IDs on the shot glasses taken from the P-Scanner at Eddie's."

Deacon rolled a cigarette between his fingers. I flicked through each holo-image, the first three containing the three dead Russians. The fourth followed, but it was blank.

"Detective Holliday," EVI said, "there were no fingerprints found on the fourth glass. Forensic analysis did discover manufactured threads of grain pigskin, consistent with heavy duty work gloves used in a variety of labor-related occupations, including, but not limited to—"

"Okay, EVI," I cut her off. "Please run the footage, starting fifteen minutes before the medical examiner's estimation of time-of-death."

A separate holo-window appeared containing an image of the taproom taken from a high vantage point. It provided a commanding view of the entrance, the long bar and several of the tables, including the high-top where the murder occurred. There was no sound, and the image quality was fair given the dim interior.

A figure of average height wearing a heavy coat and a winter hat stepped into the bar and walked over to the high-top. Although the lighting was poor, I made out Ushakov and his buddies, but the fourth figure sat in the lee of the wall, shrouded in shadow. The figure was hunched over, listening to Ushakov.

Ushakov took the bottle and filled three glasses, then placed it on the table. The fourth figure poured their own.

"EVI, please enhance imagery, and focus on this quadrant." I traced my finger in a circle around the high-top. "Account for the grade of the camera lens, the angles, pitch and shadows. Heighten all facial features and any other distinguishing marks."

Deacon and I watched in silence as the overall definition of the picture improved dramatically.

I cycled between the three Russians first. EVI highlighted each man and provided a laundry list of wrongdoing found within the ECPD database as well as information from several other enclave law enforcement agencies.

"Okay, now let's see who our mystery guest is," I said.

I brought my hand before the holo-screen and drew my fingers over the fourth figure, enlarging the image, then stopped, my hand frozen in mid-motion. I stared at the screen as if seeing a ghost.

"No," I whispered the word like a curse.

"Who is that?" Deacon asked, looking from the HUD back to me.

I locked eyes with the former Protector, the color draining from my face.

"That's John Holliday," I answered in a dead voice. "My father."

17

I couldn't tear my eyes from the frozen image of my dad, hunkered low in his chair, a black-knit winter hat crowning his head. Gray stubble lined his grim-set jaw, but his features were unmistakable. A glowing holo-window had popped up beside the image providing us the results of EVI's facial recognition analysis as well as my father's home address, criminal record, known associates and work history.

At least he hadn't moved, but the three recent disturbing the peace and disorderly conduct charges over the past four months caught my attention. They highlighted John Holliday's long and illustrious career as one of Little Odessa's least favorite malcontents. Had I decided to dig further into his record, I'd come across a report that also included my name, coinciding with the last time we'd been together.

Eight years ago.

That night hadn't ended well. The argument. Hate-filled promises. A fistfight outside Wallingbrooke, then a bloody tub, a shard of broken glass and my whole world changed forever.

A mad torrent of memory flooded me, stark impressions rife with dark and powerful emotions. Pop had finally decided to visit me at Wallingbrooke two weeks after Abner had checked me in for treatment. His appearance surprised me, given how little we'd seen each other over the years.

After my mother's murder, what little relationship he and I shared had ended. No longer was my mother's gentle hand and soft voice standing between us. There'd be nights when Pop wouldn't come home until late the following day, drunk and strung out, followed by long stretches of bitter silence and solitude. I don't remember exactly when the abuse began, only that it did. I still bore small cigarette burns on my left arm, badges of dishonor for pissing Pop off. They, like the scars on my wrists, had become symbols of who I was and where I'd been, painful mementos of how easy it was to succumb to anger and despair.

For three years, I lived in the shell of that empty house, if you call taking care of myself by age eleven, living. It wasn't long before I fell in with Ivan and his merry band of punks, raising hell in the neighborhood, and causing no small amount of trouble.

If my grandfather hadn't been there, I'd probably be dead. After the third time he checked me out from EC General for burns and broken bones, he'd seen enough. Harry waded through Social Services and a morass of bureaucratic red tape, challenging the system until finally, miraculously, he was granted custody of me.

I remember the day well. A cold morning in early February, slate gray skies, old snow and ice stubbornly clinging to the ground. We packed up what little I owned and walked out while Pop slept off another long night of bingeing in that shitty easy chair of his, blissfully ignorant that I'd left. In my hands I carried the only holo-frame in the house that contained images of my mom, to remind myself happiness wasn't a dream, and that love still endured somewhere in the world.

I owed my grandfather my life. Harry had pulled me from the brink before I did anything permanent. His steady hand had guided me through a turbulent adolescence. He, along with Abner, instilled in me a love of books, of learning, of being true to myself and taking up for the little guy. He'd been my very own guardian.

I smiled ruefully at the irony.

Pop hated me for leaving. Hell, he hated me for a lot of things. And the feeling was mutual. Eight years ago, what began as a tense conversation outside the front doors of Wallingbrooke, quickly devolved into a shouting match. Pop brought up my mother, perhaps thinking her memory would somehow bridge the gaping divide between us. But when he blamed her death as the root of all our problems, that's when I lost it.

I started the fight and John Holliday had ended it. He decked me with one punch. Pop might be an alcoholic, but he'd never been weak. The cops arrived shortly thereafter, then cuffed and carted us off in separate pods. I spent several hours stewing in general circulation at the 60th Precinct before returning to Wallingbrooke.

And had I not been in jail, I might've been there to save Kate.

Eight long, excruciating, gut-wrenching, eye-tearing, wasteful years. I hadn't seen my dad since.

Until now.

I rubbed my chin as phantom pain shot through it, then reviewed Pop's dossier again. Two of the misdemeanors had occurred at Eddie's. The third was at Caron Oceanic Container. His work history indicated he'd been employed there for the last five years. The P-Scanner had detected traces of saltwater on the taproom floor and the dead Russians' boots. There'd be plenty on the ground at a shipping yard.

Deacon was silent. He still hadn't asked any of the obvious questions, knowing my mind seethed with the same. Instead, he dashed out the cigarette, lit a fresh one and brooded.

"Detective Holliday, we have arrived," EVI reported, her voice a distant echo. "Outdoor temperature is twelve degrees Fahrenheit, with winds out of the Northwest. Chance of precipitation, one-hundred percent."

"Leyla's waiting for us," I said gruffly as I swiped the holo-windows away.

Before we left the pod, I had EVI activate the perimeter defense as a precaution. The walk to Abner's was brief, but I felt naked and unprotected. Traffic was light, as was the falling snow. Few pedestrians wandered the street, and none of them spared us a glance.

Deacon trailed me into the bookstore. Warmth surrounded us, what should've been a pleasant contrast to the bitter February morning outside, but I felt nothing. Mozart's *Piano Sonata No. 11* played, its *Alla turca* in A-major carrying little ebullience, and even less depth, as if the music had been performed on a child's toy. An old woman wrapped in a tan winter coat and a colorful scarf wandered an aisle, idly poking at books. One baleful glare from me and she hustled out the door.

We moved to the half-moon shaped wooden counter anchored at the store's center. An antique cash register rested there between a bright green cactus and a handmade sign with the words "Ring for assistance" scrawled in a handsome navy-blue script. Propping it up was a metal handbell with a worn flower-patterned plastic handle, and a pair of ceramic snowmen, or, more accurately, a snowman and his snowwoman, if the colorful *mitpachat* on her head was any indication. The snowman wore a pair of painted spectacles, a blue and white *yarmulke* on his head, and a matching *tallis* around his shoulders.

I collected the male snowman and held it in one hand, studying its face where some of the paint had chipped. The curio had a hairline scar down its left side that had been glued recently. My thumb clung to the adhesive, but I managed to peel it off without causing any damage.

Abner was very proud of his Jewish heritage, something he and my grandfather Harry had shared. I'd maintained a more neutral opinion on the divine, despite Harry's constant attempts to sway me. Life was a lot simpler without all the excess baggage any organized religion tried to pack for me. I had no issue with Jewish pragmatism or its culture, but God and I hadn't seen eye-to-eye in a long time.

Something brought you back for a fucking reason.

Deacon's words lingered in my mind. I pushed them away with a grimace.

"Mrs. Pushkin, I found Varlam Shalamov's poetry anthology you were asking after!" Abner announced brightly as he shuffled past a wrought-iron staircase spiraling up, a thick tome cradled in his hands. "The one by Robert Chandler! It was in my reserves after all, and—" The short man paused when he caught us standing by the counter, then peered past while blinking rapidly in confusion. "Oh! Tom! Deacon! Where is Mrs. Pushkin?"

"She left," I replied.

"I see." Abner frowned as he marked whatever ugly mood had taken up residence on my face. He set the book on the counter and folded his arms. "Leyla is in her workshop. She asked me to send you down."

"Thanks." I made to move past him.

"We'll talk?"

I didn't answer him.

The back room was a clusterfuck of books, periodicals, black-and-white photographs, and the occasional cat nesting on the desk, in a corner, or atop one of the bookshelves. Not an ounce of technology beyond the caged fluorescent long bulb in the ceiling was present. How Abner found anything amidst the mountain range of stacked piles was a mystery, and a testament to his precise knowledge of the store's diverse and eclectic inventory.

A short hallway adjacent to the clutter led to a tidy kitchenette, a tiny bathroom and the shuttered back door. Unlike the front, the air here was perceptibly colder as the indoor heat struggled to battle the chill seeping through the walls. A table with two chairs were by the door next to a squat refrigerator, a range insert and a rusted metal sink. Two narrow cabinets flanked a cloudy window inset in the wall. An empty coffee pot occupied one of the burners.

I glanced at the range and considered brewing a new pot but crushed the temptation in favor of catching up with Leyla.

"This don't look like no workshop," Deacon grumbled peevishly.

I moved to the door-less bathroom and studied the worn toilet. The bowl bore scrapes from numerous times a plumber had to snake the pipe to clear a clog. Square water-stained tiles the size of my fist dotted the floor, chipped and cracked from years of neglect. The inner walls were uneven and bare, compressed by the building's weight lower to the floor than the other rooms.

"I'll wait in the other room, Holliday," Deacon chuckled. "Don't think I'll ever like you enough to watch you take a shit."

I knelt by the toilet and twisted the rust-splotched spigot on the water pipe. A section of inner wall slid aside soundlessly to reveal a dark hole and the metal rungs of a ladder. Raw, arctic air blasted me, a fresh reminder of who waited below.

"Well, would you look at that," Deacon whistled.

Ice caked the rungs as we descended into the darkened sub-basement. Using my holo-phone for light, we moved down another short hallway of smooth concrete which ended at a closed metal door.

"IDENTIFY," an androgynous voice boomed suddenly from all around us.

"The fuck?" Deacon nearly jumped out of his skin.

"IDENTIFY OR BE DESTROYED!"

Twin panels to either side of the door flipped open to unveil the muzzles of high-powered weapons that zeroed in on us.

"Holliday!" the former Protector shouted in alarm. "Do something!"

"Leyla, it's us," I sighed patiently. "Open the door."

"WHAT IS THE PASSWORD?" the voice demanded.

"Seriously, Leyla?" I asked in exasperation. "I don't remember. You changed it last month and forgot to tell me."

"WHAT IS THE PASSWORD?"

"Girlie, open the goddamn door before I break it down," Deacon threatened darkly.

"AW, C'MON GUYS," it whined petulantly.

The gun panels flapped closed as the door swung open. We stepped into an icebox.

"A little help here?" I asked between chattering teeth.

"Oh, sorry," Leyla said with a negligent wave of her hand. "I've been so focused on the phone that I forgot you were coming. Give it a minute to warm up."

Heat began filtering into the small room. I left the door open to allow the colder air to evacuate briefly before closing it. Locks clicked into place. The moment the door was secured, I lost my connection to EVI.

Leyla's workshop was neat and orderly. Her portable rig was jacked into a virtual workstation comprising an entire wall opposite the door, its enhanced HUD dark. Two long metal tables covered with a cornucopia of what's-its and doodads were arranged atop each.

I had no idea what any of them were called, or their functions, other than they were part of Leyla's tricks-of-the-trade. Several devices bore long sensors, sharp, wicked looking prods and clamps, and blinking multi-colored lights. They squeaked, squawked, buzzed and whirred. Others lay dormant, brooding, hulking things with small, closed doors, virtual keyboard controls, and probably dreamed of electric sheep. Deacon wandered the workshop to admire Leyla's equipment, muttering to himself.

She once tried to explain them all to me. I reminded her that my mind was a leaky basement that easily flooded once technical things were involved. Leyla had agreed, stating it was safer for everyone concerned that I remained in the dark anyway, leaving such matters to my betters.

I hate it when she's right.

The young hacker sat before a cleared section of table. Attached to her head was a lamp that she flicked off as we approached her. Ushakov's dissected phone lay in a plastic tray next to what appeared to be a measuring instrument, if the probe and digital display were any indications. Leyla held a thin cordless soldering iron, the glow of its heating element already fading to a dull gray. Thin curls of acrid smoke wafted upward from a small, unremarkable square black metal box lying on the floor next to her chair.

"Should we be worried about something, girlie?" Deacon pointed at the box.

"Nope," she answered with an unpleasant smile. "I isolated the detonation chip just as you arrived. That phone was a nasty little bugger! Between that and the multiple layers of tracking software, it's no wonder ECPD has never been successful at hacking into the *bratva's* network."

"What did you find?" I asked gruffly, my voice hoarse and rough.

"You okay, Doc?" Leyla asked with concern.

"I'm fine," I answered, wiping at my nose, and not meeting her gaze.

"You sure?"

"I said I'm fine."

Leyla drooped as if she'd been reprimanded. I felt a momentary pang of guilt, but thoughts of Pop kept intruding in my mind. I needed to know what information Ushakov's phone held, especially if it had anything to do with my dad.

"Right." Leyla wheeled her chair over to her virtual workstation. "What did I find...what did I find..."

At her approach, several holo-windows materialized before the darkened screen, displaying a short list of phone numbers and associated outgoing and incoming calls, battery charge outputs, signal strengths and a running algorithm whose glittering lime-colored code gushed like hard-pouring rain.

"Not a lot," Leyla announced mechanically, her back to me. Her shoulders had bunched together. A thin sheen of frost covered her hair, and tiny ice fragments flitted around her. "However, my decryption program will crack it now that the detonation chip is gone."

Deacon offered me a glare that screamed "Quit being an asshole and say something nice or I'll break your face".

I sighed heavily and nodded, then stepped up beside her and laid a reassuring hand on her shoulder.

"Good work, kiddo," I said. "I don't know what I'd do without you."

"You'd fall to pieces, that's what," she grumbled without looking at me, but her body visibly relaxed. The snow shower abruptly ended. "Anyway, I've decrypted about twenty percent. I figure it'll take another eight to ten hours to get the rest, maybe longer. Their code is deep, fragmented and very complicated. However, I did get his phone records."

"Once we leave, I'll have EVI ID the numbers," I said.

"Already done." Leyla snapped her fingers, and a holo-window popped up containing a list of the owners' phone numbers.

"They all come from burner phones, just like Ushakov's. It was the first thing I checked. They were all purchased from a dozen different vendors across Empire City. No voice mails, and I doubt Ushakov's phone provider has them in their cloud, either. I have to say, Doc, I'm impressed. They really don't want anyone knowing what they're up to."

"What'd you expect," Deacon grunted. He'd lit a smoke and was filling the room with a sour white cloud. "They're a fucking criminal organization. It's what we do at Aurik, minus the criminal part."

"True," Leyla conceded. "But the *bratva's* security is meticulous, like beyond careful and deep into the land of the paranoid."

"Good security always is, girlie," the former Protector chuckled.

"Did Ushakov's phone have anything else on it?" I asked.

"Yeah." Leyla reached toward the HUD and used her fingers to withdraw a tiny holo-window that had been lurking in the background. "This."

Deacon and I studied it, a single sentence, but it was in Russian.

"Give it a second," she said.

The image rippled, transliterating the words into English.

"'Shipment departs Thursday night,'" Deacon read aloud. "What's that got to do with our killer?"

"I don't know," I replied grimly. "But I know who to ask."

18

D onald Flynn, the *bratva*, and now my dad were involved in Sanarov's murder. But how? And why? I considered Mahoney's part and how he fit in all of this. From what the Insight had shown me from Mahoney's memory, the captain had covered something up, was covering for someone, or both. EVI confirmed that Mayor Samson had been Mahoney's captain during the Flynn kidnapping case. I'd heard that he'd quickly climbed the ranks of the ECPD back in the day. Was Samson in the *bratva's* pockets, too? Was Mahoney? And what did any of them have to do with Deacon's revenant theory? The Bible verses were creepy enough but tack on the bloody brutality of the murders as well as the overwhelming sense of dread and evil, and this case had the makings of one hell of a horror holo-novel. Catching Flynn off balance at Brave New Beginnings might be the angle we needed to connect some of the dots. Or it might just piss him off enough to convince Mayor Samson into axing Special Crimes.

The thought of sitting behind a desk again, relegated to filing paperwork while Orpheus or this revenant or who knows what else worked Empire City over unsettled my stomach. Guardian or not, I was still a cop. I couldn't do that if I were off the streets. But if I wanted to unravel the truth, pushing Flynn was a risk I had to take.

Then there was Orlando Denning. When I had interviewed him at the Redeemer, the sexton had intimated nothing about knowing Sanarov, which made that a lie of omission. Was Denning one of the local crew Sanarov had run around with back in the day? And how did the Calvin Flynn kidnapping and murder fit in with all of that?

But what bothered me most was the sinking suspicion Deacon was right about Father Jack. The old pastor hadn't told me everything. What did he know? I could count on one hand the number of people that I trusted, two of whom were in this room, and the third was upstairs. Why cover up his relationship with Sanarov? Who was Father Jack protecting?

Four men were dead stemming from a thirty-year old crime. How many more would die because of lies and deceit? I ground my teeth in frustration.

Too many damn questions. No, that wasn't right. Too many damn secrets.

"*How now, you secret, black, and midnight hags? What is't you do?*" I whispered to myself then said aloud, "Keep at the encryption, kiddo. The moment you've cracked it, I want to know."

"You got it, Doc."

We exited Abner's through the kitchenette back door, walked along the rear wall before turning up the street and back to the pod. Deacon spoke quietly on his phone. I caught some of his conversation as he checked in with Mamika. I had EVI delete another voice message from Charlotte. My love-life had never been up for debate. My one and only chance had come eight years ago with Kate. The fact Charlotte had fucked me twice, once literally and the other figuratively, only proved that I wasn't meant for that kind of happiness.

"Saranda's at Brave New Beginnings," Deacon stated, stowing his phone.

I picked out the digital clock on the HUD. The day had slipped from me unnoticed. We had less than an hour to get to Brave New Beginnings. Once underway, I poured myself a healthy dose of watery brown lusciousness and closed my eyes hoping its healing magic would scare off the bad things.

It didn't.

I sighed, then filled the mug several times before returning to the front. A thin bank of gray and white smoke enveloped me as I sat down.

"You gonna talk to me now, Holliday?" Deacon asked, a smoldering cigarette between his lips. "It's plain you ain't got no love for your old man. Hell, if he's anything like mine, then I don't blame you."

For the next forty minutes, I regaled Deacon with the details of my sordid family history, all the stories he wouldn't have discovered when he scouted me for Special Crimes. By the end, he'd smoked an entire pack of cigarettes and was halfway through a second, a battalion of slain white soldiers littering the floor.

"Pop and I found her in the living room," I recounted in a detached, dead voice. "Her neck had been broken. She was naked from the waist down. I've seen those images dozens of times since, but back then, even at that age, I knew what had happened. And the look on her face..."

I lapsed into a horrified silence, the moment replaying over in my mind.

She'd been wearing one of her hand-knit blue sweaters. It had been covered in blood from her splintered nose and torn lips. Both of her eyes had been blackened, and it was clear one of the orbital bones had been broken. My mother had suffered, and whoever had done that to her still walked the streets.

"The cops never found her killer?" Deacon asked, dragging me from my reverie.

"No." My coffee had grown cold during the telling, but I hadn't felt the need to refresh it.

"You ever look into it yourself?"

My hollow laugh was short and bitter. "I did years later, but despite my clearance and street contacts, nobody in the neighborhood would talk about it, no matter how hard I squeezed them. And the local precinct had no interest in working a cold case, either. I suppose I could've pushed it. But the Brotherhood plays on a much different level from me, and I was too damn scared to chance it."

I contemplated the scars on my wrist, the years of guilt and remorse at my cowardice encasing me in brittle armor. Had Deacon punched me in the face, I would've thanked him and asked him to do it again.

"With everything that's happened in my life since that day, I guess it's no wonder I ended up doing the things that I did. It is what it is. When we're done with Brave New Beginnings, I'm going by Pop's place."

"Well, if you need backup, you just say the word," the Confederate offered.

"I appreciate that," I said, "but I won't need any. Not this time."

"Roger that." He crushed another butt on the chair's arm. A pensive expression wormed across his face. "Some things a man's gotta do by himself."

"Thanks."

I stared out the window at nothing.

"Y'know, Holliday," Deacon began quietly. "I been gone from Birmingham a long time. Left behind a few things, too. Things that needed leavin'. Went to the Euro-Bloc, and eventually met Saranda. We traveled around for a while, saw a lot of weird shit. Met a lot of people, too. Some good, some not so much. But they were just people and places, y'know? People and places. Things."

Deacon stood up and folded his arms, his shrewd brown eyes filled with an old pain, almost a mirror to my own.

"And it pisses me off that you had it that bad back when you were a kid," he continued in a thick voice. "Losing your mom like that. Living alone with your dad. Ivan, his gang, all of that shit."

He paused, then turned to gaze out the windshield as a continuous blur of light and color swept past, blending geography and movement. Shadows played with the light, and when I looked at him, he seemed to be two men—one foot in the present, and the other somewhere else.

"Just," he paused. "Damn."

I observed the internal struggle warring inside this strange, complicated man. The necklace bearing the silver lemniscate charm he wore around his neck caught the glow from the buildings and holo-ads streaming through the windshield.

"I guess what I'm trying to say here is, I got your back, okay?" he said. "Whatever you need. I got your back. So don't you go and fuck it up, Holliday. You got that?"

I nodded at him. A comforting warmth spread from my heart, enclosing some of the pitted hole that had formed there.

We arrived at Brave New Beginnings with six minutes to

spare. The non-profit was a tenant inside a broad glass and spell-forged steel eyesore occupying an entire block of West 50th Street in Midtown. Here, the sidewalks remained clear of ice and snow, as if the mere thought of frozen water defacing the architecture was an affront to the building owners' sensibilities. The mid-afternoon crowd bustled along, blithely ignoring both the single digit temperature and the blustery breezes.

As we strode through the spacious lobby, EVI's dulcet tones soothed my brain's audio center.

"Brave New Beginnings was founded by Donald and Angelina Flynn, in memory of their son Calvin, initially as a halfway house for homeless children. As funding grew, the facility was expanded to provide not only clothing, food and shelter, but educational, occupational and healthcare services. The organization fights poverty and tragedies through the gift of hope. With the assistance of other community nonprofit partners, Brave New Beginnings provides apparel, accessories, shoes, home furnishings, toys, books—"

"EVI, how much funding are we talking about here?" I murmured, exchanging a furtive glance with Deacon.

We paused by one of the elevator stacks which contained several large interactive holo-window directories. I whipped through one searching for the Brave New Beginnings main office. Deacon puffed on a cigarette, blithely ignoring the venomous glares cast by several men and women passing us to either side. All the buildings in both Downtown and Midtown were smoke-free zones, but that didn't seem to bother him.

"Over the past thirty years, more than two billion credits of donated products have been distributed through the

Brave New Beginnings network, serving the poor and disadvantaged enclave-wide," EVI replied.

I whistled low in appreciation and said, "Who are their largest donors?"

"In the prior year, the Angelina Flynn Memorial Foundation and Azyrim Technologies donated or raised more than two-hundred million credits toward all of the Brave New Beginnings programs."

At the mention of Azyrim, a chill crawled down my spine. The strange metal fragment, all that remained of Marko, an android crafted from magic and technology, and the thing responsible for murdering Vanessa Mallery and stealing her blood, came unbidden to my mind. I'd stashed it in a lead-lined lockbox at my apartment. The Insight stirred, but my eyes remained clear. I hadn't given the fragment much thought lately until now.

"Is Sanarov a part of the Game, too?" I muttered darkly.

Deacon raised his eyebrows, but I shook my head as a sudden thought hit me.

"EVI, is the Holy Redeemer Church affiliated with Brave New Beginnings?" I asked.

"The Holy Redeemer Church is not directly affiliated with Brave New Beginnings. However, the Pantry, a soup kitchen dedicated to feeding the homeless, is a joint volunteer operation between Brave New Beginnings and the Holy Redeemer Church whereby employees of Brave New Beginnings donate their time preparing and serving food at the facility three times a month. The Pantry, located at—"

"Why didn't I check into that before?" I slapped a hand to my head, disgusted.

"Check into what?" Deacon asked.

"The soup kitchen where Sanarov worked." I shifted from

the directory to observe the human traffic rumbling through the lobby. "Brave New Beginnings sends volunteers there three times a month. EVI, who is their liaison for the Pantry?"

A knot of chattering pre-teens wearing matching lime green t-shirts marched toward us, chaperoned by two matronly women. The caption on the shirts read "February Fun Day". One brown-haired boy gave me a curious look before being herded with the others toward an elevator.

"Orlando Denning, Vice President for Child Welfare and Family Services," she replied. An image of the Redeemer's sexton appeared in my retina. Using my eye, I sifted through his background. He'd been with the nonprofit since its founding. EVI provided me with multiple press releases and news briefs with associated images taken from various fundraising and other social engineering events highlighting Donald Flynn, his son James, and a cadre of Brave New Beginnings officers, including Orlando Denning.

Denning just moved to the top of my shit-list.

"Do you require anything further, Detective?" EVI asked.

"No, thanks sweetie," I replied, then nodded to Deacon to head to the elevators.

His head was cocked to one side, as if listening to a conversation only he could hear.

"Saranda's with Flynn," he stated in a dull tone, his eyes partially glazed over. "She's leading him to the elevator now."

"I really don't want to know how she does that," I muttered.

A quick ride up led to Flynn's floor. We waited in a small lobby. To our left was a pair of closed frosted glass doors bearing the Brave New Beginnings logo—a blend of children's round, smiling faces, and rays of sunshine. I was about to tell Deacon where to position himself when voices filtered to us from the faceless right hallway. Anticipation filled me as I prepared to confront the banker.

"Construction of the new facility begins next month," came Flynn's unmistakably snide tone. "Although the groundbreaking ceremony is scheduled for this Friday. I plan on personally overseeing—"

Flynn rounded the corner first, then stopped when he caught sight of us. Besim, only a step behind, glided smoothly around him to avoid any contact. Charlotte appeared soon after, her head bowed as she spoke to someone through her earpiece. She collided with Flynn, jostling them both.

"Detective Holliday," the banker choked, apprehension reflected in his eyes before he reasserted his smarmy composure. "What are you doing here?"

Charlotte gaped at me, one hand hovering near her open mouth before she mumbled something, then nodded. I maintained my professional glare on Flynn, the one I designated for hand-cuffing arrogant assholes, although my heart skipped a beat when I caught sight of her.

"Sorry to bother you, Mr. Flynn," I flashed him a disingenuous grin. "I had a few more questions I needed to ask. You weren't at your office, so I tracked you down here. I apologize for the inconvenience, but these questions couldn't wait."

"You should have contacted Charlotte," Flynn sniffed, girding his ego around himself like a smug suit of armor. "I'm happy to assist your investigation in any way I can, of course. However, I am in the middle of a very important meeting with Doctor Saranda, and—"

"Oh, this'll only take a minute," I replied evenly. Besim glanced at me and inclined her head briefly before turning her attention back to Flynn.

I caught Charlotte muttering under her breath, refusing to look at me, locked within whatever conversation she'd been holding before we arrived. I tried to formulate the questions I'd prepared for Flynn, but my mind began to wander. Seeing Charlotte had knocked me off my game. I had expected her to be with Flynn, yet I was unprepared for the deep and powerful feelings that welled up once I laid eyes on her. The Insight was also present, silver fire licking at the edges of my vision, alive and angry. A harsh sense of betrayal nearly overwhelmed me, heightened by the magic coursing through me.

"Well?" Flynn demanded.

I could barely move my swollen tongue. The world turned upside down. I staggered against the wall. Dizziness made my eyes swim with tears. I couldn't focus on anything.

"Holliday," Deacon hissed, catching me under one arm before I collapsed to the floor. "What the fuck is wrong with you?"

I ran a hand across my forehead which was slick with sweat.

"I don't have time for this." Flynn pushed past me and headed to the office doors. They opened at his approach. "Once you've pulled yourself together, you can call my office. And Detective Holliday, I assure you Harold will hear about this. Now, if you will excuse me, I would like to finish our tour. Doctor Saranda, I apologize for any inconvenience these men may have caused."

Charlotte followed, but Besim hesitated, the Vellan's layer cake makeup scarcely able to hide the color rising in her cheeks.

"Get me out of here," I whispered to Deacon before everything went dark.

19

E choes, reverberating endlessly.
Images, colors, people.
Sense and sensation.

Time.

Memories played around me, a steady stream of my own consciousness. A face without a name rippled before me, caught by an invisible current, then yanked away, to be devoured by some invisible, ravenous beast.

I was losing them.

All of them.

I screamed into the vast void.

Nothing answered.

I drifted alone, for how long I couldn't say, when realization struck.

I'd been here before.

But this time, it was different.

This *felt* different.

I was powerless.

Weightless.

Empty.

And then?

Singing.

One voice.

Not the voice from before, from when I lay dying in an elevator, poisoned by a monster.

No, this was a different voice. A singular voice, coaxing me back, tugging at the corners of my imagination. Fingers of hope replete with life, urging me to resist. To fight.

To awaken.

My eyes snapped open. Sickening fear filled my belly, and I couldn't breathe. Disoriented, I tried to move, but a thick weight on my chest kept me prone. The weight wriggled and purred.

"Hello, Carter," I mumbled.

Leyla's fat gray cat stood up, stretched and yawned, regarding me with inscrutable green eyes. He dug his paws into my chest and leapt to the floor with a soft thump, then wandered through the partially closed door and out of sight.

I was in Leyla's loft at the bookstore, sprawled in her bed. The window shade had been lowered, although pale light leaked beneath its edges. Sound filtered into the room —Deacon's gruff voice followed by Leyla and Abner, but I couldn't hear what they were saying.

My body felt leaden, as if I'd been tossed into the rinse cycle of a washing machine several times, then beaten bareknuckled by a fight club. I ran through a mental inventory of my faculties, breathing a heavy sigh when I determined each broken piece of my psyche remained in its improper place. Remnants of the song that had roused me slipped from my mind, melting away in dribs and drabs. The delicate melody had protected me, an impenetrable shield impervious to whatever force had overloaded the Insight. I sensed the fickle clairvoyance, present but resting, and imagined it asleep, curled up by some warm fireplace wrapped in a handmade afghan.

"How do you feel, Detective?" Besim asked in her soft, canorous voice.

The Vellan lurked in the corner of the room furthest from the bed, shrouded in shadow. Despite her height, she somehow appeared small and unobtrusive.

"Like someone pried open my skull, poured alcohol on my brain and lit it on fire," I replied with a painful grimace as I levered myself up against the headboard. "What happened?"

"You were subjected to a tremendous amount of raw magical feedback."

Besim glided toward the bed but refrained from sitting. In the dim light of the room, her ghastly makeup reminded me of some demonic clown, although her concerned look softened the maniacal bits.

"Your sudden appearance triggered a panicked response from Charlotte, similar to the fight-or-flight mechanism employed by wildlife," she continued. "The discharge of Nexus energy emanating from her was clumsy and shapeless, what one would expect from a brutish mind rather than an articulate one. You were fortunate she did little more than disrupt your acuity to the Insight. Had I not been so intent on Donald Flynn, I would have intervened sooner."

"Charlotte whammied me again?" I groaned, a thick lump settling in my throat.

"Correct, Detective." The consultant folded her hands before her. "I believe the Insight is hypersensitive to a multitude of external stimuli, not the least of which is eldritch power. Charlotte channeled a significant quantity of energy in a truncated moment and unleashed it upon you. The immediate backlash overstimulated your nervous system, which subsequently caused you to faint. Once I realized the source of your disruption, I disengaged from Donald Flynn and instructed Deacon Kole to transport us here. You have been in an unconscious stupor for two hours."

"Wonderful."

I swung my legs over the side of the bed and attempted to stand. The world scrambled and whirled, but I maintained my balance.

"Something needs to be done about her," I announced once my eyes had settled back into their customary setting. "Actually, something needs to be done about a lot of people. Come on."

I stumbled through the door to the landing and down the wrought-iron staircase. Abner, Leyla and Deacon conversed in a small knot by the counter. The old man sat on his stool. His bushy gray eyebrows arose in silent question when he caught sight of me.

"I'm fine," I replied, my mind scuttled with thoughts of the case, Charlotte, and the moves I wanted to make. But there was some place I had to go first.

"That's twice now I've had to drag your sorry ass from a hot situation, Holliday," Deacon stated with a sidelong grin.

"Three times, and I reckon you owe me a drink. Fuck that, at the rate you're going, I'll take that drink now."

"Any more progress with the phone?" I asked Leyla, ignoring him.

The young hacker chewed on her lower lip before responding.

"Translating the Russian was easy," she said, "but what I found was a block cypher involving number sequences. They could be dates, times, bank accounts, traffic routes, the latest Yankees' scores, pretty much anything. Usually, the sequences contain ghosts or fake sequences, to throw off cops and hackers. The blocks all follow an algorithm of some kind. I've got one of my programs working the permutations to figure it out, but the Russian block cypher is complex. This might take me months."

"I don't follow," Abner said curiously. "Are you referring to a code?"

"I'm referring to an unbreakable code," Leyla replied. "The same kind used by enclave governments to protect their most sensitive systems, such as Perimeter Defense and the EC Department of the Treasury."

"We need the key," Deacon stated flatly.

"Key?" the old man asked.

"Another code that can decrypt the cypher," Leyla explained. "Either the same key was used for both encrypting and decrypting the cypher, or there are at least two different keys. Regardless, I checked the phone's master command sequence. Ushakov's usage didn't indicate a pattern, so I couldn't backtrack on the key that way either. Either he didn't need a key to understand it, or he already knew what was on the block cypher. And I doubt I can break into the *bratva's* network to get it. Well, I could, but I don't think it's a good idea. Their watchdog programs make ECPD's look like puppies."

"Shit." Deacon lit a cigarette, then blew out a wad of smoke. "We ain't got nothin' better back at Aurik. Fuck me sideways, Holliday. How're we gonna break this cypher?"

"I don't know," I replied, rubbing my jaw.

"You all presume the cypher is salient to this investigation," Besim pointed out. "Perhaps it is meant to lure the enemies of the *bratva* into a fruitless search?"

"Maybe," I answered sourly. "But Pyotr Ushakov wasn't some low-level thug. Ivan made a statement by showing up to question us personally. Even if whatever that cypher contains has nothing to do with Sanarov's murder, it's something the Brotherhood doesn't want decrypted."

I turned to Leyla and Abner. "If Ivan sends someone here, tell them the truth. You don't know anything, you don't know where the phone is, and they can take it up with me."

"Those ruffians don't scare me, Tom," the old man said, puffing out his chest. "I've handled tough customers before."

I reached out and gripped his shoulder, locking eyes with him.

"These guys aren't just anybody, Abner," I said gently. "And they're not punks off the streets, either. They mean business, and they'll kill anyone who gets in their way."

"We'll be fine," he said. His wrinkled face broke into a reassuring smile.

A sudden chill wormed into my heart as I regarded him.

"You better be," I warned him before turning back to the others. "Anyway, thanks to Charlotte, our play with Flynn backfired. He'll be even more cautious now."

"While that is true," Besim said thoughtfully, "I did ascertain from his biorhythms an unmistakable level of fear and anxiety at your appearance. It is evident to me Donald Flynn holds secrets relevant to our investigation."

"*Our* investigation?" I raised an eyebrow.

"Naturally, I remain a consultant in such things," Besim answered with a demure smile.

"Right."

"During my tour of Brave New Beginnings, he regaled me with a variety of ongoing projects, including the recent purchase of several acres of real estate in Morris Plains," she continued, unperturbed. "Donald Flynn plans to establish a community there dedicated to children and their families who have become displaced through tragedy or financial hardship."

"Donald Flynn, a shining example of everything that's right in Empire City," I muttered. "This guy is so dirty his eyes are brown. I just can't prove it!"

"Well, I can break into his online accounts," Leyla offered with a wicked grin. "And I've always wanted to hack a major corporate bank. So many credits...I wouldn't know what to do with myself."

"Flynn's got the mayor in his back pocket," I smiled sadly. "I've already pissed him off enough, and I doubt Mahoney would give his blessing. If you got caught, I couldn't protect you."

"Fine," Leyla pouted. "But I understand. I'll check in with some of my contacts, dig through Flynn's social media presence, that sort of thing. Maybe something will pop up there."

"Since I frequent the same social circles as Donald Flynn both in Empire City and abroad, I shall communicate with associates of my own," Besim said. "Donald Flynn's late wife Angelina Devereaux was born in the Bordeaux Regime, and it is my understanding Donald and Angelina lived in the Euro-Bloc before relocating here."

"That's all well and good, Saranda," Deacon said, "but that pet witch of his needs to be neutralized. I'ma make a few calls to some law enforcement types in the Euro-Bloc that I know, too. Reckon one of them's got some shit on her."

"All right," I said. Having everyone together and working the case had burned away the haze caking my brain. "Let's meet back at L'Hotel Internacional, as long as you don't mind the company, Besim. In the meantime, I'll take Ushakov's phone. Call me if you learn anything important."

"Where are you going?" Leyla asked.

"I'm—" I began.

"Holliday's got another interview," Deacon cut in smoothly. "Schrodinger gave up the name of someone who may have worked with Sanarov in the past."

I thanked him with my eyes.

Leyla handed me Ushakov's reassembled phone.

"I wiped the drive," she said. "Oh, and I disabled the tracking protocols, although you can use it to make or receive calls, if necessary."

"Thanks, kiddo." I stowed the phone in my blazer pocket. "Okay, people, we've got work to do."

As I pushed through the front door, Besim pulled up beside me. "Detective, might I accompany you to the pod?"

"Knock yourself out," I said without looking at her.

The wind whipped down the block, its icy cold fingers knifing through my clothing. I moved briskly, my eyes tearing from the lashing. Besim kept the pace easily, her longer legs chewing up real estate with little effort. As we moved along the street, I checked in with EVI who informed me I had messages from Charlotte and Mahoney. I deleted both, unheard. I'd catch up with the two of them soon enough.

Once aboard the pod, I loaded the beverage dispenser with several scoops of Uncle Mortie's premium coffee grounds and watched the device go to work. The transport's interior quickly filled with a delicious bouquet of alchemical wonder.

"What do you want?" I said with a hard edge, my back to Besim. "If this is about Charlotte, I already told you, I'm fine."

"While her influence remains a concern, such is not my purpose for being here."

I didn't respond. The percolating machine and a subsequent stream of liquid pouring into the mug filled the silence.

"Detective Holliday, your current course of action is unwise," Besim spoke quietly. "Confronting your father will exacerbate the acrimony you already have for one another and cause irreparable damage."

"I'm not going to ask how you know that," I stated. "And my relationship with Pop is already irreparably damaged. Now leave before I say something I won't regret."

"I understand your bitterness, Detective, but I urge you to reconsider, if only to maintain your objectivity with respect to the investigation. These murders have been perpetrated by someone or something who possesses powers heretofore unseen and has killed without warning or remorse. It has touted messages whose meanings are subtle and cunning, and while I am certain you continue to puzzle through them, you do not fully understand them. Yet, you have eschewed exploring that avenue in favor of chasing after shadows. Instead of pursuing the why of the case, you are relentless in your drive toward the who. What is murder without motive? What is motive without reason? Your clinical mind, your experienced homicide investigator's acumen, is desperately needed to solve this case. However, your emotions have become an impediment, preventing you from seeing the truth behind the lies."

"Quit lecturing me, Besim," I growled. "My father is *involved*. How the fuck am I supposed to remain objective when a man I've despised for years suddenly shows up as a person of interest in my murder investigation? I'm going to get to the bottom of this, one way or another."

"You still do not see, Detective," the Vellan said sadly. "Your intimate encounter with Charlotte was contrived, a deliberate attempt to bewilder and confuse you. And it has succeeded. Whoever Charlotte is, her touch, its memory and the power that lies within it, have impacted your choices, and impeded your ability to strategize, analyze and ascertain fact from fiction. You now act like someone lost within a hall of mirrors, jumping at half-seen images whose import has lost their meaning. This is not the way of the Guardian of Empire City. And it is clearly not you, Detective Holliday."

"Are you done?" I said in a flat tone, my ears burning. "Because I'd say you are."

"If I might suggest—"

The hatchway opened. A gust of bitter air blasted us, shattering the warmth, but did little to cool my temper.

"Get out."

"Detective, please."

"*Leave.*"

"As you wish."

Once Besim left and the hatch closed, the pod flowed into motion. I took my seat up front, the coffee mug gripped in both hands. Shredded by a multitude of dark thoughts, I stared out the windshield, seeing nothing.

Time had not been kind to the old neighborhood along L Street. Gone were the homely, familiar sights of Mrs. Garcia's odd collection of pink and purple flamingoes, or the colorful pinwheels and windmills Mr. Bogomolov tended like corn in a field. Those images were drawn from a much more innocent time, witnessed through an unsullied boy's tender eyes.

Now, a rusted chain-link fence ran the length of the one-way drag, separating the small collection of ramshackle dwellings from their more neglected and decaying cousins across the way. The pitted and cracked sidewalk hadn't seen fresh concrete in decades. A dog barked somewhere, the plaintive sound decrying the maltreatment of its owners leaving the poor thing out in winter's dusk.

My hand rested heavily on the small gate. I ignored the cold threatening to bond my skin to the metal strut. The furnace roiling in my heart lent me protection against the plummeting temperature.

I considered my options.

It was a simple thing, really. Open the gate, walk three

steps forward, then a quick turn to the left and up the concrete stairs to the door.

My legs just didn't want to cooperate.

The house was smaller than I remembered. Single story, with one bedroom, a loft, a bath, kitchen and not much else. A narrow, uneven walkway led to the backyard, divided by another fence. No grass or shrubbery. No outdoor pots, furniture or toys.

Nothing.

Pop had never owned a car, even when Ma was alive. We'd walk or use mass transit pods to go places. I did have a bike once but trashed it when some street punks chased me ten blocks before I blew a tire and got the shit kicked out of me. That was right before I joined Ivan and his crew. Nobody ever messed with me after that.

Thin scales of bleached snow fluttered around me. Thick piles of the stuff had been shoveled against the fence, the result of hours of back-breaking labor. In this part of town, Empire City didn't bother to keep the streets clear of ice and snow. If you wanted to get out of your house, you were on your own.

A memory touched me then, of a time when my mother and I built a snowman in the small square of ground just past the gate I now held. Whispers of a child's laughter and the loving encouragement of my mother's voice reached inside of me before being whisked away by a sudden arctic gust.

I took in the house. It was dark, the blinds drawn, but a telltale banner of heat rippled through the window by the living room. I had called Caron Oceanic Container on my ride over and verified John Holliday wasn't on the evening shift. That meant he was either home, or out at one of his favorite gin joints happily killing his liver. Given what he'd witnessed at Eddie's, my credits were on him holing up at home with as many bottles as he could find.

My heart rattled in my chest. The Insight remained dormant. I checked the SMART gun in its shoulder rig, reassured by its familiar weight, then took a deep breath, pushed open the gate and walked to the door. Chipped and faded gray paint dotted its surface. A half-moon shaped window was inset at eye level but covered by an opaque cloth on the inside.

I raised my hand, then hesitated, inches from the wood.

Was Besim right? Was I not thinking clearly? There was only one way to find out.

I rapped my numb knuckles on the door.

"Pop," I called out, "it's Tommy."

Quiet settled on the neighborhood. Gone was the dog's barking replaced by a cold stillness.

"Pop." I glanced around. There was no one walking the block, and the closest houses sat silent. "C'mon Pop, I know you're in there."

A faint, raspy sound filtered from behind the door.

"I'm alone," I said. "Jesus, Pop, open the door, it's freezing out here!"

There was a creak, and the door cracked open. "Go away."

"Would you just let me in?" I demanded, resisting the urge to batter the damn thing down. "I need to talk to you."

Pop stared at me for a moment, bloodshot brown eyes sharp and surprisingly free from booze. He was shorter by a couple of inches, overweight but stocky, with a scattering of close cropped gray hair. His thick hands were the size of Christmas hams, scarred and calloused from years working outdoors. What my mother had seen in this decrepit old man I would never know.

He shuffled aside as I entered the house, then secured the door behind me, and stomped past without sparing me a glance. Alcohol stench and the acrid tang of unfiltered menthols stuck to him like ticks on a dog. He led me down a short hallway cluttered with discarded work boots, a heavy winter coat, two yellow hard hats, three pairs of stained denim overalls hanging on pegs, and a slew of work gloves.

The kitchen was even worse. Dozens of bottles containing some level of liquid dominated the counter space and kitchen table. The sink was stacked high with dirty dishes from half-eaten meals, and a few crawling bugs skittered away at our arrival. The place stank more than Pop.

What little furniture my father owned groveled in the living room with an assortment of containers, overflowing ashtrays, and an old-style holo-vision that still had a remote control. The 'vision was paused on a pornographic scene with three underage girls. He leered at the screen before shunting the window away with an annoyed flick of his hand, then toppled wearily into his easy chair, a faded blue and tan recliner that resembled an inverted mushroom. There were no holo-frames to speak of, or decoration of any kind on the walls, unless you counted the black mold and random holes dotting its surface. The built-in bookshelves held a small regiment of bottles and glasses in various stages of consumption. I glimpsed the bedroom through an open door and found it to be more of the same, minus a bed. The door to my old room was boarded up.

"Love what you've done with the place," I remarked, clearing some debris from the couch.

Beneath a pile of food wrappers was a twisted pair of red lace panties, partially wedged between two cushions. Cigarette burns dotted the couch's arm, and I flinched involuntarily. Pop hadn't noticed. He was busy poking through a collection of vodka bottles on the stained carpet by his chair. I decided standing was the best option. I kept the paused 'vision to my back.

Pop poured a glass from a bottle, the same brand that I'd taken as evidence from Eddie's. He crashed into his chair without spilling a drop.

"I'd offer you some, but that'd probably go against your rehab's credo," Pop chuckled derisively, his voice thick with phlegm. He coughed several times, then spat a gooey discolored wad onto the floor. "Or because you're one of those fucking cops who takes his job too seriously. Either way, I'm thirsty."

He raised the glass in salute and said, "To family," before swallowing its contents.

I balled my hands into fists but maintained my cool. "You know why I'm here."

"Maybe I do, and maybe I don't," he said. Despite the gloom, I noticed the discoloration of two burst blood vessels highlighting his cheeks. "But you're here, Tommy, so rather than stand there and judge me, just tell me what you want."

I folded my arms across my chest.

"Why were you at Eddie's with Pyotr Ushakov?" I asked. "What's your connection to the *bratva*?"

Pop regarded me with hooded eyes before pouring himself another glass.

"You're not recording this," he noted.

"Not yet."

"Fair enough." Pop knocked back the drink. "Then I want something from you first."

"This isn't a negotiation, Pop. It's a murder investigation. Tell me what I want to know, and I'll be out of here."

"Oh, but it is a negotiation," he replied evenly. "See, after all that shit went down with you at that pharmaceutical company, your image was running on all the newsfeeds for a couple of weeks. Made me proud to see my boy back where he belonged, kicking ass and at the top of his game. Looked like you'd finally gotten over that bitch you'd met at rehab. What was her name again? Courtney? Kathy? Anyway, seeing you on the 'vision, part of Mayor Samson's Special Crimes team, that filled me with pride. You have no idea how happy that made me feel, Tommy. No idea."

"I'm glad you care," I grated between clenched teeth.

"C'mon, are you still mourning that dead junkie? What'd you expect that she'd marry you? That she'd squirt out a couple of kids and the two of you would live happily ever after? You've read too many fucking books, Tommy. Harry and Abner really fucked you up, didn't they? Filled your head with all sorts of nonsense, just like your mother, God rest her soul."

His caustic laughter was cut short by more heavy coughing.

"And now you're here because some dead ex-con was found at Jack's church," Pop said once his hacking had cleared. "That fucking place! Maybe the world will finally see what kind of lying sack of shit their so-called pious pastor really is!"

"Father Jack is a great man," I snarled. "At least he was around when you weren't. Come to think of it, he was always there for me. Where were you? Oh, that's right, out fucking some whore you met at the bar, then getting so shit-faced you couldn't remember what day it was. Real classy, Pop."

"I make no pretense about what I am, boy. You could learn a thing or two from that."

He was pushing my buttons, and it was working. I needed to retake control of the interview before I lost my temper.

"I'm not here to pick a fight," I said, forcing myself to calm down. "Tell me what I want to know. You were with Pyotr Ushakov at Eddie's before he and his men were killed. Tell me what you saw."

"No." Pop poured himself a drink. "Negotiation, remember?"

"The hell with that!" I roared. "You either tell me what I want to know, or I will drag your ass down to the nearest precinct, stick you in a room, and let you sweat all that shit out of your fucking system. I don't give a flying fuck about you, Pop. That ship sailed after Ma died. Any hope I had of fixing things with you went down the goddamn toilet the night you cold-cocked me at Wallingbrooke."

Pop narrowed his eyes shrewdly.

"And, yet, here we are, bringing up your mother again, God rest her soul," he said. "You have no idea what I've been through, kid. None. There's not a day that goes by where I don't think about her. As if you could understand any of it. Jesus H. Christ. Pull your head out of your ass, Tommy! You're still so fucking naïve."

"Excuse me?" I exploded. "*I* can't understand? My mother was raped and *murdered.* In this house. In this very room. Or did you conveniently forget that? Just like how you conveniently forgot you had to raise a son. Thank God for Harry getting me out of this shithole, otherwise I'd probably be dead like Ma. Or worse, end up like you. Fuck you and the pod you rode in on."

"That's it, Tommy," Pop guffawed, his eyes gleaming bright. "Let it all out. Tell me how you really feel. Listen, kid, what happened to your mother was a tragedy, but it had shit to do with me."

"What's that supposed to mean?"

"You still don't get it." He downed the drink, then

refreshed his glass. Pop held it, swirling the vodka, a pensive look knotting his face. "Your mother's murder was a message, Tommy. To protect you."

"From whom, the *bratva*?" I was incredulous. "Why? What did I ever do to them? What did Ma do?"

Pop shifted uncomfortably in his chair. He placed the full glass onto the floor.

"Your mother didn't do anything," he answered evasively, refusing to meet my gaze. "It wasn't her fault. And you're asking the wrong guy. Look, Tommy, forget about negotiating, okay? That was me being stupid. Just ask your questions, and get out of here, okay? I, um, I've got things to do."

My father's sudden shift in behavior put me further on edge. As a former addict, I recognized his erratic conduct as his inability to handle stressful situations. But this went beyond that. Pop was struggling with something. His brows beetled together as guilt warred with his customary obstinance. But underneath that, he was scared.

The Insight stirred, sensing the moment, but remained distant, an observer, as if our roles had been reversed.

"Pop," I said, taking a half step toward him, "tell me what's going on."

He picked up the glass and swallowed its contents, hoping to draw strength from the liquid courage.

"I meet with Ushakov a few times a month at Eddie's," he said. A sheen of sweat covered his brow.

"Why?" I asked.

"Because they need me to run interference when they send out and receive shipments at the container yard."

The hair on the back of my neck stood on end.

"What kind of shipments?" I asked.

"I don't know," Pop replied forcefully, and I believed him. "I also bring them the weekly log, since I have access to the super's office when I work the nightshift. I hand Ushakov the micro-drive, he buys me a drink, and then we leave separately in case anyone gets too curious. That's it. I never know what's in the containers, I don't ask questions, and I don't get involved. They pay me, and I don't get fucking involved."

"How long have you been doing this?"

"Since I've been with the company. C'mon, Tommy, you know I've been working for them a long time. Being on Ivan's crew, you've done plenty of shitty things yourself."

"Yeah, but I got myself out of all that, Pop. You can, too. Let me help you. The ECPD—"

"Can't do shit," he finished sadly. "I'm too far in it to see the daylight, son. Besides, I'm dead already. See, I'm just living on borrowed time. I'm so sorry, Tommy. I really am."

"What's that supposed to mean?"

I hadn't heard the front door open, so intent was I on our conversation. Movement out of the corner of my eye was all the warning I got.

Yanking the SMART gun from its rig, I shouted, "Tactical!"

Instantly, the gun's three-dimensional display filled my eyes, providing me with night-vision, proximity sensors, round type, and count. I trained the gun and pulled the trigger, firing two rounds into my attacker, leveling him. Before I could reorient, a second man burst into view wielding a baton whose end crackled with bluish-white light. He rushed at me with a snarl, bringing the weapon down on my left arm I'd raised to shield me. The stun baton discharged a powerful burst of Nexus energy. Shock transfixed my body, and I dropped to the floor. I tried to raise my head, but my muscles refused to respond.

A third man arrived. He crouched down to examine me, a lit cigarette wedged between his teeth.

"We meet again, Detective," Chuckles said, offering me an unpleasant smile. He flicked hot ash in my face. "Looks like you get to pay the tax now, eh?"

I couldn't speak. Chuckles slapped my face several times, drawing blood from my nose and lip.

"Pick him up," he ordered.

Mr. Baton hefted me like yesterday's laundry.

"What are you going to do to him?" Pop asked nervously. He hadn't moved from his chair, an empty glass held in his quivering hand.

"None of your business, Holliday," snapped Chuckles. "Just keep doin' your job, and everything will be fine. We'll be back to clean this shit up, so don't touch a fuckin' thing. You hear?"

Pop didn't respond. He stared at me forlornly, a silent apology on his lips. In that moment, I don't think I could have hated him more.

"Let's go," said Chuckles.

Mr. Baton dragged me from the living room, down the hall and out into the bitter cold. I knew that a stun baton could incapacitate its target for up to ten minutes. Given how I felt, Mr. Baton must've cranked its setting to the maximum limit. The more pressing problem was the baton's discharge temporarily knocked out my connection with EVI.

I was at their mercy.

Chuckles opened the gate and led us along the block, my shoes dragging on the powdery ground. I heard the strong gurgle of a heavy engine. I tried to move my arms and legs, but nothing cooperated. Mr. Baton dumped me into the back of an empty box truck.

"You think you can take our property, asshole?" Chuckles mocked. "You think, just 'cause you got a badge, you intimidate us? You're nothin'. We own Little Odessa, and everyone in it. So fuck you, cop. Fuck your family, and fuck your life, 'cause your life ain't worth shit."

He beat me again with the baton. Satisfied, Chuckles rummaged through my clothing until he found Ushakov's phone. He activated the device, then made a call and placed it before me.

"Is it done?" a deep voice asked.

"*Dah*," Chuckles said with a wicked grin. "What do you want me to do?"

There was a pause. "Dump the body."

"You got it."

With the call ended, Mr. Baton lit a cigarette, then handed the pack to Chuckles. Blackness slid into my vision, but I forced myself to stay conscious.

A slim shadow slipped silently down from the roof of the truck and alighted in the cargo area behind the two men. Before the Russians could react, the figure lashed out, executing devastating blows to their chest and throat. The men collapsed in gurgling heaps. Chuckles struggled to rise, but the newcomer dropped him with a sharp kick to the face. With a satisfied nod, the figure picked up Ushakov's phone, then stepped past the unconscious men to squat over me.

"I need to get you out of here," Charlotte whispered.

I reached for one of my patented witty rejoinders, but unconsciousness swallowed me whole.

21

I ntense, smothering heat stole my breath. The smell of my own burnt skin made me gag. And underscoring everything, an oppressive sense of wrong.

I opened my eyes.

The room from my dreams was now an ashen ruin. Thick wooden beams had collapsed, leaning on each other like the catastrophic end to an all-night bender. Above me, the remaining supports rippled, bathed in hungry, remorseless fire.

Behold, Guardian! The price of imperfection!

That voice again, resonating everywhere, and nowhere.

"Who are you?" I demanded defiantly in my own voice, but this time its youthful timbre was defined by fresh misery grafted from the past, from my own personal hell.

I am what was, and what shall be.

Blistering agony blazed across my body. The hospital gown I wore smoldered, wispy smoke curling its fringes. The flesh beneath was charred and blackened.

"What is happening to me?" I shouted.

First you must know memory, Guardian.

A thunderous crack sounded. The support beam above me splintered from its mooring and crashed down, pinning me beneath its crushing weight.

For memory begets pain. And from pain, enlightenment.

"I...don't...understand."

Eight shall know judgment.

"Why are you doing this?" I struggled to move, my eyes swimming from the shimmering heat.

Amidst the wreckage, a brown-haired boy wandered toward me, ignoring the conflagration that raged about him. I struggled harder, but the weight was too much. The boy came closer, his young face lit with maniacal joy.

"Repay them for their deeds and for their evil work," he said, kneeling beside me. "Repay them for what their hands have done and bring back on them what they deserve."

"Who...are...you?"

The boy tilted his head to regard me.

"I am the One," he said. Movement swam behind his eyes, something dark, and sinister, and altogether inhuman. "This boy chose vengeance, and I have granted it. For upon my arrival, all will be laid to waste."

I pushed against the unbearable weight of the beam, but my world was torment and misery. The boy laughed, a chittering sound that twisted and turned my soul. He leaned closer to caress my head with leathery lips, fetid breath that reeked of worms and graves.

"Once the Bargain is fulfilled, I shall be free to devour your world," he said. "Eight to die for their crimes. Eight to suffer as he has suffered. Eight meaningless, hopeless, soulless pieces upon the Board, then none. You cannot stop me, Guardian. Nothing can."

"NO!"

I lurched awake. I felt a moist cloth press against my brow, cooling my feverish thoughts.

"It's okay, Tom," came a woman's soft voice. "It was just a dream. You're safe now."

"Orpheus?" I blinked in confusion, looking around bleary-eyed at an unfamiliar room. "Where am I?"

"At my place," Bill Mahoney said.

He sat at the foot of the bed. Charlotte occupied a chair next to me, the wet cloth clutched in one hand.

"How long have I been out?" I asked.

"A few hours," Mahoney replied.

"I don't understand." I propped myself up against the three bulky pillows arrayed behind me. "What's going on? How do you two know each other?"

"I'll explain everything later," Mahoney answered. "For now, get some rest."

"Fuck that, Bill," I snapped. Anger and clarity filled me in equal measures. "I deserve to know what the hell is going on!"

"Captain, allow me," Charlotte said.

She wore a black catsuit, which hugged her in ways that made my breath quicken. A sudden, primal urge overtook me. I reached forward and grabbed her behind the neck, then dragged her forward. The moment our lips met, invigorating energy surged into my body. The Insight burst into my eyes, tingeing everything in its silvery haze. Charlotte pushed me roughly away, gasping for air.

"What just happened?" I asked, grappling internally to control the Insight. My skin prickled with goose flesh. After a few quick breaths, the clairvoyance settled. Now it prowled on the periphery of my vision. It hadn't revealed anything about the room or the others occupying it.

"I-I don't know," Charlotte breathed, her eyes wide with

surprise and...pleasure? No, that couldn't be right. Could it? "It must be an aftereffect of my charm's backlash when you surprised me at Brave New Beginnings. It should wear off soon."

"It damn well better!" I barked bitterly. "Who the hell are you, anyway?"

Powerful, mixed desires battled for control of my heart and mind. I wanted to caress her cheek and hold her tight, as if physical contact with her would anchor me to the bedroom. I also wanted to shake her until every secret she carried tumbled out of her.

In response, Charlotte placed a simple holo-ID card on the bed. It held a plain headshot of Charlotte, her name, a serial number, and the symbol of a crown atop an enclosed garter bearing the Latin phrase *Honi soit qui mal y pense*. The symbol was flanked by a crowned lion and a chained unicorn. A banner below it contained a second Latin phrase: *Dieu et mon droit*.

God and my right.

"Jesus Christ," I muttered.

"MI6 Special Agent Charlotte Sloane, at your service," she answered with a polite incline of her head. "But, please, call me Charlie. My apologies for all the cloak and dagger, Detective Holliday, but it was necessary, given your history as a former associate of Ivan Kruchev. I needed to ascertain your intentions, if you were on the take, and whether you were running interference at Flynn's behest, the *bratva's*, or both. Thankfully, the captain has vouched for you, confirming my suspicions were unwarranted. Please accept my sincerest apologies."

I folded my arms across my chest and offered her a petulant glare. She returned it with a haughty lift of her chin.

"Charlie's been working undercover at Titan for over a

year," Mahoney supplied. "We've both tried contacting you, but you haven't bothered checking your messages. Did your phone break, Detective?"

"Sir, if you haven't noticed, I've been a little busy," I replied defensively, wondering what Mahoney may have told her about me. I turned back to Charlie. "And what was our 'date' all about? 'Emerging threat assessment?' Am I on New London's radar, too?"

Charlie had the good grace to look away.

"And since when has the Secret Intelligence Service had practitioners on the payroll?" I demanded.

"Back off, Detective," Mahoney growled. "You're out of line."

"It's all right, Captain," Charlie said, gathering up her badge. "The detective has every right to be upset with me. I know I would be were our positions reversed. Normally, my gift lulls the target into a state of light euphoria, making them more receptive to suggestion. Unfortunately, the charm's effect was far stronger on Detective Holliday than my previous targets. I haven't the foggiest idea why."

"Yeah, well, I guess I'm just lucky." I rubbed the back of my neck to ease some of the soreness.

"As to your other question," she continued without smiling, "I am with MI6's Paranormal Investigative Division, a coterie very similar to your Special Crimes. Captain Mahoney has already verified my credentials with Vauxhall Cross and cleared my presence with any pertinent Empire City authorities."

"Swell," I grumbled irritably, unimpressed so far. "Then why are you here interfering with my investigation?"

"Because you were interfering with *my* investigation of Donald Flynn and the Devereaux family," she retorted, incensed by my question.

"Devereaux," I said, tasting the name and grimacing. "As in, Angelina Devereaux? Flynn's dead wife. And?"

"And," Charlie stated coldly, drawing the word out in exasperation, "the Devereaux family has been linked to several international illegal operations that include human trafficking, international credit laundering, corporate espionage, and rare art and illicit substance smuggling, among other things. But after years of investigation, both local police and British Intelligence have come up with nothing."

I rolled my wrist for her to continue.

"You truly are incorrigible, Detective Holliday," she sniffed in indignation.

"I like to know what's going on," I shrugged. "It's part of that whole detective thing that I pretend to do."

"I should think my presence in Empire City is now obvious."

"Well, I'm not known for being the brightest lamp on the street. Sometimes, I need everything spelled out for me. It helps with my digestion."

She stared at me with an aggrieved look on her face. "You're serious."

"Charlie," I began softly, adopting a sober expression, "I don't know shit about Flynn, and even less about the Devereaux family. All I've got so far are four dead men killed by who-knows-what, the *bratva* sniffing around, and a lead suspect who appears to be clean, but is as dirty as my toilet. I just can't prove any of it. Work with me. Please."

Her eyes searched mine, gauging how much she could trust me.

"Angelina was the sole successor to the family fortune," she finally said. "Her parents died in a house fire set by her father Antoine, a man who had purportedly suffered from severe schizophrenia and depression. Several weeks before their tragic deaths, Angelina met Flynn, who had been on holiday from Empire City. They fell in love, married, and eventually moved here to start a family. Of course, you both are already familiar with what happened to their son Calvin."

I stole a glance at Mahoney who was staring at his hands. He absently twisted his golden wedding band around his finger.

"Shortly after Calvin's murder," she continued, "Angelina died in a car crash while traveling to her estate in the Hamptons. With Angelina gone, and no living challengers, Flynn claimed the Devereaux fortune, collected Angelina's life insurance, and eventually became one of Empire City's most successful businessmen and philanthropists. He is now worth billions."

"If what you say is true, why would Flynn want, or even need, to carry on the Devereaux business?" I asked.

"I'm not entirely sure," she replied with a furrowed brow. "Angelina possessed extensive real estate holdings throughout the Euro-Bloc, which transferred to her husband upon her death. Over the years, Flynn sold the land to various other interests, and shipped everything from the old Bourdeaux estate to his home in Empire City. However, I have been unable to uncover any hint of wrongdoing on Flynn's part. I inserted myself into Titan in the hopes of exposing something, but thus far, I've come up empty. However, the murder of Gustavo Sanarov, and your subsequent interview of Flynn, has changed things. His behavior has since become more erratic, to the point of paranoia.

"As for the Devereaux family, they're old money. Wineries, art collectors, horse breeders, that sort of thing. They drew their roots from King Louis XIV, if you can believe it, and flaunted their alleged aristocratic lineage to any who could stomach it. Angelina's father was a noted exporter of wine and had purchased several vineyards in New Hollywood to cultivate his interests there. It is my understanding those vineyards were eventually sold to Orpheus Financial Group, another Euro-Bloc-based enterprise that also had ties with Wrigley-Boes Pharmaceuticals, if I'm not mistaken?"

I frowned. Orpheus was that rare case of exhibitionist mixed with the power-behind-the-curtain. Her involvement would be subtle and subversive, but when she was ready to reveal herself, she'd do it in her own time, and with all the demure nuance of an exploding kitten. She might not be directly responsible for the murders, but her fingerprints were all over this.

Still, what did she gain from these killings? The murders seemed downright pedestrian compared to her bankrolling of Rumpelstiltskin's magically powered Vellan-human genetic-manipulation experiments. And what was her connection to the One? A sudden sensation of intense heat enveloped my body as the memory of the dream flitted uncomfortably through my mind.

Eight meaningless, hopeless, soulless pieces upon the Board, then none.

"Are you all right, Detective?" Charlie asked, noticing my discomfort.

"I'm fine," I answered curtly. "What makes you think Flynn's involved with the *bratva*?"

"As you know, the Brotherhood are experts in subterfuge and the dissemination of false information to keep law enforcement off balance," she replied. "MI6 has been unable to ascertain any direct connection between Flynn and the *bratva*."

"That, or they just pay off the right people," I stated flatly.

"Indeed," Charlie nodded in agreement. "However, over the past year and a half, we've intercepted eight encoded messages, all in Russian, and all originating from Bordeaux. They were transmitted to a robot server here. Each message referenced Raphael Gudarov, a well-known New London-based clothier. The rest of the message was deemed meaningless, just a series of numbers that didn't match bank account sequences, dates, times, nothing. Once I began working at Titan, I quickly learned that Flynn's suits are designed by Gudarov and shipped to his home in SoHo."

"You think Flynn's fashion sense is the link?" I scoffed. "Years of investigation with that goddamn truth charm of yours, and that's all you've got? Which reminds me, why would your Paranormal unit work this case? What's so special about Flynn that they'd send you?"

Charlie's eyes flashed dangerously.

"You've already seen how careful Flynn is," she said. "Despite my gift, I've learned nothing. Flynn has been... disinterested...in my allure. I can't determine if Flynn is somehow protected against my charm, he's in the dark, or he's clean. However, something has him spooked, and you're my best chance at cracking him."

"Oh, so I'm your asset now?" I sneered. "Look, sweetheart, I'm not your toy, and I sure as hell don't need you around to fuck things up further than you already have."

"Detective, you are to cooperate with Special Agent Sloane," Mahoney cut in forcefully. "This is now a joint investigation. Do I make myself clear?"

"C'mon, Bill!" I slapped my hands on the bed in frustration. "This is ridiculous. She's already interfered with the investigation, and maybe even compromised it! You can't expect me to share everything I've got with some foreign agent! How do we know she's not working for Flynn?"

"Detective Holliday, if it wasn't for me, you'd be at the bottom of the Hudson," Charlie pointed out archly.

"I had everything under control back there, *Special Agent*," I retaliated, my cheeks flushed. "I was about to take them both out when you showed up!"

"Oh, sod off, would you?" She folded her arms defiantly across her chest. "When I got there, you were about as threatening as a baby."

"Oh yeah? How about we go a few rounds. We'll see—"

"Enough!" Mahoney shouted in exasperation. He stood up and walked to the open doorway. "Detective, join me out here when you've cleaned yourself up."

Once Bill left me alone with the English-She-Bitch-Agent-From-Hell, I pulled myself from the bed and tottered toward the bathroom, my mind awash with conflicting emotions. I was still processing the dream, but with what Charlie had said about the Devereaux family, some pieces to the case had slid into place. However, I needed to know something first.

"So, our date, and everything that happened after that was your 'gift' overworking me, huh?" I asked. "Just business?"

Charlie moved to the door, but paused in the threshold, her face lost in shadow.

"That's right."

She left the room.

22

A fter a quick recycled water shower, I stood before the bathroom mirror to admire the road map of bruises covering my body courtesy of the Russian mob. I'd had worse, but the big purple and black one by my ribs wouldn't fade anytime soon. Sighing heavily, I got dressed, then strolled into Mahoney's living room.

It was a quaint space, and what I would expect from a man with the captain's economical personality. Everything was in its proper place. The faux leather couch was flanked by two square tables and fronted by a coffee table containing an inactive holo-novel reader, a small verdigris sculpture of Don Quixote, and an active portable holo-rig. A well-worn matching reading chair was opposite the couch. Thick, springy tan-colored carpet covered the floor, and a large darkened holo-vision hovered along one wall by French doors that led to what I presumed to be the patio. The kitchen was equally spartan, with a variety of stainless-steel pots hanging from hooks above a flat cooking-top island, and nary a crumb to be seen.

Mahoney handed me a mug before settling in his chair.

Charlie stood by a dark-paneled bookshelf, one of three inserted along the walls of the room. Holo-frames, glass curios and hardbound books populated the space, free from dust.

I wasn't surprised to discover Bill owned actual books. He was old school, right down to the reading glasses he wore. Rather than accessing my virtual record during my interview, the captain had brought a folder containing my dossier in hard copy form.

I moved to the shelf furthest from Charlie, noting the row of titles, and nodded in appreciation. Steinbeck's *Of Mice and Men* stood at attention by *Moby Dick* and *Lord of the Flies*, with *When Bad Things Happen to Good People* rounding out the set.

Curiosity got the better of me. I carefully withdrew Harold Kushner's book. A thin, glossy coat of silicon preservative protected the original cover and pages. I owned an actual copy myself, gifted to me by Rabbi Adina Adler, a close friend to both Abner and my grandfather. The concierge rabbi had hoped I might find some measure of comfort between its pages after my mother's murder. I'd read it dozens of times over the years. Kushner's elegant pragmatism still resonated with me to this day.

"*Forced to choose between a good God who is not totally powerful, or a powerful God who is not totally good, the author of the Book of Job chooses to believe in God's goodness,*" I murmured, recalling something Father Jack had said to me about his time with Gustavo Sanarov.

"What's your next move, Detective?" Mahoney asked.

I returned the book to its shelf. Charlie took a seat on the couch. The captain sat straight and tall as if he were in a courtroom facing a hostile jury.

Which, I suppose, was true.

"I'd like to know why you've been holding out on me, sir," I said.

Charlie glanced between the two of us, then settled into the cushions, arms folded across her chest. Bill nodded curtly. His wintry eyes appraised me.

"You needed to work things out on your own," he said.

"What's that supposed to mean?" I snapped back. "Is this another one of Besim's goddamn tests? You of all people should know that withholding case-critical information jeopardizes the entire investigation. If you've got something on Donald Flynn, then—"

"I don't have anything on Flynn," Mahoney cut me off sharply.

"Then what is it, sir?" I softened my tone. "What happened thirty years ago that you just can't let go?"

"I happened," he sighed. Bill's eyes glazed with emotion. He absently turned the plain gold band around his finger. "With all the good publicity the Flynn case brought to the department, I was promoted to lieutenant a few weeks after the Sanarov trial. Marla, my wife, had been so proud of me. She was like you, Tom. Always had a way with words. 'It's the beginning of your meteoric rise, Bill,' she'd say, like I was some superhero in a holo-serial."

He shook his head ruefully.

"Meteoric," he muttered, then took a deep breath and exhaled. "You have to understand, everything I did, every case I closed, every decision I ever made back then was for us. I knew the risks, and I did it anyway, because I didn't care. I only wanted what I wanted. For Marla. For my family. And he knew it."

The memory of Young Mahoney in his brown suit intruded on my thoughts.

But it's wrong. We can't do this.

"Who knew?" I asked.

"Mayor Stein," Bill barked a caustic laugh. "He was Empire City's mayor back then. He used the Flynn investigation to strengthen his own political position within the enclave. It was an election year, and Stein wanted to protect his standing with the affluent lobbying interests financing his campaign. Angelina was old money from the Euro-Bloc. Donald Flynn was a rising star in the banking world. And Stein wasn't an idiot. He wanted to secure their backing, so he used their son's kidnapping as leverage. His re-election platform included a public promise to crack down on any crime involving women and children. Closing the Flynn case became a top priority, from the D.A.'s Office on down. It was the opportunity of a lifetime. We all jumped in, from the beat cops to the support staff to the forensics teams. Everyone was on board because nobody wanted to screw up. We even worked unpaid overtime."

He paused, lost to the memory, staring unblinking at his clasped hands. I waited. Bill wanted to tell his story, his way.

"I compiled everything I had on the case," he resumed, not looking up. "All the leads, the interviews, and all the credible information we'd gathered including what we'd learned since the arrest, and helped the DA build his case to lock Gustavo Sanarov away for life. Gustavo Sanarov, the man responsible for kidnapping Calvin Flynn."

"But not the murder," I added quietly.

He regarded me. "No."

The Insight buzzed between my ears. Heat filled my chest, and my eyes burned, but there was nothing here to see. I cycled through in my mind everything I knew about the kidnapping. Mahoney had run down every known associate and lead, leaving no stone unturned, knowing that in a kidnapping case, time was of the essence. Finally, Bill and his team had caught Sanarov in the warehouse dead-to-rights with the mutilated corpse of Calvin Flynn. Then came the arraignment, the trial, and finally, the sentencing. Everything had been tied up in a nice, neat bow.

Case closed.

Why had the murder charge not stuck? Why would Mahoney close out the case and never follow up about the murder? And how could the Flynns accept Sanarov's life sentence? It couldn't have been enough for them. Yet, Flynn was also responsible for Sanarov's release through the Pieces of Eight program. What could Mahoney have done that he'd want me to find out on my own?

What was I missing?

It's tampering with an investigation.

"You flushed information," I said. "You let a lead go, something that tied to Calvin's murder. What was it?"

Mahoney didn't answer. The faint burr of the winter wind outside intruded on the silence.

"Bill, what was it?" I pressed.

"I found a foreign contaminant at the crime scene," the captain replied slowly, choosing his words with care. "A bit of hair on the victim's body. It didn't match Sanarov, or anything else we'd gathered up to that point. I ran it through the World Population Database, but never told forensics or my team about it. I wiped the entry from the WPD, and any reference to it from my report. But somehow, Samson knew."

If you want things to work, you have to make sacrifices.

Suddenly, I recognized that voice from Bill's past.

"And Samson told you to do it," I said. "Didn't he."

Mahoney nodded.

"He was my captain," he whispered, anguish printed like an Escher drawing on his worn features. "I had to tell him.

For Marla. For my family. He said I was doing the right thing."

"Did Samson threaten your family?" I asked, my mind racing.

Cocooned within his thoughts, the captain didn't answer. He stared ahead, eyes registering nothing.

"Bill, did he threaten your family?" I pushed.

"He didn't have to," Charlie answered gently, examining Mahoney with a fierce intensity. Her eyes sparkled. "He'd already made the call. The decision was his."

"Everything's politics," Bill responded woodenly, glancing up at her. "If you want to get anywhere, you've got to get in with the right people. Back then, I was still a nobody. I needed someone with enough juice to help get me to where I wanted to go. So, I did what I was told and closed the case."

You'll do this, because you know it's the right call, and because both of our careers are riding on it.

"I became the best damn investigator in Empire City," he said. "I had the office, the visibility and the rank. I had it all, until that goddamn maniac Mark Madsen took it away. Back from the dead to murder my family, then disappear without a fucking trace. That's when I pulled the pin. I turned in my badge, let it all go, and left Empire City. And now, it's happening all over again. It's all my fault. That poor kid. That poor, poor kid."

"Samson didn't threaten your family," I stated coldly. "He threatened your goddamn career! Samson dangled the promotion before you like a fucking carrot, and you took it, because it was the one thing you wanted. Jesus Christ, I've had this whole thing wrong from the start! I figured you were protecting someone, but you're a just goddamn dirty cop! By hiding the truth for thirty years, you've let the murderer of an innocent boy go because you chose your career over doing what's right!"

"I betrayed Marla," Bill replied, tears streaking his cheeks. "The department. You. Everything I once stood for."

"Is that why the *bratva* are involved?" I demanded. "Because they bought Samson and Mayor Stein? Is Flynn tied up with the Brotherhood, too?"

"I don't know, Tom."

"Who was it? Who murdered Calvin Flynn?"

"I don't know."

I stood up and began pacing the floor, trying to work it through. "Your report stated Sanarov worked alone, but he claimed to have fallen asleep, and when he came to, Calvin was dead. You knew that was a lie, so you dug deeper. Was the body even Calvin Flynn? Who else was involved? Whose DNA was connected to the hair follicle?"

"I'm telling you Tom, I don't know." Mahoney spread his hands apart.

"Do you still have the follicle?" Charlie asked.

"No," he replied, not looking at her. "It was too dangerous. I couldn't keep it around."

"Goddamn it, Bill!" I wanted to hit something but kept my anger in check. "What the fuck is going on?"

I glared at him, my mind awash with everything he'd said. Mahoney sat forlornly in the chair, wrestling with three decades of remorse. So alone and fragile, he was a man who'd lost everything.

I'd long suspected the murder of his family as the root cause, but now I knew that wasn't the entire story. Through the intervening years he'd spent hunting killers and closing cases, his conscience bore the lies, each one its own crushing weight. Mahoney was just another tool manipulated by powerful, influential people who didn't give a hot shit about the oath he'd sworn. The accolades, the recognition, the rank became hollow and meaningless, hiding a rotten shame he could never escape.

The Insight accentuated Bill's pain, conferring a portion of it to me, and dredging up memories from my own checkered past. My fall from grace, the corruption scandal that rocked the department and nearly ruined my career, and the fallout that followed were familiar burdens I carried. My ledger dripped with my indiscretions. Who was I to judge a man like Mahoney? I didn't need the Insight to tell me what Bill had done. I'd done it too.

My own hypocrisy sickened me.

A polite knock on the door drew my attention. Mahoney bowed his head. Charlie stood quietly and maneuvered around the couch to take up a position by the corner that connected the entry hallway to the living room. I instinctively reached for the SMART gun that wasn't there. Charlie signed that she'd cover me, although I didn't see her holding a weapon. After what she'd done to those thugs, she probably didn't need one.

"It's okay, Tom," Mahoney whispered into his hands. "You can let her in."

I shot him a sharp look before moving from the living room and down the hallway to open the door. A blast of arctic air buffeted me. Gray gloomy skies spat bits of ice and snow to pelt the uncaring world below. The neighborhood was quiet, blanketed by a fresh coat that sealed away any hope of warmth. And standing on the threshold was Besim.

We locked gazes, her serene gray eyes meeting my troubled stare. I could've held my ground. I could've demanded to know what she was keeping from me, but that would've been like asking the sun not to shine. Instead, I stood aside and let her pass.

She nodded her thanks, then glided forward. I closed the door and followed her. Once Besim reached the living room, she stiffened. Color darkened her cheeks, and for a moment, the composed mask she wore cracked. Fire flashed in her gray eyes, and I swear the dyed hair on her head glimmered with fire.

"You have no business here," she stated.

"I have every right to be here," Charlie sniffed haughtily. She leaned against the wall, a sly smile curling her lips. "Saving Detective Holliday from certain death at the hands of the Russian mob should count for something, should it not?"

Besim tilted her head to the side. Something passed silently between the two women. Charlie's smile slipped, her eyes filling with doubt. She rubbed her shoulders as if caught by a sudden chill.

Satisfied, Besim crossed the short distance to Bill. She knelt by him, spoke a few words I couldn't make out, and laid a light hand on his shoulder. The hair on the back of my neck prickled, and the Insight simmered in response.

"Why are you here?" I asked.

"William called to me," she replied.

"He called *to* you?" I shook my head. I'd never understand her. Instead, I motioned at the captain. "Will he be all right?"

She regarded him with an infinite sadness and said, "In time."

Besim traced the fingers of her other hand gently across Mahoney's forehead, then down his cheek and across his jawline. She repeated the movement, and his eyes closed in response. As I watched, a soft melody permeated the room. It tugged at my psyche, insistent with a gentle resonance that reached past my simmering anger, beyond my frazzled nerves, penetrating deep inside my conflicted heart. The refrain, with an ethereal pitch and rhythm the like of which I'd only heard twice before, struck within me chords replete with emotion and feeling.

Mahoney's shared agony became more intimate, intertwined with mine on a scale that reached beyond mere memory. Images appeared in my mind's eye of the man wrestling with his guilt, sleepless nights staring out darkened windows, and countless days working alongside men and women he knew were guilty of far too much. The loss of his family, his constant battle against a depression that threatened his sanity, and the end of everything he had built.

Tears fell unbidden down my face. I was a raw nerve, laid bare to every sensation, and my body shook in response. I leaned against the bookshelf but refused to fall to my knees. Gathering what will I had left to me, I stood tall against the rush of Mahoney's emotional flood unleashed by Besim's song. Sensing my resolve, her voice altered tone, drawing upon it to lend more power to her melody. Her sound soothed and strengthened, transcending the bounds of the real, and transformed into something more exquisite and profound.

Into something magical.

I closed my eyes to drink in its healing flow. The Insight responded to the magic, for it, too, had dimmed from the doubts and fears that plagued me. Many of the cares I'd worn since the case began, including my volcanic anger at Pop, sloughed from my shoulders. Mixed emotions that had clouded my judgment and ability to read this case and ferret out the clues I'd been gathering fled before the sudden torrent of clarity. The betrayal I felt toward Charlie softened as well, although the wariness remained. Besim's melody drifted into a calm silence, broken only by the ticking of an antique Telechron analogue timepiece Mahoney kept on a shelf.

I stole a quick breath, unaware that I'd been holding it, then opened my eyes. One of the holo-frames closest to me cycled between different images. Each one represented a frozen moment in Mahoney's life, of happier times during the holidays, or traveling the world back when his family was alive. Their deaths had propelled the captain to question his purpose before he chose self-imposed exile far from Empire City and the life he knew. But a so-called chance meeting with Besim in Milan had changed all that. Mahoney returned to Empire City, refreshed and focused, and with the help of Besim and Deacon, established the Special Crimes Unit. And all set in motion because of his family's brutal murder by the magical shade of a dead psychopath.

I chewed on that sudden thought. They'd been killed by a ghost. A spirit of vengeance.

A revenant.

The idea hung before me, suspended from a gossamer strand, dangling below its web of possibilities. Every hair on my body stood on end. The Insight warmed my body, and I knew I was right.

Charlie wiped tears from her eyes, staring in wonder at Besim and Bill.

Murder investigations were puzzles. Each detail, any shred of evidence found at a crime scene, every ounce of information gleaned from interviewing witnesses and reviewing the lab results, *everything* had its proper place. Gut instinct and experience filled in the gaps. Or, if you possessed a magical set of peepers like I did, well, that helped a lot, too.

"Repay them for their deeds and for their evil work," I whispered.

That sounded like more Scripture. A quick check with EVI confirmed it was from Psalms 28:4.

Father Jack and the Holy Redeemer.

The Bible on Sanarov's desk.

The one in Flynn's office.

The murdered *bratva*.

The cypher.

Numbers.

Dreams.

Messages scrawled in blood.

What did it all mean?

"*Revenge should have no bounds*," I whispered.

Hamlet was on to something.

More images of Mahoney's family cycled through the frame, but I stared at them without seeing anything.

"I still don't know who murdered Gustavo Sanarov," I stated with cold certainty. "But I know who to ask."

Both Mahoney and Besim turned their heads to regard me. The look in their eyes told me they already knew the answer. They'd known all along.

"Who?" Charlie rubbed her shoulders, discomfited by whatever emotions roiled inside of her.

"Calvin Flynn."

23

"And how do you propose to do that?" Charlie asked. "Have a time machine handy?"

"Nope," I replied with a smug grin. "I've got something better. And before you ask, it's none of your goddamn business."

Charlie glared daggers at me, but I turned and addressed Besim. "I assume you're staying here?"

The consultant's face had grown paler than usual. The dark dye coloring her hair that seemed to glow with her ire piqued, now appeared muted and dull.

"Until William has no further need of me." Her slumped shoulders and husky voice spoke of her exhaustion from the effort of her singing. "Furthermore, I do not wish to be present for what you have planned. In my current condition, the scenario would prove to be...too problematic."

"How the hell do you know what I have planned?" I stiffened, taken aback.

Besim raised her tired gray eyes to convey sardonic amusement, although no smile graced her lips. "It is not difficult to surmise you seek the services of a medium to establish a spiritual connection with the spirit of Calvin Flynn in the hopes of gleaning critical information that will help you solve the case."

My mouth hung open.

"While Deacon Kole may be in agreement with such unconventional methods," she continued placidly, "troubling the unrested is dangerous, and may not be the wisest course of action. You may discover the process more unsettling than you anticipate."

Some days, I really hated her.

"Fine," I grumbled. "I don't need you anyway. I'll make a quick call to Deacon and Leyla, and then I'm gone."

"You're going to a psychic?" Charlie scoffed in disgust. "Have you gone completely mental, Detective Holliday?"

"Only on days ending in 'y,'" I quipped, winking slyly at her. "Look, you don't have to come along either. My team can handle it."

"I had no intentions of doing so," she said. "In light of Captain Mahoney's revealing testimony, I need to further research Donald Flynn's background with respect to the Devereaux family, and how the *bratva* might be involved. It is possible Mayor Samson's connection to my case reaches further than quashing the captain's investigation from thirty years ago. Perhaps Samson is behind some of the interference that's been hindering my own."

"What are you planning on doing?" I asked.

"Nothing that will jeopardize your operation, I assure you," she affirmed with a half-smile, holding up a hand. "And certainly nothing that will obstruct your upcoming 'spiritual journey'. I truly hope it is a meaningful and fulfilling one for you, Detective Holliday. Now, if you will excuse me."

Charlie strode from the room. I rolled my eyes, refusing to admit that I liked what I saw as I watched her leave.

"Oh, Tom," she called back playfully. "I left you a present in the bedroom. Do be a good boy and make sure you keep a better eye on your toys. Next time, I may not be around to save you. You're welcome! Ta!"

The front door banged shut.

"I'm not sure who annoys me more," I muttered to no one.

I took in the room, gathering my wits as I geared up for what I was about to do next. Besim remained by Bill's side.

"You sure you don't need anything?" I asked.

"No, Detective Holliday," she replied. "We will be fine."

I nodded once, then moved to the bedroom. Both the SMART gun and Ushakov's phone lay on the bed. A stupid grin plastered my face as I slid the gun into the shoulder rig. I left Bill's place with a hop to my stride.

The half-baked idea that I'd been chewing on since Deacon mentioned the revenant angle had finally taken shape. I needed answers, but most of the people who knew the truth were dead. Although I hadn't conducted the interviews yet, I didn't think anyone at the Pantry was involved, either. The most intriguing connection was between Sanarov, Orlando Denning, the church, and Brave New Beginnings. Once aboard the pod, I had EVI cancel the interviews as the pod pulled onto the 'way.

I realized it was too late in the day to hit up Uncle Mortie's deli, but I needed to refuel. My stomach's growls were a painful reminder I hadn't eaten much since before my close encounter with Chuckles and his friends. I made a quick pitstop at the nearest twenty-four-hour Sunshine Starshine to grab a box of assorted donuts and one of their patented triple espresso lattes, then hustled off to pick up Leyla and Deacon at L'Hotel Internacional.

I filled them in on my encounter with the *bratva*, Charlie's timely arrival, and the Insight dream. However, I withheld Bill's admission of investigative obstruction. The remnants of Besim's song had softened my heart and cleared my mind. Telling Deacon and Leyla about it didn't seem like the right play. I wanted them focused on the unusual task I had planned instead.

"EVI, be a dear and take us to Madame Ruth's Psychic Parlor over in Queens," I ordered once I'd finished.

I stood behind one of the command chairs, sipping at my latte. The hotel shrank in the distance before the pod swept higher along its 'way, twisting around another massive glass monstrosity boasting dozens of holo-ads of varying colors, shapes and sizes. The varied ribbons of light bathed the cockpit in sickening technicolor. I turned before their undulating movements soured my stomach.

"MI6, eh?" Deacon remarked, propping both booted feet on the console. Small clumps of dirty snow gathered around the soles and puddled on the floor. "Explains why I couldn't find shit on her."

"I'm still not happy she charmed you, Doc," Leyla huffed. "I don't care if she was just doing her job."

"Me neither," I said. "But it's a joint op now, so let's all try to get along, okay?"

"Fine, but if she so much as looks at you funny, I'm freezing her ass."

I chuckled.

"Why are we going to this place, Doc?" Leyla asked. "I could've researched a bunch of them for you."

"I have a good feeling about this one," I said.

"Thought you didn't believe in that shit," Deacon said.

"I never said that," I said. "Besides, after working with you, I've realized I need to be more open-minded about a lot of things. The Insight reacted to the crime scene in a manner I'd never experienced before. By itself, that tells me plenty. I think this case is grounded just as much in spirits and spooks as it is in flesh and blood."

"Nice to see you finally growing a brain, Holliday," the former Protector said. "Still, we'll need to do this quickly, 'cause in my experience, some spirits' imprints don't stick around long. Might be we're already too late. Then the only impression your medium'll pick up in that church is a dead rat's fart."

"We'll see," I said. "Leyla, did you get anything else from the decryption?"

"Nope," she replied with a heavy sigh. "But my program is still running, so maybe we'll get lucky. Oh, before we went back to the hotel, a couple of Ivan's goons came by the bookstore while you were at Captain Mahoney's place."

"Why didn't you call?" I demanded. "I told you they'd—"

"Easy, Doc," she reassured me with raised hands. "Deacon was in the back in case anything got hairy. And you know I can take care of myself."

"Okay," I relented. "What did they want?"

"They asked where you were, if you were coming back, if we'd heard anything about what happened at Eddie's, that kind of thing. They knew we weren't going to say anything. They just wanted to rattle us, I guess, but you should've seen Abner, Doc. He was *pissed*! He called them 'ruffians' and 'ne'er-do-wells', too. He used some language I'd never heard him say before. Even made Deacon proud."

She grinned at us, but I wasn't amused. I needed to do something about Ivan and his crew once this business was finished. Maybe something permanent.

I shook my head, wondering where that dark thought had come from, and discarded it. We were supposedly dealing with a vengeful spirit. I didn't need to add my own dirty laundry to that list.

"Let's just get to Queens," I said, and moved to the beverage station for a gummy chocolate-frosted donut. I chose the smile-shaped one with rainbow sprinkles. The instant Proto-sugar high from eating the damn thing nearly made my head spin.

"Assuming this psychic ain't some fucking crackpot," Deacon said, lighting a new cigarette.

"If she can contact Calvin Flynn, maybe we'll get some answers," I said. "Everything about this case has been personal. It feels like revenge, but I think there's far more at play here."

"Revenge ain't worth shit, Holliday," the former Protector suddenly snapped with surprising heat. "It's empty, like that coffee mug. Fill it, and you'll never stop. Lose yourself to it, and you got shit. Like tryin' to fix somethin' that ain't broke. That's the fucking tragedy of the revenant, Holliday. Even if it kills everybody that wronged it, there ain't no closure for it once it's done. Take it from me, some wounds just never heal."

The rest of our journey was in relative silence. I combed over Mahoney's case files as well as Stentstrom's report while Leyla continued her work on her holo-rig. Deacon sat next to me surrounded by a fog bank of smoke yet cloaked more deeply in his own dark brooding.

Finally, EVI announced our arrival. "Outside temperature is eighteen degrees Fahrenheit, with a thirty percent chance of light snowfall."

We piled from the pod. Night gripped the city. Long shadows played along the building walls, dull and listless in winter's gray gloom. Streetlamps flourished as businesses flicked on their exterior lights to hawk their services to the few who wandered the streets.

Strachman's Jewelers was closed, although the interior was illuminated. As the others walked past, I paused before the storefront windows. Much of the damage the kobolds had wreaked appeared to have been cleaned up. I spied an old bald man with round glasses and a young dark-haired woman moving about the showroom, each armed with a broom. They stared at their surroundings with a mixture of anger, hurt and resolve. The old man reached out and pulled the young woman in for a hug, gently stroking her hair.

I felt a pang of remorse that we hadn't caught the furry bastards fast enough to prevent them from doing harm to the store. I vowed to do better.

I caught up to the others as we navigated the short flight of concrete steps leading up to Madame Ruth's on the second floor. As before, the curtains were drawn, but a violet holo-sign with the word *Open* in the window glimmered behind the glass. I pushed open the door and moved inside. A bell jingled merrily above me. I paused a moment so that my eyes could adjust to the dim interior. A wave of pungent incense struck me full in the face, and I started sneezing.

"Good evening," a woman's heavily accented voice floated to us from a doorway several feet opposite the entrance. Strands of colorful beads—sapphire, emerald, ruby and onyx—hung from the sill forming the image of an open eye. "Please, come in."

I recovered quickly, withdrawing my handkerchief and blowing my nose into it several times. Leyla gave me a humorous look and wandered deeper into the store. We were surrounded by displays and shelves filled with all manner of New Age relics, totems, books and baubles. I plucked at several leather necklace straps. Each held a charm bearing a unique runic mark that meant nothing to me.

A holo-ad hovered above a collection of colored mood rocks and trinkets outlining the many services Madame Ruth offered, including palmistry and tarot reading. To my untrained eye, her prices were exorbitant. Deacon had a bemused expression on his face as he thumbed through a thin pamphlet entitled *After Here, then Where? Food for After-Thought.* Depicted on the cover were expansive horizons, mythical creatures and the obligatory tarot card.

"Feel free to browse my wares," she continued pleasantly, still unseen. "And when you are ready, come join me and we will talk."

I placed her accent from one of the Eastern Euro-Bloc enclaves, although it seemed deliberate and heavy.

"Madame Ruth," I began. "I'm—"

"I know who you are, Detective Holliday," she purred.

"You do?" I asked, exchanging a surprised look with Deacon.

Leyla wandered around the showroom, at times studying the ceiling.

"Of course," Madame Ruth chuckled. "I would not be a very good psychic if I did not, yes?"

"She's got a point, Holliday," Deacon mumbled.

The Insight had been quiet since I'd left Bill's apartment. I couldn't feel its presence, but that was unsurprising given how often it would appear unbidden when I least expected. But Madame Ruth's knowledge of my name reminded me of my encounter with Orpheus and her hand-bitch Julie DeGrassi. However, unlike that meeting, and even without the Insight, I didn't sense any danger here.

"You were here earlier with the Confederate," Madame Ruth said. "At Strachman's, yes?"

"How'd you—"

"I know things, Detective Holliday. It is my way."

"She probably watched us from her window," I murmured low to Deacon.

"Or maybe she's a psychic," he countered.

"Why don't you come in and we will talk about why you are here?"

Deacon strode toward the beaded doorway and held the strands aside. "You first."

I squared my shoulders and stepped into Madame Ruth's parlor.

24

T he back room was lit in soft shades of violet, gold and blue. Thick carpet covered the floor, some faded after-market Persian knock-off that hadn't seen a vacuum since before the nukes. I waved irritably at a murky cloud of colored incense threatening to choke the life from me. Another doorway opposite the entrance was festooned with the same stringed beads, except this one combined to form a closed eye. Gold and silver-embroidered tapestries of more fantastic beasts and other-worldly imagery hung on the walls, pandering to the illusion the customer had stepped from the real into the ethereal. Low, willowy instrumental music from some unfamiliar composer warbled at the edge of my hearing. Meant to soothe and relax, the sounds set my teeth on edge. At the center of the room was a covered round table bearing a crystal globe the size of a holo-bowling ball whose interior swirled with fog and shifting colored lights.

Madame Ruth hunched in a tall, stiff-backed wooden chair. Swathed in a violet and gold kimono, she reminded me of an ancient prune that had spent too many hours in a tanning booth with the setting at maximum. A pair of chop-sticks jutted from the bun of her glossy black wig. The psychic's wrinkled features creased into a smile as her sparkling brown eyes caught sight of me.

"Ah, Detective Holliday," she crooned through red-rouged lips, her accent at odds with her attire. "Please. Come. Sit. Be welcome."

I hesitated before taking one of the three unoccupied chairs arrayed around the table.

"Friends," she called, glancing past my shoulder. "Do not be afraid. Sit. Sit, and listen."

Deacon and Leyla joined me at the table. The former Protector glared at the crystal ball, his dark eyes flitting around the room before settling on Madame Ruth. For her part, Leyla seemed at ease, an amused expression on her face.

"Good," Madame Ruth said. "Now we can begin."

The music swelled at her pronouncement, the lights dimmed further, and the air grew thicker and warm. I'd begun to sweat and shrugged off my blazer.

The medium's eyes closed. She mumbled an incantation of unintelligible words while placing both hands over the crystal ball. Its smoky interior swirled faster, spinning the lights in mesmerizing patterns.

"You need my help," Madame Ruth intoned, her eyes moving beneath the lids. "There is something out there. Dark, and dangerous. Lurking. Waiting. Something from the long ago past. Something desperate. Something—"

She paused dramatically, then her eyes flashed open and locked with mine.

"Evil."

I drew in a sharp breath.

"Murder," she whispered. "And death."

"What can you tell us?" Deacon demanded. "What do you see?"

Madame Ruth regarded the three of us with a mysterious smile. The lights from the crystal ball glittered against the ceiling and walls. The tapestry threads glimmered in response.

She let out a throaty chuckle and said, "It is close. It surrounds us. It wants something."

"And?" Deacon prompted her, leaning forward in anticipation.

"It wants," Madame Ruth frowned in consternation, tilting her head to the side as if listening to something. The expression reminded me of Besim. "It wants…"

"What?" I exclaimed, rising from my chair to plant both open hands on the table. My heart hammered in my chest. "What does it want?"

"It wants," she repeated, staring at me with the intensity of someone about to reveal the secrets of the universe.

"Can the act, Ruth," Leyla interrupted. "We don't have time for this."

The music cut out to a strangled warble before dying as normal lighting activated, blinding me. Deacon coughed, equally bewildered. A fresh breath of cold air cleared away the cloying incense. I looked at Leyla who wiggled her fingers. Flecks of frost glittered below her hands.

"I *had* them," Madame Ruth whined, a petulant look on her face. Her former accent was gone, replaced by pure, homegrown, unadulterated Queens. "I had them! They were *this* close! Everything was working, and then you just had to ruin it, didn't you?"

"Whatever," Leyla said disdainfully, placing her holophone on the table. "Save it for your next mark. We're busy, and don't have time for your melodramatic bullshit."

"What's that?" I asked, rubbing my eyes with the edge of my shirt cuff. Several small frames floated above its screen, but my eyes were too watery to make out what they were. "And how do the two of you know each other?"

"Never met her before today," Leyla said with a nod at the disgruntled psychic, "but Ruthie here operates a neat little operation. She fills the place with incense, plays the music, dims the lights, fakes the accent, wears that ridiculous costume, and sets everything up so that the two of you idiots can admire her ball. Meanwhile, she's taking your images from one of a dozen cameras hidden throughout the store, runs them through her not-very-legal access to the World Population Database, then uses the information to prep the rest of her performance. After that, she checks the 'Net to get whatever current info there is on her 'clients' and figures out the rest. I've run into a bunch of amateurs over the years, but Ruthie's setup here is grade-A, first-class bullshit."

Madame Ruth slumped in her chair like a popped balloon. She chewed on one of her long faux fingernails, glaring daggers at Leyla, then mumbled something under her breath.

"What's that, hon?" Leyla asked sweetly.

"I said, you've got a lot of goddamn nerve," Ruth shot back. Leyla laughed while retrieving her phone.

"This was all an act?" Deacon bristled.

"'Fraid so," Leyla replied. "Ruthie has about as much 'talent' as that chair. We should go. I've already put together a list of replacements. We can hit them up and then grab a late dinner."

"Yeah, get the hell outta my shop," Madame Ruth glowered. "And don't come back!"

It took me a moment to recover both my vision and my

pride. Leyla and Deacon had already vacated the room, leaving me alone with the miserable hack.

"You're not arresting me, right?" Madame Ruth asked plaintively. "It's just all part of the performance. People want the show. The lights, and the music and the mood, y'know? Everyone who comes in here, they're looking for answers, and even if they don't get exactly what they wanted, they still leave satisfied, like they still got something from it."

I donned my blazer without looking at her and checked my pockets to make sure I hadn't lost anything.

"And I'll pay for the WPD access this month, I swear I will," she added nervously. "I run an honest business here, Detective Holliday. I always pay my taxes on time, and all my permits are legit."

"I'm sure they are," I said, rubbing at my itchy nose.

"But it was a good performance, though, right?" Madame Ruth asked with a hopeful smile, straightening her posture in the chair.

"You had me fooled," I replied, turning from her. "I'll see myself out."

I shook my head, disgusted at myself. What a huge waste of time. Besim had been right. What the hell was I thinking?

"She's wrong, you know," the medium said in a soft voice. "I do have talent."

I glanced back to see Madame Ruth draw her fingers above the crystal ball. Colors and smoke began twirling beneath the glass. Shaking my head again, I turned to leave.

"*A fool thinks himself to be wise, but a wise man knows himself to be a fool*," an old man's voice said from behind me.

A familiar tingling formed at the base of my neck. Silver heat waves danced at the edge of my vision. I rounded on Madame Ruth who wore a mysterious smile.

"Holliday," Deacon called from the other room. "You comin'?"

"In a minute," I responded distractedly as I stared at the medium.

Madame Ruth peered into the depths of the crystal ball, the fingers of her right hand caressing the air above its curved glass. The hair on the back of my neck stood tall.

"What is a man without character?" the same old man's voice asked through Madame Ruth's lips.

"What is this?" I demanded.

"C'mon Tommy," she urged. "Think. Use that *keppy* of yours."

Subtle changes had emerged on her face—a slight quirk as she smiled, a broadening of her nose, and her posture was different, less feminine, and more frumpish.

I took a menacing step forward. "What the hell are you doing?"

"Tommy, Tommy, Tommy," she chided with a heavy sigh, in a familiar voice whose gentleness and wisdom had carried me through so many dark days growing up without my mother. "My little Brighton Beach Flash."

"*Zeyde?*" I asked, my voice barely above a whisper.

"*There* he is." Madame Ruth smiled at me with a pride I hadn't seen in decades. Her hand continued to trail around the crystal ball. "My *luftmensch*. My little Tommy. Always wandering and wondering. Or was it the other way around? I could never remember."

"What trick is this?" I hissed.

"This?" The psychic gestured broadly with her other hand. "This is nothing. Air and sound. Light and music. The trappings of a would-be charlatan who is anything but. You, however, my boy, you are very real. And we haven't a lot of time."

My mind refused to register what was happening. Yet, that voice from a man who I had loved unequivocally, whose voice I hadn't heard in forever, was speaking to me as if it were only yesterday.

"What did I used to teach you?" Harry asked through Madame Ruth. "Do you remember?"

My brow furrowed in concentration. I shuffled my nearly forty-year-old feet as if they were a quarter the age of what they were.

"To ignore the *mishegoss*," I said slowly, my heart pounding in my chest. "Stay out of trouble because there's too many bad guys and grifters out there, and not enough honest men."

"That's right!" the medium chuckled fondly. "And to walk with your eyes open, and your head out of the clouds. Well, Ruthie here still pulled one over on you and your friend, eh? Thankfully, you have that Leyla. She's such a good girl, Tommy. Such a *shayna madeil*. But she has a darkness inside of her, too. A terrible darkness. Someday soon, she's going to need you. She'll need all three of you."

"Three of us?" I asked in surprise. "What do you mean? *Zeyde*, what's going on?"

"Besim made that clear to you," Madame Ruth said, "at Mortie's, and then at the church. And after everything you've been through. With your mother. With Kate and Vanessa and Patricia. Why do you still not believe?"

"*Zeyde*, I'm just not ready. I'm—"

"*To thine own self be true,*" my grandfather said from the mouth of the medium. "*And it must follow, as the night the day, thou canst not then be false to any man.*"

"*Farewell, my blessing season this in thee,*" I finished mechanically.

Madame Ruth offered me a sad smile. "I have to go now, Tommy."

"What?" I cried, tears streaming down my face. "Wait! You can't go! *Zeyde*, you can't go now!"

"I love you."

Madame Ruth exhaled slowly and blinked several times. I took a shuddering breath, then wiped my nose with the back of my hand.

"How?" I started, unsure what to ask.

"I told you already," Madame Ruth answered. She clasped both her hands together and set them on the table. "I wasn't kidding. Most of the time, it's all stagecraft and theater. But once in a while, the readings are real. And the, um, other things? Well, those are real too. That's how I've stayed in business. Don't get me wrong, Detective. I read about you too, just like the girl said. But I knew you were coming here the moment I saw you outside Strachman's. It was a premonition, a feeling. And here you are."

The Insight didn't pour into my eyes. There was nothing to see here, but it was present, intent upon Madame Ruth. I sensed the truth of her words.

"I've worked with PI's before," she continued. "The occasional call-in when the cops got weirded out by something and dropped the case, but the victim's family needed closure. I never overcharge for those. I know what it's like to be on the wrong side of something bad."

I observed her in silence, my thoughts awhirl with what I'd just experienced. With the lights on, I noticed Madame Ruth's wrinkles were part of her costume, along with the wig and clothes. I guessed her real age was somewhere older than Leyla and younger than me, but not the wizened crone she portrayed.

"You do need me to find someone," the medium

asserted. "Or something. I'm not sure what, but I do know it involves something from the past. Do you need me to contact a dead relative? A cold case, maybe?"

"No," I said, reasserting firm control over my reeling emotions. Thinking about her objectively as a resource to assist me with a case helped me get my shit together. "I need you to contact the murderer."

Her eyes slipped up to meet mine. Within them, I saw my reflection, and the shadow of something else. I couldn't make it out, but it stood behind me, and I sensed in it a deep and abiding patience and wisdom. But then the moment was gone.

"That's a new one," Madame Ruth said dryly with raised eyebrows. "How can you arrest someone who's already dead?"

"We believe this killer is special," I said. "Something called a revenant. Ever hear of that?"

"Ah." The medium drew the word out. "A spirit caught between worlds. I understand now. And this revenant is at the church?"

"Yeah, how'd you—" I paused, then chuckled. "The Dose article, right?"

"That's right," Ruth smiled, adjusting her wig. "Little Odessa, Holy Redeemer Church, and not much more than that, other than some background on your victim, Gustavo Sanarov. But it was enough to get me started. Let me get a few of my things. I'll only be a minute."

I used my handkerchief to clean myself up, hoping the dim interior would hide the red around my eyes. Right then I didn't need a dose of Deacon's special brand of pity.

Leyla and the former Protector waited by the front door. The Confederate frowned at the sight of the medium who puttered behind the sales counter.

"What the fuck's she doin'?" he demanded.

"She's coming with us," I answered, then lowered my voice as I approached them. "The Insight gave me a good feeling about her."

Deacon glared over my shoulder, reassessing the diminutive psychic.

"But it was all a show, Doc," Leyla said, gesturing at the store's interior. "You sure about this?"

"I am. Thanks for pointing it all out, kiddo. I would never have guessed."

She patted me on the chest. "That's because you're both gullible. Cute, but gullible."

"What the fuck are you yammerin' on about, girl." Deacon stiffened with indignation. "I didn't just fall off the goddamn turnip truck. I knew the score. Was just playin' along, is all."

"Sure." Leyla winked slyly at me, then pushed open the door. "I'll wait for you and the turnip outside."

25

M adame Ruth's choice of apparel would've given Besim a run for her credits. The medium was decked out in a teal winter coat, yellow and orange scarf, and fluffy purple gloves. Her ensemble reminded me of a flower garden tended by the Mad Hatter. She dragged a plain travel suitcase on rollers behind her. By the way she huffed and puffed as she struggled with the luggage, her entire store must've been packed inside.

"Now, Detective Holliday," the psychic began. "Before we do anything else, there's the matter of my fee."

"Fee?" Deacon grated. "There ain't no fucking fee. This one's on the house."

"Detective!" Madame Ruth gave me a stricken look.

"Think of it as performing a public service," I said, not bothering to inform her that our CI budget was non-existent. "Or we could just shut your little psychic con-shop down. Your choice."

"That's blackmail," she huffed with indignation.

"Tomayto, tomahto," I shrugged.

"If this works, I promise I'll post glowing reviews on a

bunch of tourist sites, as well as a couple of holo-chats I'm in," Leyla offered. "That should drive business to your shop."

Madame Ruth was unconvinced but relented as she boarded the pod.

On the way to the Holy Redeemer, I called Father Jack to let him know we'd be arriving shortly but didn't give him any details on what I was doing or who was with me. I felt a twinge of remorse, but knew he'd strongly veto what I had in mind. And after recent events, I had neither the time nor inclination to be as forthcoming with the pastor as I might normally be.

He'd forgive me.

Eventually.

A steady snow shower heralded our arrival in Little Odessa. Our walk to the church was frigid and slippery. The falling snow cocooned the world in its simple quietude, muffling the distant rush of a Metro pod as it slipped along its 'way.

The church parking lot was empty. Father Jack had closed the building to evening worshippers. I scanned the area, wondering if Rena skulked nearby, but didn't see her broom's smoky black vapor trail in the sky. Hopefully, she'd already found another story to sink her fangs into that was far from here and didn't involve me.

The pastor waited outside the entrance. I made with the quick introductions. He held the door open but gave me a disapproving frown as I went past. Once inside, he engaged Leyla and Madame Ruth in small talk, but never made eye contact with Deacon. For his part, the former Protector said nothing, content to walk with his hands in his jeans and his eyes straight ahead.

"You have a beautiful church," Leyla remarked as she admired the walls and stained glass.

"Thank you," he smiled, then indicated with a wave of his hand some of the more ornate artwork the church contained. "It's been my home for over forty years. Many of our families have been a part of this congregation several times longer than that. It's a testament to their love and devotion to our Lord Jesus Christ, who welcomes all with an open hand and a loving heart. And through His teachings, we find hope and inspiration, bearing witness to the power of the Lord working in our lives. For within these walls, we believe in the sanctity and salvation of the soul."

He directed that last part at Deacon.

"I been around the world," the Confederate grunted. "Lived in a bunch of places, too. Worship comes in all flavors. Just 'cause it ain't yours, don't make it no less important or relevant."

"That is true," Father Jack replied. "However, there should be an accounting for how it is taught. The word of the Lord is not some hammer to bludgeon and bloody. It is a welcome embrace, to nurture and encourage. Families should never live in fear of the Lord, or anyone, for that matter."

Deacon stopped. "You got somethin' you wanna say, then fucking say it, old man. Otherwise, I ain't got time for this."

"I merely wanted to share that we at the Redeemer encourage openness and diversity," the pastor said mildly. "Ours is not to force a twisted and perverted view of Scripture upon a helpless populace. We strive to educate and accept, rather than belittle and persecute. And, in so doing, we promote a spiritually and emotionally healthy congregation."

"Oh, but judgin's okay, right?" Deacon retorted. "You think you know everything about me, just 'cause I'm from Birmingham and all? You don't know shit, Jack. Some people don't get the luxury of a nice house or worship at a big fucking church. Or livin' behind goddamn mile-high, spell-forged steel walls. Some people live with fear 'cause it's all they fucking know. And maybe, just maybe, Scripture is there to help them cope with the horrors that walk the world in the daylight."

"That shouldn't be an excuse to excise anyone's rights and treat them like cattle based upon their differing beliefs, their sexual orientation, or the color of their skin," the pastor countered with a flinty stare. "The church is a bastion of hope, a beacon of light. It is not, and should never be, a prison. And megalomaniacs such as your High Inquisitor employing the word of the Lord to oppress others for monetary gain or temporal power is wrong."

Deacon stepped up to Father Jack, so they were nose-to-nose. "Well then you can thank Jesus Christ our Lord and fucking Savior that we ain't in Birmingham. 'Cause if we were, you'd be burning at the stake right now."

"Violence accomplishes nothing," the pastor said calmly. "Nor does vilifying the sanctity of our Lord or taking His name in vain. Both of which prove my point."

"Gentlemen, please, let's not do anything we might regret," I warned.

The two men were locked in a staring contest. The rage rolling off Deacon was palpable. There was an angry darkness in his eyes I'd never seen before.

"Let's finish the job and get the fuck out of here," Deacon muttered, then stormed off to Sanarov's room.

Leyla glared at Father Jack before running after Deacon. Madame Ruth gave us an uneasy smile and trundled her suitcase down the hallway.

"I warned you earlier not to bring him here," the pastor said. "He, and his 'brethren' in Birmingham, represent everything this house stands against."

"Couldn't you shelve the anti-Tribulation rhetoric for another day?" I asked. "I need Deacon to be focused, and now he's a mess!"

Father Jack clasped his hands behind his back. "Tom, I cannot abide intolerance and tyranny. No one should. Those poor people in the Confederate States suffer daily. The atrocities that enclave have committed against humanity are beyond outrageous. We have to make a stand against that brand of evil."

"I don't disagree," I said, running a hand over my face before pinching the bridge of my nose. "But today isn't that day. Please restrain yourself until after we leave, okay?"

"I will do no such thing," the pastor huffed in indignation. "That man needs to leave at once!"

"You don't know the first thing about—"

"His presence is an affront. I will not allow him to sully our good name by strutting around our halls spouting his antithetical beliefs!"

I jabbed a finger down the hallway and said, "That man is my *partner*. I love and respect you, Jack. But your emotions are now interfering with my murder investigation. I need Deacon to help me track down a killer. And the longer we stand here arguing, the more time the killer has in getting away. Which is more important to you: proving your point, or solving Gustavo's murder?"

"How dare you ask me such a question, Thomas Henry Holliday!" Father Jack exclaimed. "You, of all people!"

"Decide," I said, then softened my voice. "Please."

The old pastor stared at me hard for a long moment.

"I want no part in what you are about to do," Father Jack

said. He strode toward the sanctuary. "I will neither interfere, nor offer my blessing. If you need to speak with me, I will be in one of the classrooms preparing for tomorrow's Bible study. Once you're finished with whatever it is you are doing, you can see yourselves out. Good night."

I watched him go. My duty to the job outweighed the guilt I felt. Father Jack had no idea the kinds of things I'd encountered during my short tenure with SCU. He couldn't possibly understand what it took to hunt down the scumbags of Empire City, be they supernatural or otherwise. While I appreciated his strong feelings toward Deacon and the Church of the Tribulation, I wouldn't let them stop me from doing the right thing.

By the time I caught up to the others, Madame Ruth had removed her coat, hat and gloves, and laid her suitcase on the floor. Its dual-fold interior contained a large colorful cloth bag with a draw string. She knelt by the open suitcase reading from a plain violet book that reminded me of a diary. Deacon and Leyla were speaking quietly further down the hallway.

Inside Sanarov's room, I heard the splash of water and the clang of something metallic. When I reached the doorway, I saw Orlando Denning strain a mop into an old metal bucket. He wore worker's gloves, a flannel shirt, jeans and heavy work boots. His dark skin shone with sweat. Crimson rain fell from the mop's cloth tentacles showering the bucket's interior. I stopped and stared but recovered quickly and adopted my professional I'm-a-detective-investigating-yet-another-homicide expression.

"Good to see you again, Detective Holliday," Denning said. "Thought I'd finally take care of the mess in there."

He dropped the mop into the bucket, removed his gloves

and stuffed them into a back pocket. He offered me his hand in greeting. I didn't take it.

"Did you know Gus?" I asked, placing my hands on my hips.

He eyed me curiously, then dropped his hand.

"Met him after he arrived here," he answered. "Would see him around occasionally but didn't talk to him much."

"You've never met him before?"

Denning blinked once. "No sir."

I nodded, pursing my lips. "You from the neighborhood, Mr. Denning?"

"I grew up in one of the low-income complexes over by Ocean Parkway," he replied. "Took over the place after my mom passed. That was, let me think, fifteen years ago. It's not much, but it's enough for me."

"Right." I drew out the word. Deacon and Leyla remained locked in conversation. Madame Ruth flipped through more pages of her book. "You married, Mr. Denning?"

"No, Detective," he answered sheepishly. "Just never found someone what liked me enough to stick around, y'know?"

"I know what you mean," I said with a false smile. "Mr. Denning, Father Davis tells me you're the Brave New Beginnings liaison with the Pantry. As you know, Gus worked there, too. How long have you been with Brave New Beginnings?"

"Well, from the beginning, if you pardon the pun," he answered with pride. "Back then, I needed a job and they was looking for someone. Things just worked out, y'know? Started as a stock boy in one of their food banks, then became a supervisor, and eventually got involved with the kids and placing them into homes. Talk about hard work!

Some of those kids, man, they was addicts and trouble-makers and brought all sorts of problems with them. But they was still kids. They just needed love. A good home. A push in the right direction. Someone to care about them, about who they was, that wasn't a needle or a quick hit."

If I hadn't seen his mug in Stacey Schrodinger's holo-frame, I'd almost believe him. But the bullshit he shoveled just kept piling up, and I wasn't buying any of it. I just had to figure out what part he played in all this.

"When was the last time you saw Gus?" I asked.

He leaned on the mop handle as he considered the question. It creaked beneath his weight.

"Last Thursday, before the first morning service," he replied. "I'd just come in to do a quick once-over upstairs. We got a custodial service to really clean things up, but I like to come around and do my part, too. Sweeping and vacuum-ing, y'know? Gus was in one of the pews, toward the front. I waved. He waved. Then I went about my business."

"He ever get any visitors?"

The sexton shrugged and said, "None that I know of. As far as I knew, the man was a loner. But I'm usually here in the mornings and on Tuesdays and Thursdays after Father Davis has closed up for the night."

"You weren't here the night of the murder then?"

"No, Detective, I wasn't here."

Madame Ruth placed the book carefully on the floor, then retrieved a small velvet bag from inside the cloth bag. Gathering the book, she stood up and gave me an expectant look. I'd have to cut Denning's interview short.

"Okay, Mr. Denning, thanks for cleaning up," I said. "We'll take it from here."

Denning wheeled the bucket past me.

"No problem," he said. "Just watch out for some of the

wet spots in there. Oh, and I used a lot of bleach to get the stains out of the walls and the floor. I chased it with lemon freshener to cut down the smell. Hope you don't mind."

"I don't think we'll be in there long," I grunted sourly, recalling the last time I'd encountered a similar fragrance. "Thanks again."

Denning waved farewell over his shoulder and disappeared around the corner with the bucket in tow. Deacon and Leyla joined us.

"Learn anything?" the Confederate asked, twirling an unlit cigarette between his fingers.

"Denning lied again about not knowing Sanarov," I replied grimly.

"Let me dig into him, Doc," Leyla offered. "Maybe his online footprint leads to somewhere juicy?"

"Not a bad idea, kiddo," I said. "Once we're done here, see what you can find out."

"Detective Holliday," Madame Ruth interrupted. "I'm ready when you are."

I gestured to the ladies, then followed them into the room. Denning had done a good job cleaning up the blood, although I nearly gagged on the stench of the cleaning products. The medium wandered around, studying the bed first, the closet and then the workstation. She stopped before the empty chair that had held Sanarov's body.

"This is where you found him?" she asked me.

I nodded. Madame Ruth drew in a slow, deep breath, as if tasting the air. Goose prickles danced along my arms.

"I can feel it," she said in a hushed tone. "The workstation, too."

I exchanged a look with Leyla. Deacon leaned against the doorway, lost in thought.

"The two of you, stand with him," Madame Ruth instructed, nodding at Deacon.

She handed me her book. It had no title. I opened the cover and glanced at a few pages, admiring the hand-written drawings and symbols whose meanings I didn't understand.

"Once I begin, do not interfere," she said. "No matter what happens to me, don't move or do anything. Just ask your questions. It'll be over quickly. I think."

"You think?" Deacon exploded. "You don't know? Holliday, you sure she's for real?"

"Speaking with the dead isn't an exact science," she bristled. "You want me to do this or not?"

Deacon dismissed her with a disgusted wave and folded his arms.

"Okay, then," the medium said. "I just need to set a few things up. Won't take long."

Madame Ruth removed a chipped and scratched wooden curio box from the velvet bag. She placed it carefully on a dry spot of the floor by the chair. Next, she withdrew from the cloth bag four votive candles attached to small silver holders and arranged them around the box, one at each cardinal point. Finally, she lay the larger empty bag on the floor and settled on top of it. She reached into her kimono, then patted herself down, a frown of concern on her face.

"Do any of you have a lighter?" Madame Ruth asked hopefully.

"Oh, for fuck's sake," Deacon grumbled, and tossed his to her.

Madame Ruth lit the candles. Once the flames appeared, I felt a cold chill crawl down my spine. Deacon shifted uneasily, the truncheon now in hand. No fire played along its length. Leyla stood next to me caught in rapt attention.

Madame Ruth called out to the room with her head bowed. A slight breeze stirred the air, tickling my face. I glanced down the hallway, but no one was there. The medium continued her incantation undisturbed. She leaned forward and flipped open the top of the curio box. Music began filtering around the room. Tinkling chimes stuttered along in a discordant and unfamiliar tune. My ears ached from the strange sound, but the Insight flickered to life, responding to Madame Ruth's ritual.

"Who are you?" the medium called.

The lights dimmed. My breath streamed out before me as the temperature plummeted. The breeze picked up, growing stronger.

"Hearken unto my voice!" the psychic urged.

I stole a glance at Leyla. The young hacker's eyes had turned white. The runes on Deacon's truncheon began to glow.

"Show yourself and be known!" Madame Ruth shouted.

And then, something answered.

26

Madame Ruth stiffened, then turned a coy eye on me.

"Guardian of Empire City," she rasped in a voice crawling with barren things long dead. "I see you."

"Uh, Ruth, I think you dialed the wrong number," I said nervously.

"She ain't there no more, Holliday," Deacon cautioned.

The little woman's pallor had grown several shades lighter, its color now that of curdled glue. When she wasn't speaking, her lips worked, locked within some silent conversation.

A chill breeze bled around us, ruffling my hair and clothes, yet I couldn't determine its source. The Insight wormed into my vision, as it had when I first stood in Sanarov's room. It revealed nothing, despite my instincts screaming to the contrary.

The music continued unabated. The jarring sounds had transformed into soft, dulcet crooning, meant to calm and soothe, yet my heart felt heavy, and full of dread. Leyla was rooted to the floor. Taut and still, I don't think I could've pushed her over had I tried. The sclera of both her eyes had been devoured by snow white.

"Kiddo." I waved my hand before her face, then snapped my fingers. "Hey! Leyla! Now isn't a good time to check out. We need you. Kiddo?"

She didn't respond. I exchanged an uneasy look with Deacon. The medium smiled, a cruel expression that held no warmth, only the promise of a slow, excruciating death.

"That ain't our dead kid, Holliday," Deacon warned, gripping the truncheon. White fire licked along its length as the engraved runes glimmered in response to whatever had possessed Madame Ruth. A corona of steam encased both the former Protector's hand and the weapon he held.

"What do I do now?" I asked, at a loss.

"The fuck if I know. Talk to it. Say something. But make it quick, 'cause you can bet your ass it ain't friendly."

"Right." I set my shoulders, took a deep breath, and faced Madame Ruth. "I want to speak with Calvin Flynn."

"No," the medium sneered.

"I want to speak with Calvin Flynn," I repeated with less authority and more humility, then added, "Please?"

"Seriously, Holliday," Deacon uttered an exasperated sigh. "It's a goddamn miracle you're still alive."

I shrugged sheepishly.

"Who the hell are you?" Deacon demanded. "What do you want?"

"I am the One," she purred with dark pleasure. "Where I tread, misery and death follow. I am the Scourge, the Devourer, the Destroyer. To those who have transgressed, I dispense justice by my righteous will. And in their glorious death, shall they find absolution. The guilty shall answer for their crimes in the flames of perfidy!"

"Gustavo Sanarov already paid for the kidnapping of

Calvin Flynn," I answered. "He did his time. Thirty years in prison. Isn't that enough?"

Whatever this thing occupying Madame Ruth was, its raw power enveloped the room, a palpable energy that sapped at my resolve. The Insight quavered, either unable or unwilling to reveal the truth. I had to work this out on my own.

"Your law failed the boy, Guardian," she intoned. "Your justice is flawed. Broken. Righteous retribution was served and shall be served again. Four are gone. Four remain. Such is the price for lies and deceit."

I frowned. Something wasn't right here. The One's speech held the proper amount of pedantic, over-the-top melodrama I'd expect from a vengeful spirit. Not that I had had much experience with them. And it was also in keeping with the Biblical verses from the crime scenes. However, listening to them live and not while caught in some crazy dreamscape, the One's words felt hollow and meaningless, lacking any real punch, like some classic Vaudeville holo-act staged for this very moment. I wasn't buying any of it but decided to play along and act dumb.

Because I'm good at that sort of thing.

I concentrated on the little woman. Reality rippled and wavered around her small frame. The room's temperature plunged further. The breeze howled, whipped to a frenzy, and stinging my eyes.

"Who are the remaining four?" I asked, rubbing my arms against my chest in a vain attempt to generate warmth.

"Those who have transgressed against their own," she replied. The sound of her hatred made my frozen skin crawl. "Peddlers of flesh. Purveyors of sin. Thieves and killers, charlatans and false prophets, suckling upon the teat of the fallen. Blood on their names, damnation in their hearts, and treachery in their souls."

"Why are you doin' this?" Deacon asked. "What's it to you?"

"He has been wronged," she answered. "And he has suffered for far too long."

"Where is Calvin Flynn?" I asked, my breath streaming before me in ghostly clouds. "Is he alive? Let me speak to him."

"No," she smiled.

"Then let me help you," I urged. "I'll find those responsible. I'll put them away, so they won't hurt anyone ever again. I can end the killing. But I need to know who they are. Help me. Give me time, and I'll—"

Madame Ruth rose to her feet. The mirage effect had spread further, encompassing the room. I felt it brush against me and stepped back, fearful that if I let it touch me again, I'd be transported somewhere unpleasant.

"Your path is not vengeance, Guardian," she said. "Yours is to stand against the Dark. To protect those who cannot defend themselves. The task before me is mine to complete, not yours."

"I can't let you do that," I stated resolutely. "I don't know who or what you think you are, but murder is not justice. And if that's your plan, then you're damn right I'll stand against you, the Dark, and anyone else."

Deacon moved beside me. The truncheon's heat chased the unnatural chill away, relieving my body with its comforting warmth. The Insight drank in the weapon's glow, drawing courage from the purifying flame.

"I am the One," Madame Ruth said. "What comes cannot be undone. Blood for blood. Eight lives for one. Corruption for salvation. Oppose me at your mortal peril,

Guardian. God will not save you. Nothing can. You have been warned."

"What the fuck do you know about God?" Deacon fired back, eyes ablaze with fury. He pointed the truncheon at the diminutive psychic. "And shovellin' Scripture like you were sellin' it on a fucking street corner don't make you no saint. That ain't justice or God's will, and it sure as shit ain't what's drivin' you."

"Ah, the fallen Protector," Madame Ruth sneered. "You, who have transgressed so fully. Fleeing from a life of acrimony and hate in the hopes that one day you will find absolution? Do you truly believe standing beside the Guardian will return you unto God's good graces? You are nothing. Damaged. Disowned. Disavowed. Disgraced. Your soul tainted beyond repair. Perhaps my vengeance shall turn upon you afore I am done."

"I'd like to see you try," Deacon growled. He took a menacing step toward the medium.

"A demonstration, then," she said. "So be it."

Madame Ruth's eyes snapped open. Soulless black pits stared back at us. I reached for the SMART gun. She raised one hand, then curled it into a fist. I collapsed to the floor as the breath was stolen from my lungs. I clutched at my throat, gasping for air.

Deacon swung the flaming truncheon at her wrist. A loud crack, a blinding flash, and the Confederate was hurled backwards to crash hard against the wall. He staggered to his feet, then rushed at her. The medium raised her other hand, palm outward, and Deacon smashed against an invisible barrier. She lowered her hand slowly. He struggled against her power but fell to one knee as an inexorable force pressed him down.

Infuriated by my helplessness, I latched onto my anger, all the frustration, bitterness, fear and doubt I'd stored since the case started. I used it as fuel, incensing my negative emotions further. My sight shifted spectrums. I noticed thin strands of loose colors—violet, blue and red—had been wrapped cocoon-like around my arms, my body and my legs. Somehow, these filaments had dulled my instincts, twisted my emotions, and ensnared my senses. Where they had come from, I could only guess. Armed with this new knowledge, the Insight burst out, freed from some enchanted prison. Its power coursed through my body, saturating my eyes with cleansing silver and white fire, and strengthening my resistance against whatever fell magic was arrayed against me. Sweet, wonderful air rushed into my lungs. I gulped at it greedily as I clambered to my feet. The room returned to focus as I began to perceive what truly lay before me.

A monstrous silhouette hung suspended behind and above Madame Ruth. I concentrated harder, swallowing more air, and willed the Insight to penetrate whatever glamour shrouded her. The medium's power over me weakened further. Finally, I tore through the illusion it wore to reveal the wretched and foul thing underneath.

It was a spider.

Long, spindly legs protruded from a thick and bulbous torso that gleamed with shadowy, swirling energies. The creature hung from a silken strand woven from ethereal light whose opposite end was tethered to the back of Madame Ruth's head. The thread stretched up and beyond the room's ceiling, and into a vast glittering web of space. Before I became lost in the galaxy of stars, movement caught my eye, and I was drawn back to the monster. Within its abdomen were thousands of tiny spiders writhing beneath the surface. Their desire to devour and destroy nearly overran my senses.

The spider's eight eyes glistened with an awful, alien intelligence. I knew then it was no avenging spirit. It was a killer, a destroyer of lives and worlds. It spouted lies, cunningly woven epithets meant to confound and confuse, another illusion to hide its true intentions. The One was ancient, its origin lost to time. Whatever this thing was, whatever it pretended to be, it wasn't a local. The Insight showed me how the creature traveled between worlds, bending the dimensions of space, folding it to create doorways allowing it to skitter from one place to the next. Images crowded my mind of billions of its victims, from places too fantastic for my brain to register, lost souls devoured by the One and its ravenous children. Alternate Earths, parallel dimensions, all similar to ours, yet different in ways beyond compare.

The memory of Orpheus' mocking voice haunted me.

Old things return that have not seen this sun in an age.

Another twisted Piece in her goddamn Game. Her laughter echoed in the deepest, darkest reaches of my mind.

And that really pissed me off.

The Insight seared my vision. I cried out in pain at the clarity it bestowed. Madame Ruth was caught within the One's shadowy web. Her eyes stared at an unseen horror while her mouth shrieked a silent scream. More of the One's children ran the length of the medium's helpless body adding additional threads to her gossamer prison. Enervated by the little creatures' paralytic venom, Ruth's struggles grew weaker with every heartbeat. If we didn't free her soon, she'd die. Hell, if we didn't do something soon, we'd all die.

I trained the SMART gun on the One, and shouted, "Heavy ordnance!"

The gun's targeting system activated in my eye providing me with dozens of tactical details. The Insight did nothing to enhance the data stream, but an energy surge rushed down my left arm and into the weapon, suffusing it with a lambent silvery glow before dissipating.

A fierce grin curved my lips. Now that was more like it.

With the creature's glamour defeated, the fear and doubt that had gnawed at both the Insight and me evaporated. I straightened my back and held my ground.

"Let them go," I commanded.

"Oh, no, my delicious Guardian," the One replied, its true voice a chittering, petulant hiss. "And have you ruin my fun? I think not. My children are hungry. They must feed."

Hundreds of tiny spiders burst from the One's body to swarm over the helpless medium. Faint whimpers escaped her lips, desperate eyes pleading with me. Deacon grunted beneath the invisible weight crushing him. However, I couldn't shoot the damn thing without harming Madame Ruth. Somehow, I had to remove the spiders, and send the One and its legion of eight-legged doom packing. The problem was, I had no idea what to do.

As if reading my thoughts, the One's legs wrapped possessively around Madame Ruth. "This wretched flesh husk is mine, as is your fallen Protector. The Bargain that was struck, eight lives for one, will soon be complete. Then the portal will open, and my children and I shall feast upon your world. There is nothing you can do to stop me."

"You've said that already," I retorted. Sweat covered my brow. We were out of time. "But I'm going to find one, just to piss you the hell off."

"We shall see, Guardian," it cackled gleefully. "Your suffering will be the most delicious of all."

The room's temperature plummeted. I gasped as the sudden drop ripped the heat from my body.

"Release them!"

Leyla moved to my side, her pale features ablaze with icy fury, a vast shadow with broad wings limned behind her. I ducked my head, uncertain whether the Insight could shield me from the full brunt of whatever that thing was.

"Ah, the Daughter of Night," the One acknowledged with grudging respect. "This matter does not concern you."

"Release them," she thundered again. Was it my imagination, or had the room shook? "They belong to me."

"We do?" I asked.

"They interfere in my designs," the foul creature bellowed. The spiders crawling over Madame Ruth grew agitated. "The Bargain struck—"

"I care naught for your plans," Leyla sneered in disdain. "There is only one Board, and one Game. Nothing else matters. Find another world upon which to sate your hunger. Tempt not my wrath, fiend."

"But this Earth is ripe," the spider wheeled and whined like a petulant child. "It is the Prime. Only the Guardian stands in my path. My hunger demands—"

"ENOUGH!"

A rush of arctic wind raced from Leyla's outstretched hands to curl around Madame Ruth's body. Where touched, tiny spiders withered and died, littering the floor with their quivering corpses. The medium's hair frosted, the wetness in her eyes frozen. Her lips turned a dull blue. What few spiders remained on her body rushed back to its master. Freed from them, Ruth crumpled to the floor.

"My children!" the One roared. "How dare you? HOW DARE YOU?"

Released by the One's broken concentration, Deacon rolled to his left and out from under the invisible force pinning him to the floor. He scrambled to his feet, then pressed his back against the wall. The truncheon's fire continued its writhing dance.

"You shall pay for that slight, Daughter of Night," the spider vowed. The stars above dimmed as the One drew strength from ancient suns it had devoured long ago. "Even you must honor a Bargain made. It is the Way of Things, so written for a thousand generations and more."

"The boy is innocent, for he knows not what he has done." Leyla bore a mocking smile. "Your Bargain is false. The Guardian will see to that. Now, return to your Prison, and trouble us no longer!"

The spider wailed, a singsong dirge that spoke of its overwhelming hunger and an eternal need to devour and destroy. Hundreds more of its children bubbled through its abdomen and spilled to the floor. The shadows around us deepened as an icy wind seethed. What little light the room held dimmed in response, drawn toward the mammoth thing veiling Leyla. She exhaled a fine shadowy mist filled with pea-sized shards of sharpened ice. Leyla flicked her fingers forward, directing the deadly cloud toward the oncoming rush threatening to overwhelm us. Dozens of creatures were impaled by the tiny daggers, yet their advance continued. While much of the wave came for Leyla, the rest surged toward Deacon and me.

"Deacon, what do we do?" I yelled.

He pointed at the music box and shouted, "Destroy the anchor, Holliday!"

My ears caught the warble of music above the din of

impending death. I trained the gun at it and fired, but missed, blasting the floor, and destroying most of Sanarov's workstation.

"Jesus Christ, Holliday!" Deacon yelled in exasperation. "Shoot the goddamn box!"

Spiders crawled on my shoes, beneath my pants and up my legs. Tiny creepy-crawlies wriggled, each one a violation of my flesh. It was like waking from a ghostly nightmare only to discover the horror was all too real. The vicious arachnids burrowed into my skin. Blistering pain scorched my body. Ignoring the sensation as best I could, I took aim, exhaled, and fired. The heavy round obliterated the wooden memento, the candles, a bunch of spiders, and a three-foot swathe of concrete, narrowly missing Madame Ruth. The silence which followed echoed into eternity.

"Four left to find, four soon to die," the One sang. "The Bargain upheld, and this world shall be mine!"

Leyla puddled unconscious to the floor. Cold fled the room. The One's chant faded, and the spiders melted away as if they had never been.

27

"More coffee?" I asked solicitously.

Madame Ruth jerked her head up and down as if she'd been electrocuted. I had stripped the blanket from the bed, wrapped her in it, then led carried from Sanarov's room to the kitchen. Leyla occupied a chair opposite her. The young hacker's head was cradled in her arms on the table. Her eyes had reverted to normal, but she hadn't said anything since the One vanished. Despite the cold and snow, Deacon was smoking outside. Father Jack's arrival at Sanarov's room had given the Confederate all the excuse he needed to get some air.

The old pastor lurked in the doorway of the kitchen like some wayward shadow that had become detached from its person. He wiped his nose with a handkerchief as his red-rimmed eyes stared daggers at both women.

I refilled Madame Ruth's cup followed by my own. After a few fortifying sips of the rejuvenating roasted beans, I was almost ready to face the world again.

"I'm so sorry," the little woman whispered tremulously. "It was unlike anything I'd ever experienced! That...*thing*...

took me over completely. I felt its hunger, the things it's done, *everything*, as if I was a part of it. There's not enough alcohol in the world to get rid of that."

I mustered a reassuring smile. "It's not your fault. None of us knew what we were in for. I'm just glad I broke the connection before the One did any real harm. Sorry about your music box and candles, though."

"I don't think I'll be reaching out to the deceased anytime soon," Madame Ruth grimaced. Her trembling had subsided to an intermittent tremor. "I'm closing the shop for a few weeks. I need time, y'know, to process things?"

"Believe me, I understand," I said. "We'll take you back once you're up to it. Thanks again for doing this. You've helped the investigation tremendously."

Her face blossomed with color and hope. "I did?"

"You did," I nodded. "And I'll make sure SCU compensates you fully for your time."

"Tom," Father Jack interjected. "A word, please?"

I hesitated, drawn by the need to stand by Leyla, to shield her from the pastor's biting recrimination that still hadn't come. After refilling my mug for a fourth time, I followed Father Jack to one of the classrooms. He activated its light and gestured politely for me to enter. Once inside, he closed the door and stood before it, hands clasped behind his back.

"I'll pay for the damage," I began.

Father Jack held up a forestalling hand. He seemed wasted, like a weathered boulder that had been worn down through time and the elements. It reminded me of how Mahoney looked before I'd left his apartment.

"Aren't you at least curious?" I asked. "Don't you want to know what happened?"

"No, I most certainly do not."

"You can't live with your head in the clouds forever," I snapped. Although the magically induced negativity had disappeared, his response rekindled some of that anger. "You've heard me say it before, ever since the Vanessa Mallery case. The dark things that are out there are very real. You can't ignore—"

"I am not a fool, Tom," Father Jack interrupted harshly. "Please don't take me for one. I am fully aware of the kind of world in which we live. Nexus nodes, Vellans, parallel worlds, magic. Creatures from stories and nightmares. But you? You brought those things *here*! You used powers beyond your ken and cavalierly put innocent lives at risk. Did you ever consider the consequences of your actions? Did it occur to you that someone would get hurt, or worse? My goodness! If your mother were alive, God rest her soul, she'd be appalled!"

"My mother?" I asked, taken aback. "What's she got to do with any of this?"

He glared at me but didn't respond.

"Look, Jack, I get that you're pissed that I shot up your basement and had Ruth channel an alien entity hell-bent on eating everyone on Earth," I continued, the embers of my anger fanning brighter. "Even Deacon would agree that wasn't my best idea. But I've gained vital information about this case that I think will help us stop that thing from killing again!"

"Ah, yes, the Tribulation Protector," Father Jack spat out the title as if he'd swallowed day old puke. "I warned you not to bring him here. But you didn't listen to me, blinded by this crusade of yours to catch Gus's killer."

"Jesus Christ, Jack!" I retorted. "I'm a goddamn homicide detective! What I do isn't about feelings or playing nice with the other kids in the sandbox. It's about hunting down remorseless, diabolical killers. It's about doing a job that, quite frankly, few people are equipped to handle. And if that means stepping on people along the way, then so be it.

"You're right, I don't give a damn about your feelings. All I care about is stopping the thing that murdered a man who you took in and provided sanctuary. That should be enough motivation for you to help me. This isn't about religion, or who holds the moral high ground, or the reputation of this church! It's about decency, of what it means to be human. Of protecting the sanctity of life and preserving it against something that has no qualms about taking it away. Because, let me tell you, evil is *very* real. And this thing, this One, is as bad as they come."

"Don't lecture me!" the old pastor fumed. "After everything I've ever done for you. Everything I've ever taught you! *How dare you.* I was there for you after Elaine died. Can John Holliday say that? I looked after you, kept my eye on you when you attended school here. And even after you checked into Wallingbrooke, did I ignore you? Whenever you needed me, did I ever say no to you? Have I ever closed my door to you?"

"That's not the point," I answered. "I'm conducting a murder investigation. And I've just learned there's a time limit on it that, if not stopped, will bring something truly terrible into our world. We aren't just talking one or two lives anymore. We're talking millions. This investigation has grown so much bigger than Calvin Flynn and Gustavo Sanarov. It's bigger than you, me, this church, and every clueless, ignorant person living in Empire City! And all you're doing is making it harder for me to do my job!"

"Then do your job," he hissed in a low voice. "But do it somewhere else."

He turned to leave.

"You're involved in this," I stated flatly.

Father Jack rounded on me, his face flushing a deep, sullen red. The pastor's gentle brown eyes grew hard.

"Am I a suspect, Detective Holliday?" he asked. "Are you recording me now?"

That stung, but I kept my emotions in check. "That depends on you."

"I didn't murder Gus."

"I know that."

"Then what do you want?"

"The truth."

"I've got better things to do than listen to another one of your made-up stories." He shook his head in disgust and yanked the door open. "Now, if you will excuse me."

"*O, that way madness lies,*" I whispered.

"Excuse me?" the old pastor shot back. "Did you say something?"

"I saw you," I said quietly, yet my emotions charged my words, imbuing them with authority and power. "You, Orlando Denning and Pyotr Ushakov. All three of you at Sanarov's wedding. I have the holo-frame."

Jack froze in mid-step.

"You lied to me," I continued. "You lied to me about knowing Sanarov, and I'd like to know why."

He took a deep breath, held it, then exhaled slowly, releasing all the piss and vinegar he'd been channeling a moment before.

"I never lied," he said. "I just never said how long I'd known him."

"Semantics, Jack," I waved away his comment. "Omission is still a lie, especially to a cop investigating a murder, so let me fill in the blanks. You knew about his placement in the Pieces of Eight program. After his release from New

Rikers, you offered him a place to stay. That sound about right so far?"

Through the open door, I noticed Leyla wandering aimlessly toward us. She appeared lost and fragile, as if recently awakened from a bad dream, which I suppose wasn't far from the truth. When she caught sight of me, her face brightened until I made a slight negating gesture with my hand. She nodded once and stopped.

"We all grew up in the neighborhood," Jack started slowly. "Gus, Pyotr, Orlando, your father, and me. Living here was hard then, and it hasn't gotten any better now. And when we were teenagers, Gus, Pyotr and John got involved with the wrong people. I didn't want any part of it, but they were still my friends. We had each other's backs. Swore we'd be there for each other if we ever needed it."

"What does any of that have to do with Calvin Flynn?" I asked.

"I was recently ordained when Gus married Stacey," the pastor said softly, his eyes misting over with memory. "He asked me to preside over his wedding, but I didn't want to impose. We were all invited, you see, even your parents, who were also recently married. I remember dear, sweet Elaine, so beautiful with those blue eyes of hers. So full of life! It was a joyful occasion. New beginnings. We were all young and idealistic. I was fortunate enough to join the Holy Redeemer earlier that year. I wanted to stay in Brighton Beach rather than go abroad like so many of my colleagues. I'd always dreamt of using my position at the church to help the less fortunate, the spiritually dispossessed, even the morally challenged, and help them find hope in the teachings of our Lord. But I couldn't leave Elaine, or any of my other friends behind. They were family. And this was my home."

I folded my arms but kept my expression neutral.

"I tried to help Gus," Father Jack lamented. "When he lost his job and fell on hard times, I tried to get him something here, but he refused. His pride wouldn't let him accept charity. Instead, he fell in further with *them*. We had so many arguments over it!"

His bitter laugh turned into a coughing fit. He retrieved a handkerchief from his trousers' pocket and spat into it. Blood colored the cloth in dark red splotches. Concerned, I took a step toward him.

"It's nothing." He wiped his mouth, then folded the handkerchief and returned it to the pocket. "I'm fine. Just getting over the flu, that's all."

Father Jack ran a hand across his slick forehead. I hadn't noticed before the fever hiding behind his eyes, or how he wheezed whenever he spoke.

"Gus owed the *bratva* a lot of credits," he said after clearing his throat. "His marriage was failing, and there was nothing I could do. One night, Pyotr Ushakov visits me and says I can help Gus repay all his debts if I do him a small favor. It was no secret Pyotr was a rising star in the organization, but I harbored hope that our mutual friendship with Gus was what motivated him to make the offer. I should've known better. The *bratva* owned Gus's soul, just like they owned most of Little Odessa."

"What did he want you to do?" I asked.

The Insight stirred. The hair on the back of my neck stood on end.

"To hide someone," he answered sadly. "To keep them here and out of sight for a few days. And to not get curious. If I kept to myself, then Gus's debt would be absolved, and the church would receive a substantial sum of credits in return. I was such a fool."

"When was this?"

"You know when it was, Tommy."

I stared at him.

"Calvin Flynn was here?"

"In the very room that Gus was murdered."

I studied Jack, recalling the details of the kidnapping from Mahoney's report as some of the pieces fell into place. Sanarov's testimony never accounted for the missing time, nor did Mahoney's investigation provide the DA with sufficient evidence to convict him for murder. Ushakov and his two dead friends from Eddie's must've somehow infiltrated the warehouse, knocked Sanarov out and taken Calvin Flynn, leaving behind the other body.

But why? What did the *bratva* gain from the kidnapping? The more I chewed on it, the further I was convinced Donald Flynn was the key.

"Did you know who it was?" I asked. "Did you see him?"

Father Jack shook his head. "No, but I suspected. Pyotr and two of his men arrived here late that night. I had given him the alarm code and left the back entrance unlocked. I watched the footage the following day but deleted it and the archives as Pyotr instructed so the records would be lost. They stayed in the basement for three days. I kept everyone out, claiming we'd had a burst pipe and the damage hadn't been cleaned up yet. After three days had passed, I went into the basement, but they were gone. Everything had been scoured clean, the bed sheets taken, as if no one had ever been down there. A week later, a hand-written note had been slipped beneath my office door. It said the credits would be deposited into the church's account via a series of donations spread out over the course of the year. And if I wanted the donations to continue, all I had to do was keep my mouth shut."

Father Jack clasped both hands in front of him. His body trembled.

"I've kept my mouth shut for over thirty years," he said. "I haven't spoken to Pyotr Ushakov since then."

"What about Orlando Denning?" I asked, my mind racing as I tried to connect the dots. "What's his part in this?"

"I don't know. But he was close with Pyotr. Orlando is also the one who established our relationship with Brave New Beginnings, ironic given the circumstances. I've caught him here on occasion speaking to others who I know work for the Brotherhood. They're members of this very congregation! It galls me whenever I see them, as they sit and pray and ask for forgiveness, pretending to be pious when I know evil dwells in their hearts."

"Why didn't you tell me any of this before?" I asked. "I could've helped you!"

"I'm sorry, Tom," he answered sadly, echoing Mahoney's admission of guilt. "I...I didn't know what to do. What you would think of me if you knew the truth. I was ashamed. Afraid. I just thought that by doing Pyotr's favor, it would help Gus, and maybe even free him from the *bratva*. But when I saw the newsfeed the next morning that the police had arrested him, I..."

He gestured vaguely with one hand, at a loss for words.

"You should've come to me," I growled, my heart pounding in my chest. "You should've trusted me! You always have a choice, Jack! Isn't that what you taught me? You make your own destiny, whether you trust in a higher power or not. We're given one life, and in that life, we have a responsibility to make choices that not only impact ourselves, but the world around us. And if we unwittingly choose to do evil, and then do nothing to stop it, we become the very thing we hate!"

"Tom, I—"

"Father John Davis, I'm going to need your official testimony," I stated, mentally activating EVI to record. "By the power vested in me by the Mayor's office and the enclave of Empire City, you are hereby under arrest, and charged with accessory after the fact to the kidnapping and murder of Calvin Flynn."

28

I dropped Madame Ruth off outside of her shop. The others remained inside the pod, leaving me her sole escort. I reiterated my promise of compensation for her time.

"Thank you, Detective Holliday." She gave me an exhausted smile.

"If there's anything I can do," I said earnestly. "Anything at all, please don't hesitate to contact me."

I offered her my hand. She gripped it with trepidation, as if touching me would bring about another supernatural disaster. I didn't blame her.

"Thank you," Madame Ruth replied, her haunted eyes darting around. "Right now, I just want the world to leave me the hell alone."

She chuckled ruefully, then beat a hasty retreat into her shop. The lights never came on inside.

"That is one fucked up woman," Deacon commented after I closed the hatch. The Confederate's booted feet were propped atop the command console, a lit cigarette between his fingers.

"Just like the rest of us," I said. "EVI, please take us to Abner's."

I positioned myself behind the chair next to Deacon, my hands resting on its curved back. Beyond the windshield, Empire City blurred, blended streaks of shifting colors without beginning or end. Night had long fallen, soaking the world beneath a snowy abstract blanket where truth slept with lies and deceit. So many thoughts crowded my mind vying for my attention: the Flynns, the One, Pop, Ivan and the *bratva*, Jack, Mahoney, my feelings for Charlie.

And Leyla.

"*It is of the highest importance, therefore, not to have useless facts elbowing out the useful ones,*" I quoted quietly.

I shook my head in bemusement. Sir Arthur Conan Doyle had been right. My brain-attic was near capacity. Questions bounced around in my mind, banging off of dusty facts, clues, details and other minutiae, a vast amorphous jumble that up until now, had formulated little to no answers.

"You put the old man on house arrest?" Deacon asked, breaking me from my reverie.

"At worst he's an accomplice, and at best, a witness, thirty years removed from the crime," I replied.

"You reckon that's a good idea, leavin' him alone and all after everything that happened today?"

"He's not a flight risk," I said. "EVI recorded his statement and then I had her dispatch surveillance drones to the church to keep an eye on things. Father Jack isn't going anywhere. If he does, I'll know about it. And if someone pays him a visit, all the better."

"Fair enough," Deacon said. "Saranda called while you were out. Said Mahoney's doing better, whatever the fuck that means. Also said she'll meet us at the bookstore."

I meandered over to the beverage station to pour myself another round of liquid sanity. Leyla sat alone in the furthest seat of the pod facing the rear wall. Once I'd taken care of Father Jack, the young hacker informed me her holo-phone had pinged with a message announcing the decryption program had cracked the rest of the code. She said she needed to run a final diagnostic, which meant traveling back to Abner's.

I emptied my mug in two quick gulps, refilled it, then moved over to take the chair next to her. Leyla held her knees to her chin and stared sightlessly ahead.

"Hey, kiddo, how you holding up?" I asked.

For a moment, I thought she hadn't heard me, but then she sighed. "Is Madame Ruth okay?"

"Seems to be." I set the mug on the chair's tray table. "Although I don't think she'll be doing any readings for a while."

"It's all my fault."

"Hey now," I said, placing my hand on her shoulder. A deep chill rushed up my arm, and I shivered at the contact. "First off, it's my fault for bringing her into this. You did nothing wrong."

"Yeah, but you had no idea what would happen."

"True. None of us did, not even Deacon. But thanks to Madame Ruth, we learned quite a bit back there. I've got a crazy theory about what's going on now, although I'm still not sure what the connection is between Donald Flynn, the Russian mob and some malevolent dimensional alien hell-bent on eating all of us for breakfast."

Leyla didn't laugh.

"I don't know what's happening to me," she whispered in a small voice.

"What do you remember?" Deacon asked, turning the

chair to face us. "'Cause I ain't never seen nothin' like the shit you pulled back there."

Leyla's face scrunched in concentration. Her blue eyes darkened with the memory.

"Once the music started, I sort of fell into a deep waking sleep," she said. "I was there with you, and then I wasn't. It was like someone else had entered my mind and shoved me aside. I saw everything, but I couldn't do anything about it, like watching a holo-show on my rig. The gunshot somehow brought me back."

"Something possessed you?" I exchanged a worried glance with Deacon. He folded his arms across his chest.

"I-I guess?"

"Does 'Daughter of Night' mean anything to you?" Deacon asked.

"No, I've never heard that name before today," Leyla said, her eyes filling with icy tears. "Doc? Deacon? What's happening to me?"

"I don't know, kiddo." I drew her toward me and hugged her close as she cried into my chest. My body grew numb, but I held on despite the cold. "But we'll figure this out. Together."

I again recalled the winged shadow I'd seen through the Insight at Kraze, and the power Leyla had wielded in the fight with the vampires, as well as our encounter with Marko the killer android.

But she has a darkness inside of her, too, Tommy. A terrible darkness. Someday soon, she's going to need you. She'll need all three of you.

My grandfather's words had been more than a warning. Whatever darkness lived inside of Leyla wasn't some random event brought on by stress or anger. There was a sinister intelligence behind it, a purpose whose design we had yet to see. And its power was growing.

Leyla pushed me gently away, wiping at her nose and eyes with her hand.

"We don't have the time to waste on me right now." She took a deep steadying breath.

"You're damn right we don't," Deacon rumbled. "But that don't change the fact you're a goddamn witch. When Holliday blew that music box to hell, it severed the connection between whatever the fuck's inside of you and here, too. But that ain't the only time. Sure, it's helped us in a pinch, but if you keep doing that kind of magic, bad shit will surely follow. And I ain't interested in bein' on the wrong end of that someday, neither. I've said it before, and I'll say it again —everything's got a price. Everything."

"Such is the price for lies and deceit," I wondered aloud, the One's words echoing what Deacon had said.

"And?" Deacon scoffed. "That spider thing sounded like one of the High Inquisitor's sermons. That goddamn blowhard sure did love to talk about the end of days, and how every sinner would get their comeuppance, and that right soon. Hallelujah!" He raised his arms above his head and wriggled his fingers dramatically.

"Yeah, but none of those jives with what the Insight has shown me," I pointed out. "The One is a formidable creature with unimaginable power who has destroyed every parallel world it encountered. I doubt it possesses a moral compass, let alone anything resembling human emotion or belief. And why didn't it just kill us out of hand? Why let us live?"

"Prolly 'cause it likes playin' with its food," Deacon grimaced.

"Or maybe it can't," Leyla countered. "Maybe this Bargain won't let it. And why would it use those Biblical verses at the crime scenes? Why bother with the holier-than-thou pretense at all? I mean it kind of reminded me of Madame Ruth's show back at her shop."

"Maybe," I said, and stood up. Warmth returned to my limbs in a hurry as a jumble of ideas formulated in my mind. "Or maybe Calvin Flynn was trying to tell us something."

I started pacing to help my thoughts gain momentum.

"The One said, 'peddlers of flesh' and 'purveyors of sin,'" I continued. "'Thieves and killers.'"

"Yeah, as if that would make us think it was doing the world a favor, using God as an excuse," Leyla said.

"There's more to it than that," I said. "What bargain did it make with Calvin Flynn? And what does it get from it?"

"That thing murdered very specific targets," Deacon said. "Like following some goddamn recipe."

"A list," Leyla supplied.

"Calvin's hit list," I finished. "Everyone involved with his kidnapping from thirty years ago. Sanarov, Ushakov and his two pals were just the beginning. He's arranged his own dead pool and made a deal with the devil to do it."

"Well, there's four more to go." Deacon lit another cigarette. "Who you got?"

"Denning has to be one of them," I answered. "Between his friendship with Sanarov, and his position at Brave New Beginnings, that's enough of a connection to link him to all of this."

"Five down." Deacon blew a long stream of smoke from his nostrils.

"What about Mrs. Sanarov?" Leyla asked.

"Schrodinger?" the former Protector replied. "She didn't know shit."

"Okay, then who else?" she asked.

"Whoever organized and planned the kidnapping," I replied. "Ushakov was high up in the organization, but back then, he was just another thug. He wouldn't have come up with that kind of operation on his own. Someone gave him the order."

"Or paid him to do it," Leyla said in a quiet voice.

I stared at her as the realization struck me full in the face.

"Donald Flynn," I said slowly, allowing more of the case details to fall into place.

"Why would that rich fuck do all that?" Deacon asked.

"I don't know." I scooped up my mug and drained its contents, then moved to the beverage station for a refill. "But I bet credits to donuts it's got something to do with whatever Charlie is investigating. I'm thinking her arrival in Empire City is no coincidence. She knows more than she's letting on."

"You think?" Deacon scoffed. "That twat's been using you from the start, Holliday. She's hopin' you'll crack these murders to give her everything she needs to bring down Flynn. You do all the work, and she reaps the glory. Maybe if you pulled your head out of your pants, you'd see that."

"I get that," I said, angry heat inflaming my face. "I don't need the reminder."

"Guys, guys," Leyla pleaded. "Stay on point here, will you please?"

I glared at Deacon who returned it with a placid one of his own. He must've been taking lessons from Besim.

Asshole.

"Which leaves your old man, Mahoney and the pastor," Deacon finished. "Unless we're missing somebody, time's runnin' out for two of them."

"Yeah," I sighed. "But which two?"

My annoyance evaporated in an instant, leaving behind a sick, awful dread that settled in the pit of my stomach. I'd known the moment Leyla brought up the list but refused to acknowledge it until now. Something must have shown on my face because the young hacker rushed over to gather me in a frigid hug.

"Oh, Doc, I'm so sorry!" she sobbed.

"It's okay, kiddo." I stroked her hair, trying to find courage among the tiny ice crystals fluttering around my fingers. "Besides, Deacon's right. There could be others involved that we haven't determined yet. I'm not giving up on any of them, even Pop. And if we can put a stop to the One, no one else has to die."

I disengaged from her embrace. Seeing the resolve in my eyes, she nodded sharply and returned to her seat.

"Okay, we know what the One is, and what it wants," I said. "What does it want with Calvin Flynn?"

"Ruth called on the dead kid, and that fucking thing answered instead," Deacon stated. "Revenants don't work like that, Holliday, least not in my experience. But if that big fucker is doin' all the killin', how's it gettin' around in the first place? 'Cause I doubt it's got its own pet psychic to summon it. Irregardless, the kid and that thing are bound together."

"Irregardless isn't a word," Leyla said.

"Whatever, girlie."

"Bound?" I asked. "As in, soul-bound?"

I stared ahead, contemplating the Biblical verses at the crime scene and the faux holy pretense the One had hidden behind before the Insight revealed everything to me.

"*Solamen miseris socios habuisse dolors,*" I stated quietly.

"What does that mean?" Leyla asked.

"It means 'misery loves company,' girlie," Deacon replied. "Mephistopheles, right?"

"You know Marlowe?" I asked in surprise. "I studied Dr. Faustus my second year at ECU."

"You'd be surprised what I like to do in my spare time, Holliday," the Confederate quipped.

"I don't get it," Leyla said. "What does some dusty old book have to do with this case?"

"It's a tragic cautionary tale about making a deal with the Devil, among other motifs," I explained. "Faustus was a bored, yet ambitious German scholar who coveted magic. He made a deal with Lucifer, offering his soul in exchange for twenty-four years of having Mephistopheles and all his magical knowledge at Faustus' disposal. Problem is, Faustus was blind and wasteful of the gifts he was given. In the end, he's torn apart by the devils sent to claim his soul."

"Yikes," Leyla shivered. "Tough lesson."

"Yeah," Deacon grimaced. "Don't fuck with the Devil."

"This whole thing reminds me of Faustus," I said thoughtfully. "I wonder what kind of collateral a kid dead thirty years has to offer?"

The Confederate flicked ash from the end of his cigarette and said, "Unless he ain't dead."

"If that's true, then where has he been all this time?" I countered.

"Beats the fuck out of me."

"What if he never moved on?" Leyla suggested. "What if Calvin Flynn died, but his soul remained behind? Could his ghost make that kind of deal? Deacon, you said it yourself that the spirit is anchored somewhere. What if he didn't die in the warehouse? If we can figure out where he is, maybe we can stop him."

"*There are more things in heaven and earth, Horatio, than*

are dreamt of in your philosophy," I quoted the Bard. "We know what Calvin's getting from this, but what does the One want, besides devouring Earth?"

"The fucking thing can't cross over," Deacon declared, then looked at Leyla. "When you were this Daughter of Night, you mentioned a prison. Somehow, it needs Calvin to create a bridge between worlds."

"The One's bargain must be to kill everyone responsible for Calvin's kidnapping, and whatever else that entailed, in exchange for passage to our world," Leyla said. "That has to be it!"

My mouth hung open as the implication hit me. Father Jack's confession had cracked opened the door. And what the One had said meant more than a mind-numbing, horrific threat. There had been something else hidden behind those apocryphal words, a subtle message not even that dreadful monster realized it had conveyed to us.

"Calvin was trying to warn us," I said. "Somehow, he's figured out what the spider wanted and—"

Suddenly, a powerful blast hammered the pod followed by a second that sent our transport careening from its *'way* to smash into the ground below.

29

D eacon shouted something at me, but the ringing in my ears overpowered everything. I lay against the rear wall of the transport. Every part of my body ached. I raised a shaky hand before my face, grateful my fingers still worked. A smoky haze filled the compartment. Exposed circuitry fizzled and died amidst chunks of glass and twisted metal. My eyes teared from the ash and heat.

"Holliday, move your ass!" Deacon repeated as he extended a helping hand, his voice now a muffled echo.

The former Protector hauled me up, sporting a shallow cut above one eye that bled freely. Covered in dust and debris, he appeared otherwise unharmed.

"Leyla?" I managed, tasting blood in my mouth. I ran my tongue along my teeth to confirm none of them were missing.

"Girlie's fine," Deacon responded harshly as sound returned to normal. "Now shut up and move!"

He half-pulled and half-dragged me from the wreckage. An ugly rent in the side of the pod spilled into an abandoned restaurant. All the hardware and machinery had been removed leaving behind a derelict space with broken cabinets, a moldy sink and fresh piles of rat shit. Leyla was by the kitchen entrance, although several bloody scrapes dotted her worried face.

"What the hell happened?" I asked as the three of us moved deeper into the kitchen. I dug a finger in each ear, then moved my jaw around to clear the popping.

"Some motherfucker hit us with heavy ordnance," Deacon said. "We've got to find some cover before—"

"Too late!" Leyla shouted.

I heard the incoming shriek seconds before the shell detonated. Hot shrapnel exploded through the crumbling walls of the restaurant. The force of the blast hurled us back several feet before we crashed to the floor, momentarily stunned. The walls were just thick enough to absorb the attack, otherwise rescue teams would be scooping up our remains with micro-spatulas.

I labored to my knees and tried to get my bearings. Leyla and Deacon were a tumble of legs and arms as they disentangled themselves from each other. The young hacker coughed to clear her throat. Deacon wiped blood from two fresh cuts on his cheek and chin.

"EVI, status report," I ordered aloud.

"Pod 041407 has sustained terminal damage to all systems," she answered in my ear. "At 19:24 Empire City Standard Time, pod external cameras captured two heavy projectiles discharged from an alleyway adjacent to our destination, Abner's Vintage Books—"

"EVI, code 30. Repeat, code 30," I said quickly. "SCU officers under heavy fire and need immediate assistance. Repeat—"

"Move!" Deacon barked, then grabbed Leyla under the arm and yanked her through the back door.

Another scream followed a heartbeat later. I scrambled forward just before the shell struck home and rolled low as the ceiling collapsed behind me with a rush and a roar.

I counted to ten. Acrid smoke stung my eyes, and I was bathed in sweat. Crumbled drywall fragments and shards of broken concrete showered the ground as I shakily returned to my feet. We were in a combined storage and bathroom attached to a short hallway that led from the ruined kitchen. The rest of the hallway ended at a closed door, our only means of escape.

"Officers have been dispatched, Detective Holliday," EVI said. "However, due to the icy 'way conditions, a thirty minute minimum arrival time is estimated."

"Shit, shit, shit," I said, exchanging a worried look with Leyla. "Calvary's going to be late."

"Oh, God, I hope Abner's okay," she cried. Icy tears mixed with the blood, soot and dust on her cheeks.

"Clean-up crew will be arrivin' soon, Holliday!" Deacon cast around with a wild look in his eyes.

I coughed, spitting out bloody phlegm and said, "EVI, give me the floor plan and engineering for our current position in Brighton Beach, and include every commercial or living space connected to it."

Instantly, the old building's three-dimensional layout played in my eye, providing every access point, floor height and design. I scanned it, taking note of the choke points. Whoever had attacked us had picked their spot well.

"There's got to be something we can do!" Leyla worried. "We can't just sit here!"

"We're like fish in a fucking barrel," Deacon spat with cold fury. He held the flameless truncheon in a white-knuckled grip. "Only choice we got left is to make these goddamn motherfuckers hurt."

As if on cue, the rear door blew off its hinges, spraying the hallway with scraps of wood and metal.

"Everyone, behind me," I ordered grimly, gripping the SMART gun. "Tactical."

The building layout was replaced by the weapon's strategic center, providing me with short range distances between ingress and egress, stand-alone objects and heat signatures as well as its own status. Two colorless dots appeared, converging on our position.

"Two bogeys," I whispered to the others.

The dots approached the opening side-by-side, heedless of their own safety, presuming we'd been reduced to bloody smears.

Fucking amateurs.

"Ricochet," I muttered.

After I'd downloaded the latest firmware upgrade a few weeks ago, the SMART gun now had motion sensors up to twenty-five feet from my position in all directions. I also splurged on a couple of new rounds, although the cost forced me to miss last month's rent. I was supposed to get paid later this week and made a mental note to transfer the credits to my landlady, presuming we survived today.

I'm usually an optimist, but only on days ending in I'm-Not-About-To-Die-In-A- Gunfight.

The SMART gun's targeting system locked on two points through the doorway against the opposite wall at specific angles. Two green dotted lines raced forward, demonstrating the projected trajectories and expected results. I exhaled a slow breath and squeezed the trigger. The weapon's muzzle roared twice, firing two ionized rubber bullets the size of my thumb at the precise tracks outlined by the tactical. The projectiles hurtled forward, connecting with the wall, bouncing off the exposed concrete at their respective angles, then against the opposite wall and finally into each assailant. Two soft thuds from the hallway brought a fierce grin to my lips. No more blips appeared on the SMART gun's sensor array.

"Clear," I announced.

Deacon pushed past me, with Leyla close behind. Sprawled on the ruined floor were two unconscious men I didn't recognize. A sawed-off shotgun and a .32 ACP lay nearby. Deacon retrieved both and stuck the smaller weapon behind his jeans belt. I used zip ties I kept in my inner blazer pocket and wrapped their wrists behind their backs to their ankles. A brief search revealed no holophones. EVI confirmed their facial IDs as low-level thugs from somewhere in East Brooklyn. Another cell of the *bratva*, no doubt.

"Let's go," I ordered.

We exited the building, me in the lead, Leyla in the middle, and Deacon taking up the rear, shotgun cocked and ready. Sleet pelted us, the *tap-tap-tap* dancing a quick staccato on my head and shoulders. The sharp cold outdoors erased the heat from the closed quarters of the explosion. Sweat froze on my brow, and my breath streamed ahead of me. I kept low and to the near side of the brick wall, moving swiftly. No light illuminated the alley, affording us some cover. We reached the corner without incident.

Despite the explosions, no traffic ran along the street. Other than the icy patter, the neighborhood kept silent. In most parts of Little Odessa, the neighbors weren't stupid. They were either laying low or had already fled. Involvement around here meant getting hurt, or worse. I had my doubts about whether the backup I'd requested would even show up.

I edged around the corner. No answering shower of bullets or singing holo-grams greeted me. The lonely street-lamp standing guard outside Abner's shed its off-white circle on an empty icy sidewalk. According to EVI, whoever had attacked the pod had been stationed in the alleyway adjacent to the bookstore. Somewhere out there was a third assailant, armed with a rocket launcher and who knew what else.

So why hadn't they hit us yet?

I scanned both sides of the street, up and down its length, but didn't see anything. Other than the merry pop and sizzle from the destroyed pod and restaurant, the area appeared deserted. The gun's motion sensor registered only the three of us. Switching to night-vision, the grainy green feed didn't uncover anyone lurking in the shadows.

"Anything?" Deacon asked in a low voice.

I was about to respond, when my holo-phone vibrated in my pocket.

"Incoming call from an unlisted number," EVI announced in my ear. "I am unable to trace its source."

I pulled the phone out and stared at it, my jaw clenching.

"EVI, set to record," I ordered aloud while activating the speaker function. "Patch it through."

"Thomas."

A ghostly, faceless image appeared above the display, cloaked by whatever scrambling program he employed.

"Ivan, if all you really wanted to do was talk, a phone call would've been fine," I quipped. "The pod's going to need one helluva paint job."

"I already tried that, but you would not listen, Thomas. And so, I chose a more direct approach."

"Well, you've got my attention. What the hell do you want?"

"I thought we were friends, Thomas. But these past few days have shown me that I was mistaken. I was content to let you hunt the killer of our men. Instead, you have chosen to involve yourself in our business. This is most unfortunate."

"Yeah, well I have a tendency to muck things up. It's a gift."

"Thomas, you were once very loyal to me," Ivan sighed dramatically. "You knew when to interfere. When to talk. When it was wise to leave things to your betters. And for your troubles, whatever you desired, we provided for you. Protected you. Guided you. Nurtured you. How many can say these things? A little gratitude is in order."

"So sorry to disappoint you, but I've done that to a lot of people lately."

Deacon and Leyla kept a sharp eye out, although I didn't expect anything to happen. Ivan wanted his say, and I was willing to give it to him, if only to figure out his play.

"And what of your father?" he continued. "He has been employed for many years. He has his house. Friends. Even after the tragedy of your poor mother, he has learned to appreciate the benefits of loyalty to his other family. John has been a good man for us, Thomas. You would be wise to learn from his example."

My hand holding the holo-phone shook. Rage warred with shame, years of harsh memories from growing up without a mother while an abusive alcoholic took out his anger on his defenseless son. Of running around the neighborhood with the likes of Ivan and his goons, trying to emulate the tougher, older kids, and nearly losing myself in the process, if not for Harry, Abner and Father Jack.

"That little thief you are so fond of, have we not allowed her to do as she pleases?" Ivan asked. Leyla regarded me with a mixture of shock and concern. I turned from her and back to the bookstore, afraid to meet her gaze. "All these years, and still Abner and his bookstore remain untouched. This, Thomas. This is what good friends do for one another. Loyal, reliable friends. We look out for one another. We treat one another with respect. A respect that you seem to have forgotten. Your time spent in rehabilitation has changed you. Made you soft. Careless. Stupid. Now, I must take measures."

"I'm cold and getting rained on, Ivan," I retorted. "What the fuck do you want?"

"You lied to me, Thomas. When I asked how my men had died. The Albanian Syndicate is not involved. And then I find out you took Pyotr's phone. That is theft of property, Detective. Is against the law, no? And, so, I have run out of patience. I want it back. You will give it to me. You will give it to me, because I am no longer asking. You will give it to me, because that is how to conduct proper business. You will give it to me, because you know it is the right thing to do."

"And if I don't?"

"Then Abner and the Vellan will die."

30

"**I**f you touch a hair on either one of them—" I threatened, but Ivan's deep, throaty chuckle full of malice cut me off.

"Thomas, my old friend, why make this difficult by over-complicating matters? You are in no position to threaten me. Bring me Pyotr's phone, and all will be forgiven."

"Give me time to find it," I urged, sudden desperation coloring my tone.

"Do not patronize me, Thomas. It is beneath you. Since you disabled its tracker, you either have it with you, or it has been secured elsewhere. However, knowing you as I do, I believe you have it on you now. And, so, you will go into the bookstore and give my men Pyotr's phone, or your friends die. The choice is yours."

The audio cleared as the empty image winked out, and my phone went dark. I bit back the scream threatening to crawl from my throat, then pounded the brick wall with my closed fist.

"That's it," Leyla declared, striding past me. Intense cold wept from her in waves. The brittle air around us crackled.

"Where are you goin'?" Deacon demanded.

"In there," she answered in a grim, dead voice. The sclera was rapidly overtaking her eyes. Sleet pelted us like tiny bullets, frozen solid by Leyla's rage. "And then I'm going to fuck their shit up. Nobody threatens my family, Deacon. Nobody."

"Don't be an idiot," he said, flicking a warning glance at me. Wisps of white tickled the business end of the truncheon in his hand. "We got no idea what their situation is in there. If you go rushin' in, they'll kill everyone before you can say 'freeze.'"

"I don't care, Deacon. Move."

"He's right, kiddo." I interposed myself between Leyla and Deacon, then placed my hand on her shoulder, squeezing gently. Instant cold shot up my arm and into my chest, stealing my breath. My eyes teared from its intensity. I gritted my teeth and forged ahead. "We've got to come up with a plan."

"Doc, there's no time," Leyla said. Her voice had deepened, adopting a timbre I'd never heard from her before. "Abner and Besim's lives are at stake! We can't talk our way out of this one. We have to do something!"

"Girlie, pull yourself together," Deacon said. The truncheon flared brighter, its flickering brilliance bathing the dull red of the brick wall in white. "This ain't right!"

"No."

The finality of that word frightened me to my core. I felt a sudden presence, awful, dark and malevolent, a crushing weight against my soul. That's when I saw it. The winged shadow draped around and over Leyla, reminiscent of Madame Ruth and the One back at the church. I imagined its breath on my flesh and shrank from its phantasmagorical touch. My mind shrieked from the shadow's enormity, retreating to the furthest corner of my psyche in the desperate hope it could hide from whatever this thing was.

Instantly, the Insight responded, flooding my senses with preternatural clarity, and filling me with resolve, as it rose to meet the shadow's challenge. Time slowed. Sensation intensified. My fear diminished. I studied slivers of sleet as they spat from the sky, admiring their unique crystalline forms. I saw the individual cracks within the bricks where the stone had weakened to the point of near collapse. I smelled human consumption and loss, a foul odor that had seeped into the pavement from centuries of abuse and neglect. I tasted bitterness and decline, of failed human enterprise and the extinguished hopes for a better tomorrow, and of the struggle to make something good from a neighborhood that cared about nothing and no one. Emotions that weren't mine warred with the tactile sensations from ghosts long dead, people who had once lived and worked here, now reduced to ash and memory. Their forgotten history permeated the very air, and all of it crashed against me in one massive emotional wave.

The sensory overload was too much, exacerbated by the shadow and whatever was happening inside of Leyla. I crashed against the wall, struggling to stabilize my heart and mind as both the shadow and Insight overwhelmed me.

"Leyla," the former Protector warned in a dangerously quiet tone, the flaming truncheon brandished before him. White fire roared along its length. "Think about what you're doin' before somebody gets hurt."

If I didn't get my shit together and defuse whatever was happening with Leyla, we'd be dealing with something far worse than the hostage situation in the bookstore. The Insight roiled around my mind, licking at my consciousness, urging me to confront and do battle against the thing that had taken her over. I clamped my eyes shut, refusing to give in to the desire. I was out of my depth, ill-prepared for what might come next, so I went back to the basics. No matter what occupied Leyla now, she was still in there, and I was determined to bring her back to us.

I took a deep breath and pushed myself upright. With great effort, I forced the Insight aside for the moment. My vision dulled to near normalcy.

"You're right, kiddo," I said. "But stop and think for a second. Why does Ivan need the phone? What's so important about it? Whatever your decryption uncovered is valuable enough that he's willing to act openly. That's out of character for him. He'd rather work from behind the scenes. It's how the *bratva* operate. Maybe we can use that to our advantage."

"How?" she cried, her stricken voice mixed with another. The blue of her irises was nearly gone.

"I'm not sure yet, but I need you to trust me," I answered. Frost caked everything. I stepped in closer, then reached out slowly to grip both of her shoulders, bending low so we were nose-to-nose. "But whatever we do, we'll do together. Because we're a team. Because we're family."

"Family," she whispered.

"You, me, Abner, Deacon. Even Besim. We're all family. We take care of each other. Protect each other. Because that's what families do. But we don't run in blindly. We stop and we think and we plan."

"Family," she repeated.

"You got it, kiddo. We're in this together. All of us. And we're going to save Abner and Besim. But we need you to find yourself, okay? We need you to look deep inside yourself and remember who you are. Can you do that for me, Leyla?"

"Remember."

Her eyes softened. Wet tears formed at the corners. The Insight settled into a restless prowl. The shadow faded, now little more than a stain.

"Yes, remember," I urged. "Isn't that right, Deacon?"

The former Protector was about to respond when his face went slack. He stumbled backwards, dropping the truncheon as if burned by its touch. Ice and snow melted around it with a loud hiss.

"Deacon?" Leyla asked, momentarily distracted.

He bent over, both hands on his knees, and shook his head shouting, "No, no, NO!"

Something tickled my mind, a light, familiar whisper wafting along the winter breeze. Leyla tilted her head to the side. The Insight relaxed, calmed by a soothing presence. Deacon stood up, ran his hands down his leather jacket to straighten it, then strode purposefully toward us. He glanced at the truncheon but made no move to retrieve it.

"There are three assailants inside the bookstore, Detective Holliday," Deacon said.

Leyla gaped at the Confederate. Her eyes had returned to their normal state. The temperature followed suit. Fitful flakes of snow replaced the sleet. The winged shadow was gone. I breathed a heavy sigh of relief.

"They bear handguns," he continued. "One man is positioned six and one quarter feet inside the entry, to your left facing, and has secreted himself behind a bookshelf, ostensibly for cover. The second maintains tight watch over us by the central checkout kiosk. He holds a weapon to my back and is the *de facto* leader of the group by the manner in which he directs the others. He also wears an earpiece, with an active connection to Ivan Kruchev. The third is at the top of the stairs. A large projectile device is near him, presumably the weapon which disabled your transport. I have been unable to ascertain their names, although their intentions are quite clear."

"How are you doing this?" I asked.

"That is not relevant to the current situation, Detective," Deacon admonished me as if I were a ten-year-old returning home with bad grades on my report card. "However, what is of paramount importance is the condition of Abner. He lies unconscious on the floor three and three-quarters feet to my left. He has sustained significant trauma around his abdomen, face and neck and requires immediate medical attention. Whatever you plan to do, I suggest you do so quickly."

"Right." I returned the phone to my pocket as a misguided idea formulated in my pea-sized brain. "Besim, let Deacon go. I need him to listen."

"As you wish."

A heartbeat later, Deacon's face resumed its customary scowl.

"I hate it when she does that," he muttered darkly.

"You okay?" I asked.

"Shut the fuck up, Holliday, and just tell us the goddamn plan."

"We get captured," I said. Warmth and feeling returned to my body as adrenaline took hold. "Leyla, you bring one of them with you to get the phone. Once underground, take him out."

A slow, devious smile crept along her face.

"Then what?" Deacon fumed. "Our fucking hands will be tied! We're just going to sit around and wait—" His face went slack again. "What would you have me do, Detective?"

"Remember Rumpelstiltskin?" I grinned fiercely.

Deacon nodded once and was released.

I pulled out Ushakov's phone and laid it carefully on the ground. The cold and snow wouldn't do it any favors but leaving it behind would reinforce the fiction the phone was in Leyla's workshop. The young hacker glanced at it, then me, and nodded. Deacon, freed from Besim's whatever-the-fuck-that-was, recovered the now flameless truncheon.

We crossed the street, heedless of our safety. My eyes swept the area but saw nothing. Snow wafted around us, an eerie silence descending like the last curtain call from a Greek tragedy. My heart raced, sweat coating my brow despite the cold. The Insight had energized me, but that didn't remove the fear gripping my heart. I held the SMART gun's barrel up, and my other hand raised with an open palm. Deacon and Leyla followed suit. The bookstore windows were thick with frost and fog. I couldn't make out the perp I knew hid beyond the glass. I slowly lowered my empty hand and opened the door. Warmth exhaled around us in a billowing breath, the strains from Tchaikovsky's violin concerto in D major wafting toward us, caught *allegro vivacissimo.*

"That's far enough," a familiar voice wheezed. "Drop your weapons."

"Chuckles!" I greeted the thug with false cheer as I placed the SMART gun on the floor. "What's it like knowing you got your ass kicked by a girl? Didn't think Ivan employed pussies, but who am I to judge?"

His buddies snickered. I glanced to my left then back to Chuckles, using the SMART gun's still-active tactical to gauge distances. The Russian stood behind Besim, his splotchy, bruised face and broken nose a bold testament to the beating he'd taken. The third man leaned against the cast-iron railing at the top of the spiral stairs.

Chuckles glared daggers at me. "Shut the fuck up. Now,

kick gun and baton there." He indicated with his chin. We did as we were told. "Keep hands where I can see them. Dimitri!"

The second man stepped out from behind the bookshelf and moved to frisk each of us. He withdrew our holo-phones, showed them to Chuckles, and placed them in his pocket. Then he bound our hands behind us with my remaining zip ties.

"Clean," Dimitri announced.

"You come forward, slowly," Chuckles instructed. "No sudden moves, or you're all dead. If any cops show, you're all dead. If you don't do as I say, you're—"

"We're all dead," I grumbled. "Yeah, yeah, we get it."

We crossed the floor to Chuckles and Besim. She dwarfed the Russian, more than half a head taller than him. In any other situation, I would've cracked a joke about her taste in men.

"Are you all right?" I asked her instead.

"I am unharmed, Detective Holliday," Besim replied serenely. I noticed her hands were not tied. Despite a gun pressed to her back, she regarded me with her strange almond-shaped eyes without a hint of fear in them.

Leyla sucked in a sharp breath. Abner lay in an unmoving heap just as Besim had described. My heart clenched at the sight, and I nearly lost my nerve, but then the old man coughed twice, a wracking sound full of fluid.

"Let me call an ambulance," I urged. "He needs to go to the hospital."

"Fuck him and fuck you, Holliday. Give me Ushakov's phone. Then maybe we leave." Chuckles ogled Leyla with a sly, sickening grin. "After we have some fun."

"You goddamn sonofabitch!" Deacon roared, his face reddening as the cords around his neck bulged.

"You wanna dance with me, tough guy?" Chuckles taunted. He looked past us. "Dimitri, shoot him."

I heard the cocking of a gun behind me.

"Wait!" I shouted. "You need the phone. That's why we're here. That's the deal I made with Ivan. Shooting any of us won't get you closer to that."

"But it will make me laugh," Chuckles grinned. "So. Where is phone?"

"I have it," Leyla answered. "It's in my workshop. In the basement. I'll get it for you."

Chuckles studied me, suspicion plain on his face. I kept my expression neutral.

"Alexei, go with her," he said.

The third man clambered down the stairs, his gun trained on Leyla. I began a silent count.

"She does anything stupid, shoot her."

Leyla led Alexei into the back room and out of sight.

"Where's Ivan?" I asked, stalling for time.

"Not your business," Chuckles grunted.

"At least let me help Abner."

"No."

"C'mon, man. He's dying."

"So?"

"So? Don't you have a grandfather?" I tested the zip tie binding me, but the plastic bit into both wrists, secured tight. "An uncle? Someone you care about?"

"No."

"What the hell do you think I'm going to do with my hands tied behind my back? For Christ's sake man, he's from the neighborhood!"

"He fucked with the wrong people. Lied to us. He got what he deserves."

"You're a real humanitarian, Chuckles. A goddamn saint."

"Fuck off, Holliday. None of this happens if you hadn't fucked with us."

Suddenly, icy cold bled from the floor and up my legs.

"Now," I said.

"Now?" Chuckles asked curiously.

I shot Besim a meaningful look. "Now."

The Vellan opened her mouth and shrieked.

Despite the small pieces of my torn shirt that I'd pressed into my ears before we left the alleyway, the awful sound of Besim's voice dropped me to my knees. Both Russians planted their hands against the sides of their heads, their faces contorting in agony. Blood burst from Dimitri's nose, and he collapsed against a bookshelf, dragging against it a few feet as he stumbled away. Deacon, seemingly unaffected by the sound, moved quickly to engage the beleaguered Russian. The former Protector kicked Dimitri hard into another bookshelf. The gun tumbled to the floor. Deacon kept at him, roaring unintelligibly as he kicked the other man into bloody submission.

From my knees, I lowered my shoulder and rushed Chuckles, driving him hard against the sales counter. Before he could recover, I swept his legs out from under him, then drove my heel toward his head, but he rolled to the side. Chuckles squeezed the trigger, but the bullet whizzed past, missing me by inches. Heedless of my own safety, I dove atop him, slamming my head into his face, and shattering his already broken nose further with a satisfying crunch. He screamed. Pressing my advantage, I drove my knee into his chest, but he smashed the gun against the side of my head, forcing me off him. Dazed and tasting blood, I lurched against another bookshelf, spilling books to the floor. He fired again, but I dove behind a shelf as the bullets massacred wood and paper. Deacon maneuvered around the other side of the store, ducking low as Chuckles shot at him.

"Come out, Holliday," the Russian jeered. I heard a clip release and the inset click of its replacement.

Peering over the top of the bookshelf, Chuckles had regained his feet, eyes squinting against the blood and bone bits clinging to his face. Besim hovered protectively over Abner, her voice forgotten. Seeing her, Chuckles smiled cruelly and lowered the gun at her head. My heart seized in my throat.

"NO!"

Icy shards of jagged shadow perforated Chuckles, through his chest and throat. A crimson spray showered the checkout desk. The light left his eyes as blood streamed from his mouth, the gun dropping from nerveless fingers. I moved forward and kicked the weapon away.

Besim left Abner to kneel beside Chuckles. She removed his earpiece and holo-phone, then inserted the device in her own ear and activated the phone.

"What are you—" I demanded, but she gestured in a firm, commanding motion for silence.

"We have Pyotr's phone," she said, perfectly mimicking Chuckles' voice. "I killed Holliday myself. They are all dead."

I stared.

"Understood. *Proschay.*" Besim deactivated the phone and placed it and the earpiece in the front pocket of her coat.

"That is one scary neat trick," I huffed, looking wildly around. "Is everyone okay?"

"Doc!" Leyla warned.

In the confusion, I hadn't noticed Dimitri had recovered his gun.

BANG.

I expected the bullet to rip through me, my life blinking to a sudden end, but it didn't. Instead, Dimitri fell backwards, crimson flowering his chest from where he'd been shot.

"Get the hell out of my store," Abner wheezed from behind me, tottering on his feet, Chuckles' gun clutched in both shaking hands.

I raced over as he collapsed into my arms.

31

N ursing my lukewarm coffee in both hands, I sat beside Leyla on the third rung from the bottom of the wrought-iron staircase while Besim's people worked the bookstore. Lying between us was Ushakov's phone. I had retrieved it when I made the call to Doctor Stentstrom. The two thugs I'd incapacitated were long gone. Deacon was near the entrance, issuing animated instructions to the severe-faced woman dressed in a gray suit.

Gaff. Or was it Bryant? I always forgot.

Abner had been stuffed into an Emergency Medical Pod and dispatched to EC General. He hadn't regained consciousness, but both the EMTs and Besim assured me he'd be all right. Stentstrom's people had lugged the two dead Russians from the scene in their own personalized travel rubbers. I explained to him that both had been righteous kills. Stentstrom hadn't questioned any of it. Working with Special Crimes had that effect on people. I'd file the appropriate report with EVI and dish the full details to him when I had the time.

There was no immediate media coverage, either. Apparently, shootings and explosions in Little Odessa didn't generate ratings. I also hadn't reached out to Mahoney. The backup I'd requested earlier never arrived, which told me all I needed to know.

A dozen men and women in gray suits milled about, armed with cloths, brooms, cleaning chemicals and equipment, and the determined efficiency of a well-oiled machine. Abner's clock showed more than two hours had passed since all hell had broken loose in the store. At the speed Besim's people worked, they'd be finished shortly. The consultant had also mentioned replacement bookshelves would arrive tomorrow morning, along with a new stool. I'd smashed Abner's old stool in my tussle with Chuckles. That stunk. Abner had loved that stool.

Any of Abner's higher quality volumes that might have been damaged in the fight had been taken to the Metropolitan Museum. Because of course Besim knew the Head of the Sherman Fairchild Conservator in Charge of Works on Paper there. Didn't everybody?

She'd taken care of everything.

Again.

Besim stood apart, overseeing the restoration with a calm detachment, as if the blood puddle that had belonged to Chuckles was merely an annoying wine stain on her genuine Persian rug. I studied her, and not for the first time attempted to understand who she was and why she was here, all the Guardian of Empire City bullshit notwithstanding. She caught me looking at her, and nodded once without any change in expression, acknowledging the jumbled thoughts billowing in my tired brain. I rolled my eyes in exasperation, then turned my attention to Leyla.

The young hacker leaned forward, elbows on knees, and

her chin cradled in both hands. She stared ahead, nibbling on her lower lip pensively as the events of what had transpired replayed in her mind. Thankfully, the winged shadow hadn't appeared when Leyla turned Chuckles into a *pinata*. One less problem to deal with, for now.

Still, I knew that familiar countenance well. It was part of the job. I hunted murderers, and sometimes coming face-to-face with them ended badly. Killing anyone was never easy, unless you were the type that enjoyed it. Pulling the trigger tested a cop's character, that fundamental part of what made us human. Killing stretched your belief in the sanctity of life, even your place in the world. Some people never shook the doubt, self-recrimination and guilt. They couldn't. They turned in their badge and left the game. They had no choice, if they wanted to function in the so-called "real world". Their new normal was neither new nor normal. Sure, the department helped where they could, offering counseling services and that sort of thing, but it was up to the individual to fight the good fight in their own mind. In their own soul.

At the end of the day, killing was a lonely business.

Imagine my surprise when I discovered you needed people if you wanted to get through it. Even after my old friends and colleagues dumped me, some people still had your back, no matter the circumstances. And those folks, the Abners and Leylas of the world, they were the ones that made the fight bearable, the long days tolerable, and everything that followed, livable. Abner and my grandfather Harry had kept me going after I'd fallen from grace all those years ago, and I wasn't about to let Leyla do the same, either. In my experience, love and compassion didn't solve everything, but they were damn nice things to share.

"How you holding up, kiddo?" I draped my arm gently

over her shoulders. Only a slight chill invaded my touch, bearable for the moment.

"Empty," Leyla whispered, then sighed. "How do you do it, Doc? Does it ever go away?"

"No." I drew her close and kissed the top of her head. "But it does get easier, over time."

"He—" She choked on a sob. Crystal tears glittered down her cheeks. "He was going to kill you. And—"

"And you didn't let him. Remember how you stood up to Marko? You didn't let that thing kill Deacon and me, either."

"But he could have!"

"But he didn't." I gave her shoulder a gentle squeeze. "You're my little sister, Leyla. I will always have your back. Always. And I know you'll always have mine."

I fished my handkerchief from the inner pocket of my blazer and handed it to her. She took it and smiled, then dabbed at her eyes before wiping her nose.

"So, what now?" she sniffled.

"Now, we find out what's so important about Ushakov's phone and why Ivan was willing to murder us to get it back."

Besim glided over, with Deacon a few steps behind her.

"Detective Holliday, the bookstore is secure," she proclaimed. "I also took the liberty of contacting the nearest fire department to extinguish the blaze caused by the destruction of the pod. Should that fire spread, the ensuing damage would become catastrophic."

"Fuck this neighborhood," Deacon grunted sourly. "It could use a good cleansing."

"I was debating calling this one in," I admitted, "but if FDEC is on site containing that fire, protocol requires ECPD to respond, as well. I'll contact Bill and get him to play interference for us." I paused, then gestured broadly at the bookstore. "Thanks, Besim. For this, and for—"

"Your thanks, while appreciated, is not necessary, Detective," Besim answered primly. "The damage wrought here is unfortunate, but not irreparable. My people will see to its complete restoration. And do not fret about the cost. Aurik will 'foot the bill,' I believe is the expression? It is the least I can do."

Leyla surged to her feet and engulfed the much taller woman in a hug. Besim stiffened momentarily, then placed a tentative hand above Leyla's head, fingers extended, unsure what to do. For a moment, her customary aloof mask faltered, revealing a powerful emotion Besim buried everyday behind cold logic, excessive makeup and her personal rebellion against a culture I knew very little about. However, I'd seen her tragic visage before, the devastating loss of her only daughter that she'd kept hidden from everyone, including Deacon.

We exchanged a knowing look.

"Thank you," Leyla cried.

"Of course," Besim managed.

And then the moment was gone, her understated equanimity restored like death and taxes. Leyla released Besim, held her hand an instant longer, then resumed her seat beside me.

"Alexei is still frozen to the wall outside my workshop," Leyla said. "You may want to have someone check on him."

Deacon nodded across the room to Gaffbryant or Bryantgaff or whatever the hell her name was, then pointed to the floor. She somehow knew exactly what he meant and made a beeline past us and into the back room. I shook my head. I really needed to work on my unspoken commands.

I shifted my weight to get more comfortable, then brought Besim up to speed with what we knew.

"I believe someone replaced Calvin with a mutilated

body double," I finished. "Sanarov took the fall, but never talked. I think it's because he made a deal where Flynn took care of his house's mortgage as long as he kept his mouth shut. Thirty years later, and thanks to the Pieces of Eight program, he was released."

"You're skipping the whole vengeful-spirit-in-the-form-of-an-interdimensional-giant-world-eating-spider-murdering-people-and-then-disappearing-without-a-trace-but-leaving-behind-a-bloody-mess part," Leyla pointed out.

"One thing at a time, kiddo," I sighed dramatically.

Besim's eyes narrowed, but she didn't interrupt.

"Thirty years later, Sanarov is released," I plowed ahead. "Meanwhile, Donald Flynn, a key member of the Pieces of Eight program, portrays the role of the bereaved father who has come to terms with the murder of his first-born as if he were poised to walk the red carpet in New Hollywood. Our friendly neighborhood British agent Charlie Sloane mentions something about Flynn's wife dying in a car crash, and Flynn's extended family that has a long and storied history of extreme mental illness. Throw in Ivan's lethal interest in Ushakov's phone, and we've got ourselves one fucked up mess. Oh, and my dad is somehow involved, too. How are these things connected, and why?"

"Perhaps if I understood the importance of the holo-phone, I might be able to ascertain relevant relationships," Besim offered.

Leyla took her cue and said, "Aside from the note about a shipment arriving Thursday, which, in case you were wondering, is today, the only other apparently relevant information on it were a short series of numbers, and what I believe to be the password for an electronic passkey."

She withdrew her holo-phone, made a series of quick commands, then flicked the phone outward as if trying to wipe a bug off the display. One ghostly holo-window hovered before us, a dark screen with three sets of white numbers: *284, 413, 117* and the word *silver.*

"That's it?" Deacon scoffed. "Three fucking numbers? Silver? What the hell does any of it mean?"

Besim stepped toward the floating window, her brow furrowed in concentration.

"How do you figure 'silver' is a passkey?" I asked.

"The code it was embedded in was a continuous loop that produced nothing," Leyla replied. "However, my decryption found a backdoor sub-routine hidden within the loop, behind which was that word. Thankfully, my decryption program is *very* smart, and knew to continue searching, eventually discovering that within the actual letters, there's additional code which corresponds to some real fancy passkey tech, the kind you see the military and top-end corporations use. I bet 'silver' accesses whatever those numbers are. I've just shared the key to the SCU cloud so we all now have access to it."

"SCU cloud?" I blinked in confusion. "When did we get an SCU cloud?"

"I made one right after we closed our first case," the young hacker dimpled with pride. "When you had EVI access my surveillance signal tracking program back in October, I did a little extra work simultaneously behind the scenes to get my fingers inside ECPD. Considering how that bitch Flanagan fucked your AI, I thought it prudent to have our own safety measures in place. Anyway, I've poured our data from our subsequent cases in there, including the kobold jewel thieves, and everything you've investigated to date on this one."

"You hacked into EVI," I said slowly, as the realization of what Leyla had done dawned on me.

Deacon nodded his approval. "Clever."

"Thanks," she beamed at him, then sobered when she caught sight of me. "I haven't done anything with it, Doc. I'm just piggybacking on top of EVI, strictly under your SCU clearance that the captain gave you. Even ECPD's routine diagnostics won't know I'm there."

"It's a damn good idea, Holliday," Deacon added. "Girlie here knows her shit, and SCU could use its own dedicated and secure space."

"Besides, I've got the information bouncing off of at least twelve different satellites, plus several servers hidden throughout Empire City," she said. "Nobody's going to find our cache."

"Sure," I sighed. "You know, you could've told me all this."

"I know." Leyla fidgeted with her phone. "And I've been meaning to, but we've all been so busy, and then this case came along. If it makes you feel any better, anyone that does come looking, I have traps and early warning protocols in place that'll give me plenty of lead time to shut it all down and remove the programs."

Besim ignored us, instead studying the numbers, her arms folded across her chest and the index finger of her right hand tapping her pursed lips.

"Perhaps they are from a bank account?" she posited.

"Too few characters," Leyla replied. "Even if I added in the appropriate zeroes, they don't correspond with any local or international bank. And they don't correspond to any social security number. I thought they might be coordinates on a map, but if they are, two of the three are outside the wall and several hundred miles away. Then I got creative, thought maybe they were astronomical coordinates, but, nope, struck out there, too."

"A mathematical formula of some kind, then?" Besim's frown deepened.

"Nope," Leyla shook her head. "I checked with my cute ex Leigh who used to be in the Applied Mathematics department at ECU, and she confirmed it wasn't from any known formula she's ever seen."

"The shipment arrives Thursday," I muttered aloud. "Wherever Ivan called us from, credits to donuts that's where the shipment is coming in. But a shipment of what? And how is it being transported? Hover-Pod? Rail? Water?"

I paused. The color drained from my face.

"Christ," I swore softly. "That's why he's involved in this."

Deacon nodded as his mouth formed into a grim line.

"Explains a lot," he said.

"Who's involved?" Leyla asked.

"My dad," I replied. "He works at Caron Oceanic Container over in Red Hook. That's why the *bratva* needed him. They must be smuggling something through the container yard, and my dad is the gatekeeper. That place will be an armed encampment."

"What's the play?" Deacon asked.

I glanced at the clock again and said, "Ivan wanted the phone. It must have something to do with this shipment. In the dead of night, and with this weather, the harbor patrols won't be as frequent. We need to get over there, catch them in the act, and find out what they've got coming in or going out."

"Great plan, Holliday, except how the fuck are we getting there?" Deacon lit another cigarette. "Our ride is still on fire. Can Mahoney get us a replacement pod this late? 'Cause we're gonna need us some serious firepower."

"We'll confiscate the guns here," I said. "However, pod travel is just asking for trouble. They're on the lookout for us. No, we need something inconspicuous. Something that nobody will expect."

"None of my local personal conveyances would meet that requirement," Besim said. "However, I could make a few calls and see what I can arrange?"

I was about to agree when Leyla piped in, "I've got a better idea."

She stood up, then moved to the sales counter and rummaged through a variety of drawers, tossing all manner of miscellaneous paraphernalia, writing instruments, and notepads behind her.

"Found 'em!" A set of metal keys jingled merrily in her hand. "Follow me!"

Leyla ran out the back, with Besim trailing her. Deacon barked final orders to his cleanup crew, then he and I gathered up the Russians' weapons and pushed after them.

Outside, an icy wind whipped small flakes into our faces, channeled by the short breezeway that connected a side street to the main drag out front. Leyla turned right, and we followed. Fitful light from the few working lamps along the street gave the impression of a dying search and rescue operation.

After half a block, she turned right again into a short driveway ending at a closed garage door. A heavy padlock and chain wrapped around the handle. Leyla inserted a key and turned it, then yanked off the padlock and chain. With a slight heave, she lifted the garage door. The track must have been greased regularly because the door's rising made little noise. A light winked on inside, revealing a bulky mass covered by an old and grimy blue tarp. The scent of old oil, mildew and rust permeated the air.

"Ta-dah!" Leyla flourished with a grin and a pirouette.

Deacon and I removed the tarp to reveal a large faded

black van with a red racing stripe and a sliding door. I surveyed the vehicle. Several fine spiderweb cracks had matriculated across half the windshield. It was also missing one wiper, and all four hubcaps.

"Meet Stella," Leyla announced happily. "She can go from zero to forty-two in a minute. Less, if she's warmed up. And she can fit up to six comfortably."

"This piece of shit actually runs?" Deacon asked dubiously.

"She sure does," the young hacker affirmed. "So, what do you think?"

"I think we're all going to die," the former Protector stated. "Holliday?"

I ran my hand along the sliding door. "She's perfect. Get in."

32

S tella roared along Ocean Parkway, and Hell followed with her. Or in our case, a thick cloud of dirty exhaust.

The old girl handled like a hooker well past her prime —rough and sloppy. Still, she bravely chewed up the distance we needed to cover, at times losing traction whenever she hit a sneaky patch of black ice along the pitted road. Squinting between the crisscrossed fissures covering Stella's foggy windshield, I somehow maneuvered around what little gas-powered traffic there was without getting us killed.

The ancient heating system had failed two minutes after we had cleared the garage. But who needed heat when the joyful threat of imminent doom lurked behind each and every goddamn pothole I managed to hit along the way?

Deacon occupied the front passenger seat, entombed within a gray cloud of cigarette smoke. He studied the layout of Caron Oceanic Container on his holo-phone, anticipating Ivan's security measures.

"When did you learn to drive one of these things?" he

asked after a long drag, seemingly unconcerned for our safety or my considerable lack of driving prowess.

"My grandfather," I replied. My teeth clacked together audibly as I found yet another bump in the road. "He taught me right after I turned sixteen. Stick and automatic. He used to say Renaissance men were a dying breed, so he showed me a bunch of things, including how to change a flat. Unfortunately, he sold the car to some antique car aficionado in Brooklyn right after I joined the Police Academy. He said the maintenance was killer, so he had to get rid of it."

"The only thing mine ever showed me was how to dress whatever we'd killed on the land he owned a few miles outside of Mercy," the former Protector said. "Did a lot of walkin' and ridin', but ain't never done no drivin'. What kind of ride was it?"

"An off-colored green Buick Skylark convertible whose top mechanicals never worked properly," I answered with a fond, if shaky smile. "Every spring and summer, we'd roll along the Brighton Beach Boardwalk 'cruisin' for *shiksas*.' That's, um, Yiddish for non-Jewish girls. Anyway, he always said they looked better in bikinis than the ladies at his bridge club. Man, I miss that car. V6 engine, a manual 3-gear box, and handled like a dream. But no posi-traction."

"Posi-whatsit?" he asked.

"Posi-traction," I repeated. "You never got stuck in Birmingham mud? It's, oh, never mind. What you got there?"

"Looks like there're three roads in and out of Caron," Deacon replied. He adjusted the controls to increase the size of the satellite imagery displaying roads and buildings in the area around the container yard. I stole quick glances at the glowing map hovering above his phone while maintaining my tenuous control of Stella. I didn't want EVI showing me the route while I drove. I figured running us off the road before we had a chance to uncover Ivan's operation at Caron Container was a bad idea.

Because I'm smart like that.

"If Saranda convinced Ivan we're all dead, his security will be tight, but they won't be lookin' for us," the Confederate continued. "Drop me off at the corner of Imlay and Bowne. There's a lot of real estate for them to cover, and I know how to move quiet-like. I'll get in and find a spot high up where I can keep an eye on things. You come in from the northeast along Van Brunt. I reckon the place is fenced with wire, but girlie here can freeze part of it so you can get in. Then she and Saranda stay in the van, in case shit goes sideways, which, this bein' us, it probably will."

"I'm coming with Doc," Leyla proclaimed from the bench seat behind us. She'd set up her portable rig next to her as she tried to solve the riddle of the numbers. "I'm not sitting this one out."

"Girlie, these Russians got orders to shoot-to-kill," Deacon said, lighting a new cigarette. "Didn't the bookstore teach you nothin'?"

"I'm not leaving Doc," she said with a stubborn frown.

"Your funeral," Deacon replied before jabbing his fingers that gripped the cigarette at me. "And your fucking responsibility. Again."

"What else is new," I muttered darkly. "Leyla, stick close to me, okay? I'm working on something with EVI that will help us get in there. Any luck with those numbers?"

"Nope," she said. "I've checked phone directories in thirty different enclaves so far, and the numbers don't correspond to anything. Twenty-two more to go! My rig will ping my phone if the program gets any hits."

"What about your dad?" Deacon asked grimly.

I pointed at the largest structure inside the yard located

closest to the main entrance. "Pop's the night watchman and should be in the central administration building, there. He'll have access to all the surveillance cameras, recent cargo manifests, and communications. At a guess, he's directing traffic and keeping the waterways clear in case harbor patrol or the Coast Guard decide to show up. We sneak to the admin building, and then I'll get Pop talking, find out what the hell is going on."

"He let those motherfuckers into his house, Holliday," Deacon pointed out. "What makes you think he won't sell you out again?"

I frowned. "Pop is an alcoholic and a bully, but he's not stupid. He'll weigh the odds that I brought back-up with me, and that Ivan's whole operation is about to go down in flames. He'll cooperate."

"And if he still don't?"

"Then I'll give him no choice."

"Fair enough," Deacon said, then spoke over his shoulder. "Saranda you're stayin' put. You're the only one on the outside in case we need a quick evac. You got that? Saranda?"

Besim's soft voice floated to us from the back of the main cab behind the first row of seats.

"I will not attempt entry into the container yard unless granted permission to do so." The consultant sounded distracted, but I chalked it up to her focus on the investigation. She hadn't said a word since we left Abner's.

"Should we have a code word in case we run into trouble?" Leyla asked.

"Yeah," Deacon growled. "It's called 'help.' Just keep your fucking head down, girlie. Thanks to Holliday, we ain't got no backup around to yank our nuts from the fire."

Everyone lapsed into an uneasy silence. I concentrated

on my driving. I'd chosen not to call the Organized Crime Taskforce, gambling that the *bratva's* potential connections inside ECPD would tip them off about our plan. I grimaced at the thought. Although EVI's security had received a significant upgrade after the discovery that the late Lieutenant Joan Flanagan had compromised her programming last October, not all ECPD was rotten, but many of these criminal organizations thrived despite the department's best efforts. I couldn't risk it.

Not for the fifth time since we left Abner's, I wished for coffee and a heaping plate of Uncle Mortie's chocolate rugelach. I was running on a steady diet of Sunshine Starshine donuts and coffee. Working homicide cases had their drawbacks, like fighting bio-engineered vampires, getting blown up by Russians, and a distinct lack of good coffee whenever you needed it. Maybe that's why I was so skinny?

I pulled off the road and drove along quiet side streets until we reached our destination. Deacon hopped out and surveyed the snowy area before moving around the van. He opened the back to retrieve the Russian's missile launcher and slung the strap around his chest.

"If bad shit goes down, I'm lighting this place up like a fucking Christmas tree," he stated. "Keep your eyes open, stay smart, and don't fuck anything up."

He shut the door and disappeared along the street in the direction of the yard, melting into the drifting snow and darkness like he was born to it.

I turned the van around and retraced my route. After several minutes, I picked up I-278 and drove north to give us some distance before steering Stella on an indirect path back to Van Brunt. I parked in an abandoned lot between two ramshackle buildings that were once affordable housing by the looks of them. Boarded up windows and empty doorways that were covered with grime and snow gave the illusion of two headless, eyeless mutes left for dead. A few pinpricks of light inside the top floor of one suggested life of some kind. I killed the engine but left the keys in place, then turned to my passengers.

"I do not like this, Detective," Besim said. She stood in the back, bent at the waist to prevent her head from touching the van's roof. "There is a foulness to this place. And something else..."

Her voice trailed off. The Insight had lain dormant since the fight at Abner's ended. The moment I parked Stella, it stirred, sensing something, a strange familiarity I couldn't place.

"I haven't forgotten Calvin or the One," I said. "They're still out there, and if I'm right, the One's clock is ticking. Whatever bargain Calvin made with it is coming to a head. We need to stay sharp, just like Deacon said. But if the shit hits the fan, I want you to leave Stella and call your people to get you the hell out of here."

Leyla slid the door open and hopped outside.

"I understand, Detective." Besim nodded. "*Fortune favors the bold.*"

"More like the foolish," I returned with a half-smile.

Arctic wind mixed with the salty tang of the nearby harbor cut through my clothing. Leyla and I stole along a row of buildings, shunning the light. The container yard had floodlights, but they were directed inside to provide ample illumination. Out here, it was a ghost town. Municipal plows had left piles of hard-packed snow hunched in ugly, darkened lumps to allow for the passage of occasional ground traffic. The nearest Metro station was several blocks east. Across the street, a twenty-foot-tall chain-linked fence

topped with barbed wire and covered in a privacy windscreen ran the length of Van Brunt. I paused in a breezeway
between two darkened buildings. Leyla, my shorter shadow,
kept close to my side.

"EVI," I breathed quietly aloud. "Please tell me I have
access."

"Affirmative, Detective Holliday," she replied.
"Uploading the data to your retinal interface now."

"Patch it thru to all registered SCU devices."

The same satellite imagery that had appeared on
Deacon's phone now filled my visual center. However, this
feed was live, directed from one of Empire City's Perimeter
Defense satellites. Overlaid on top of it were red heat signa-
ture dots—twenty-two in total. Twelve were arrayed evenly
around the perimeter of the yard near the fence. They were
stationary, which I took to be a good sign. Nine clustered at
the edge of the quay by a trio of enormous container cranes,
heavy-duty equipment resembling elephant trunks each
capable of lifting several tons. A lone dot nestled inside a
small group of containers.

"Swanky," Leyla marveled, concealing her phone behind
my back to prevent the glow from exposing us. "How'd you
get this?"

"Made a call to my buddy Jon Scarl with Perimeter." I
leaned against the frigid brick of the building for support.
Even with EVI stuffed inside my head, I needed an extra
minute to acclimate to the additional data stream overtaking
my synapses. "He's a commander now, does external sweeps
hunting Jumpers with a bunch of trigger-happy lunatics.
You'd like Scarl. He's Deacon, except fatter, meaner and
missing an eye."

"My kind of guy," Leyla chuckled.

"Deacon, Besim, you two getting this?" I asked.

"Yes, Detective," the consultant replied. "I shall continue monitoring your situation from here."

"Nice work, Holliday." The Confederate's feed crackled with static. "I'm between two container walls, about thirty yards west of the target. They're packin' semi-automatics, probably connected wirelessly with earpieces, too, so keep that in mind. They're careful, but they ain't paranoid, so I reckon Ivan still thinks we're dead."

"Understood," I said. "Going dark. See you on the other side."

"Copy that."

"Now what?" Leyla asked me.

"We look for the weak point and get inside."

I studied a section of fence on the map that had demonstrated no red dot movement, then gestured for Leyla to follow. After another half-block, we crossed the street, using the snow piles for cover. Thin flakes fell from above, hinting at further accumulation. I drew the SMART gun and kept watch. Leyla used her holo-phone to illuminate the windscreen before us.

"Doesn't feel like there's current here," she observed, kneeling before the fence. "This shouldn't take long."

The temperature around me dropped. Snow froze and ice splintered. My eyes teared, and I couldn't stop my body from shivering. Leyla placed her outstretched right hand against the windscreen, then lowered her head in concentration. A blue and white nimbus materialized around her hand, as if she wielded winter's power itself. Maybe she did. The glow saturated both fabric and metal. She drew her fingers in a circle three times. With each pass, the glow brightened. I hoped no one saw it from the opposite side or my plan was toast.

She exhaled slowly. "Done."

I released my breath, unaware I'd been holding it, my shoulders bunched in knots. The glow dispersed. I stowed the gun and reached forward with fingers and thumb. When I touched the windscreen, it shattered in a thousand tiny fragments. The metal links of the fence snapped with little effort.

"Now comes the fun part," I said.

I tore a hole large enough for us to pass through. Leyla went first, saying nothing, her blue eyes tracking the area, and I followed on her heels. A horn blared forlornly in the distance. The floodlights were fewer here.

We found ourselves in a graveyard for misfit cargo transport toys. Trucks of all shapes and sizes were arranged in haphazard clusters, many of them in severe disrepair. Rust covered most of them, their empty windshields grinning at us like crazed ghouls. Stacks of unused rubber tires more than twice my height filled the section closest to our destination. I consulted the map. None of Ivan's goons had moved in our direction, although several had shifted positions. We snaked through the bones of long-dead trucks and into the maze of tires, keeping low, until we reached the end of the line. About a hundred feet to our right was a single-story building with closed bay doors which housed the yard's maintenance and repair facility. Half that distance and directly across from our position was a split two-story brick affair. The black and red logo of Caron Container was painted across one broad wall. Exterior lights were bright, exposing any incoming or outgoing traffic, although nothing was currently in view. An uneasy feeling settled over me. I was missing something, some small detail, but I couldn't remember what.

"We're in," I whispered through the comm. "Looks like we'll have a ten-second window to cross the open stretch between here and the admin building. Should be plenty of time, right?"

"Yeah, unless one of them turns around," Deacon growled. "Don't fuck this up, Holliday."

"No pressure," I muttered.

Leyla and I huddled in the shadow of the tire wall, waiting. The horn sounded again, closer than before. A ship was coming into port. All the dots by the cranes converged on one of the berths. Two guards halted their movements at the corner of our side of the repair shop. A minute went by, but they hadn't moved. Instead, they lit up cigarettes and became locked in conversation. The snowfall increased, and with it, my anxiety.

"I have an idea," Leyla said. She bowed her head. No white and blue glow this time. The wind off the harbor grew in intensity, whipping into us despite the partial cover afforded by the tire stacks. It billowed with a strange ebb and flow, as if directed, which was precisely what Leyla intended.

She extended a hand, then slowly drew her fingers from left to right across her body. A strong gust swirled around the two men, shoving both against the building. Startled, the two men scrambled forward, then rounded the corner of the building to use the wall as a buffer against the breeze.

A whisper brushed my mind.

Here.

"Did you say something?" I looked at Leyla.

"No." The young hacker regarded me, the blue irises of her eyes scintillatingly bright. "Let's go."

She reached for my hand which I took, shocked by the intense cold racing up my arm. Lurching forward, Leyla and I loped across the open ground, exposed and vulnerable, the wind buffeting the yard. My heart pounded hard enough I

thought it'd burst from my chest. I kept my eyes on the door
to the admin building. No sudden squall of screaming cats
tore us to pieces. No outcry of discovery. Nothing.

At the building, I grabbed the door handle and yanked,
but it was locked. Leyla pressed a glowing hand against the
lock. I heard something snap. She pushed the door inward
and we slipped inside the lit foyer. After passing through a
short series of corridors, we made it to the door outside the
control room. That's when it hit me. I'd forgotten about the
exterior cameras on the admin building itself. I was
reaching for my gun when I heard another cocked from
behind us.

"That's far enough."

33

"Put it on the floor," Pop ordered. "And keep your hands where I can see them. You too, girl. Now, turn around. Slowly."

I lowered the SMART gun, never taking my eyes off him. Pop wore his work uniform, a brown and yellow canvas jumpsuit with plenty of pockets to stow small bottles of gin, or whatever the fuck he decided to drink during his shift. He held his old 9mm, and by the looks of it, probably the only clean thing he kept at the house. Pop's hand shook, but his bloodshot eyes were alert.

"Security cam, right?" I asked. "On the corner of the building? I knew I'd missed something."

"For all the book smarts you got at that goddamn university, you've never really been that bright, Tommy," Pop sneered. "And who's your little girlfriend? She another sorry piece of ass from rehab that you fooled into thinking you're some kind of hero? Well, I've got news for you, sweetheart, Tommy's just like me—a whole lot of nothin'. He's just too stubborn to see it."

My temper flared, erasing the chill from my limbs, but I

held it in check. Leyla remained silent, although I felt the temperature drop several degrees.

"Probably the only thing we have in common," I returned.

Pop flinched as if I'd struck a nerve. I felt a perverse pleasure in hurting him, but one pointed look from Leyla brought me back to the present.

"Ain't nobody convergin' on your position yet, Holliday," Deacon said quietly through my earpiece. "Container ship's coming in, though. Reckon you got ten, maybe fifteen minutes, tops. Say the word, and I'll take him out."

I ignored Deacon and mentally set EVI to record.

"Sounds like a ship's out there," I said. "Let me guess. You cook-the-books so nobody sees anything, right? Control the entry logs, allay any curious call-ins, that sort of thing?"

Pop puffed out his chest. "It's an important job. Ivan doesn't just let anyone do it."

"Wow, Pop, does Ivan pat you on the head, too? You must be very proud. I know I am."

He flexed his arm so that the gun was now pointed at my face.

"Where's the welcoming committee?" I glanced around nonchalantly, lowering my arms to shoulder height. "I knew you were a first-class asshole Pop, but I never thought you'd sell out your own son for a bottle of booze."

"I had no choice!" Pop wiped his nose with his other hand. "They swore they weren't going to hurt you. They said you had some property of theirs, and they wanted it back. What was I supposed to do?"

"Wrap this shit up, Holliday," Deacon warned.

"I'm surprised they're not already here," I said, feeling time's fingers crawling down my back. "I figured you put in the call to Ivan the moment you saw us on your feed."

"I'll call him when I'm fucking ready," Pop retorted. "And get your hands higher!"

"What is it, then?" I demanded, ignoring the order.

"I said, put your hands up, Tommy!"

I shook my head. "Or what? You'll shoot us? I don't think so. What's really going on, Pop? You looking to impart some long overdue fatherly wisdom on me? That'd be a joke. Tell me I made a mistake in coming here? That you won't be able to protect me from the *bratva* anymore? Maybe put a cigarette out on my arm, just for old time's sake?"

"Fuck you, Tommy," he said. "I warned you back at the house. Told you I was on borrowed time. But you wouldn't listen. You never have."

"Borrowed time?" I barked in derision. "What is this, some holo-show melodrama? Is this the part where you tell me that you have a fatal disease and only weeks to live?"

His face soured with contempt. "I don't have some goddamn disease. Jesus Christ, Tommy!"

"Then tell me what the hell it is that you want."

Pop washed a nervous hand across his jaw and cheek. I'd catch him stealing glances through the long window and into the control room behind us. What was his game? Why was he doing this? And what was up with that strange whispering I'd heard outside?

Suddenly, the Insight simmered, prowling at the periphery, in anticipation of something. But what?

"Tommy, you still don't get it," Pop said, his face wrung with a mixture of worry and frustration. "Did you ever get in trouble, in *serious* trouble, growing up? Of course not. Because you were protected. Protected by me. Protected by my position in the organization. Anytime the cops picked you up, Harry bailed you out, but I kept all that bad shit from you. Me, Tommy. Not Harry, not Abner, and especially not goddamn John holier-than-thou Davis. It was me. You were always an ungrateful punk. I gave you a roof, a bed, three square meals, and this is the thanks I get? Jesus H. Christ."

"You think I owe you?" I jeered. "What a crock of shit! News flash, Pop, you're not some concerned dad hoping to keep his son out of jail through tough love. You're a two-bit, low-level scumbag working for an organization built by greed and blood. But maybe you're right, Pop. Maybe I've been looking at this whole thing all wrong. Maybe I should thank you. I mean, without you and mom's murder, I never would have become a goddamn cop in the first place!"

"I get it," he said. His voice quavered with anger and regret. "I wasn't the greatest father figure, what with working all the time, and your mom gone. But I tried, Tommy. I really tried so hard."

"YOU?" I roared incredulously. "I lived in fear every day of my life after Ma died! How drunk were you going to be tonight? When was I going to get hit or burned or ignored? Jesus, Pop, if it weren't for Harry and Abner, I'd be dead! *You* tried? Spare me your sanctimonious bullshit, please!"

"Doc—" Leyla began, but Pop cut her off.

"Shut the fuck up, girl!"

"Don't you dare talk to her, Pop, or I swear I'll—"

"You'll do what, Tommy?" He stepped forward so that the gun was inches away. "I've got the gun. This is my turn. Mine! Just shut up for once and listen! Okay? Just listen."

"Fine, Pop," I relented. "You've got my attention. I won't make any trouble, okay?"

He stared at me, struggling with whatever it was he wanted to say. However, despite his white-knuckled grip on the gun, I didn't think he would shoot.

"You know," he began in a hoarse whisper, "every time I

looked at you, every time you gave me lip. Every single goddamn time, all I'd see was her."

"We both know the *bratva* murdered Ma," I hissed with barely suppressed rage, trying to maintain a level tone. "Maybe it wasn't Ivan, but it was one of his gang. And someday soon, I'm going to put whoever did it in the ground."

The approaching ship's horn sounded again, two long bursts followed by a quick one, then repeated twice, what must be a coded signal to Ivan and his men waiting on the pier.

The Insight sharpened in response, intensifying my senses. I heard Pop's heartbeat, the tonal quality of his words, and the slight click of his thumb as it trembled against the trigger. I felt Leyla's unease, her concern for me overshadowing her apprehension about the container yard, and something else, some other consciousness, subtle, dark and mysterious underlying it all.

I saw Pop through the Insight's mystical lens, a broken, flawed man, whose alcoholism, guilt and remorse had consumed him ages ago. His pain was palpable and raw, a rotting sweetness laced with spilled blood and irredeemable regret. The sickness of his addictions clawed deep, dredging up my own sordid past. Revulsion, bitterness, doubt, shame, anger, and so many other thoughts, all old, familiar bedfellows of mine. It had taken Harry, Abner and Leyla, my turn at Wallingbrooke, my love for Kate, her suicide, and the arrival of Mahoney and the others to set me straight again. But these images and sensations weren't anything I didn't already know about Pop or myself. There was more here, but whatever it was, I couldn't see it.

"That's where you're wrong, Tommy," Pop said. "You've

always been wrong about that. I protected you from the truth."

The Insight pushed, growing more insistent, its silver fire coursing through my mind, urging me to move beyond this wretched man. Yet, nothing changed. Pop remained an aging, squat, ruined sack of shit that used to beat me for failing to take out the trash on Thursday nights. He treated me as the unwanted burden he'd never asked for, the surviving legacy of a murdered wife. So much time wasted, growing up in an empty household devoid of a parent's compassion and love. A dismal place where my upbringing was ignored in favor of Pop's never-ending search for solace and the sweet oblivion found in every drop he drank.

Fire burned in my gut, in that place where you hid all your innermost hatred and rage. My eyes narrowed as I studied Pop. He could drop dead of a heart attack, and I wouldn't care. He didn't deserve my piss on his grave, let alone anyone remembering him long after he was gone. My body trembled, and I became vaguely aware of Deacon's voice in my ear, but I couldn't hear him. Hot blood pounded in my ears, drowning out everything. My hands balled into fists. Right then, all I wanted was to beat Pop until there was nothing left but a pulpy mess.

"Doc!" Leyla shouted from a great distance. "What are you doing?"

She gripped one of my arms. Cold careened through me, but my rage remained immune to her icy touch. I snarled, an animal's sound without words, but replete with meaning. Leyla spun me around, her clear blue eyes beseeching mine.

"Doc," she pleaded.

Heartbeats passed. I stared through her. Twisted and bent, the dark thing that thundered inside me craved its release. I wanted to give in, unleash my savage rage, satiate my overwhelming desire to hurt this man, this putrid piece of dog shit, and delight in his ruin.

I took a menacing step toward him.

"Please," Leyla said.

Intense cold shot up my arm. I faltered as two more freezing bursts followed in quick succession. The shock to my system reset my faculties, and the world crashed back into focus. Blinking rapidly, I sucked in several breaths. Leyla released my arm. My hands unclenched. My heart rate slowed. Sound returned to normal. Understanding slowly dawned on me as I realized what I had nearly done, and why.

There was no opposite number, no external force working against me or the Insight's power. Nor was the clairvoyance acting mysterious or fickle, as it had so many instances before. There was nothing else at play here, no hidden, unknown magic deliberately obfuscating the truth.

The Insight wasn't showing me everything because it wouldn't. It wasn't showing me everything because it couldn't.

My anger had clouded my perception, impairing my judgment. Deacon had been right. I was too close to the situation, too emotionally invested in my confrontation with Pop to see the forest for the trees. Gustavo Sanarov, the One, Charlie, Mahoney, Father Jack, Calvin and Donald Flynn, none of them had influenced my ability to see the truth. It was my stubborn refusal to push past my own prejudices and allow the Insight into the walled off parts of myself that I'd kept remote from everyone. For the Insight to reveal the truth about Pop, I first had to accept one very ugly truth about myself.

Despite everything this man had ever done to me, all the

pain and suffering at his hands, the arguments, the fighting and the silence, at the heart of it all, he was family.

My family.

And the one thing I cherished above all else, the one bright spot in my life, the memories I'd clung to which had helped steer me through the worst moments of my life, was family. My mother and grandfather, Kate, Father Jack, Abner, Leyla and Deacon, they were all a part of that family. And, yet, in some strange, twisted sense, Pop was, too.

Because no matter how much I hated him, John Holliday was still my father.

I exhaled, giving in to the Insight, allowing its magic to purge the fury from my system. Pop stepped back, unsure of what was happening, his gun now pointed at the floor. He had no knowledge of the Insight, but I could only imagine what he saw when he looked at me.

"A little more than kin, and less than kind," I whispered.

As my mental balance returned, I focused on what the Insight had been trying to show me. My eyes widened with surprise. I had expected the magic to reveal a monster, perhaps another *fetch,* some hideous thing that had grafted itself to Pop, the root of all his evil. But that wasn't it. Instead, a tiny pinpoint of brilliance flashed in his chest, a beacon of light that radiated a powerful emotion.

Love.

It was the love he still nurtured for my mother. A pure and unquenchable flame. It filled me with warmth and compassion, and a tenderness Pop had never shown me. A rush of images came to me, and time slowed to a crawl. I witnessed a catalogue of touching moments between my parents before they were married, each one now an indelible and beautiful imprint on my soul.

Yet, soldered to that, marring everything and tainting the

memories with violence, was an unforgivable betrayal I could not discern. One striking instance—a heated argument between the two of them in the same living room where my mother's body would later be found that same day—that had pushed Pop to become the man who stood before me now.

The Insight evaporated, leaving me enervated. My knees buckled. Leyla reacted, grabbing me under the shoulder to prevent my sudden collapse. I looked up. Pop's eyes were lost to memory and pain, both arms lowered, the gun no longer pointed at me.

"What the hell are you talking about?" I whispered hoarsely.

"Elaine was an angel," Pop answered, his anger gone. "She saw the good in people, to a fucking fault. She trusted them too much. I loved your mother, Tommy. I know you don't believe me, but it's true. It killed me to know about..." He trailed off, struggling to find the words.

"Know about what?" I asked.

"It doesn't matter anymore," he muttered, almost to himself.

"Pop, I don't understand. What aren't you telling me? What doesn't matter?"

"The ship is almost here, son," Pop smiled sadly. "Denning will call in soon. I need to be at the desk when he does. There's no time. Get inside. Please."

Pop surrendered his gun to Leyla, then moved past us and into the control room. With Leyla's help, I regained my feet, my energy slowly returning.

"You okay?" she asked, her concern evident.

"I don't know," I replied shakily. "The Insight tried to show me something, but I couldn't understand it. And the things he was saying! What the hell is going on?"

34

My legs wobbled as Leyla and I entered a heated space that reminded me of archival footage from the long-defunct control rooms at NASA. On the opposite wall hovered a dozen large holo-screens that cycled through various grainy angles of the container yard. At the room's center was the command module. It rested on a thin metal platform ten feet above an otherwise empty floor. A broad staircase accessed the platform, which held little more than the operator's workstation, a high-backed office chair on rollers, and a trash can. I followed Pop up the stairs, gripping the railing as if my life depended on it. Leyla had to push me the final few steps. I sank gratefully into the chair and looked around.

The workstation was the centerpiece for the yard's integrated command center. The operator controlled a variety of quayside robotic cranes, as well as self-driving flatbed trucks used to transport containers to and from the yard. A wireless joystick with three buttons—white, blue and red—sat on the desk next to an open holo-phone. The enlarged holo-screen hovering above it spat logistical data across its surface. From the platform, Pop supervised the automated loading and unloading of containers in the stacking areas, as well as vessel traffic services. The joystick offered him manual-override capability for all the external operating machinery should their auto-function run into any problems. This included the heavy gantries at the end of the quay as well as the various tractors, reach-stackers, forklifts and other terminal yard vehicles. However, Pop's primary responsibilities revolved around perimeter security. If he saw anything out of the ordinary, it was his job to call it in to the EC Port Authority.

Or Ivan Kruchev.

"Now what?" I rubbed my legs to get the blood flowing again.

Pop pointed at the landline and said, "Denning is calling any minute. No imaging, so he won't see you. Just keep quiet and let me do the talking."

"Are they picking up or dropping off?" Leyla asked. She studied the module's controls with interest.

"Picking up," Pop replied. "Three containers tonight. That's a big shipment for them. Usually, it's one or two. They must really need to move something."

"Do you know what's in them?" I asked.

He shifted his weight. I arched an eyebrow.

"It's need-to-know," he replied defensively. "They don't tell me, and I don't ask. I'm here to watch the yard and make sure the gantries do their job. Then I download the information to a micro-drive, wipe the logs and reset everything."

"Sounds like hard work, Pop."

"It's a living."

"Not a good one."

"Don't start with me again, boy."

"Come on, Pop, you must have some idea what's—"

The phone rang, a jarring sound that echoed throughout the room. Pop shushed me, then activated it with a quick wave of his hand before I could respond.

"Johnny H, we a go?"

The familiar baritone of Orlando Denning came through clear, as if he were standing in the room with us.

"Event site is clear," Pop replied nervously. "Advise parcels."

There was a pause on the other line.

"Everything okay up there, buddy?" Denning asked.

"All good." Pop offered me a crooked smile. His flushed face beaded with sweat. "Just came back from the john. Fucking pipes froze again."

"No shit," Denning chuckled. "I damn near froze my nuts off waiting for the boat! When we're done here, I'm coming by. Brought a bottle of something tasty for us. To celebrate."

"Celebrate what?" Pop asked.

"This is the Big One, my man!" Denning crooned. "The one we been waitin' for! We are gonna get *paid*! I'll explain when I get there."

"Uh...um...yeah, you better not come by, O," Pop spluttered. "I couldn't flush the can so the whole place stinks. It's real bad here. I'm gonna have to plunge it, man."

"Well, then clean that shit up," Denning said as he chortled at his own dumb joke. "I can wait. The boys here said the cargo is special, so it'll take longer than usual to get everything settled before they shove off again."

An accented voice in the background spoke to Denning, but I couldn't hear what was said.

"Okay, okay. I got this." Denning sounded rushed. There was a pause before he came back on the line. "We're on the clock, Johnny. Parcels are two-eight-four, four-one-three and eleven-seven. Confirm."

Pop shot me a "What-the-fuck-do-I-do-now look?". I rolled my hand, then gestured at the console. He nodded, inhaled, and blew out air in a low gust. Glancing at the scrolling data, Pop manipulated the workstation controls. The screen's streaming halted, focusing on three numbers highlighted in yellow. One of the large wall screen's images shifted, providing a view of three stacked containers shrouded in shadow. A large gantry crane appeared in the distant background, and beyond it, the dark and rusted hull of a container ship.

Here.

The whisper caught me off guard. Suddenly, the Insight rushed into me. I jolted upright. My scalp tingled. Energy filled my body. I stared at the holo-screen as the external camera zoomed in on the numbers painted in white at the upper right of each container.

Two-eight-four.

Four-one-three.

Eleven-seven.

"Holy shit!" Leyla exclaimed when she caught sight of the numbers.

"Repeat, Johnny H," Denning piped up. "You say something?"

"Uh, negative, O," Pop stammered, the color drained from his face. "Just mumbling to myself."

"Well, hurry it up, Johnny. We got some antsy folk here wanting to get out of the cold."

"Copy that. Just give me a second."

I waved Pop to continue. He nodded uncertainly.

"Uh, parcels two-eight-four, four-one-three and eleven-seven, confirmed," Pop said.

"Load 'em up and send 'em over, Johnny H!" Denning shouted with glee. "Let's get this party started!"

"You got it. Activating transport."

Pop killed the call. He ran a trembling hand across his jaw.

"*He repays everyone for what they have done,*" I murmured, awestruck by what was on the screen. "*And no creature is hidden from his sight, but all are naked and exposed to the eyes of him to whom we must give account. And when they have finished their testimony, the beast that rises from the bottomless pit will make war on them and conquer them and kill them.*"

"The Scripture!" Deacon exploded in my ear. "It's a fucking code!"

"That couldn't be part of Calvin's bargain with the One," Leyla said. "It doesn't fit. What do those containers have to do with his murder?"

"No idea, kiddo," I said, thinking furiously, "but Calvin wants us to keep them in Empire City. Pop, where is that stack?"

"Not too far," he replied. Using the workstation controls, he extended his fingers so one hand was splayed wide. The image holding the container stack expanded exposing more of its surroundings. Leyla showed him the yard map on her phone.

He pointed a finger at a section of it and said, "Go out the back and you'll be there in a couple of minutes. Once I activate the robot, it'll take another five to load and secure the containers onto the flatbed, then five more to the quay."

I had EVI assign a red "X" to the spot Pop had indicated. The approaching ship appeared as a giant blip. I counted ten more heat dots on its deck. Combining them with the numbers in the yard, we were woefully outgunned, if it came down to a fight. And it always came down to a fight.

We needed help. Whether it would get here in time was a different problem.

"EVI, please contact Port Authority and let them know we have a potential situation over at Caron Container," I ordered aloud. "Tell them there is a ship pulling in that is under suspicion of having a falsified registration and manifest and engaged in smuggling operations. I count thirty hostiles on board and at the yard, and all are presumed armed and dangerous. Have them get over here as soon as they can. Give them whatever the hell Mahoney uses to identify SCU to push it through."

"Affirmative, Detective," she replied in my ear.

"Deacon, head over to the cranes and keep an eye on Ivan and that ship," I continued. Pop started dry washing his hands. "The moment he detects anything wrong, we need to move fast."

"Copy that," Deacon said.

"Decision time," I addressed Pop quietly. "I need to get into the containers without Ivan knowing. Whatever they're doing, it's connected to your old pals Gus Sanarov and Pyotr Ushakov. You can turn us in, or you can let us do our job."

He dug his hands into his pant pockets, a deep frown furrowing his brow.

"Think about that murdered kid," I pressed. "Calvin Flynn. The little boy Sanarov paid time for. He's part of what's going on here. Whoever really murdered him, I can't let them walk, Pop. I can't. It's too much like what happened to Ma. Help me, Pop. Help me catch Calvin Flynn's killer."

John Holliday hesitated, his frantic, bloodshot eyes working the room, weighing his options as his mind struggled to choose between his fucked-up loyalties. Pop glanced at my hand, then up to my face, finally registering the stern resolve he found there.

"Pop, I need your help," I urged, then softened my tone. "Please."

"Okay, Tommy," he nodded. "For that kid. I'll do it for the kid. I'll stall a few more minutes, but that's it."

"It'll be enough." I squeezed his arm before releasing it. "Thank you."

He hesitated, then asked, "You still have Ushakov's phone on you?" I narrowed my eyes as I pulled it from my pocket. He gestured at the holo-window with the three containers. "It's a key. Ushakov uses it to unlock their containers. Ivan has one, too. Each container has a numeric randomizer combination lock. You bring this to one of the locks and it activates the opening sequence."

"It only generates the correct sequence when it's in contact with the lock it's meant to open?" Leyla asked.

"That's right," he said.

"Pop, I don't know what to say," I began, taken aback. Perhaps there was hope for him after all? "I'll make sure to keep you out of the prosecution's crosshairs. But if Ivan finds out, he'll—"

"Go fuck yourself, Tommy." He pierced me with a sullen glare, his voice laden with scorn. "Fuck the ECPD and Special Crimes, too. I'm not doing it for you. I'm doing it for them. For Gus and that kid. Gus deserved better. That kid, too. Maybe this'll help even things up a little."

There we go. Just when I'd harbored the slimmest, slightest hope, the universe kicked me square in the cookies again. I'll never learn.

"The back door's over there." Pop pointed to his right at a darkened doorway beneath the screen holding the container stack image. "Oh, and one more thing. Hit me with the gun. At least make it look like I stood up to you. Because if you fuck this up, I'm dead too."

I stared at him. He didn't meet my eyes. So many things I could say but wouldn't. Because there was no point.

"Get your ass in gear, Holliday," Deacon said. "I'm nearly in position."

Leyla handed me Pop's gun. I held it a moment, then placed it on the table by the joystick. Without looking back, I led Leyla down the stairs, across the floor and through the doorway. A short, faceless corridor ended at a heavy metal door with a single barred window. The yard map showed no one nearby.

I pushed the door open slowly, the SMART gun at the ready. Frigid air accosted us. The thin flakes from earlier had developed into a steady icy snowfall. Judging by my footprint, an inch had accumulated since we'd been inside, but the impression was already filling in with new powder. The wind off the water gusted and swirled, issuing strange sounds as it breathed between loose bits of concrete and around rusted metal. The world felt muted, cocooned by the relative silence of the yard and the tumbling white. We became Theseus, racing from the admin building and into the regimented maze of stacks, hunted by the dreaded Minotaur. Except this monster carried guns instead of horns. Death came calling regardless of the method, and we needed to be quick and quiet if we were getting out of here alive.

I focused on the yard map. Port Authority hover-copters and drones couldn't fly in this, which meant our backup was coming via water or land. My heart raced, emboldened by the Insight, and a growing sense of anticipation and uneasiness quickened my pace. Whatever Ivan was transporting, it went beyond this case. Something else was going on.

"Those motherfuckers came to play, Holliday," Deacon interrupted my thoughts. "Looks like a goddamn security detail for the fucking High Inquisitor! I'm seeing automatics, and there's one with a sniper rifle just outside the bridge of the ship. That'd be handy to have right about now."

"Don't do anything stupid, Deacon," Leyla warned. "There's a lot more of them than there are of you."

"Oh, don't you worry none, girlie," he chuckled mirthlessly. "Like I told you in the van, when things go sideways, I'm lighting that fucker up."

"Port Authority should be mobilizing by now," I said, "but it'll take them time to get here because of all the ice in the bay. Just sit tight. We're almost at the stack."

We reached the end of the row. The forty-foot-long containers had been piled closest to the edge of the quay. A silver padlock with a digital display and no keyhole hung from both pull-handles.

Here.

"Eleven-seven," I said, almost in answer to the whisper wavering in the wind.

"Look at that." Leyla pointed at the side wall of the first container. It held two small square boxes, reminiscent of chillers used in preventing frozen food from spoiling. A low buzzing sound carried over to us presumably from the internal fans used to circulate air.

"Why aren't they on top?" I mused.

I handed Ushakov's phone to Leyla. She activated it, approached the door and presented it to the padlock. The phone's display worked its numbers, rifling through a myriad of eight-digit combinations. Similar numbers generated on the lock display. I held the SMART gun in a two-handed grip, my head on a swivel scanning everywhere at once. The yard map showed no sign of anyone alerted to our presence.

"Come on, come on," Leyla urged.

The lock clicked the moment a set of eight digits settled into place, matched by the same sequence on Ushakov's phone. Holstering the gun, I stepped forward and yanked the lock from the handles. I grabbed the long metal bolt securing the door and pulled it back, then did the same for its twin, and with great effort, hauled one of the doors open. Rusty hinges groaned in protest, but the door opened. Some instinct made me remove my SCU badge. I held it aloft as its soft silver illumination brightened the darkness that had swallowed the interior.

"Oh my God," Leyla cried, holding her own holo-phone aloft.

More than a dozen pale and frightened faces met our light. Dressed in flimsy pajamas, the boys and girls huddled together for warmth at the center of the metal container. I immediately recognized them all as the troop of kids wearing the green t-shirts from Brave New Beginnings. There was no telling how long the kids had been in here, although none of them appeared abused or malnourished.

I stepped forward, a grim countenance on my face.

"We're all going home," I growled with barely suppressed rage.

A cold touch on my hand drew my attention, sending shivers throughout my body. The Insight responded, empowering my outrage and restoring my determination with a heat that banished the uneasiness I'd been experiencing. I looked down, startled by the familiar face regarding me, a face I thought I'd never see again.

"Here," Nine whispered.

35

"How are you here?" I breathed, my eyes filled with wonder.

Nine was taller than I remembered, caught in that ungainly stage between adolescence and teenager. She had been one of more than two dozen young girls and women enslaved by Rumpelstiltskin that we had liberated from his underground goldjoy lab last October. At the time, her name had come from the ink that had marked her forehead. If I hadn't met her before, I could have easily mistaken Nine for a boy. A slip of a girl, her hair hadn't grown back much, the strands thin, colorless and airy. Her large pale eyes reflected the light of my badge, liquid pools of silver, mysterious and unreadable. I realized I still held her hand, and let it go with a gentle smile. She didn't seem to mind. The other children surrounded us, anxious and afraid. Outside, a heavy rumbling announced the arrival of the robotic reach-picker attached to the back of a self-driving flatbed. Leyla tore her surprised eyes away from Nine and said something to me, but I didn't catch it.

"What's that?" I asked absently.

"I said, how are we getting them out of here?" she repeated.

"Working on that."

Nine never blinked. I wasn't sure if she could.

"Okay, then how are we getting past the Russians?" Leyla asked.

"Working on that, too."

I lost the staring contest, unable to meet Nine's gaze any longer. Was that a ghost of a smile on her lips? The other kids pressed close, shunting her aside, and began asking a bundle of questions to which I had no answers. Nine hovered on the fringe, watching me without expression.

"Everybody, listen up," I addressed the kids. "My name is Detective Tom Holliday with the Empire City Special Crimes Unit. This is my partner, Leyla. We're going to get you out of here, but you need to stay close and do exactly as we say. Okay?"

Nervous nods followed. Nine simply watched me, as if I were the answer to the meaning of life. As if I filled her entire world.

Non-plussed, I moved beyond the knot of kids to shine the badge light at the container's rear. Four unmarked plastic-wrapped rubber tubs sat there. I approached one and tore into it before popping the top open. Air hissed as the vacuum seal broke. Inside were small parcels taped in bubble wrap, the kind used for fragile goods. I reached in and hefted one, allowing the weight to drag my hand down. I ripped off the tape and pulled back the wrap to reveal a tan sack the size of my fist. Shifting it in my palm, I heard the telltale jingle of coin.

"Ivan, you son of a bitch," I murmured.

"Holliday, what the fuck's happening over there?" Deacon demanded. "Something's stirred the Russians. That big fucker just gave some orders, and his men are on the move."

"The cypher locks must've transmitted an 'all clear' signal to Ivan once they deactivated," Leyla said. "I should've thought of that!"

"Don't fucking matter none now, girlie," the Confederate grated. "You've got five headed your way."

EVI's map confirmed five heat dots converging on our position. It also showed the perimeter guards had resumed their posts. Pop hadn't activated the reach picker yet, buying us a little more time. I moved from the container and located a surveillance camera attached to a metal pole at the end of the row. I flicked two fingers off my forehead in acknowledgement, hoping Pop caught the gesture. It was time to go.

"Right." I cleared my throat, running through our limited options in my mind as I scanned the yard map. "Here's what we're going to do. Deacon, I need a diversion, something big and loud that'll draw these guys from us and keep them busy."

"Show time," he chuckled. "I got just the thing."

I turned to Leyla. "We need to commandeer the flatbed. Can you override the automated control so I can drive it?"

"Self-driving programming isn't complicated," she replied. "As long as your dad hasn't switched it to remote control while I'm doing it, this shouldn't take long."

"Make it happen, kiddo."

Leyla flashed me a bright grin, then sprinted to the idling truck outside. I returned to the kids with what I hoped was a reassuring smile of my own.

"When I give the word, I want you all to climb aboard the truck," I instructed in as calm a voice as I could muster.

"Stay low, and hold onto each other to keep warm, and so you don't fall. Can you do that for me?"

"Holliday, are you out of your goddamn mind?" Deacon blurted in my ear. "You're just going to drive out the front gate?"

"Damn right I am," I replied and activated the SMART gun's tactical interface. "We all are. Come on, kids. And Deacon, on my signal, unleash whatever the hell it is you've got."

Leyla had already disconnected the reach-picker from the rear hitch of the flatbed to make room for the kids. As they clambered aboard, a brilliant white flash burst to our right by the moored container ship, along with a muffled boom that sounded more like snow thunder than the expended shell from a missile launcher. Several kids stopped to wonder at it. A second flash and explosion followed, lighting up the leaden sky. The yard map shimmered as the intense heat from the explosions wiped out many of the dots clustered by the quayside cranes. Deacon must've hit something flammable either aboard the ship, or by the cranes.

"Eyes on me!" I ordered. "Eyes on me! Get on the truck. Let's go!"

I helped anyone who wasn't tall enough to scramble aboard. Nine was last. I hefted her easily, her eyes never leaving me. My heart pounded. With the truck to my back and the reach-picker idling nearby, I faced the yard, clutching the gun with both hands. I searched the shadows but saw nothing. Some of the heat dots along the perimeter behind us had separated. The approaching five also split up. Three maneuvered around the container stacks hoping to outflank us.

"I don't think so," I growled. "Ricochet."

The gun's tactical confirmed the order, then calculated distances and trajectories as the dots closed in on us.

"Kids!" I shouted. "Cover your ears!"

Without waiting to see who listened, I pivoted in the opposite direction and fired three quick bursts. The gun roared, a bold klaxon in the night heralding our intention to stand and fight. Children shrieked from the explosive echoes of the gun's discharge, but there was nothing I could do about that. As the third round left the chamber, I whipped around and unloaded two more. A heartbeat later, all five dots halted movement.

"Five down," I announced. "I'm out of ricochet rounds. How's that override coming along?"

"Almost got it," Leyla shouted from inside the truck's single cab. "Just a few more seconds."

"Holliday, I lost track of that sniper on the ship," Deacon said. "One minute he was there, and the next, he's gone. Stay sharp."

"Copy that," I said. "What's your status?"

"Took a nice chunk out of that ship," Deacon answered with a satisfied chuckle. "Goddamn thing is on fire, too."

Gunfire erupted on the line, drowning out whatever Deacon said next.

"Deacon!" I shouted. "Deacon, do you copy?"

"It comes," Nine whispered.

At her pronouncement, anticipation and dread settled over me. A tingling sensation rippled through my body. Fear gnawed at my insides. I shut my eyes and bowed my head, trying to get a grip on the sudden rush of emotions.

"Drop the gun," Orlando Denning ordered. He stood before the open door of the container, a Colt 45 in his hand and trained on me. "I won't shoot the kids. They're far too valuable. But I won't hesitate to blow a hole through your motherfucking face."

The hair on my arms and the back of my neck rose as if I was near a live wire. I glanced past Denning's shoulder as a strange shimmering rustled the air behind him. He didn't notice, so intent was he on me.

"Don't you know it's bad luck to steal another man's property?" he asked.

"Fuck you, Denning," I retorted hotly. "Using your position at Brave New Beginnings to traffic innocent kids? That already puts you below the lowest ring in Hell. The Coast Guard will be here soon. Be smart and let us go. I'll even cut you a deal with the D.A.'s Office, if you give up Ivan and cooperate."

The wind from the bay whipped around us. Frosty white ground powder plumed at my feet, driven by the wind's arctic fury.

"And fuck up this score?" Denning scoffed. The good guy act he had put on at the Redeemer was long gone. "Get real, man. I don't give a fuck about these orphans. Nobody wanted them in the first place. At least I'm doing them all a favor by sending them somewhere where they'll be useful."

"By selling them into slavery!" I shot back.

"Whatever, man," he laughed. "I don't give a shit what the end-buyer wants. I just care about the ones and zeroes."

"Actually," I said with a pointed glance at the strange portal forming next to him, "you've got a much bigger problem now."

The shimmering brightened, then parted, a vertical tear in the fabric of reality.

"What the—" Denning jerked around to face it.

Calvin Flynn stepped through, the boy from my dream. Dressed in a light blue hospital gown, his body crawled with thumbnail-sized objects. Bile rose in my throat at the sight of them.

"And for the sin of kidnapping and murder, Orlando Denning, you have been found guilty," Calvin declared, his youthful voice echoing with the alien resonance of the One. "Your time is mine. A life, for a life."

Denning cried out. He pulled the trigger, firing several shots. The bullets struck the undulating shield of tiny spiders protecting Calvin and dropped harmlessly to the ground.

"What the hell?" Denning emptied the gun, only to watch in horror as each new round met a similar fate.

A sly, oily smile spread over Calvin's face. Paralyzed by terror, I could only watch. Dozens of spiders leapt from the boy onto the shocked man, each connected by a silky filament that reflected the light. Denning screamed, a piercing, ululating wail of panic and agony. He wiped at his body, frantic to dislodge the small invaders, but they clung tenaciously to him, bonding to his flesh. Calvin raised his hand, then gestured a languid come hither. Denning was dragged toward the gaping rent. He struggled, but the spiders held him fast, finally yanking him through the glittering portal.

"Guardian of Empire City," Calvin addressed me, his boyish smile oozing malice. I felt the promise of violence in the air. "This Bargain is nearly settled. Five have been served retribution. Three remain. Face me at the beginning of all things. The Daughter of Night cannot aid you. Deny me at your peril."

"You've said that before," I challenged, summoning a bravado that didn't match my fear. "I'll be there. And I'll stop you."

"Then you shall fall."

The boy retreated, swallowed by the glimmering aperture, which closed as if it had never been. The buffeting wind died. However, a glutinous residue slickened the container doors, dripping down the rusted metal. With a start, I realized I'd seen that gelatinous shit before.

"Doc, get on the truck!" Leyla yelled.

"I'll drive!" I shouted.

"No time! Get on!"

My legs quivered into action. I threw myself onto the flatbed as Leyla slammed down the accelerator. The truck barreled ahead, hitting the biggest pothole the world had ever created. I instantly lost my balance, falling to the side. The kids managed to pull me back before I went ass-over-teakettle to the frozen ground. I stood, one hand holding the SMART gun and the other gripping a metal strut along the roof. My eyes teared as Leyla gunned it, pushing the truck to its top speed. We fishtailed sharply from right to left, threatening to tip over along the icy ground. The young hacker did well for having never driven anything in her life, but if she didn't get her shit together soon, this would be the shortest getaway ride in the history of daring escapes.

"Deacon!" I shouted over the roaring engine. "Where are you?"

Nothing. Worry cut at me. Deacon was one of the few constants in my little universe. If something had happened to that crusty son of a bitch...I couldn't finish the thought.

Leyla rounded a sharp turn, the truck's wheels screeching in protest. To our left was the admin building, and to our right, several more container stacks, some piles of rubble, and the perimeter fence. We had a clear path to the gate. The explosion flare on the yard map hadn't cleared. I shunted it aside in favor of the SMART gun's tactical. Six dots were spread throughout the stacks to our right. Three more appeared amidst the tire graveyard to our left, using the mounds of cast-off treads for cover.

It wouldn't be enough.

"Armor piercing!" I bellowed and unloaded everything I had.

Remorseless incendiaries detonated on impact, blasting people-sized holes through the container walls, obliterating old tires and dead vehicles, and igniting everything in sight. Chunks of melted rubber and shrapnel rained down in fiery blazes. Small infernos raged where our attackers had been.

"Punch it, Leyla!" I shouted.

The truck chewed up the distance separating us from the outside and freedom. We were too exposed, but there was no helping it. Speed and momentum were our only allies in this race to escape. I checked the ammunition counter. I'd expended all the ricochet and armor piercing rounds. Eight regular rounds remained.

As I bent low to check on the kids, a whizzing bullet grazed me high in the left shoulder. The force shoved me back, and I bounced hard against the cab. A second bullet shattered the window where my head had been, showering me in glass fragments. Turned around and disoriented, I staggered forward then fell from the flatbed to bounce hard against the unforgiving ground.

Leyla slammed on the brakes. The truck skidded along a small patch of black ice, but she managed to keep it and all the kids upright. However, they remained trapped in the yard.

I spat out blood mixed with crumbled gravel and snow. More blood soaked my shirt and blazer. The warm wound stung badly. I rolled onto my side to see someone approach from the admin building. I jarred myself to my feet, swaying in the wintry breeze.

"Thomas," Ivan greeted. "So nice of you to drop by."

Man, I hated bad puns, almost as much as child kidnappers, lazy writing, and murderers.

Ivan sauntered over and casually drove his fist into my face. My lip split in a few places, dribbling blood. I toppled to the earth like an old fourth-world government. Pretty stars swirled in my vision. Ivan grabbed me by my wounded shoulder and squeezed, admiring the crimson stream flowering between his thick fingers. I screamed, nearly blacking out from the pain.

"This is what happens when you interfere with our business," he declared, and squeezed again. I struggled futilely against his implant-enhanced grip.

"I warned you," he said, a sad smile crossing his lips. "I take no pleasure in this, Thomas. I truly do not. We were friends once. Brothers. You see the tragedy in this, yes? Now, I must punish you and your little friends here. Then I will find the Vellan and the old man, and I will kill them, too."

"Detective, perhaps I may be of assistance?" Besim's melodious voice in my ear cut through the red haze of pain. I'd completely forgotten about her in all the hullabaloo. "Deacon Kole is alive, but unconscious," she continued, as if describing a live cat dissection. "He sustained minor injuries after falling from his sentry perch. I have attempted to revive him, but at my current location, I am too distant to be effective. I respectfully request your permission to enter the container yard so that I may see to both yours and his safe recovery."

"You what?" I blurted out, spitting blood on the front of Ivan's dark coat.

"I said I am going to kill you now, Thomas," the big Russian said, his brow knotted in consternation. He backhanded me in the face. My neck popped from the force of it.

"This is one of your problems, Thomas. You never listen. Even when it is for your own good."

"I respectfully request your—" Besim repeated.

"A little...busy...right now," I managed. "How...you plan on...getting here? Air mail?"

"I will accept your response as acquiescence to my request," she said.

"Who are you talking to?" Ivan demanded, hurling me into one of the flatbed's tires.

The kids gathered above me, urging me to get up, their panic evident. Ivan advanced, both fists clenched, and his face burning a dull scarlet. Even if I'd been at full strength, I was no match for his implant-augmented muscle. I pushed myself up, raised both hands in a pugilist's pose, and prepared to give a full accounting of myself before Ivan pummeled me into paste.

"How quaint," Ivan chuckled. "Unfortunately, Thomas, this is—"

Suddenly, the metal security gate burst apart with a bang as Stella blasted through the opening. The van expertly maneuvered around the flatbed, then swung sharply to the right, and smashed into Ivan with the heaviest part of its rear end. The collision launched him into the air. He landed hard, and I heard something break.

"Goodbye," I finished with a bloody grin.

36

Besim extricated herself from Stella, unfolding her long legs gingerly from beneath the van's steering wheel. The children watched in awe as she approached, a giant in their midst. The consultant offered them a friendly smile in return. However, the layers of makeup caking her face, and the fiery glare from the wreckage-strewn backdrop around us, transformed it into a hellish expression. Uncertainty and anxiety held the kids back. They clung to one another, all except Nine. She stepped forward to regard Besim with a tilt of her head. The little girl's eyes offered nothing. The consultant paused, a raised eyebrow the only indication of her surprise.

"Are you hurt, Detective?" Besim asked. She gripped my outstretched hand, then drew me to my feet with a strength that belied her thin frame.

"Nothing aspirin and nine cups of black with a mountain of proto-sugar can't cure," I grimaced. Adrenaline continued to burn through me, but I knew that energy burst would be short-lived. The intense winter cold coupled with the biting wind off the harbor wasn't helping my cuts, grazed shoulder, bumps and bruises, but it beat the alternative. At least my bloody lip had frozen over, although there wasn't a washing machine on Earth that could save my stained shirt. I glanced forlornly at the torn and dirtied sleeves of my brown blazer and sighed. Sometimes this job really sucked.

"I apologize for my tardiness," Besim said. She frowned and gestured at Stella with her long fingers. "Abner's conveyance is...temperamental. However, once I explained my intentions, she settled down, and we became as one."

"Right," I nodded, pretending as if I understood what she had said. "So, um, when did you learn to drive like that?"

"On our journey here," she answered placidly. "I observed your movements, how you manipulated the steering and administered the pedals. The inclement conditions made observing the rules of the road somewhat of a challenge, but, in the end, it was not difficult to master. Your choice in music, however, leaves much to be desired."

"Hey, show some respect for the classics," I bristled. "Steppenwolf is great driving music."

A blur of white pushed past me and engulfed Besim in a much shorter bear hug.

"You did it!" Leyla exulted with a broad grin, squeezing the consultant tight.

Besim froze. A whisper of the Insight touched my vision. Leyla was unchanged, yet strands of translucent shadow dripped from her arms, reaching for the Vellan. Sudden revulsion and pain flashed across her face. Breaking free from Leyla's embrace, Besim recovered quickly, her customary indifference restored. The Insight vanished, along with the strange umbra.

"I merely accomplished what the situation required," Besim said, clasping her hands together.

"I didn't mean to—" the young hacker began.

Besim faced me, ignoring Leyla's entreaty. "Detective, we must locate Deacon Kole. And these children have been exposed to the harsh elements for far too long. We must remove them from this place at once."

Crestfallen, Leyla said, "Doc, I'll take the kids inside where it's warm."

"Good idea." I glanced at the admin building but didn't see anyone. Pop was no fool. He'd be long gone by now to work on his alibi. "EVI, please contact Emergency and Social Services. Have them get here on the double and let them know the Coast Guard is rounding up Ivan's crew."

I turned to the flatbed to find Nine holding the SMART gun with both hands.

"Uh...thanks," I said, carefully relieving her of the weapon. Nine's arms dropped mechanically to her side, her task completed.

I studied her as I holstered the gun. What were the odds that she would be one of the Brave New Beginnings' kids found at Caron Container? A bajillion to one? More?

In the weeks since I'd closed the Vanessa Mallery murder, I had wondered after Nine and the other lost and abused people Rumpelstiltskin had enslaved but had never investigated their status in the enclave's social welfare system. I presumed they had all been reunited with family, or at least found a safe place to call home.

Nine hadn't displayed any emotion during our wild ride across the container yard. Now, she simply stared back at me, without a hint of reproach or recrimination in her eyes. Had Besim been right? Down in the goldjoy laboratory, she had tried and failed to heal Nine with her voice. Was the little girl's soul, her "light" as Besim had called it, truly gone? I turned away from Nine, struggling with the sudden guilt crowding my heart, and exchanged a look with Besim.

"Only time will tell, Detective," she said cryptically.

Nine wandered over to Leyla who was leading the children toward the admin building. A brief pang of doubt crept into my heart, but I discarded it. If Leyla was still under the influence of that winged shadow, the Insight wouldn't have disappeared. That said, worry tugged at me. Something terrible was going on with her. The Sanarov murder investigation took top priority, but once we closed this case, she and I would get together for a private heart-to-heart.

"After I locate Deacon, I'll remain with the kids until Emergency Services arrives," I said. "You and Leyla should head back to L'Hotel Internacional—"

"Detective," Besim interrupted me for the millionth time. "Mamika and her team are to rendezvous with us here shortly. I took the liberty of contacting my major domo once the children were discovered and felt it wise to expedite an emergency response. They will transport the children to my apartments where my medical staff will oversee to their injuries, provide a warm meal, clothing, toiletries and appropriate sleeping arrangements. Your Social Services may contact Mamika after such time she has deemed the children are in no further danger."

"Detective Holliday," EVI announced. "I have received a priority message from Captain Mahoney. He will be arriving with Emergency Services soon."

I glanced at Ivan who lay prone and unmoving. A thin layer of white had formed on his clothes. I resisted the urge to run over and kick the ever-living shit out of him. Instead, I unhooked the spell-forged steel handcuffs I kept on my belt, strode over, and knelt by his side. He moaned. Blood caked the side of his head and face where they had kissed the ground. One arm was bent at a wrong angle. I caught a whiff of burnt flesh and circuitry. The implants in his broken arm had fractured from the impact. Several of the fingers on that hand spasmed. There was no telling what kind of internal damage had been done to his nervous system, or whether it would be permanent.

I yanked both of his arms behind his back and cuffed the bastard. He howled in pain, but judging by his vacant, unfocused stare, he'd also suffered a serious concussion.

"Ivan Kruchev," I said pleasantly. "You're under arrest for smuggling, trafficking, kidnapping, the attempted murder of an SCU officer, and a bunch of other felonies that I'm too tired to list right now." I read him his rights. He groaned again. I took that to mean he waived them. "Don't go anywhere." I patted him on the cheek, then stood.

Switching from the gun's tactical to EVI's yard map showed a Coast Guard cutter anchored beside the container ship. The heat glare had finally cleared. New dots milled around the quayside cranes. EVI had colored them blue.

That's my girl.

"Where's Deacon?" I called over to Besim.

Her eyes closed. An icy wind picked up, swirling bits of snow and ice around my face. Goose pimples flocked along my arms. Besim raised her arm and pointed toward the quay. She strode purposefully down the main drag between the admin building and the repair shop.

"Detective," EVI said. "Captain of the Port Greta Banks wishes to speak with you. She is the commanding officer of the USCGC *Enterprise*, the vessel deployed to Caron Container."

"Good," I huffed as I tried to keep pace with Besim. I really needed to work on my cardio. After we closed this case, I vowed to get a gym membership. A cheap one. With workout machines. Whichever ones I needed that would help me keep up with long-legged, pain-in-the-ass consultants. "Please inform Captain Banks that I'm engaged in a search for one of my people. I'll be happy to debrief her once he's been found."

Besim pointed at a large field of containers, and I headed that way, leaving her behind. The heavy metal boxes were stacked five and six tall. Shadows lay deep and heavy. The air was thick with a cloudy haze from the fires burning along the quay. I heard a male voice issuing instructions to the captured crew of the container ship, his voice amplified by the cutter's communications array. By the sound of things, Captain Banks' people had everything well in hand. One less thing to worry about, at least.

A section at the end of the row was full of twisted metal and debris. Stale smoke lingered like a bad dream. Something had hit this area hard. Several containers had been blown to the ground. I heard a groan beneath a mound of scrap and junk. Rushing forward, I handled the largest piece and tried dragging it toward me, but to no avail. I cried out from the intense pain radiating from my wounded shoulder. I tried again, but failed, grown weaker with the effort. Fresh blood dribbled from my wound. I staggered backwards, the pain and the futility of trying to move the damn thing sapping my resolve. Hot anger welled up inside of me. Deacon needed my help. I couldn't leave him buried beneath the rubble. Despite my flagging strength, I refused to give in to my failing body. I knew Deacon would never give up on me, no matter the cost. And I'd never give up on him.

Sensing my need, the Insight responded in kind.

Energy infused my body, saturating me with fresh

adrenaline mixed with something far more potent, a magic born from the enigmatic clairvoyance. Joy and life coursed through my veins. I pulled away two more pieces, cutting my fingers and palms on the jagged edges, but I didn't care. Finally, a bloody hand reached for me from beneath chunks of rubble. I gripped it, then helped a beaten and battered Deacon to his feet.

"About goddamn time, Holliday," he coughed. The former Protector's ash-covered face split into a tired grin. "Thought y'all had forgotten about me."

"You'll never be that lucky," I chuckled. The Insight hadn't dissipated. Instead, it simmered along my arms, into my chest, and down my legs. "What the hell happened?"

He dusted himself off. "Couple of them trigger-happy motherfuckers tossed some grenades at me. I ducked just as they hit. I'm lucky I still got everything attached. You get the kids?"

"We did." I clapped the other man on the shoulder. He winced. "You all right?"

"I ain't fucking fragile like you, Holliday."

We shared a laugh and limped back to the others. An unmarked silver bus, the kind employed by traveling entertainers and celebrities with inflated egos, idled next to the flatbed, along with a personnel carrier. Men and women in dull gray suits milled about, ushering the kids onto the bus. They'd already formed a perimeter around the vehicles, although none of Besim's people were visibly armed. I saw Mamika speaking with Leyla, their white breaths mingling together.

"I guess you aren't dead," Leyla addressed Deacon as we joined her, the relief plain in her eyes.

"The story of my demise was greatly exaggerated," the

Confederate drawled with a playful smile. "Looks like you were busy. Where's the big Russian?"

"In the building," she replied. "Two of Mamika's people are watching him, although he still hasn't regained consciousness. I figured we didn't want him to die of frostbite before the arraignment. Oh, and Doc, your dad's gone."

"Not a surprise," I said. "He probably bolted the second after the shooting started."

Blue and red lights bathed the entrance to Caron Container as ECPD and Emergency Services arrived. A man and woman, both wearing heavy coats and white naval caps, came into view walking up the road from the main yard. I waved them over as Besim joined us.

"Looks like the gang's all here," I said, rubbing my hands together.

I felt great. No, that wasn't right. I felt better than that. The Insight had temporarily rekindled in me hope and purpose, replacing the antipathy brought about by my encounters with the One, my meetings with Pop and Ivan, and my tumultuous feelings for Charlie. I knew we were close to the finish line. We'd figure out what was going on, take down the One and...

"Detective, if I might—" Besim began.

A sharp crack split the air. Besim shifted her body, side-stepping a hair to her left. Something whizzed past her, grazing my cheek, narrowly missing muscle and bone by millimeters. The force of the bullet spun me around before I collapsed to the ground.

"Doc!" Leyla called out to me in a voice not her own.

My eyes, suffused with the Insight, connected with hers. She hovered beside me, but the winged shadow loomed above her, a harbinger of shadow, cold and death. It filled my vision, sinister and formidable. Writhing tendrils of darkness and frost enshrouded the young hacker's body. Two sets of eyes regarded me—one, icy blue and familiar, brimming with love and compassion, and the other black, endless and cunning, a cruel intelligence rife with heartless recognition.

"Guardian," they whispered simultaneously. "Beware the Light to which you serve. It made you. It has used you. And it will be your undoing."

A second gunshot rang out, and before I could shout a warning, Leyla collapsed, clutching at her chest.

37

D oc!
Echoes. Racing footsteps. Roaring engines.
Your time is mine. A life for a life.
Shots fired. Light blurred.

Echoes.

Burgeoning sounds, distinct and intimate, ebbed and flowed, yet everything and everywhere was unfocused, unregistered, uncertain. Edges of what might have been bled in and out of vague shadows without form or substance. Faces appeared then dissolved, both familiar and alien.

Echoes.

Darkness. Despair, and then...

Singing.

Their light is gone.

Mocking laughter. Subtle cunning. Emerald fire. A singular flaw.

Old things return that have not seen this sun in an age.

Echoes and sensations. Intense cold. Paralyzing fear. Betrayal.

Doc!

And pain.

"Tom?"

A light touch on my shoulder startled me from the nightmare. Anxiety and apprehension draped me like old bedfellows. Unsure of my surroundings, I tumbled from an uncomfortable seat to a cold floor. Sterile smells assaulted me—the sharp tang of bleach, ammonia, and dried paint. My jaw and nose were stiff and swollen. Half my face and my left shoulder were numb.

"Are you all right?"

Dim light filtered between the closed slats of a single window on the far wall. I reached out blindly and encountered a soft and thinly woven material. Bunching it in a fist, I blinked away half-baked shadows. Yet the dregs from the dream persisted, clutching my mind and refusing to let go.

Beware the Light to which you serve. It made you. It has used you. And it will be your undoing.

A steady beep and the ragged rasp of a breathing tube brought reality crashing back. Harsh memory quickly followed.

Leyla sprawled on the frozen ground.

First responders shouldering past me.

Blinding red and blue flashing lights.

Besim stunned, yet unharmed.

An enraged Deacon bellowing orders to his team, pointing in the direction from where the shots originated.

And me, staggering forward, eyes tearing, blood streaming from the hot gash in my torn cheek, the gruesome trophy of a life nearly taken.

Bill appeared as if summoned. Gruff and bristly, the captain assumed immediate command of the situation while he consulted with Captain Banks and her lieutenant. I never saw Ivan or the other Russians. Besim's people had escorted the children from the yard. The EMTs whisked me from the scene to EC General. There, a nice nurse administered a local anesthetic to dull the pain, but all it did was ladle more broth onto the chicken soup blanketing my brain. By then, the Insight had long vanished. At least, so I thought. All the pounding my body had taken at Caron Container returned, magnified a hundredfold. I plummeted into a lightless oblivion.

Time blurred.

I awoke in a hospital room and recalled Abner had also been taken to EC General. After wrangling his location from a different and very uncooperative nurse, I lurched through the halls until I found him. The old man had been plugged into an elegant array of medical apparatus. All his numbers appeared low. A breathing tube filled his mouth. The room smelled empty, bleak, bereft of hope. I took the old man's hand. No strength. No recognition. Just feather-light, and cold.

Guilt ravaged me. In my relentless pursuit of the murder investigation, I hadn't spared him a second thought since we'd left the bookstore. Solving the Sanarov case had consumed me. My epiphany about family and its paramount importance in my raggedy life now tasted rank and bitter. I was a hypocrite, no better than that piece of shit I called a father.

I had rubbed Abner's fingers, my wishful thinking that physical contact would somehow magically restore him to health.

I couldn't say how long I stood there, only that I eventually crashed in the chair by his bed. Sleep claimed me once more until the new voice roused me from my stupor.

"Who's there?" I asked, bleary-eyed.

A diminutive woman had entered the room. She closed the door behind her. Dressed in a bulky gray winter coat, a pink and white knit scarf was wrapped around her neck, but her head was bare. In response to her arrival, soft ceiling lights blessed the room. I struggled to my feet. She came forward and helped me regain my seat.

"Looks like you've had a rough night," she remarked dryly.

Rabbi Adina Adler was a few years short of Abner, but you'd never know it by looking at her. Neatly kept brown hair flecked with silver ran to the nape of her neck, giving her a boyish appearance. She possessed a slim, athletic body that had avoided overindulgence and the decadent pleasures of bagels, *babka* and *hamantashen*. And a wit sharp enough to slice deli.

Nowadays, online, ala carte, and concierge Judaism was available, considered passably chic by many who wished to pay token homage to their ancestors. However, I knew of a few local families that had banded together to keep the flame alive. Called a *chavurah*, or "fellowship," these like-minded groups assembled to share communal experiences, ensuring the Jewish religion's rich culture, its heritage, traditions and holidays remained hale and whole. My mother, grandfather and Abner had been a part of one, along with Uncle Mortie, Myrna and their children.

As for Rabbi Adler, she held Rosh Hashanah, Yom Kippur and every other holiday service at her small and well-kept brownstone in Seagate. She cared for two Torahs, the ancient and revered prayer scrolls that contained the Jewish laws as recorded in the first five books of the Old Testament. One came from Dresden, a survivor of the *Kristallnacht* in Nazi Germany and the Holocaust during World War II, as well as the worldwide nukes and pandemics that eventually followed. The other had been hidden and moved several times during the violent Race Riots that had plagued Empire City just after its establishment. This was before the Vellans arrived, when the world still teetered on the brink of a catastrophic second Dark Age.

While I'd spend most days skipping classes at the Redeemer's parochial school, my grandfather did his damnedest to impart to me as much Jewish pragmatism as he could. And when he ran out of stories (and patience), he brought me to Rabbi Adler. Under her tutelage, she filled in all the gaps of my formative Jewish education, including presiding over my bar mitzvah, and my mother's funeral.

"I've been better," I grimaced. The dull throb in my nose suggested the anesthetic was wearing off. "What time is it?"

I could've asked EVI, but in that moment, I craved human interaction. The outside world could go to hell.

Rabbi Adler's warm brown eyes studied me. Liver spots had burrowed through her trackless laugh lines. She never missed much, but she was also wise enough not to press. People came to her, in time. She placed her coat and scarf on a second chair, then regarded Abner, her concern evident. The two had grown up together in the old neighborhood. I always suspected she had a soft spot for the old bibliophile. Then again, who didn't?

"A little after ten," she replied. "Do you mind if I dim the lights?"

"Knock yourself out."

The rabbi adjusted the environmental holo-control on the command pad next to the door. The light receded to a gentle glimmer.

"I'm sorry I couldn't visit him earlier," I admitted as if I'd been caught stealing, spreading my hands wide. "I've been, um, busy, you know, working a case. Another murder investigation."

"Of course."

I stared at the wall behind her. Stress and anxiety anchored my body. Exhaustion was the cherry on top.

"It's a tough one, too," I continued in a rush, fearful that if I stopped speaking, the ensuing silence would overwhelm me. "Kidnapping and murder from thirty years ago. Somehow, the victim is back from the dead and killing everyone involved in that old crime. Gustavo Sanarov, Pyotr Ushakov and some of his men."

My voice trailed off. I didn't care whether Rabbi Adler knew any of the players. I just needed to keep talking. The older woman moved to Abner's side.

"I mean, the One's taken out some very bad people," I mused. "Hell, if it hadn't, we would never have discovered Ivan's operation at the container yard. Or Denning's involvement. The connection to Brave New Beginnings, too."

She smoothed the bedspread I'd rumpled earlier. Was it my imagination, or had Abner's ragged breathing softened?

I squinted at the ceiling. "We saved a lot of innocent kids last night. Credits to donuts those coins were part of the silver stolen from the Spanish exhibits I'd heard about. Between that and everything else, it should be enough to lock Ivan and his crew away for a long time."

The rabbi stroked Abner's cheek.

"Still, it's not right." I wrung my hands, exposing the puckered white scars on my wrists. "Not that I'd classify the One as a vigilante. A crime's a crime. And it's my job to enforce the law, but...well, even I've done things I'm not proud of. Convinced myself they were for the right reasons. Manipulated situations to ensure some scumbag never saw the light of day. And some other things..." My voice trailed away.

Rabbi Adler bent low and whispered something to Abner, but I couldn't hear it.

"But everyone should be held accountable," I resumed. "Everyone should be held to a higher moral standard, especially me. But I'm not foolish enough to think the past never catches up with you. Which I guess is what's happening now, and yet..."

I broke off and glanced at the rabbi. She was a slouched silhouette paired against the austere white of the bed and the ghostly holo-windows monitoring Abner. She drew her fingers gently across his brow. The gesture reminded me of Besim.

"What Calvin Flynn and the One are doing goes against everything I've trained for, the shield, the reasons I became a cop," I said. "So why do I feel like I should be thanking them?"

Both crime scenes replayed in my mind's eye. The victims, Sanarov sprawled in his chair, the Russians splayed on the floor, their bodies corrupted and broken. The messages of retribution, one scrawled in blood, macabre calling cards heralding further violence. Yet, these were also men who had harmed others, unabashedly ruthless and cruel.

"*Tzedek, tzedek tirdof,*" the rabbi said softly.

"Excuse me?" I regarded the older woman. "I don't understand."

"It means 'justice, justice shall you pursue,'" she replied with a fond smile. "It comes from the Book of Deuteronomy. It means there is a fine line between seeking *tzedek*, seeking justice, and *naqam*, seeking vengeance. Sin creates an imbalance in any moral universe, but *naqam* is something far more personal. Justified or not, their lust for vengeance, all the pain and rage which stirs in the hearts of these people you are pursuing, this Calvin Flynn and the One, has become all-consuming to them. These things drive them to hurt and to hate, overwhelming rational thought. *Ayin tachat ayin*. 'An eye for an eye only brings blindness for all.'"

She paused to let her words sink in. I bowed my head and pressed the palms of my hands against my eyes, rubbing at the ache and exhaustion I couldn't shake.

"But there is always hope," the rabbi continued. "Compassion is one thing that separates *tzedek* from *naqam*. Your compassion, Tom, not only as an officer of the law, but as a caring person. Right now, you are hurt, and angry. You wish to fight injustice in a morally appropriate manner but are still bound by the constraints of the law. To make the hard choices between what your mind knows, and how your heart feels. It is part of what makes us all human. However, doing what is necessary versus doing what is right is not always one and the same."

I raised my head and gestured angrily at the old man lying helplessly in the bed.

"They hurt Abner," I said. Hot, guilty tears streamed down my face. "And Leyla. I don't even know if she's going to make it. And if she doesn't, I don't know what I'd do."

"They both knew the risks," the rabbi said. "Abner has told me as much whenever we've met for tea. Consider for a moment where Abner makes his home. Crime is rampant there, yet he continues to open the doors to the bookstore six days a week despite everything. Having the freedom to make those choices, knowing that some are good, some bad, and understanding the difference."

"And all of them hard," I finished, but was unable to contain the bitterness in my tone.

The older woman smiled and said, "Yet another part of what makes us human. Life is about making choices, and the faith and trust you pour into them. The faith and trust you have in yourself. The faith and trust both Abner and Leyla have in you. You can't blame yourself for the choices that others make. Are there unintentional consequences? Of course. To think otherwise is arrogant, short-sighted and foolish. However, to do what you do, willingly and knowingly placing yourself in danger to protect the people of Empire City, these are choices that you make, and not lightly. Abner and Leyla have done the same. They live in your world, and they understand. As for these killers you hunt, and their victims, they understand this, too. However, they are the other side of the same coin. Opposite you, opposed to you, yet the same."

"How will I know the difference?" I scowled, frustrated. "How do I know that I'm doing the right thing?"

"You once told me that investigating murders is both art and science," she replied. "The forensic evidence tells one story, but logic married with instinct and experience fills in the gaps. You live and die by your instincts, Tom. So, what are they telling you?"

I considered her question. I believed the One was somehow using Calvin to create a bridge to our world. If that happened, it and its eight-legged children would devour us all. This had evolved beyond a mere homicide investigation. More than meting out justice for a horrible crime perpetrated thirty years before. And more than my guilt for allowing Abner and Leyla to get hurt, Mahoney's shame, my muddled romantic attachment for Charlie, the personal vendetta I had for Ivan, or even the anger and resentment I felt toward Pop. Whatever the details were behind the bargain Calvin and the One had struck, that monster's intent was clear.

I'd already taken down Rumpelstiltskin and his vampires four months ago. If "Old things" were returning like Orpheus had said, then someone had to stand up to them. Besides, if I truly was the Guardian of Empire City, I had damned well better start acting like it.

I shunted my feelings aside, calming my mind to draw upon the facts of the case as I knew them. My emotions settled. Cold logic took hold, and I felt a measure of peace.

"Calvin Flynn and the One must be stopped," I finally answered.

"Then stop them."

38

T he Ninth Pod Platform found at the midway point
between the third and fourth floors was the least
used of the ten Metro and Emergency stations
attached to EC General Hospital. High enough above the
swarming ground traffic to avoid much of the acidic stench
of exhaust and the toxic allure of human waste, the Ninth
offered a broad view of the Lower East Side and the East
River.

I stood alone inside an enclosed heated waiting area
staring out the reinforced glass windows at a world cloaked
in white. A steady snow shower filtered endlessly from the
leaden afternoon sky. At least two inches of cover had fallen
since I'd been standing here, and at its current rate, another
six wasn't far behind.

I'd left Rabbi Adler and a slumbering Abner, promising
to attend Passover seder at her home in late March, something I hadn't done since before Harry died. She had reassured me Abner was in good hands, then reminded me to
bundle up against the cold before I went outside.

There was no arguing. Jewish mothering was

inescapable. You either obeyed, or you were guilt-ridden for life.

On my way out, I had checked my messages. The first was from the captain. The other confiscated containers held more stolen property from the museum heist. Ivan's crew had been rounded up, although no one was talking. They were being held at the Coast Guard's station on Staten Island, far enough removed from the rest of Ivan's pals in Brighton Beach for now. I expected the *bratva's* lawyers would come calling soon enough. Still, despite their interference, and given everything we had found at Caron Container, I didn't think Ivan was wriggling out of this one anytime soon. Mahoney also said that without Orlando Denning and any incriminating testimony he might have given, there wasn't enough evidence at the container yard to implicate Donald Flynn. Until we had something concrete, we couldn't touch him.

The second came from Deacon. Leyla had been taken to one of Besim's private medical facilities. A team of specialists was doing everything they could, but the bullet had caused significant internal and structural damage, and she remained in critical condition. His grim tone spoke volumes. I ground my teeth in frustration and moved on to the final message.

"Tom, it's Charlie. Call me. Please."

I stared at her image on my holo-phone, locked in indecision. What did she mean to me? A brief respite from a life devoid of emotional attachments? Or was there something more? After Kate, I'd given up on everything. Then, one night with Charlie, and suddenly vibrancy and color had returned to my world. She'd made it abundantly clear at Mahoney's apartment that I was an asset, a means to an end, another avenue of getting to Donald Flynn. Was she that good of an actress, using her magic and training as an MI6 agent to play upon my feelings to get what she wanted?

I flicked Charlie's image aside and brought up Deacon. He had answered before the first ring had finished and instructed me to meet him at the Metro platform in twenty minutes. We disconnected, and then I had wandered aimlessly around the hospital until a nice nurse pointed me in the right direction.

Feeling antsy, I moved from the heated waiting area. My breath billowed and died on the air like vanishing ghosts, remnants of life drawn into the frozen embrace of winter.

The 'way shuddered beneath the weight of an oncoming westbound Metro pod. A half-second passed before it hurtled by me. I was blasted by the sudden gust of cold air mixed with icy wetness. I raised my hand to cover my face. Shadows danced before me, blotchy spots of amorphous silver and gray, summoned by the blur of the fast-moving glass and spell-forged steel carrier. I turned to protect my wounded nose and cheek, but something caught my eye.

A figure waited on the opposite platform, separated by the dual tracks.

The scars on my wrist itched just as the Insight crackled to life. I squinted against the stinging wind, trying to catch a glimpse of whoever it was. But once the pod cleared, my heart shattered into a million forlorn fragments.

Kate Foster stood there, just as I remembered her, dressed in the same clothes she wore the night she died.

"Beware the Stones, Guardian," she called out. "They have been perverted to serve the Others now. However, the Stones will fail them when they need them most. Seek the flaw to unravel their designs. For truth without meaning, without substance, without a soul, is empty, worthless, phantasms constructed by your enemies to subvert and control you. Only when your heart and mind act as one will you prevail against them."

"Stones, what stones?" I stammered. My breathing quickened. I wanted to leap across the 'way, gather her in my arms, and hold her forever. "What are you doing here? How is this possible?"

Her face softened. Despite the distance separating us, real tears welled in her eyes.

"Help him see to end his pain," she said.

"Kate, I don't understand. Help who see?"

The thunderous roar heralding the arrival of another pod drowned out all other sound. I shouted Kate's name, my throat raw with emotion. Her lips moved, but I heard nothing. The pod shot past, and a moment later, both it, and Kate Foster, were gone.

"No," I whispered hoarsely, staring at nothing.

The Insight evaporated. Only emptiness remained. Each agonized breath I took tasted of despair. The bitter tears I'd shed had frozen on my cheeks. I wiped at them absently, wondering at the strangeness of my life. I didn't doubt what I'd seen. Kate had been no mirage, no construct from my wishful imagination. Why she appeared now, when the last I'd dreamt of her had been as I lay dying from overexposure from goldjoy, had everything to do with what lay ahead. I'd listened to her then, and I'd be damned if I didn't do the same now.

My mind worked through what she'd said. There was only one "Stone" that I'd encountered in my brief tenure with Special Crimes—the whammy-inducing emerald Orpheus had worn on her finger. I recalled diving into its green depths to discover the hairline fracture at its center. If there were more of those objects in play, that meant Orpheus wasn't too far behind. But where were they? How would I even know what to look for? Everything I'd investigated thus far showed no direct correlation between that smug-faced bitch, the *bratva*, Brave New Beginnings, Calvin Flynn or the One. What did it mean? What was going on? My cheek hurt, my head hurt, the thing thudding in my chest hurt, and I had no answers. Cinching up the broken pieces of my heart, I concentrated on the second part of Kate's message. As I did so, the platform trembled, stronger than before, which meant the northbound pod had finally arrived. However, what showed up was anything but ordinary.

The transport was silver and sleek, smaller than a Metro pod both in length and width, but larger than most executive private pods owned by Empire City's elite. It resembled one of the segments from a hyper-speed bullet transport contracted for long distance overland travel.

The hatchway popped open with a hiss of released hydraulics. Deacon stood in the entry, decked out in black fatigues and combat boots. His truncheon hung in a leather harness against his body. The former Protector glared at me, his bruised expression caught somewhere between annoyance and a general disgust of everything. Once aboard, he closed the door, and we slid forward without so much as a tremor of motion. Deacon lit a cigarette, then stomped to the front.

I whistled appreciatively, distracted by my lavish surroundings, my encounter with Kate momentarily forgotten. The interior matched the exterior—spotless, functionally pristine, and drenched in wealth. It even sported one of those super-duper beverage dispensers that made three dozen different gourmet coffees from around the world. The glorious aromas of various European blends tickled my fancy in a much-needed way, putting all the shitty gastronomical horrors at Fernand's and Armin's Coffee House to shame. I took a moment of silence in memory of the trusty old beverage dispenser, now a twisted ruin in some inglorious salvage yard, lost and forgotten along with the remains of our destroyed police pod.

Deacon consulted a large colorful heads-up-display sprawled across the opaque windshield. It indicated active traffic patterns for this quadrant of Empire City and included private access 'ways independent of the main municipal tracks used by the general populace.

"Good morning, Detective Holliday," Mamika said, gesturing for me to sit in one of four comfortable-looking passenger seats set in the center of the pod. "May I offer you breakfast?"

She stood by the spacious beverage station which also included a flat cooking surface, a sink, and built-in cabinetry and refrigerator. She, too, wore black fatigues, although she appeared unarmed.

"Please, and thank you," I said as I claimed a chair.

Besim sat opposite me, bedecked in her black longshoreman's coat over an orange and yellow peasant's shirt, and an aqua blue on a field of green paisley bandana around her head. She'd refreshed her makeup, judging by the unsettled flecks of white and beige powder around her cheeks and nose, but traces of uncertainty mixed with curiosity clouded her strange, almond-shaped gray eyes.

Mamika carefully placed a breakfast tray in my lap whose top contained a starched dinner napkin, gleaming silverware, a mug of life-altering java, and a steaming plate of fried proto-eggs, burnt bacon and a toasted pumpernickel bagel. Ravenous at the sight of fresh food, I tore into it with gusto.

"Where we going?" I mumbled between a mouthful of much-needed deliciousness.

"L'Hotel Internacional," the consultant replied. She sipped from a large teacup held in both hands. "William is awaiting us. Given the recent encounter with Ivan Kruchev and the *bratva*, I thought—"

"I don't give a damn what you thought," I interrupted coldly. "Right now, all I care about is Leyla. Where is she?"

"Safe, and under exceptional medical care." She countered my hostile mien with a placid one of her own. Her uncertainty had been replaced by detachment.

"Why wasn't she taken to EC General?" I demanded.

Deacon hadn't moved from his post at the front of the pod, but I could tell by his posture he was paying more attention to us than the HUD. Mamika remained at a respectful distance by the kitchenette.

"I should think the answer to that was obvious," Besim responded while placing her teacup on a side table beside her chair. "Given Leyla's singular abilities, it would be unwise for anyone to examine her at your hospitals. Complications would arise, which would subsequently expose William, the Special Crimes Unit, and yourself to unwanted scrutiny. I assure you she is in excellent hands. The facility contains the highest standards in both medical and trauma technology."

I swallowed the hot retort on my lips. The demure consultant's simple logic was spot-on, and the fact I hadn't even considered Leyla's abilities embarrassed me. While we lived in a new age powered by magic from the Nexus nodes, the truth was active practitioners were rare. Most people turned a blind eye to reports of magic use, content to believe everything was as it should be, the natural order was maintained, and there were no such things as warlocks and witches. That, and the authorities would keep the peace by taking care of anything that ever got out of hand so that the rest of the populace could get on with their regular, mundane lives.

I shook my head more for my stupidity than anything else. Deacon laughed derisively, sparing me a glance before turning back to the HUD.

Mamika offered me a fresh mug of coffee. I accepted it with a rueful smile. She returned it with a knowing look before returning to her previous position.

"What about the shooter?" I called out to Deacon.

"A goddamn ghost," he replied, dashing his spent cigarette on the command console in obvious frustration. He lit a fresh one. "My people searched the rooftops. They found shit. No bullets or casings neither, which means a pro. And Saranda's surgeons didn't find no bullets or fragments or anything after Leyla's surgery. I'm thinkin' acid-eaters or some other kind of corrosive that disintegrates the bullet upon impact with the target. I reckon the shooter was that sniper I saw on the Russian's boat."

"What's Ivan doing with a sniper?" I asked, more to myself than to the others. "Who was he expecting? He had a small army at the yard, enough to frighten anyone dumb enough to come calling. Besides us, of course. Because we make dumb look bright."

"Beats the fuck out of me, Holliday," Deacon grated in between puffs of his smoke. "But I'm startin' to think this motherfucker wasn't invited to the party."

"A contract killer?" I mulled it over in my mind. "Then who was the target?"

"Perhaps the target was me," Besim suggested. "My many business interests, and subsequent influence in international circles, creates its share of corporate enemies.

However, none of them have resorted to violence in the past. Financial gains and losses are how those battles are waged. Thankfully, my hearing alerted me to the incoming projectile milliseconds before its arrival, which allowed me to evade it, with the unfortunate result of the bullet grazing you."

"If you're right, then how the hell can I conduct an investigation if I have to constantly worry about getting shot by one of your pissed off competitors?" I demanded.

"Calm the fuck down, Holliday," Deacon said. "Saranda's never been shot at before. No, this is something else. I'm institutin' more security around here just to be safe. But if there is someone out there gunnin' for her, they'll have to go through us first."

"Gee, I feel so much better now." I gestured to Mamika to refill my cup.

We arrived at the hotel a short time later. Rather than pull into the gaudy main entrance with all its fake pomp and circumstance, Deacon directed the pod around the back to a separate and nondescript underground parking garage. Four of Deacon's gray-suited security met us at our own private berth. They ushered us inside a faceless elevator that sped to the penthouse. We stepped from the elevator car into the foyer, where Deacon dismissed our little retinue.

Mahoney occupied one of the couches and stood up as we entered the sitting room. His blue eyes were clear, but his unresolved guilt and remorse armored him like the deep gloom of winter.

"Tom, I—" he began.

"Sir, we all make mistakes," I said. "Given my life's choices, I'm not the one who should be throwing stones here."

He nodded, then pointed at my face and said, "That hurt?"

"Looks worse than it feels," I grimaced. "Chicks dig scars, right?"

The captain chuckled and moved to the holo-vision. The empty screen sprang to life at his approach, generating several split screens depicting images of the Flynn family, the dead Russians, Ivan, Denning, Pop, and Gustavo Sanarov. He folded his arms and studied the information. Deacon stood behind one of the couches, eyeing the screens with a baleful glare. Besim issued quiet instructions to Mamika, who then left the room without a word.

With Mamika gone, I explained what had transpired since the investigation first began, as well as my theory behind Calvin's bargain with the One. Besim shifted in her seat. It was a subtle movement, but I'd learned last October that the consultant amassed secrets like a high-priced call girl collected johns. It would be just like her to know some-thing about this business that she hadn't bothered to tell me.

"Calvin wants revenge, and the One is giving it to him," I finished, rather than allowing her cue to sidetrack me. I deliberately left out my encounter with Kate. No one needed to know about that right now. "By my count, three targets remain, assuming Denning is dead, and even if he isn't, he's probably as good as."

"Do you know who they are?" Mahoney asked.

"Anyone directly associated with the Flynn kidnapping." I hesitated, but the look from the captain confirmed he shared my suspicions.

"I can take care of myself," he said.

"Not against this fucking thing, Bill," Deacon growled.

"It ain't like that serial psycho that murdered your family. That monster ain't like nothin' you ever seen. It's—"

"Old magic," Besim stated solemnly, piercing me with a penetrating stare. "The One is a thing of nightmare and death. A remorseless destroyer of worlds. In my tongue, it is called *Velos Aad,* the Endless Spider, for its children are without count. My people faced it once, long ago. We repelled it, but not without cost. Many Vellans perished performing the banishing ritual necessary to cast *Velos Aad* into the Void."

"That confirms our theory about it bein' imprisoned, Holliday," Deacon said.

"Why didn't you mention this earlier?" I demanded, glaring at Besim.

"I required time to properly assimilate the information from your encounter at the church," she replied, but I sensed her hesitation.

"Okay, well, if you beat it once, then we can do it again, right?" I pressed. A slim hope had blossomed in my chest. "What do we need?"

"Such magic is found within the Hall of Adepts, in Vellas," Besim replied with a downcast glance at the carpet.

"Then use whatever pull you've got and give the home-land a call," I urged. "We need some serious help."

"Were it so simple," Besim murmured, raising her head to grace me with a wan smile. Her gray eyes glistened. "As you are aware, my standing within the *Al-Aquibas* is... complicated, at best. And, even if I were able to call upon the Adepts, the banishing ritual requires more than one hundred of them to be present, singing in unison. I am afraid it cannot be done."

"Then how the hell are we supposed to beat that thing?" I threw up my hands in frustration.

"These apartments have been warded against such beings, Detective." Besim gestured at the room with both hands. "It cannot enter. We are safe here."

A million and one questions clamored in my mind, each one begging to be uttered. However, before I could ask, the flames from the fireplace died, plunging the room in deep shadow. The Insight roared through me, responding to the unexpected threat. Silver fire blazed around my eyes, granting me clear vision despite the darkness. A shimmering tear in the wall appeared beneath the dimmed holo-vision. I sensed more than saw Calvin and the One's shadow on the other side.

"What the fuck?" exclaimed Deacon, truncheon in hand. It burned with white fire, illuminating the former Protector in a silver nimbus.

"And for the sin of lies, William Mahoney, you have been found guilty," Calvin Flynn boomed. "Your reckoning is at hand."

I shouted a warning. Dozens of tiny spiders shot through the opening and engulfed Bill. The web strands attached to each creature pulled taut, dragging the helpless man back through the portal before anyone could react. Once it closed, the hearth blazed to life.

Hot anger seared my heart, cauterizing the fear I had once felt in the presence of Calvin and the One. I stepped to the wall, and slammed my fist against it, taking note of the viscous ectoplasm oozing down its surface.

"Not this time, you son of a bitch!" I declared with all the righteous rage of a man on a mission. "I know how to find you. And I'm coming."

39

I pointed at the slick transparent slime oozing down the wall. "Deacon, recognize that?"

His eyes lit up. "It's them goddamn motherfucking kobolds!" he snarled. "You tellin' me they're back from the dead, too?"

"You only killed three of them," I replied. Between the Insight's magic and the quarts of caffeine coursing through my veins, I could've leapt from the rooftop and landed on my feet without a scratch. "Leyla said they run in packs of four."

I began pacing, hoping the movement would further fuel my raging synapses.

"Back at Strachman's, Mr. Shotgun said to me, 'You not the One.' At the time, I discarded it, because I had no idea what it meant. Now I do. The One must have the fourth kobold and has been using its translocation ability to get around and murder people. And credits-to-donuts kobolds aren't 'old magic,' either."

Besim shook her head dismally. "They are not."

"Which is why the fucking wards didn't keep that thing

out!" Deacon slapped the flameless truncheon into his open palm with a loud thwack.

"EVI, show Captain Mahoney's location," I ordered aloud.

"Unable to comply, Detective Holliday," she replied in my ear. "Captain Mahoney never reinstated his chip upon his return from retirement."

"Dammit!" I swore. I moved to the coffee pot and gave my mug a healthy pour. "Okay folks, we can't use EVI, but we still know how to track the kobold."

"Goddamn right we do," Deacon said. He ran his truncheon against the stained wall, gathering up a large disgusting dollop. "I'll dump this shit into Saranda's bioanalyzer and upload the results to Leyla's modified sniffer program. Shouldn't take long. And once we find Calvin and the One, then what?"

"No idea," I scowled. "We'll just have to figure something out on the way."

"Meaning, we're fucked," Deacon chuckled mirthlessly as he strode from the living room.

"I didn't say that."

"Hard to un-fuck something once it's been fucked, Holliday," the Confederate shouted cheerfully from the hallway.

Excitement boiled through me. I should've been frightened, but I wasn't. The Insight had quelled my anxiety and banished my fear by accentuating my burgeoning belief we were finally on the right track. Yet far too many questions lingered, not the least of which was how to stop a ravening monster from destroying the world.

Because that's what all homicide detectives did, right? Solve murders, arrest the bad guys, and prevent spider monsters from eating planets.

Yeah, my normal issues just picked up a new subscription.

Besim drifted over to the wall beneath the holo-vision. The kobold's secretion had evaporated. Her fingers drew a line partway down where the aperture had been.

"Leyla's sniffer found the kobolds once," I said. "It'll find them again."

She bent close, turning her head to the side and pressed her ear against the wall.

"What are you doing?" I asked.

"Listening."

That grabbed my attention.

"Listening for what?"

"Leyla's tracking program is partially predicated upon the Vellan scientific theory that portals and similar gateways create a sudden release of energy in the *aether* akin to tectonic plate movements, or seismic waves."

"The what?" I blinked.

"*Aether.*" Besim waved her hand dismissively without turning around. "The reality to which the six senses are attuned and anchored. When a portal appears, it creates a rent in the *aether* similar to an earthquake. Ripples follow, invisible to the naked eye. These ripples create waves, expanding outward in concentric rings, until they dissipate. Several of the instruments in my laboratory are sensitive to such things. The bio-analyzer that Deacon Kole referenced previously is one of them. However, the disbursement of most energy also generates an echo. And within this echo, other sounds can be trapped within, providing a hint of both its origin point, as well as any other ambient tones or vibrations. They are quite faint and difficult to hear, and certainly beyond human capability. Complete and utter silence is essential if one is to capture the echo."

"So you're asking me to shut up."

"I did not say that, Detective."

"So you're asking me to shut up."

"It would be the most efficacious use of our current time."

"I'll shut up now."

"Thank you, Detective."

I drank my coffee while Besim lowered herself to a few inches above the carpet. The countdown to doomsday was ticking away. Other than the faint howl of the winter wind outside, the crackle of the fire, and the mad screaming in my head, the living room was still.

Okay, I made that third part up.

The lack of sound and movement bothered me. And patience had never been one of my virtues. I needed to work out more of the case, and I couldn't do that standing idly by while Besim used her super-hearing on the wall.

"What I want to know is how Calvin Flynn became involved with that thing in the first place," I said pensively. "How does a murdered boy make a deal with the Devil?"

"Your question is predicated upon the supposition that Calvin Flynn was deceased when the bargain was struck," Besim stated, her back to me. "Perhaps Calvin Flynn died, but his eternal soul, his very essence, never passed on to the next plane."

"That's impossible," I scoffed. "Besides, it's been over thirty years since anyone has heard of or seen Calvin. Then the kid appears out of nowhere, as if no time has passed, and he's bonded to a giant eight-legged killing machine ripped straight from a bad holo-film!"

"Improbable, yes," the consultant said. "Impossible? We live in a world where magic makes anything possible, Detective. You yourself have experienced enough in your short tenure with the Special Crimes Unit to accept that the word 'impossible' holds little weight."

Besim pulled away from the wall, although her hand maintained its contact.

"Eight lives for one," she mused, almost to herself. "Detective Holliday, *Velos Aad* is a creature of magic and lies, hailing from a place of nightmare and suffering. Vellan history tells of how the Spider nearly destroyed Avenir, the Vellan home-world. It beguiled a young and idealistic Acolyte through trickery, honeyed words and false promises. Only when the Acolyte realized her folly could the Circle intervene, and *Velos Aad* hurled into the Void. But what would Calvin Flynn, a child of eight years, know of vengeance? Of retribution? How could he bear such hatred in his heart that he would wish death upon those who had wronged him? Somehow, and at some point, Calvin Flynn and the Spider intersected. And when they did, Gustavo Sanarov and the other victims were butchered. To my mind, this suggests their union is recent, promulgated by some heretofore unknown circumstance that brought them together. If you can deduce when and where this transpired, you will find the answers you seek."

Besim was right, but I couldn't shake the feeling that I was missing something, a crucial detail which would help me understand why thirty years before, an eight-year old boy was kidnapped and murdered. I sipped at my coffee, savoring its flavor, and took in the room. As I did so, the events from last October reared their ugly head. I glanced at the table where I'd left the last bottle of wine containing a mysterious enzyme that spelled life or death for an innocent young woman.

Thoughts of Vanessa Mallery and Patricia Sullinger entered my mind. Two young women at the heart of an ancient magical conspiracy, with their lives as the spoils. I'd been used from the start. When I had finally uncovered the truth, Besim denied nothing. She'd wagered on a reformed addict and disgraced homicide detective, someone whose jigsaw puzzle of a life would keep it together long enough to unravel the mystery and bring justice to her own daughter's tragic end. That I'd jump at a second chance to hunt down killers, rather than waste the rest of my career, hell, the rest of my life, at a dead-end precinct.

That I'd blindly accept the role as Guardian of Empire City.

Well, she'd been partially right, but at what cost? I had trust issues which was why I had so few friends. However, I couldn't deny the thrill I'd felt at being back in the game. At being relevant again. And the weird shit I'd encountered since the first day I'd met Deacon, Bill and Besim hadn't been boring. A tangle of twisted, fiery emotions welled in my heart, yet their heat quickly faded. Maybe I should cut Besim some slack? The elephant in the room stared down its trunk at me, expectation in its shrewd eyes.

"Patricia Sullinger is well," Besim spoke softly, as if reading my thoughts. Her melodic voice resonated with melancholy and grief. "I thought you would be interested in knowing such."

"I'm glad," I said with genuine feeling. "She's been through a lot. Have you seen her?"

"No."

Besim's terse response spoke volumes, the word mingled with a multitude of complications. By her own admission, Besim was considered a pariah among her people. Between the hair, the clothing and the cosmetics, she had flipped her culture off in the most overt and insulting way possible. It was strange, but we shared that in common. I'd been the outsider at the 98th. The other cops had tolerated me, but nobody really wanted me around. Now that I was with SCU, we both got what we wanted.

I studied the tall woman. She appeared ashen despite the layers of makeup crusting her face. Fearful cracks had appeared where aloof equanimity normally presided. The One's invasion of Besim's home had struck deep, with hidden implications of which I could only guess. I'd never fully understood Besim's relationship with Mahoney. Theirs was an unlikely friendship. And after seeing the consultant care for Bill back at his apartment, I wondered if there was more to it.

"We're getting him back," I reassured her.

"Of course."

"And I'm going to stop the One."

She turned from the wall to face me and said, "Of that, I have little doubt, Detective."

"Did you catch the echo?"

"I did. It spoke of earth and loam, of places buried from the light. Of a fire long extinguished. Of ghosts and tombs. A place of tragedy."

"And that means what?"

"I do not know."

"That's not helpful."

"Detective Holliday," EVI interrupted in my ear. "Incoming call from Charlotte Sloane. Shall I direct it to voice mail?"

"No," I answered aloud, then produced my holo-phone from my inner coat pocket. Besim tilted her head to the side, studying me, curiosity overcoming her sorrow. "Patch it through via speaker."

I swiped the window, activating the function. I also

disabled the visuals so I wouldn't have to see Charlie's image.

"Holliday here."

"Tom, it's Charlie." Besim narrowed her eyes, but otherwise betrayed no emotion. "I've been trying to reach you. What's wrong with your holo-phone? I can't see you."

"I've been busy," I replied in a neutral tone that sounded more like the love child between a dumped, bitter boyfriend and sour grapes. Fine, I'm no poker player. I wore my heart on my sleeve and sang Broadway showtunes in the shower. Loudly. Sue me. "You know, investigating murders, fighting Russians, getting shot at. My phone was damaged. Sorry I haven't called you back."

"I, too, have been busy," she said archly. "I can only surmise that these are the same Russians the Coast Guard apprehended yesterday at the container yard?"

"Wow, what great detective work, Special Agent Sloane. You really should get a job in law enforcement, you know that? I hear British Intelligence is hiring."

There was a pregnant pause from the other line. Besim narrowed her eyes, listening intently. I strained my ears but heard nothing.

"Are you quite finished taking the piss?" Charlie asked.

"For now. What do you want?"

"Flynn has surrounded himself with lawyers and private security. While this is not unusual, it appears he has brought his entire retinue with him, as if he is expecting some manner of action. He appears agitated and has asked me to verify the day's schedule several times already. Would this have anything to do with your altercation?"

"Could be," I replied, then summarized the events from Caron Container, omitting Calvin and the One. "He's in cahoots with the Brotherhood, although how far up their collective asses he is, I still don't know."

"And you think the Russians were smuggling the stolen silver and the children to the Euro-Bloc?" Charlie asked.

"Those containers were earmarked for overseas travel. And the hardware the Russians carried made it clear they didn't want the Coast Guard or anyone else snooping around. I think Flynn's been leading a double life. I bet he took over his late wife's shady family business after her death. His position at the bank is window dressing for his an illicit and illegal private lifestyle. And he's been using Brave New Beginnings as a front to conduct business both in Empire City and abroad for decades. Denning's involvement is one bridge that connects Flynn to the *bratva,* but I think there's more."

"That's all circumstantial, at best," Charlie said. "You still don't have any hard evidence linking Flynn directly with anything."

"Not yet," I conceded. "But I'm close. The murders I'm investigating are all linked to Flynn and the Russians. I'm about to track down a lead that should put it all together. Where is Flynn?"

"Today is the ground-breaking ceremony for the future site of the Brave New Beginnings headquarters in Morris Plains. Flynn purchased a property there nearly a year ago, and they recently began part of the demolition. Despite the inclement weather, the media and guests are still arriving. The event will begin in a few hours."

I recalled Besim's recap of her meeting with the banker.

A sudden thought hit me.

"What was it before Flynn bought the property?" I asked.

"A psychiatric hospital that had been closed for decades," she replied. "Why do you ask?"

I traded a knowing look with Besim. "No reason. Have fun today."

"I'll inform you should I learn anything new," Charlie said and disconnected the call.

Besim wore a troubled frown.

"What is it?" I asked.

"I heard whispers shadowing her voice but was unable to ascertain their message," the consultant said. "It appeared as if Special Agent Sloane had been receiving instructions amidst your conversation."

"It's probably MI6's version of EVI." I crossed my arms over my chest. "Either that, or background noise."

Her frown deepened as she considered my comment. "A distinct possibility, Detective. However, I am able to discern your conversations with great efficacy. These sounds were unintelligible."

"You've listened in on me?" My cheeks burned with anger. Just when I thought I could forgive Besim, she drops another bombshell on me. "That's official business, which makes it none of yours!"

"Please allow me to clarify, Detective," Besim gave me a deprecating smile. "As a consultant to the Special Crimes Unit, I have used my hearing to assist with the case to which I have been assigned. For example, I uncovered critical evidence during our review of Vanessa Mallery's home where I discovered the micro-cameras. During those times, and only then, has my hearing intercepted any dedicated conversations between EVI and yourself. I assure you I have not memorized any of them, nor do I think—"

"I don't give a rat's ass what you think. Stay the fuck out of my head!"

"My apologies, Detective." Besim sounded contrite, but there was a hint of steel underneath.

Deacon returned to the living room carrying Leyla's satchel containing her portable holo-rig.

"Program's ready to roll." He glanced between the two of us. "Who pissed in your coffee, Holliday?"

"It's nothing," I muttered. "Let's just get the hell out of here."

40

The silver bullet flew along the elevated private 'way as if shot from a giant gun. A quick check with EVI confirmed the temperature had risen to a hair above freezing. Apparently, a new challenger had entered the fray—a southern warm front had unexpectedly arrived weakening winter's grasp over the enclave. Still, sleet made travel treacherous, although the forecast did say the warmth would be short-lived. Winter's reign was absolute, and she wasn't about to give it up to Spring without a damn good fight. With my luck, the cold and snow would linger through July and beyond, not uncommon in the years following the nuclear aftermath back in the day.

Despite the high probability of ice and snow accumulations during winter, not all of the enclave 'ways were heated. Consistent maintenance of the 'ways was spotty at best, and an expensive proposition. The further out one traveled from the main beehive, the worse the infrastructure might get, depending upon the affluence of the zone.

EVI announced that we were passing over the Hudson River. As I peered out the long portside windshield, the snowfall had transformed into a steady rain. Flecks of wet ice splattered against the reinforced glass, deflected into oblivion. I took note of the thick, enormous spell-mixed concrete pilings that had been driven deep into the bottom of the waterway to ensure the wide track's stability. The massive skyscrapers, holo-ads and suspension bridges of Manhattan melted behind us, forgotten memories guarded by the frozen river more than a hundred feet below. Ahead, the appearance of a regimented grid of buildings, each layered atop the other like ancient pyramids laid out by a careless pharaoh, marked our crossover into Newark Major. A bustling industrial sprawl, and Empire City's central hub for manufacturing and robotics, Newark Major stretched for miles, encompassing what used to be Jersey City, Passaic to its north, Orange to the west, and Elizabeth to the south. Past Orange, we'd pick up Route 10 and head to Morris Plains. The maze of pyramids, transmission towers and smokestacks would eventually thin out to make room for Newark Minor, a series of massive residential and retail centers, conglomerates that offered all the "big city" lifestyle situated in cozy, suburban settings. That is, if you enjoyed living in cubes the size of my apartment with a few hundred of your closest neighbors dwelling above, below and beside you.

Fifty miles to the west of Morris Plains and hugging the Delaware River lurked the mile-high, spell-forged steel walls that both protected and insulated Empire City from the horrors of the past. Manning those walls was Perimeter Defense, twenty-thousand brave men and women whose daily job ensured the more dangerous portal Jumpers stayed out. Beyond the walls lay miles of shattered ruins and the old bones of what once was, horrific mementos of where humanity might have gone if not for the return of magic, the discovery of the Nexus nodes, and the fortuitous arrival of the Vellans.

I regarded the HUD filling the forward curved windshield with a detailed map of northern New Jersey. Morris Plains comprised a tiny section highlighted in blue. A separate holo-window held a variety of weather, municipal and public traffic data.

"What kind of a moron does a ground-breaking ceremony in the middle of a fucking ice storm?" Deacon asked, his lit cigarette filling the command area with a dull gray haze.

"The kind who won't let his ego back down." I checked the readout of the fully charged and reloaded SMART gun in its shoulder rig. I didn't know what we'd be facing but I sure as hell wanted to be the one bringing a bazooka to a knife fight. "Charlie told me Flynn is commemorating the new facility to Calvin and Angelina."

"So why not bring the fucker in for questioning?" the former Protector asked curiously.

"Because I'd much rather have Flynn apprehensive, exposed and vulnerable," I replied with a grim smile. "By now he knows we're closing in on him. However, none of the Russians have talked, and Denning is gone, so no one has given him up, yet. Can I have EVI access your pod's port? I need to check something."

"It is already done, Detective," Besim replied from one of the passenger chairs, a porcelain teacup held in one hand. If Bill's abduction still bothered her, those emotions had been bottled up and thrown into the sun. "As part of the Special Crimes Unit's unique mission, William anticipated the eventual need for an upgrade in transportation and consulted with me. He felt Special Crimes should achieve an additional level of separation from the more mundane aspects of your law enforcement. This transport is officially licensed and sanctioned with Empire City as an unmarked, clandestine vehicle. In order to deflect the curious should we be scanned, it bears an appropriate identification number and parking address that corresponds with a privately owned and operated transportation service rather than law enforcement. And after your unfortunate encounter with the Russian gunmen *en route* to rescuing Abner and myself, donating this vehicle was the obvious choice."

"Of course it was," I grumbled.

"Do not be fooled by the comfort that you see, Detective." She gestured with her other hand at the pod's interior. "Both Deacon and I oversaw its special modifications personally. It possesses all the appropriate security clearances your previous vehicle had, along with several useful utility functions including fire suppression, defensive countermeasures, and emergency medical facilities. It can also act as a temporary submersible."

"This thing goes underwater?" My eyebrows lifted with surprise as I reassessed the transport's cozy interior.

"If necessary," she replied while sipping nonchalantly at her tea.

"Well, let's hope we never need that," I said. "EVI, please provide background analysis for Morris Plains."

"Accessing," the AI's soft voice issued from hidden speakers throughout the pod's interior. "Morris Plains is a privately held settlement of three thousand two hundred and sixty-eight residents as of the previous year's census."

"Who owns it?" I asked.

"Darby Wistermoor, a retired psychiatrist now turned agro-dealer of strawberries, soybean, corn and wheat. Her family purchased Morris Plains ten years after the establishment of Empire City."

"Old money," I muttered.

When an ECPD investigation involved a privately held settlement, it was customary to reach out to the local authorities to coordinate how it would be handled and avoid any conflicts. Naturally, I hadn't bothered. The locals could clean up the mess after we were gone.

Although I spent most of my time in the Five Boroughs, I'd ventured out to the more rural parts of Empire City on occasion. A large stretch of northern and western New Jersey had been transformed into indoor and outdoor agricultural centers. While hydroponics, animal cloning and vertical farming were essential to feeding Empire City's population, dozens of smaller agro-businesses had popped up over the years outside the main metropolitan center. These facilities grew all manner of natural and proto-products, and all for a profit. Over the years, parts of New Jersey had literally been transformed into a garden state in more than name.

Morris Plains, and places like it, had grown into mini fiefdoms, ostensibly under the jurisdiction of Empire City's constitution and mayoral hegemony. Each landowner held a vote in both the enclave's council and the electoral college. They also ran their own local government, which included a real estate tithe for anyone not employed by the landowner, as well as maintaining their own private security to keep the peace. It wasn't the old Wild West by any stretch, but some settlements were known to be prickly whenever outsiders ventured into town. However, all these landowners kissed Mayor Samson's office since he had direct oversight of the border wall and Perimeter Defense.

And his guns were a lot bigger.

"Please check Wistermoor's public records," I instructed. "Cross reference the following key words—Donald Flynn, *bratva,* Pyotr Ushakov, Ivan Kruchev, Gustavo Sanarov, Orlando Denning, Titan Bank, Brave New Beginnings, Calvin Flynn."

A new holo-window flickered to life, displaying Flynn's recent purchase records for twenty acres of undeveloped land and all associated buildings located at the Darby Psychiatric Hospital in Morris Plains. Another window popped up to reveal several newsfeed puff pieces highlighting the sale of the property and Flynn's grandiose plans to demolish the derelict buildings and replace them with a new state-of-the-art Brave New Beginnings facility.

I scoured the e-docs, taking special note of the defunct property's images, forgotten by time, and covered in creeping vines. The main four-story brick hospital had been expansive, with eight separate wings connected to a central hub. However, one section drew my attention. The roof and portions of both walls had collapsed, the result of some old catastrophic event.

"EVI, what happened to the east wing?" I pointed at the screen.

A new window appeared containing a vid-feed from a hand-held device. The recording's image trembled, the apparent work of an amateur filmmaker. The time stamp was from five years ago.

"Overcrowding was Darby's downfall," a young woman outlined in a sing-song voice, the kind you'd hear in holo-documentaries. "The quality of life for those receiving treatment there had greatly deteriorated. This unfortunate state-of-affairs was the impetus for several riots. It was during one of the more violent uprisings nearly twenty-five years ago that a fire broke out in the east wing. Due to an unseasonably dry spring and a catastrophic sprinkler system failure, the entire east wing was destroyed. Two hundred lives were tragically lost. After a short investigation, the hospital was closed permanently, and the remaining residents relocated. However, the 'East Wing Burning,' as it was later called, did help to inspire and inform an enclave-wide institutional reform."

I waved my hand to halt the streaming.

"A psychiatric hospital with eight parts," I mused aloud. "What are the odds?"

"Puts that fire around thirty years ago." Deacon crushed his cigarette against the console. "And Flynn's here today. That ain't no coincidence."

I nodded in agreement and said, "Springtime, after the February kidnapping, but in the same year. Charlie said Angelina Devereaux' parents died in a house fire set by her dad. The man had suffered from severe depression and schizophrenia. What if..." My voice trailed off as I considered the leap I was about to make, sewing together the miscellaneous evidence we'd gathered throughout the investigation. "Why would Flynn buy this property? Why Morris Plains? Why not something closer to the city?"

"Perhaps the purchase price was attractive," Besim offered. "Between his position at the bank, and the many business contacts he has cultivated over his career, Donald Flynn is privy to a tremendous amount of real estate information."

"Maybe." I moved to the beverage station and filled a fresh mug. "But Morris Plains is a long ride from Titan and all of Flynn's rich pals. No, I think we need to look at this another way. Sanarov wakes up to find a mutilated body, who is later identified as Calvin Flynn. He's sent to New Rikers for kidnapping, but the murder charge never stuck because there hadn't been enough evidence. From the testimony I read, he was as shocked as anyone that the boy was dead. Now there's Mahoney who destroyed evidence because his former captain, a man who we now know to be Empire City's own Mayor Samson, and a close friend to Flynn, ordered him to do it. On the same night Sanarov is apprehended, Father Jack revealed to me that Pyotr Ushakov and his two men arrived at the Redeemer with someone who he suspected was Calvin. We have a run-in at Caron Container with Orlando Denning, who is a longtime employee of both Brave New Beginnings and the church. This is all related, and it starts with Calvin, Angelina's parents, and Darby Psychiatric Hospital. What if Flynn was afraid Calvin had inherited his maternal grandfather's mental health disorder and believed the boy would become another Antoine Devereaux?"

"You think Flynn faked his own kid's abduction?" Deacon asked in disgust. "What kind of sick fuck does that to his own kid?"

"Someone consumed by vanity and hubris," Besim answered.

"*Pride went before,*" I stated softly. "*Ambition follows him.*"

Besim acknowledged me with an incline of her head. "Angelina bore the stigma of her parents, something she could neither escape nor leave behind. By fabricating Calvin's abduction, they would curry both favor and sympathy with Empire City's elite."

"So the Russians take the kid from Sanarov, hole up at the church for a few days to make sure Mahoney's investigation stays fixed on the kidnapper, then they dump Calvin at a psychiatric hospital," the Confederate said. "That dog still don't hunt, Holliday. With all of Flynn's wealth between him and his wife, why not just smuggle Calvin out of Empire City like they tried to do with them orphans?"

"At a guess, to keep an eye on him," I answered. "But it's

more than that. The Devereaux family had long been the target of British Intelligence. Maybe Flynn also wanted to create separation between the Devereaux family mental history, and their new life together in Empire City?"

Deacon tapped out the cigarette, lit a new one, then took a long drag before saying, "You can ask him after we get there."

The bullet's interior grew quiet as we all marinated in our own juices. I sat beside Deacon who was monitoring the progress of Leyla's kobold sniffer program. From the look of the data output, no ripples had been detected.

Thinking about the young hacker sequestered in one of Besim's medical facilities rekindled the cold rage brewing in my gut. Were the consultant's medical personnel doing everything they could?

I should be there with you right now.

"Stop it, Doc," she'd say.

But I let you get hurt, kiddo.

"It's not your fault."

How can I be the Guardian of Empire City if I can't protect the people I love?

"Remember what Rabbi Adler said? Sometimes bad shit just happens. Now you go and be a detective. I'll be waiting for you when you get back."

Once this case was closed, I'd make it my business to hunt down the son of a bitch who had shot her.

"EVI, access my private collection," I said after a moment, then ran through the robust artist list before making my selection.

As I settled into my chair, a haunting saxophone's singular cry permeated the pod's interior, followed by the steady riff of a bass guitar as Bob Seger sang about loneliness, pain and the long road traveled.

41

D espite the rain, we made good time. Once the municipal 'way ran out of track, the silver bullet transformed into an eight-wheel road vehicle and we merged with Route 10. The poor weather conditions made visibility rough, and the roads were dotted with downed tree branches and potholes. At the outskirts of Morris Plains, however, the rain let up, the clouds parted, and fitful bursts of dappled sunlight blessed the frozen landscape. Eventually, the hills flattened into acres of heated glass and steel greenhouses stretching north and south in regimented rows. Robotic pickers and covered containers used to harvest the yields trundled along the metal tracks running between the low-rise buildings for transport back to one of several packaging and distribution hubs.

"Detective Holliday, Morris Plains peacekeepers have registered this vehicle and are requesting identification," EVI announced.

"Put them through," I said, then quickly added, "audio only."

"Good afternoon Citizens, and welcome to Morris

Plains," a woman's voice droned over the internal comm. She sounded about as friendly as a canker sore. "I'm Officer Pearson. Please state your business."

"Good afternoon Officer Pearson," Besim answered before I could respond, leaning heavily on her accent. "I am Doctor Besim Saranda from Aurik. We are guests of Donald Flynn who is holding a ground-breaking ceremony at his new facility today."

"You're late, Doctor Saranda," Pearson grunted. "They began five minutes ago."

"My sincerest apologies for our tardiness," the consultant said, adding the right amount of embarrassment to her voice. "The weather out of Manhattan was atrocious."

"Please provide your authenticator for validation," instructed the officer.

Besim reached toward the HUD and opened the access menu. From there, she pulled up her electronic messages, then sifted through a series of correspondence between herself and Flynn relating to her earlier tour of Brave New Beginnings. The final message contained the link to a personalized invitation written in gold calligraphy, which she illuminated with a flick of her fingers. A new holo-window appeared to the side of the main screen bearing Empire City's official seal as well as the Morris Plains police department header. Besim drew the invitation into the new holo-window, and an eye blink later, both images disappeared.

"Thank you," Pearson said. "Mind the speed limit and enjoy your visit."

The communication terminated. Tension descended upon my shoulders like unpaid alimony.

"When were you planning on telling us you'd already been invited to this?" I demanded.

"When the need arose," she replied placidly. "As I had no intention of attending the event, it did not seem relevant at the time. Rather fortuitous given our investigation has led us to Morris Plains."

"Not the 'f' word I would've used." I stomped over to the beverage station and poured myself a full mug. "You heard the peacekeeper, EVI. Mind the speed limit."

"Acknowledged, Detective."

After turning left onto Route 202, EVI eventually steered the bullet from the main drag to smaller and better kept surface roads. Unlike the residential and industrial centers that we'd passed through on the way in, Morris Plains had managed to retain some of its late twentieth century character. Individual homes dotted the landscape, each surrounded by thick clusters of maple and alder trees whose leaves had long succumbed to the season.

"Ain't nothin' registered to Leyla's sniffer so far, Holliday," Deacon said at one point. The former Protector drew over a holo-window containing the active search program to the forefront of the windshield's screen. "Flynn's been there awhile, so the One's had plenty of opportunity to bag the fucker. You reckon it's waitin' for somethin'?"

"Yeah." I downed half the mug in a single gulp. "Us."

I had just finished pouring myself another healthy jolt of java when the silver bullet's proximity scans revealed we had arrived at the outskirts of the Darby property. Ahead of us, four dour-faced men and women in heavy winter coats had set up a temporary security checkpoint. I had EVI slow us down in anticipation of another credential verification, but one of the suits merely waved us through instead.

"Sauce for the goose," I muttered, eyeing the four people as the bullet rolled by them.

Tall, thin sentinel trees guarded both sides of the cleared

gravel road, their gnarled and bony branches bent from the memory of winters' past. I finished the coffee, then placed the empty mug by the beverage station. I was about as wired as I was going to get. I checked the SMART gun for the twentieth time since we had arrived at the settlement.

"Relax, Holliday," Deacon drawled. He leaned back in the command chair with both of his combat boots propped on the console. "It'll all be over soon."

"That's what worries me," I said.

The end of his cigarette burned bright as he took a long drag from it. "You said it yourself," he said. "The One is waitin' for us. We'll fuck it up, bag Flynn, save Mahoney and call it a day."

"You make it sound so easy," I grumbled. "If I'm right, then we're about to go up against something that took a hundred Vellans to banish."

"Yep," Deacon nodded his agreement.

"And we don't have the faintest idea how to stop it," I added.

"Right again," he said.

"So why aren't you concerned?" I asked.

"'Cause I ain't," he shrugged.

"Gee, that's so helpful," I muttered.

"Lighten up, Holliday," the Confederate said. He dropped the expired cigarette to the floor, then crushed it beneath his boot. "I've been in worse scrapes and had a lot less to work with. Besides, I reckon between Saranda's brains, my truncheon, and your Insight, we'll figure somethin' out."

"I hope you're right," I said. "Without Leyla with us—"

I couldn't finish the thought. My heart grew heavy as new anxiety ate at me.

"Well she ain't comin'," the former Protector stated

quietly. "C'mon, Holliday. Keep it together. If we fail, it don't matter none what happens to Leyla, 'cause there won't be an Empire City left for anyone to live in anyway."

As we passed beyond the trees, the land opened around us. A frozen lake occupied much of the space, its dull surface glinting sadly in the fitful sunlight. To the right, the land had been cleared to make room for a regiment of inert heavy construction machinery. Ahead loomed the Darby Psychiatric Hospital, a monstrous collection of vine-covered brick and glass that resembled a forbidding fortress rather than a former bastion of mental health. The ruins of the east wing were in plain view, piles of cracked and broken stone like the unearthed bones from some ancient beast.

EVI directed the bullet into a parking lot that had been established several yards from the lake's edge. A colorful open-air pavilion with tall metal space-heaters and dozens of chairs had been set up before the hospital entrance. White-shirted servers with black bowties shuffled around offering food and drink to the guests. More security suits lurked among the attendees and servers, dead-eyed sharks swimming with the minnows.

I donned my rumpled brown blazer, and we exited the pod, with Besim in the lead. As we crossed the tramped-down grassy field toward the pavilion, I could just make out the hazy outline of the Perimeter Wall on the horizon. Even from here I felt its presence, a stark shadowy line of untarnished spell-forged steel, all that stood between our so-called "civilization" and memories best forgotten.

"Look alive, Holliday," Deacon warned.

I felt dozens of curious eyes descend on us. We stood out like a birthday cake that had been lit on fire. Four thick-bodied, steely-eyed security personnel converged as we neared the entrance. Both Deacon and I kept our arms by our side, although our weapons were within easy reach. Besim glided ahead unconcerned as if she owned the place, blissful insouciance and a lazy half-smile on her heavily-rouged face.

A sudden stabbing pain in my chest made me stagger. I managed to keep my balance, but then I stumbled to the side as if the world's axis had shifted beneath my feet. Deacon grabbed my arm to steady me.

"What the hell's wrong with you?" he hissed.

My eyes blurred with tears as the Insight seared them, although my vision hadn't changed. Goose prickles flocked along my body. Warm sweat beaded down my back. My body shivered.

"I'm not sure," I managed. "Something's sparked the Insight. Something in the pavilion."

"The One?" The former Protector cast about searching for threats.

"I don't think so," I murmured. "This feels...different. Stay sharp, Deacon." I stood up, cleared my throat loudly, and waved at everyone with a sheepish smile.

Besim hadn't turned, seemingly oblivious to what had happened. A barrel-chested man with a handlebar mustache and squinty pig eyes intercepted her before she could enter the pavilion. The other four suits hovered nearby.

Handlebar held up a forestalling hand and said, "This a closed event."

"I am Doctor Besim Saranda," she replied frostily. "These are my retainers. Please consult your list."

"One moment." Handlebar's eyes glazed over a moment, then he nodded. "Ah, yes, Mr. Flynn has been expecting you. Follow me, please."

Besim ducked her head as Handlebar escorted us into

the pavilion. The other suits kept pace. The sweeping susurration of guests buzzed loudly at the sight of a Vellan in their midst. We were subjected to more than a few curious glances, but Besim ignored them all. Instead, she was content to be led by Handlebar to the far end of the pavilion where Donald Flynn held court.

The banker wore a classic charcoal and pinstriped three-piece suit and crimson power tie, more in line with a board-room than an outdoor ceremony. Five other similarly attired sycophants flittered around Flynn like a gaggle of school-yard flunkies. A broad smile spread across his lips as he registered our arrival.

My heart skipped a beat as I caught a quick glimpse of Charlie off to the right engaged in conversation with some-one, but a large throng of people blocked my view. She held a full glass of sparkling wine, laughing in delight at some-thing she'd just heard. I caught her eye, but she made no move toward us. A server bearing a silver tray offered Besim and I chilled shrimp cocktail before presenting it to Deacon.

"Fuck off," the former Protector growled.

"Ah, Doctor Saranda," Flynn gushed as the server blanched whiter than her shirt and skulked away. "So good of you to come. And I see you have brought unexpected guests."

"Mr. Flynn," I said. The Insight simmered, but it wasn't directed at him.

The other men who had been talking with the busi-nessman mumbled their goodbyes and melted back into the cesspool of guests.

"Detective Holliday, come to witness the end of the old and the start of something brave and new?" Flynn asked lightly, although the anger in his eyes said otherwise. He sipped at his champagne, then glanced at me, a mocking smile riding his face. "I'd offer you a drink, but then I wouldn't want you to check back into rehab."

"I'm so glad you care," I said, trying to keep my flaring anger under wraps. "This isn't a social call."

"Then you can speak with one of my lawyers, Detective," Flynn said, gesturing airily in the direction of the open bar. "They're here somewhere and will happily answer all of your questions."

"I'm sure," I said. I made a show of looking around. "I'm surprised Orlando Denning isn't here. Given all he's done for you and the family business over the years, I figured he'd want to be. Don't you?"

Despite the alcohol flowing through his bloodstream, Flynn paled. I grabbed a couple of small pastry quiche from a passing server, then popped one in my mouth. It was warm and savory, but no substitute for one of Uncle Mortie's knishes.

"You picked a nice day for it, too," I continued.

"Yes, the weather has held off, thankfully," Flynn said, trying to recover. "Once we've torn down the old hospital, a state-of-the-art facility will take its place. It will be the premier center for children's advocacy and welfare in the western hemisphere."

"That's not what I meant," I said. "Isn't today also the anniversary of your son's kidnapping?"

"And his tragic death, Detective Holliday," Flynn replied. "Why, I remember—"

"No, Mr. Flynn," I interrupted forcefully, raising my voice. "Today is the day you *faked* your son's 'tragic death.' You hired Gustavo Sanarov to kidnap Calvin. Then you had Pyotr Ushakov and his men take him from the warehouse in Red Hook. From there, they brought him to the Holy

Redeemer Church in Brighton Beach, before transporting him here a few days later."

"I have no idea what you're talking about." Flynn waved at some new arrivals behind me, feigning indifference.

Besim stepped forward, her size and proximity pushing Flynn closer to a space heater. Perspiration appeared on his brow. One of his sculpted eyebrows twitched.

"Must've cost a shit-ton of credits to keep everyone quiet," Deacon added grimly. "Sanarov, his wife, the medical staff at Darby. And even more to falsify Calvin's medical records, enclave ID and everything else, too."

"One thing I still don't understand," I continued before Flynn could respond. "Why not have Ushakov kill Calvin and let Sanarov take the fall? That would've been so much cleaner. Sanarov gets the chair, so no chance of parole. Or did you figure with so many people in your pocket, you didn't want to add murder to your laundry list of other crimes?"

"Ain't no use hidin' behind your money now, Flynn," Deacon grated. "We've got Denning and the Russians at the container yard, and all them orphans from Brave New Beginnings the *bratva* tried to smuggle out of Empire City."

"That's right," I said. "It won't take the D.A.'s Office much to connect you to all of it and make it stick. So maybe you should grab all of your lawyers, because I'd say you are about to be well and truly fucked."

"Donald is everything all right?" a new voice interrupted.

Charlie and two men joined our group. Her eyes flashed me an apology and a warning.

"Ah, Harold," Flynn breathed. The sight of his relieved reptilian smile filled my mouth with bile and half-eaten quiche. "Thank you for coming. I believe you are already acquainted with Detective Holliday and his vaunted Special Crimes team?"

Harold Samson was my height, thin and white-haired, with an aristocrat's nose, high cheekbones and shit-brown eyes. I'd met him a few times in my early days working the homicide table downtown. Back then, he was on the city council. A politician's politician, known for his skillful negotiations and hardline stance on anything that went against his policies. He hadn't changed since he'd been elected to the highest office in the enclave.

But he wasn't the one who had grabbed my attention.

"Alan Azyrim," greeted the other man. "It is my distinct pleasure to finally meet you, Detective Holliday. I have heard so much about you."

He was a tall, strikingly handsome man with glossy hair the color of midnight, a strong jaw and a predator's easy smile. But it was his heterochromia which captivated me. One eye glittered a startling blue, while the other smoldered a deep amber. The Insight writhed as if entranced by a snake charmer's tune.

Azyrim offered me his hand in greeting. I studied it, noting how his palm appeared surprisingly soft and smooth. A faint part of my mind wondered how often he moisturized. After a heartbeat, he lowered his hand, but the sardonic smile remained.

"Detective Holliday, shouldn't you be out hunting ghosts or arresting vampires or some such nonsense today?" Mayor Samson demanded. "And where the hell is Mahoney?"

Whatever witty comeback I'd normally employ died on my lips, buried beneath the Insight's reaction. I tried concentrating, but a powerful sense of inadequacy had debilitated me.

"Donald, my sincerest apologies, but I must depart,"

Azyrim said. His deep, compelling voice was both strong and seductive. If he told me right then to take a swan dive from the roof of his corporate office, I might have considered it. "I have matters to attend to at my office that require my immediate attention. Ladies and gentlemen, I bid you a good day."

Azyrim left us with a polite and deliberate nod to Besim. She stared back at him stony-faced, her gray eyes hard as diamonds. My mouth hung open. A hand clasped my shoulder firmly, and I met Charlie's worried look. At her touch, warmth coursed through my body, dispelling the paralysis. The syrup filling my brain evaporated, and I had command of my faculties once again.

"Now then," Flynn huffed with indignation. He made a move to get around me. "If you'll excuse me, I have a ceremony to finish."

"You couldn't do it yourself, could you," I blurted out, desperately trying to regain our momentum. "You were overcome by the shame and ridicule you knew you'd have to face because of Calvin's mental illness. It was the same sickness that took Angelina's father. So, you decided to fake his death. I'd like to know why."

The banker hesitated, then gestured to Handlebar and his security detail. They pushed their way between us to form a protective ring around their boss. Deacon reached for his truncheon. Handlebar glared at him, daring the Confederate to make the next move.

"These spurious accusations are going to cost you your career, Detective," Flynn spat as his men cleared a lane. Once free, he stepped up to the podium. Beside it lay a large square of fresh dirt, and a shovel planted spade-first in the ground.

The assembled guests had been drawn to our verbal

sparring, including members of the media. I realized that our entire exchange was being livestreamed on dozens of newsfeeds and social media channels.

"You disgust me, Flynn," I continued in a hard voice, the slow burn of the Insight churning my gut and stirring my fury. "You're just a soulless coward."

"And you're out of line, Detective," Mayor Samson warned. "You're casting aspersions on a man held in the highest regard by the Empire City constituency, including myself. His philanthropic efforts have helped thousands of dispossessed and orphaned children for nearly three decades. If you don't have anything more concrete than words, I suggest you leave Mr. Flynn alone until such time that you can present credible evidence for review."

"With all due respect Mr. Mayor, I don't give a flying fuck what you think," I shot back. "Your friend Donald Flynn is a liar and a murderer."

"Then prove it to me, Detective," Samson declared. "Otherwise, get the hell out of my sight."

Handlebar stepped in my space. "Time for all of you to leave," he ordered.

"Detective Holliday speaks truth, Mayor Samson," Besim stated suddenly. "Donald Flynn invited us here to prove to everyone how his wealth will safeguard him against the rightful hand of justice."

Besim's words trembled on the air, resonant with power, drawing everyone's eyes to her. Everyone, that is, except for Deacon and me who watched the telltale shimmering that had begun to creep around the earthen square on the ground.

"Stay close," I muttered, edging toward the ceremonial plot. "We'll only get one shot at this."

Deacon nodded.

"It is the hope of Donald Flynn that Detective Holliday will protect him against a being that seeks vengeance," Besim continued. The shimmering grew more pronounced, but Flynn and the others were so engaged by her voice, they failed to notice. "It cares nothing for his accolades, nor his influence. It knows only death and destruction. It feeds upon the frailties of others, their lies, their guilt, and their despair. For this creature has subverted the soul of poor Calvin Flynn to allow it entry into your world. And now, Donald Flynn, it, and your son, come for you."

At her pronouncement, tiny spiders boiled up from the ethereal tear in the ground. The arachnids swarmed the area around Flynn, instantly consuming Handlebar and his men, their shrieks echoing sharply before being silenced in death. The crowd of guests and media burst into a fleeing mob, screaming in terror where moments before they were enthralled spectators.

Calvin arose from the earth to stand beside his father, a grim specter glistening with hundreds of eight-legged horrors. Flynn stared, stunned by the apparition of his son given terrible form.

"Donald Flynn, your day of reckoning is at hand," the boy declared in the voice of the One. "Atone for your sins and burn in perdition's flame."

Calvin embraced his father. With a legion of spiders crawling over them both, they sank into the ground, swallowed by the hungry darkness.

42

I vomited a second time, painting a Picasso knockoff on the wall and floor. Deacon stood several paces from me, disgust plain on his face. He held his holo-phone aloft, bathing parts of the room in its glow.

Deacon and I had leapt after Calvin and the One seconds before the aperture closed. The instant we entered the strange null space created by the kobold's ectoplasm, our reality had shifted and churned, stretched and shrank, and careened in a million colors and directions all at once. Vertigo had quickly overwhelmed me to the point where I couldn't figure out where up ended and down began. An eye blink later, and we were wherever the hell here was.

I stumbled over to a cleaner wall, then slid to the floor. The cool surface stabilized me as I watched the Confederate roam about. Debris and dust cluttered the floor from bits of concrete that had fallen from the ceiling. The air by one wall shimmered like a heat mirage. I blinked, and it vanished. My stomach gurgled in mild protest.

"You fixin' to sprout roots, or are you gonna get your ass up?" Deacon asked.

"Just give me a second," I wheezed, then belched. Thankfully, that settled some of the queasiness in my gut. "Where are we?"

"Sub-level, I reckon," he replied. "Definitely below grade, judgin' by the thick concrete. There're light fixtures on the ceiling, but the bulbs are gone. Anyway, while you were redecoratin' the place, I wandered around a bit. We got two exits out of here, and both lead to adjoining corridors with more rooms in the same condition as this one. No elevators, though. Didn't want to go too far in case somethin' decided to sneak in here and eat your face."

"Thanks." I took several deep breaths, exhaling through my mouth after each one. The world had stopped performing cartwheels before my eyes. The shimmering hadn't returned. "Where's the One? Why did we appear in here?"

Deacon shrugged. "Maybe the kobold portal don't work like that."

He directed light around the room to reveal the exits. A hulking figure overshadowed one doorway. I jerked against the wall, yanking the SMART gun from its holster.

"Perhaps Calvin Flynn influenced the jump by redirecting us here," the figure said, resolving itself into Besim as she entered the room to stand beside Deacon.

Charlie appeared behind the consultant. In one hand was her holo-phone, and in the other, a gun whose make I'd never seen before. The weapon was compact like a .22, but oddly translucent, as if made from glass. Bleeding throughout its interior were the three primary colors of red, yellow and blue, yet the "pigments" never mixed.

"Glad to see you've finally managed to contain yourself, Detective," Charlie remarked with a sly grin.

I lowered the gun. "How'd you get here?"

"I reached out to Deacon Kole moments before your leap," Besim explained. Her face held little expression. She smoothed the front of her longshoreman's coat with a steady hand. "Special Agent Sloane had a similar idea. An unfortunate oversight on my part."

"My sincerest apologies, Doctor Saranda." Charlie's smile widened, never reaching her eyes. "As I informed you previously, Donald Flynn is mine. Special Crimes can't have all the glory."

"Suit yourself, Sloane," Deacon grunted.

He moved by Charlie, who turned to follow him. Besim glided past me. Without Deacon's holo-phone, the room plunged into darkness. Before I joined them, I reached beneath my shirt collar and pulled out the SCU badge, laying it over the front of my shirt. Its soft silver radiance enshrouded me, a tiny aisle of light in an ocean of black. I levered myself unsteadily to my feet.

"Hey Holliday," Deacon called out. "You comin'?" His voice echoed once before it disappeared.

"Deacon?" I shuffled forward and entered an empty hallway. "Besim? Where are you?"

My badge lit up the corridor in both directions, chasing away some of the darkness. Thick roots had burst through the concrete in places, twisted warnings that nothing humanity ever made was permanent. Musty smells permeated the air, a mixture of mildew, wood rot, and old ash. Water dripped in the distance, and I wondered if a root had pierced a pipe. I pulled out my holo-phone, but it wouldn't activate.

"EVI?" I couldn't feel her stuffy presence in my head, either.

The Insight simmered, patient and aware. A thrill of anticipation shuttled through me, as if the magical perception was preparing to reveal to me a carefully guarded secret. The Insight purged the last vestiges of vertigo from my body to fill me with fresh energy. All my senses sharpened, but apprehension gnawed at me.

Had the others inadvertently stepped through another kobold portal? Had I? Or worse, had the One captured them?

I'd known we were headed into a trap ever since the One had abducted Mahoney, but I still felt uneasy and unprepared. The question remained of how I was supposed to stop a creature that had eaten parallel Earths for breakfast. That stuff was reserved for wise-cracking wizards and sword-swinging heroes from holo-fantasies. I was just some poor schmuck with a gun, a pair of handcuffs, and magic true sight. How could any of those things help me against something like that? It had easily manhandled us back at the church. Had it not been for Leyla's intervention, we'd be dead, too.

I needed all my marbles now and couldn't let panic unsettle me. Closing my eyes, I focused on the Insight. Its presence quelled my fear, clearing my mind of the phantoms plaguing it.

When I opened them, Nine stood at the edge of the silver light.

You are In-Between.

Her mouth hadn't moved.

"What does that mean?" I asked, nonplussed by her sudden appearance.

There is little time.

"Who are you?"

Help them see.

She stepped into the darkness.

I drew the SMART gun. I didn't need online access or its

wireless capability to shoot something. Glancing down the opposite way revealed no change. I turned back to where Nine had been and moved in that direction.

The extensive network of hallways held no common areas. Broken doorways marked more empty rooms, but I ignored them. There was no sign of Deacon or the others. I'd pause at each split and turn, trusting the Insight to guide me. Its insistent tug pulled me along, growing stronger with each passing moment, and with it, the scent of ash, and something else.

Something old and foul.

Warmth crept into the hallway, growing in intensity the further along I moved. A dull red haze glowered ahead from an open doorway. Smoke billowed outward to crawl along the ceiling. I coughed, choking from the grit, and pressed forward, holstering the gun. Thick, heavy air and raging heat surrounded me. Sweat soaked my clothing. I hesitated, the swelter unbearable, but I sucked up my courage and forged ahead. I held my arm before my face, squinting against the intense crimson glare.

Part of the ceiling in the chamber I entered had collapsed, toppling the remains of whatever the room above it had contained. Piles of rubble and rotted support beams mingled with the fragments of the past. Scraps of demolished bed frames and shards of glass poked out from the rubble. Everything was bathed in the color of spilled blood. Yet there was something both alien and familiar about its hue. Something I'd encountered once before. The Insight seethed, dancing along my skin, reacting to its presence as if readying for a fight.

"Is someone there?" a tremulous voice croaked.

"Calvin?" I called out.

"Help me."

"Hang on, Calvin!" I picked my way through the debris. "I'm coming!"

My exposed skin blistered and cracked. My hair, my eyebrows, even the stubble on my cheeks felt abused and singed. My clothing smoldered. The soles of my shoes began to melt. I clutched the SCU badge, brandishing it before me like a talisman to guard me against the hell seeking my destruction. Blooming red flogged hungrily at the silver aegis, yet somehow, I was protected from the worst of it.

"Help me."

A crimson film billowed before me like an ancient clipper ship's sail, rippling with the heated current. A few feet beyond it lay a figure beneath the rubble, but my seared, dry eyes couldn't penetrate the haze. I knew that if I pushed through this veil before me, my life would end. But I also knew that if I didn't try, whoever it was on the other side would die.

Life was never simple, so why should death be any different?

I closed my eyes and stepped beyond the translucent barrier, and shrieked as if I had stepped into the sun. What courage, strength and fortitude I had left was stripped from the very pores of my skin. This was worse than being shot, slicing my wrist with a broken shard of glass, or watching the love of my life die before my eyes. Every painful sensation, every slight, every heart-wrenching moment, every defeat, every mistake, every wrong decision I'd ever made all coalesced in a sheet of unsurpassed failure. My soul was flogged and flayed, torn asunder, remade and ripped anew as I experienced each memory again and again, and each time sickeningly slow and unforgivably intimate. Whatever I'd passed through, it was sentient, and knew me in ways that perhaps even I didn't. Yet, somehow, despite this excruciating torment, I forced my legs forward. I refused to allow it to beat me. Someone needed me, and I couldn't let them down.

"Not him," the voice rasped. "Jesus Christ, not him."

I opened my eyes.

Pop lay beneath a pile of split wood and fallen masonry. Blood ran from his mouth, and bone protruded through his left arm. Soot and ash covered his charred face, but his angry eyes were fixed on me.

"Leave," Pop croaked through blistered lips. "There's... nothing...you can do."

"I'm getting you out of here," I swore.

I tore my blazer off and wrapped my hands in its fabric. Grabbing a smoking beam, I heaved, but the immense weight defied me. Again I tried, shouting my frustration, and wasting precious air. Defeated, I punched the immovable object, then slid to the floor by Pop's side.

His good hand snaked out to grip my arm.

"S'just like you," Pop wheezed. "Too weak...to do shit. Just like...when you were...a kid. And now you're going to die here...with me."

"Why do you have to be such a goddamn prick?" I yelled. "I'm trying to help you! Don't you see that?"

"'Cause you're just like...your mother," he laughed. "You care...too much...about everyone...even the ones...who don't...deserve it."

My old anger burst to the surface, erasing the exhaustion and pain. A deep, dark red stained the corners of my vision, slowly consuming the Insight's white fire. I staggered to my feet, glaring at him, my eyes narrowed and brimming with hatred. Pop met mine, taunting me with a mocking half-smile as his life seeped from his mangled body. He was helpless, crushed beneath the weight of the ceiling, yet still the same salty son of a bitch who never missed a chance to tell me that I wasn't good enough. That I didn't deserve to be loved or respected.

That I just wasn't worthy of anything. I waved my hand dismissively. I couldn't help him. No, that wasn't right. I wouldn't help him. In that awful moment, I considered his pitiful plight, the irreparable damage to his body, and the sense of relief I'd feel once Pop had finally left the land of the living.

It would be a simple thing.

Walk away.

Do nothing.

And just let John Holliday die.

Help them see.

I hesitated.

Pop's smile faltered. The red haze around my eyes wavered.

"Don't listen to her, Tommy," he urged. "She's trying to trick you! She's always trying to trick you!"

Make them whole.

"It's too late for them," Pop wheedled, as if he was trying to bargain with someone else, his voice taut and sibilant. The red faded further. "Don't you see? You're all too late. Listen to me, Tommy. All of this is real. All of it! Your friends are dead. You let them die, remember? They disappeared, and you couldn't find them. That thing got them. But you can get out! You can still save yourself!"

I staggered back a few steps. "This isn't right," I murmured uncertainly, running a shaking hand across my face.

"Wake up, you ungrateful little shit!" Pop screamed.

"Isn't this what you've always wanted? Walk away, Tommy! Walk away and you'll finally be free!"

"No."

I felt like I was a blind man haunted by echoing voices, drowning in feelings replete with venomous heat, but lacking bearing and substance. Something external had flooded my senses all at once, hoping my mind would unravel from the overload, that I'd bury myself inside my personal demons and forsake my rational self. It wanted me to give in to my despair and lash out, thereby controlling me. I realized then that everything I had been experiencing was manufactured, the mad concoction of a dark, alien mind seeking to tear me apart for its own twisted amusement.

I was trapped within its finely crafted illusion, a phantasm of incredible depth and detail. Like my experience with Pop in the control room at Caron Container, the Insight couldn't penetrate the glamour because I refused to see it. The clairvoyance relied on both my vision and my mind working in tandem to process whatever I saw. This went beyond the One. Whatever this effect was, it had somehow exploited my own memories and emotions to circumvent the Insight and prevent me from seeing the truth.

"This. Isn't. REAL!" I shouted in defiance.

The Insight railed against the red stain until only white fire remained. Suddenly, the smoke and heat vanished. Cold descended upon me. Darkness settled in place of light, except for a passage of silver surrounding me. Pop and my imagined wounds disappeared.

I stood a few steps inside a massive underground chamber whose left half had been shorn away long ago to plunge into a spiraling aurora of nothing. Hoary walls hugged the rest of the chamber, scored by time and the natural movement of earth and stone. Parts of the ceiling had caved in, revealing the scorched hospital room above where Calvin Flynn had been imprisoned thirty years ago, and was burned alive because of it.

Portions of the old drywall, support beams and concrete had collapsed to mingle with the old stones. It was a dichotomy of manmade construction and the natural shaping of the underground, blended by something powerful enough to wreak havoc on both. That's when I remembered the heavy equipment parked by the hospital. Flynn's contractors must've broken the seal to this chamber when they began their demolition, awakening whatever had been contained here.

To my left, five human-sized cocoons depended from thin strands of translucent webbing embedded in the ceiling. They hung at the edge of the endless swirling night below. My connection with EVI remained quiet. I put my blazer on, then unholstered the SMART gun and manually switched rounds. I slid closer to the nearest cocoon, never moving my eyes from what waited for me at the center of the chamber.

Calvin Flynn stood behind a chest-high stone pedestal that appeared to have been shaped from the earth itself. Strange patterns roamed around its surface. I couldn't tell if they were letters or images or both. They shivered whenever I looked at them, merging into one another.

Floating above the top of the pedestal, and the source of the ruddy incandescence blanketing the chamber, was what appeared to be a glittering ruby. Calvin's fingertips caressed the gem's edges almost reverently. The boy's eyes stared unseeing ahead. Frozen fire blazed around his body like an unholy aura trapped in amber, raging moments captured in time.

Settled behind Calvin at the center of its giant web was the massive chitinous thorax of the One. The terrible arachnid's bulbous form was covered in hundreds of tiny, slithering, skittering creatures. The rustle of their movement composed a sinister symphony, heralding horrible things yet to pass. Its eight arms were poised protectively around the fiery aspect insulating Calvin, yet never touching it.

"Welcome, Guardian of Empire City," boomed the One. "Welcome to our Ascension!"

43

"Let them go!" I shouted, training the gun on the spider. The Insight gathered itself, dripping strength into my arms and legs as it prepared me for battle.

"You pose no threat to us, Guardian," the One said. "You and the rest of your wretched species are cattle for the slaughter. So easily manipulated, and so easily broken. Humanity is a blight, a disease that infests this world, living in disharmony with it, plundering its resources and riches with little remorse and offers nothing in return. Humanity harms its own for the pleasure of it! Consider this speck of life, a mere child who wanted nothing more than to be loved! Kidnapped, betrayed, spirited away to a place of so-called healing. Ignored, unwanted, and spurned by the very parents that bore it! When the seal was broken, it found the Stone, and together, they cried out to the Void. How could I not answer? Once bonded, I feasted upon its sullied innocence. Now, the child is trapped In-Between, fearful to pass beyond the veil, neither here, nor there, or anywhere. And its hatred, Guardian! Oh, its hatred is unparalleled! So young, yet so exquisite! In all my travels, I had never considered the limitless power of a child's suffering and fury!"

The Spider cackled with awful delight. I moved to the nearest cocoon. It hung from the ceiling by a strand as thick as my wrist.

"You okay in there?" I whispered out of the corner of my mouth.

"Our circumstances could be improved, Detective." Besim's muffled murmur barely touched my hearing.

"I'm working on it."

"We appear to have little time."

"Tell me something I don't know."

"I, and my children, are the instrument of this child's vengeance," the One continued. "Once the Bargain is complete, we will be freed! My children will pour into your world and ease its pain by erasing humanity's very existence from all places and all times. It shall be a kindness. Only then will this child know peace."

"By laying waste to everything and everyone Calvin knew?" I shot back. The narrow curve of the SCU badge caught my eye. I slipped the device from around my neck. "And speaking of the 'Bargain,' aren't you missing somebody? Sanarov, Ushakov and his two men, Denning, Mahoney and Flynn. Where's the eighth?"

The Spider's chittering laugh grew low and menacing. "And here I believed you to be worthy prey, Guardian," it said slyly. "Yet still you do not see that which is right before your very eyes?"

"*I'm* the eighth?" I blinked in confusion. "What do I have to do with Calvin Flynn?"

The calculus made no sense. The only remaining person to have had a direct hand in the kidnapping plot from thirty years ago was inexplicably missing. What the hell was going on? "You are all that stands between us and our freedom from the Void," the One said. "Your companions have been neutralized. Your mortal weapon cannot harm me. And the Daughter of Night is not here to protect you. You are at our mercy. Your cause is hopeless, Guardian. Give in to the inevitable, and I shall make your death a painless one."

"Gee, that makes me feel so much better," I muttered, desperately weighing my options. None of them held a happy ending for the good guys. The fight in the Redeemer's basement had proven the One outmatched me. Not only was I not in its league, I wasn't even in its own universe. I needed to even the odds. But how?

Help him see.

I stole a glance at Calvin. The Insight sharpened. The boy had cocked his head as if listening. It was the first movement I'd registered from him since the illusion lifted. A slow warmth filled my belly, and for the first time since this goddamn case began, I nurtured a tiny glimmer of hope. I didn't know shit about magic bargains, but I'd read Marlowe. And I knew that once you broke a deal with the Devil, he always got his due.

"You had no intention of honoring the terms of your Bargain with Calvin, did you," I said. "You've just been using Calvin to find me so you and your offspring can get out of jail. Calvin might not realize it, but I do. You lied to him, counting on his anger and pain. You fed him false hope and empty promises. You're not his instrument of vengeance. You're just another goddamn pusher selling damaged goods."

"Empty words, Guardian," the One spat. "I have given the child everything it desired."

"All any child wants is to be loved and feel safe," I said, drawing on my own fractured emotions for strength. "Vengeance is no surrogate for that. Murdering those responsible won't change what happened. All it'll do is dig a deep enough hole where no light can ever shine. Quote the Bible all you want about mercy, retribution, and humanity's frailties and failures, but the truth is Calvin just wants to understand why he wasn't good enough for his parents."

"Spare us your human sentimentality," the One mocked. "It is beneath you, Guardian. Yes, this youngling was foolish and naive. It knows nothing of magic, the ways of the multi-verse, and the powers that dwell within it. What will it matter to a dead little boy once everything it has ever known is reduced to dust? We have tasted glory, the delicacies of worlds unknown to you and yours, now lost and adrift. And we shall do so again!"

Calvin flinched. One hand slipped from the ruby. The ruddy haze dimmed. EVI's stuffy presence reasserted itself, pressing against my brain. The SMART gun's tactical appeared in my eye. Ignoring the data stream, I focused on what the Insight showed me.

Nexus energy flowed between Calvin, the One and the strange ruby, raw and powerful. It cycled between the three of them, a constant rush of dazzling color. The energy had become a living current, and through it, they were bound together, with Calvin as the anchor.

Suddenly, yet another in a long and storied history of ridiculous ideas formed in my head.

"You've been sitting in stir for a long time," I said. "When the Vellans sent you packing from their homeworld, that must've really pissed you off. Stuck in-between time and space, unable to feed, incapable of doing anything except stew in your juices. Although I guess with ten million of your hungry children to keep you company, you were never bored."

Calvin lowered his head to his chest. The flow of energy hadn't abated, but I sensed another subtle change, as if Calvin was siphoning off a portion of it.

"Vellans!" the Spider snarled. "Their beloved world of Avenir is gone, thanks to the Adversary. Yet they managed to find refuge here. An unexpected boon. I shall delight in their destruction! Still, it is a curious thing, Guardian. Despite all the pain and anguish you have suffered. Despite everything both humans and the Vellan have ever done to you, still, you desire to protect them?"

"Yeah," I growled defiantly. "Because that's what I do."

I fired.

Heavy ordnance flew at the grotesque monstrosity, showering it in a blaze of fiery incandescence...and did absolutely nothing.

"Oh shit."

The powerful explosions echoed, pounding my ear drums with their concussive thunder. Thick debris tumbled from the ceiling, and the ground shook. The seizures forced me to my knees. The floor fissured wide, separating me from Calvin and the One. I regained my feet, then slashed down the length of the cocoon with the sharp edge of the SCU badge, freeing Besim.

"Feed!" the One raged.

Hundreds of wriggling bodies scurried from the arachnid to race toward us but were stymied by the newly formed crevasse. They surged into one another, running along the length of the break, unable to cross.

Besim regained her feet, then used her own badge to free the others. Flynn and Mahoney were unconscious, each sporting a swollen purple bite on their neck. Besim quickly examined each man. A low humming issued from her lips. I sensed more than saw the healing flow of her song.

"This distraction will not save you, Guardian," the One mocked. I watched as the spiders, acting in concert, constructed a chain out of their own bodies to cross the gap.

"We've got company!" I pointed at the wave of great icky death headed our way.

"Good," Deacon grinned, his truncheon ablaze with white fire. "Been itchin' for a rematch with this motherfucker." An aura of strength surrounded him, bathing us all in its confident glow.

"Allow me," Charlie said.

The MI6 agent aimed her glitter gun, whispered words that melted the moment they touched my ears, and pulled the trigger. A light popping sound followed, like bubbles bursting. Colors jetted from its barrel in a barrage of yellow and blue. They arced over the crevasse, melding to one another until they formed a green outstretched hand the size of an auto-cab. Charlie growled something low and unintelligible. The hand swatted the little fuckers into the fissure, breaking the formation. An instant later, the hand dissolved, the colors raining down into the darkness. Charlie bore a satisfied smirk.

"While an impressive and overindulgent display, Special Agent Sloane, nothing about our dire situation has improved," Besim observed dryly. "You may have eliminated hundreds, but thousands remain."

As she spoke, four new chains appeared across the gap. Two bands broke off from the swarm and rushed toward the walls, while the cavernous ceiling above writhed with movement.

"We can't leave Calvin," I said, thinking furiously. The only visible exit was dozens of feet above us. Everywhere else either led down into the unknown or lost within the ruddy haze permeating the chamber. I had to get over there. Something within the web near the One, hidden previously by the spider's prodigious girth, caught my attention. It was a cocoon, smaller than the ones that had entrapped Besim and the others. A viscous ooze seeped from its bottom.

The fourth kobold.

I added a new wrinkle to my plan.

"What the fuck is that?" Deacon pointed across the chasm.

Orlando Denning emerged from the shadows, nearly every part of him crawling with spiders. He joined the horde of spiders and stepped onto the chain. It surged forward, ferrying him swiftly toward us. Charlie raised her gun and fired again. Two bursts of red and yellow formed streaking fire arrows. Denning took them both in the chest, the flames barbecuing him like a 4th of July cookout. The force knocked him backward, yet the creatures kept him upright. He paused, hugged himself, then threw his arms wide, scattering roasted spiders in all directions.

"That's not right," Charlie said, horror etched on her face.

Denning arrived on our side of the crevasse, an armada of arachnids awash at his feet. Deacon strode out to meet him.

"*Imperet illi Deus, supplices deprecamur!*" he shouted, brandishing the truncheon, a halo of pearly luminescence enshrouding him.

The Insight swelled in response. A howling breeze swept the chamber, rising from the shadowy depths of the chasm behind us. Ghostly wings sprouted from Deacon's back. His body became clad in armor fashioned of silver and white light, and the truncheon lengthened into a gleaming sword.

"*Tuque, Princeps militiae coelestis, Satanam aliosque spiritus malignos, qui ad perditionem animarum pervagantur in mundo, divina virtute, in infernum detrude. Amen!*"

With both hands on its haft, Deacon drove the weapon downward, splitting the ground. A resplendent dome of argent flame erupted before us, a scintillating barrier gleaming with flickering absolution. Spiders hurled themselves at the protective dome but were turned to ash the moment they touched it. With his power spent, the archangel imagery receded from the former Protector.

Charlie clustered closer to me. Besim observed the conflagration in silence, her eyes narrowed, head tilted in her familiar pose of listening.

Suddenly, she stiffened.

"Beware, Protector!" Besim warned.

Denning leapt through the flames. Spiders armored his body, their meagre lives spent to see him safely through. Open wounds, akin to those found on Sanarov and the others, covered his exposed flesh. Where his eyes had been, only empty sockets remained. Moving with alarming celerity, Denning closed with Deacon before either Charlie or I could shoot him.

Deacon brought the restored truncheon to bear, striking Denning in the arms and upper torso, but the blows had no effect. Denning's hand shot out and grasped Deacon's leather jacket. The Confederate kicked at Denning's legs, hoping to trip him, but the sexton's feet were rooted to the ground. He hurled the former Protector against a rubble pile. Deacon struggled to rise, wiping dirt and dust from his bloodied face. As Denning made to move against the shaken Confederate, Charlie and I unloaded our weapons.

Flame arrows and bullets hammered him, scoring angry burns and gaping wounds across his body. The fiery barrage severed his right arm, forcing him back and through the argent wall of fire. As he was engulfed by the flames, Denning unleashed an inhuman wail that nearly made my ears bleed. Burnt beyond all recognition, he stumbled free of the white fire before collapsing in a twitching heap, then lay still.

I turned away from the wreckage that had once been Denning, and exchanged a fierce grin with Charlie, who returned it with a suggestive wink. But before I could respond, a loud series of sickening snaps from behind me made the smile slip from my face. Whipping around, I watched in horror as eight long spindly legs burst out from Denning's skin. His neck and spine cracked like peanut shells before his head twisted around at an impossible angle. What little bits of Orlando Denning that remained had become unrecognizable. With its transformation complete, the horrible creature began scuttling toward us.

"Armor piercing!" I roared and opened fire.

It deftly avoided the bullets with inhuman dexterity, moving faster than the SMART gun's tactical could track. The ammunition counter reached zero, automatically switching back to regular rounds.

Deacon burst into view. He lowered his shoulder and hurtled into the creature, knocking it aside. Charlie's gun fired crystal blue arrows that froze its legs to the uneven ground, allowing the bruised and battered Confederate to rejoin our group. The four of us huddled together, our backs to the darkened chasm behind us. I surveyed the scene. Deacon's shield had weakened, although it was enough that the undulating wave of spiders kept their distance. An air of eager anticipation rustled through them.

"Your resistance is amusing, but futile, Guardian," the One said. "Surrender yourself to the inevitable, and I shall allow your companions a swift death. The choice is yours."

The Denning creature tore its legs off, freeing itself from the ice trapping it. An instant later, new legs grew from the ruined stubs of the old, and the monster was whole again.

"This has to end," I stated grimly. "One way or another, this has to end. I'll surrender to buy everyone time to escape."

"No, Tom, we will find a way as we have done so before," Besim said, placing a firm hand on my shoulder. "Together."

"You heard that bloody thing," Charlie said. "It's going to kill all of us! We have to get out of here!"

"Fuck that, I ain't goin' nowhere." Deacon offered me a tired, determined grin. We locked eyes, sharing the moment. "Besides, we've been in worse shit than this. What's the plan, Holliday?"

Mahoney had regained consciousness. Besim checked on him, but he waved her away, stood up and joined our group. Flynn hadn't moved.

"Sir—" I started, my eyes wide with relief and concern.

"I'm alive, Detective," he grunted gruffly. "Tell us what you've got."

I nodded, then shared my plan that would probably get us all killed.

44

"That's it? That's your fucking plan?" Deacon stared at me as if I'd lost my mind, which, to be fair, I probably had.

"You're a bloody nutter," Charlie marveled at my brave stupidity. The fright that had briefly taken hold of her lessened when she saw the determination in my eyes. She grabbed the front of my blazer, dragged me to her, and kissed me full on the mouth. "For luck."

I stared at her, but no words came. Deacon chuckled. Besim pursed her lips but said nothing. Charlie patted me on the chest, grabbed my arm and twirled me around to face the horror that awaited me. Brain function soon followed.

"You win," I called out. "I surrender."

"A wise decision, Guardian," the Spider said. "Bring forward the flesh known as Donald Flynn and William Mahoney. It is time."

"Whoa, whoa, whoa!" I held up my hands. "That wasn't part of the deal."

"Bring them to me," it said. "Now."

I bit back the hot retort on my lips. Arguing with that

thing was pointless. If there was any chance of surviving this, I had to give in to the monster's demands. Besides, I had to be in spitting distance for my ridiculous plan to work. And, if I was right, Calvin wanted me close by, too. I gathered up Flynn, slinging one of his arms around my shoulder. His head lolled to the side. The bite on his neck wasn't as angry as it had appeared before Besim's song. Mahoney came over. He looked haggard and exhausted.

"Sir, you don't have to do this," I said.

His sunken blue eyes lit up. "Detective, let's show this goddamn parasite how we do things in our town."

I nodded grimly and said, "Deacon, make a lane."

The former Protector held up his left hand and traced an incomplete circle with two fingers. A narrow opening appeared at ground level in the flaming dome.

As I guided Flynn forward, my thoughts traveled to Abner and Leyla again, how they'd each put themselves in harm's way because they believed it was the right thing to do yet had suffered as a result. Rabbi Adler had been right. It had been their choice to stand beside me during my darkest moments, propping me up, believing in me as both a cop and as a person, and showering me with an unwavering love that not even the One could break. I paused, then turned back to regard my companions.

The irrepressible Confederate.

The alluring British agent.

The enigmatic Vellan.

They all had faith in me, be it misplaced, misguided, or otherwise. I couldn't let them down.

The Insight bolstered my courage and sheared away the fear threatening to overtake me. I took a deep breath, exhaled slowly, and resumed my march of doom toward Calvin and the One. As I approached the crevasse, a mass of the squirming fuckers formed a bridge wide enough for me to cross.

I hesitated, eyeing them with suspicion, and asked, "How do I know they won't drop us?"

"As you are the eighth, your life's essence is forfeit to me, thus fulfilling the means of our escape," the One responded with gleeful malice. "While amusing, allowing you to fall to your death would be self-defeating."

"Oh," I gulped. "I guess that makes sense."

The closer I approximated to the source of the ruddy haze and flow of Nexus energies, the more caustic the air surrounding me became. My skin grew raw from the exposure. The chittering flow of spiders beneath my shoes nearly turned my stomach.

Once across, I dumped Flynn before the pedestal, close enough that I could touch both him and the boy. Calvin hadn't acknowledged our arrival. One hand cupped part of the ruby while the other rested by his side. His body was unblemished by the ravages of time, yet his eyes were distant and lost.

I quickly studied the scene through the Insight's lens. The One clung to a translucent web whose strands were as thick as my arm. Its immense form possessed depth and size, yet midway up its torso, the Spider became incorporeal. The One's body quivered with excitement and longing. Its eyes fixated on us. Slavering fangs glistened with a violet venom. Its children skimmed the lower webs in droves, but the moment any of them passed beyond the invisible border above them, they winked from existence before reappearing as ghostly shadows.

Nine's voice fluttered into my memory.

You are In-Between.

"What's going on?" Flynn mumbled, rubbing at his eyes

with hands caked in cavern dust. He struggled to rise, then collapsed. "Holliday? What the hell have you done to me? Why is it so dark in here? Where are we?"

I slipped my arm beneath his shoulder and drew him to his feet. He blinked several times, trying to clear the cobwebs.

Pun intended.

"Donald Flynn, say hello to your son." I gestured at the macabre tableau before us.

"My...son?" The businessman gaped. I held him steady. "Calvin, is that really you? What is that thing?"

"See now the face of vengeance, Donald Flynn," the One intoned. "The face of your son, the boy you left to die!"

"Holliday!" Flynn panicked. "What in God's name is happening? Do something!"

My heart rate accelerated. The Insight roiled. Silver fire suffused the crimson miasma the gemstone generated.

I am here, Detective.

Besim's calm whisper tickled the corners of my mind. I shivered, unnerved by the sensation. Unlike my stuffy connection with EVI, this felt like the consultant's fingers were inside my head fondling my brain. No wonder Deacon appeared discomfited by the experience! If Besim ever decided to rearrange my mental decor, I only hoped the carpet matched the drapes.

"Calvin Flynn, I have been your loyal instrument," the One spoke in silken tones. "Five times, justice was met. Five corrupt, sinful, evil men brought low. All but three remain, and they stand before you. Now, release your righteous wrath! Command me, and I shall bring upon them such ruin that they will never harm another man, woman or child ever again!"

"Son, listen to me," Flynn pleaded. He tried to approach

Calvin, but my grip held him back. "You don't understand! Your mother and I adored you! What happened to you was a tragedy! We never wanted you hurt! We only wanted you to be safe! Calvin, please, listen to me! I'm your father, Calvin! Listen to me!"

Calvin dipped his head, and a dark foreboding swept over my heart. His other hand reached up and resumed its place by the stone. The chamber thrummed with renewed power, removing the silver stain the Insight had wrought, and restoring the ruddy glow to its former measure. I glanced behind me. Deacon's argent shield dimmed as the gem's influence seeped into it. His steady eyes were fixed on me. Charlie had moved to the far side of the dome. She gripped her gun with both hands, nervously shifting her weight. Besim was alone, hands clasped before her, and head bowed.

"This child cares nothing for your honeyed words and false promises!" the One spat with genuine acrimony. "Deceiver! Liar! You forsook it, cast it aside and hurled it away! You let it die. And for that, you have been found guilty! Now, Calvin Flynn, finish what was started! Fill me with your hatred and rage and consummate our Bargain!"

Mahoney inched beside me. We exchanged a knowing look. He reached into his coat to palm his 9mm.

"I'm sorry, Calvin," Flynn cried. "I'm so, so sorry! I didn't know there would be a fire! I thought this place was safe! I didn't know! For the love of God, please forgive me!"

The boy raised his head and directed his vacant stare at Flynn. Spiders swarmed down the web, along the One's body and dropped to the floor. They were on us in seconds. It took every ounce of my training and self-control not to swat at them, or leap into the crevasse behind me. They bounded up my legs, digging beneath my clothing, everywhere at once, to slip into every nook and cranny. The creatures spread past my shirt collar, flowing along my neck, over my cheeks and into my hair. They secured themselves to my exposed flesh.

Then they began to feed.

I screamed. Agony flayed my body as the spiders burrowed into my skin. With one arm around Flynn, I thrust my other through the aura surrounding Calvin. Unnatural heat blistered my arm, but I managed to clasp the boy's hand, connecting the father to the son.

"*All live to die, and rise to fall,*" I groaned Marlowe's quote like an incantation.

Besim began to sing. The Insight surged, using me as a bridge connecting her voice to both Calvin and Donald Flynn. The chamber, and everyone in it, disappeared.

And everything changed.

Daylight filtered through the barred windows of the room. There were twenty beds in here, but nobody ever used them. Well, nobody except me. I had three people who visited me. They never told me their names, but they all knew mine.

The Nurse With The Ugly Wart On Her Face would yell at me a lot if I didn't do what she said. And then the Mean Doctor With All The Needles would show up and poke me with them. After that, everything always got real fuzzy. And then I'd see the ghosts walking through the walls. I'd talk to them sometimes. They'd tell me stories about the hospital, and all the bad things that had happened to them here. They were so sad. I wish I could make them happy. But I couldn't. I never made anyone happy. Well, except Mom, but she wasn't here. She left me, just like everyone else.

"Why are you crying?" The Tall Man Who Wasn't A Doctor sat next to me. He wore black clothes and had kind brown eyes.

"Because I'm lonely," I said. "I want to see my mom and dad."

"We've gone over this before, Calvin," the Tall Man Who Wasn't A Doctor replied gently. He smiled at everyone, but whenever he smiled at me, it was a special, secret smile. It always scared me. "You need to get better first. Once you're better, then you can see them."

"When will I get better?" I asked.

"In time." He patted my leg. His fingers were always warm. I never liked it when he touched me there, or any other place he liked touching me. Or when he'd tell me to take off my pants. Or when he wanted me to touch him. I didn't understand how that was supposed to help me, but he said that when we did stuff like that, it made the bad feelings go away. But they never went away for me. They always got worse.

"Why don't we read?" He pointed with his other hand at the big black book lying on my bed.

I picked it up and looked at its cover, but it didn't have a name on it. It was an old book, and a lot of the pages had writing on them. The Tall Man Who Wasn't A Doctor would tell me that the book was the answer to all of my problems, but I never believed him. He said that God punished the bad people, but if I behaved like a good boy and listened, then God would never punish me. I always did everything that the Tall Man Who Wasn't A Doctor and the other people here told me to do. But I was still stuck here, and nobody would let me see my mom and dad anymore. So why was God being so mean to me? I thought God was supposed to be good. And all the stories we ever read together were scary too, like the one about the man who wrestled with the angel, or the other one about all those people turning to stone. How were those stories supposed to make everything better?

"What should I read?" I asked.

The Tall Man Who Wasn't A Doctor scrunched up his face as he thought about it. His other hand had moved up my leg. I tried to get away, but I was squashed against the end of the bed and there was nowhere to go.

"How about something inspirational," he smiled, that awful, scary smile. "Let's read about Job."

Help them see.

Blood covered the carpet. Ma lay in the middle of it. Her open eyes stared at the ceiling. The room stank. Ma wasn't wearing her shoes. She always wore shoes. Where were her shoes?

Pop was there, just staring at her. Then the cops showed up. Voices came and went, but I couldn't hear what they said. I turned around and looked in the kitchen. I smelled coffee. Two mugs were on the table. One had pretty flowers on it. That was Ma's. She loved flowers. She used to plant them in the garden next to the house. The other mug was black and white, the one she'd take out for visitors.

I turned back to the living room. The cops were busy taking images. They didn't talk to me. Pop hadn't moved. I walked over to him. He never looked at me. I tried to hold his hand, but he pulled it away, like he didn't want to touch me. I tried talking to him, but he ignored me. He just stood there, staring at her.

Like I wasn't even there.

Help them see.

We'd met in a cute little Parisian café—the willful debutante from the Bordeaux Regime, and the up-and-coming banker from Empire City. Our whirlwind romance took us all over the Euro-Bloc, ending with marriage in New London. Months later, we returned to Empire City, the seat of the financial world.

The social circles here had little use for the foolish and the weak. Love to them was an afterthought, yet another commodity to be bought or sold. Naturally, I fit right in from the start. My attraction to Angelina came from her inheritance, and a lucrative, if sordid family business, the kind law enforcement frowned upon. However, for my legacy to endure meant maintaining above-

board appearances. And, so, I lived a life that was as full and imaginative as any Walter Mitty daydream.

Besides, Angelina's indulgences were a poorly kept secret. Her insatiable hungers for the pleasures of the flesh, the drugs, the booze, they were all symptoms of the depression she fought every day. She used anything to chase away the shadow cast by her family demons. And I encouraged her rank behavior. After all, wasn't that what doting, supportive husbands were supposed to do?

When she became pregnant, Angelina changed. She adored Calvin, convinced that he would be free from the madness that had claimed her father. He became her redemption story. To my mind, it was a fantastical contrivance, the desperate hope of a woman clinging to the misguided belief that love saved all. Despite our many arguments, Angelina slowly divested herself from the family business, severing long-standing ties with both her Euro-Bloc and Empire City associates. The dissolute woman was hell-bent on dismembering our carefully laid plans and ruin everything! It was all so short-sighted and pedestrian. She failed to see the potential in what we could accomplish. I knew her love for Calvin would be the downfall of everything we had built together.

However, what came as a complete surprise to me was the love that I, too, would feel for my son. My boy, my heir, the one who would carry on the Flynn legacy long after I was gone.

I was meant for greatness. To want for nothing. To suck the marrow out of life, and damn anyone who stood in my way. The same would be said for my son, and Angelina be damned!

But I was no fool. The Devereaux madness had been all too real. The house fire set by Antoine which claimed the lives of both of Angelina's parents wasn't something I could, or would, ignore. I formulated a plan that would ensure Calvin was spared that horror.

After months of discreet and painstaking research, I settled on the Darby Psychiatric Hospital in Morris Plains. Their doctors had achieved promising results with individuals afflicted with similar mental health issues. Under their care, Calvin would overcome his grandfather's disastrous disability and rejoin upper society, no matter the cost.

The plan was brutally efficient. Contracting with the bratva's go-between in Brighton Beach was a simple matter. He had promised a swift and untraceable solution, and all for the price of assisting the kidnapper's wife with her mortgage, among other things. Strange what friendship will do, but I never questioned the arrangement. I just needed it done.

Meanwhile, the additional arrangement I'd brokered with them involving Brave New Beginnings and my other phil-anthropic operations would eventually become a very lucrative sidecar. Angelina would never know.

But then the fire happened at Darby, and everything changed.

After that disastrous day, Angelina never wanted another child. She claimed she had poured all her love and devotion into Calvin and had nothing left to give. Losing a child did that to some people, or so I've been told. Blinded by grief, Angelina grew worse, jeopardizing my plans. Something had to be done.

Our dinner party tonight knew I had to catch an early trans-port to New London. Raphael had tailored several new suits. Working via holo was no good. I needed to be there in person for the proper fitting.

Raphael had also connected me with that delightfully devilish woman named after some dusty Greek tragedy. Her counsel regarding my own business strategies had been instru-mental in getting me to where I was today. But it was her simple suggestion about Calvin that had helped me formulate the plan in the first place. My son needed proper care, and I'd be damned if I wouldn't move heaven and earth to get it for him.

Naturally, everyone at dinner understood because that was what Empire City's elite did.

Such fools.

I put on the act, apologized profusely, kissed Angelina on the cheek, and left, but not before deftly slipping the sleep supplement into her drink. I then disabled the auto-navigation to her car and drove away. Even in an age where self-driving vehicles kept most people safe, the arrogant stupidity of many who wished to operate theirs while impaired still prevailed.

An hour later, Angelina wrapped her car around a tree, and the deed was done.

A police investigation was inevitable. However, the toxicology report would reveal the high levels of sleep supplements and alcohol in her bloodstream. Captain Samson would control the situation, as he always did, and I would see to his political ambitions. Another fair trade in an enclave that thrived on its backroom deals.

As I watched the crimson and orange plumes balloon skyward, I imagined the flames at Darby. Calvin's body had never been recovered, burned to ash along with his memory.

Still, I vowed to find a way to use his death, and the tragic loss of Angelina, to my advantage. I had little doubt that the Flynn legacy, MY legacy, would endure.

James Thurber was right. Dreams were meant to be lived.

And now, you see.

45

S weet relief washed over me. The excruciating pain had vanished. The Insight was a gentle flicker around the corners of my eyes. I hugged myself, thankful I was still alive.

I had returned to the cavern, minus the spiders, my friends, Charlie, Donald Flynn, and the hellish glow. The SCU badge on my chest colored me with its soft, milky luminescence. I clasped the device, surprised by its soothing warmth coursing through my fingers. I studied the Empire City sigil embossed on the front of it—the scales of justice held between two toga-clad women, one blindfolded, the other bearing a curved sword pointed down.

Make them whole.

Apparently, my magical mystery tour wasn't over yet.

"It's okay, Detective Holliday," a young voice said. "Kal can't hurt you. It's just us now."

Calvin stood behind the pedestal-like rock formation, both of his hands lightly touching the fiery ruby that floated inches above its surface.

"Kal?" I asked absently.

"Kal Arach." Calvin regarded me with innocent curiosity, a departure from the remote expression he'd worn earlier. "Kal said it means 'One Above All.'"

"Is that right?" I released the badge, but its soothing touch lingered. The SCU shield had never done that before. Yet another mystery to unravel someday, when I had spare time and an endless supply of Uncle Mortie's coffee. Thinking of the deli centered me. I shrugged off the last of the malaise scrambling my eggs to focus on the present.

The boy nodded and said, "Yeah, Kal told me when we first met."

I raised my eyes to the hole in the ceiling dozens of feet above me. I'd need a grapnel gun and rope to get us out of here, both of which were in short supply.

"Your friend said you would be safe here, too," Calvin added.

"Friend?" I cast a startled glance at the boy. "What friend?"

"The one that's been talking to me," Calvin replied cheerfully. "Right after you showed up in my fire dreams. She's really nice. She was talking to me while Kal was shouting and hurting you and your friends with the little spiders. I'm really sorry he did that, Detective Holliday."

"Have you seen her?" I asked.

"Oh, no, she's just a voice." Calvin's demeanor brightened as he spoke. "She's been telling me all about you. Stuff like, I can trust you, and that you're the Guardian of Empire City, which sounds really cool! Oh, and that you'll make the bad things go away. Kind of like one of those knights from the adventure holo-stories Mom and me used to watch together. Except, instead of fighting with a sword, you fight with your eyes. Magic eyes. Like you're some kind of wizard!"

I stood there dumbfounded. My encounter at the hospital transit station loomed large in my mind.

Kate, what the hell are you doing?

"I'm just a police officer, kid," I said with a wry smile, infected by Calvin's enthusiasm.

"She said you can use your magic eyes to see why I'm stuck to the glowing rock." He gestured at the ruby with his chin. "I want to let go, but it won't let me because it said it doesn't know how. She also said Kal's using me to help him kill everything, and not just the bad people, but the good ones too."

"She's right about that," I said grimly. "Did she mention anything else?"

"She told me everything would be okay because you're the Guardian of Empire City and you protect kids like me. She also said you don't believe in yourself. How do you not believe in yourself, Detective Holliday? You don't look make-believe to me."

I shook my head and said, "You and me both, kid."

"You know, she cares about you a lot. She didn't say that, but I could tell by how she talked about you. Like she was smiling." Calvin's face clouded over. "Detective Holliday, was that lady lying on the floor your mom?"

My heart clenched. "You saw that?"

"I saw everything."

"Me too, kid. And, yeah, that was her."

"I'm sorry. She looked like a real nice lady."

"She was. So was yours."

"Yeah." Calvin grew somber, but then he perked up. "Hey, you know what?"

"What's that?"

"You and me and the ruby, we're all the same."

"Yeah, kid. I guess we are."

"The ruby told me it doesn't want to hurt anyone anymore. And I don't want Kal to hurt anyone anymore either."

"That's a good thing, Calvin. Too many people have already been hurt."

"I know. We're really sorry about that."

"I believe you. Both of you."

"She said that you'd show me the truth about what happened to me and my mom." His body trembled, but his hands wouldn't release the stone. "My dad is a really bad man, isn't he? And so is that other man. The one at the hospital."

Father Jack.

My smile vanished as my hands balled into fists. That unimaginable horror, a stunning revelation born from the Insight's truth, would haunt me forever. How could Jack have done such a reprehensible thing? He helped raise me, for fuck's sake! Worse, how did I never see it? How could I have been so blind? I had entrusted him with everything. Father Jack's betrayal merged with the white-hot anger churning in the pit of my stomach.

"*We know what we are, but know not what we may be,*" I whispered.

Make them whole.

No shit, Kate, I projected back. *I'm working on it.*

"Do you think you can help us?" Calvin asked.

I released the breath I'd been holding, then willed my hands to unclench. My eyes strayed to the gem cupped between Calvin's hands.

"Yeah, kid," I said. "I'm going to help you."

The Insight's silver fire melded with my vision, clarifying, cauterizing and capturing everything in my sight. I concentrated on the ruby. Suddenly, I was inside its glittering facets, swimming in a swirling crimson sea.

Seek the flaw to unravel their designs.

I dove deep, heedless of my safety and without need of breath, for the Insight preserved my senses, shielding me from the gem's despairing influence. My own painful memories, scoured in red and shadow, drove at me, false phantasms crafted by the ruby to dissemble and destroy anyone foolish enough to enter its demesne. Touch and taste, sound and emotion, thought and vision, all were recreated by the ruby's magic to trick and derail me from seeing the truth. They appeared as real as memory—my mother at the park, stolen moments with Kate at Wallingbrooke, eating lunch with Leyla at Uncle Mortie's, reading at Abner's, walking with my grandfather—yet hollow and empty, revealed to be false by the Insight's flame.

Finally, I arrived at the ruby's heart, a crystalline formation so beautiful and intricate, I couldn't see where it ended or began. I gathered the Insight, coaxing its fire brighter, then concentrated until the stone's flaw was revealed, a nearly imperceptible blemish identical to the one within the emerald Orpheus had worn on her finger. Armed with the fiery clairvoyance burning my eyes, and desperate for answers, I had unfettered access to study the secret that lay at the ruby's center.

The gemstone housed the fading sentience of a Nexus node, one of the transluminal eldritch shells containing the naturally occurring magical energy that powered nearly everything on Earth. It once held a spectrum of color, full of life, acuity and dimension, and a sense of belonging, for no one hue defined it. Then its brightness was taken, although how or when this happened, I couldn't see. Now bereft and forlorn, it burned with a desolate rage, lashing out at anything it encountered to assuage its own pain and loss.

The gem communicated its agony in striking fashion. Hundreds of images flashed before me, almost too swift for my Insight-infused mind to process. They offered me a cracked and broken window into the stone's murky past. I learned the Nexus nodes were part of an intimate symbiotic relationship with all living organisms. They acted as conduits for the transference of life energy from one being to the next, replenished by the return of energy when something died. It wasn't a reference to the soul because the nodes didn't recognize the concept. Instead, it was a process akin to photosynthesis in plants, and part of the natural order of things.

Nexus nodes weren't bound by distance. Instead, they were all linked by an abstract latticework of unimaginable depth and magnitude, pulled along a multidimensional axis invisible to the eye. There was no society, no caste, no culture or anything like civilization as I understood it. The bigger the node, the greater its draw, like the gravity well of a planet, pushing and pulling nodes across the multiverse of parallel worlds. Whenever a Nexus node collided with another, a tremendous amount of energy was released. From that connection, portals appeared, rents in the fabric of reality.

Despite my best attempts to interpret the rush of images flooding my mind's eye, whatever had happened to the ruby remained unclear. Once a thriving, sentient energy, this stone, and three others like it, had been drained of its essence as a result of some vast, enormous endeavor. All four were damaged in the attempt, subverted by whoever or whatever had harmed them. They weren't from around here, but I couldn't determine their point of origin. The stones arrived on Earth an indeterminate time ago because our world was the central hub of an extraordinary existential multidimensional wheel in both time and space. Reduced to nearly empty husks, they'd been cast aside, their apparent usefulness exhausted.

Which was far from the truth.

The process used to drain the stones had split them into something else, shadowy reflections of their former selves. Each aspect had its opposite number, yet they remained inextricably linked as only light and dark could be. But their individual halves defined each node: Desire and Harmony, Deceit and Truth, Despair and Hope, and Malice and Justice.

As I stared into the ruby's heart, understanding blossomed in my mind. What I believed to be a flaw was an old and excruciating wound, a literal tear to its very metaphysical being. The red crystal encasing it was a scab to protect its essence from further harm.

Hurt beyond anything it had ever known, the ruby had drifted, burying itself beneath the ground, but even there, it couldn't deny its transformed nature. It sought out those similarly afflicted and somehow traveled beneath the earth until it encountered the Darby Psychiatric Hospital. There, it fed upon the dregs of the patients' suffering above, soaking in their tortured madness and pain, but not enough to restore the stone to its former balance. The need to reunite with its own kind was both undeniable and unbearable, but in the stone's current condition, equally impossible. Caught between a half-life it couldn't escape, the node gave into despair.

Suddenly, the images faltered, melting in a crimson haze. The traumatic echoes rippled the space around me. I was buffeted in their wake, yet the Insight's silver fire protected me, a mystical barrier against the onslaught. Once the ripples receded, the images returned to reveal the rest of the story.

I witnessed the fire to Darby's east wing. Although I never found its cause, I knew Orpheus was behind it. The conflagration had weakened the room's integrity above, thereby breaking the seal to the chamber the ruby had created beneath the hospital. Calvin, barely alive and his body broken, fell into it when the floor disintegrated. The ruby reacted instantly, adhering to its primal nature as a conduit to reclaim and transfer energy.

But then the unexpected happened. By bonding with Calvin, the stone had discovered a kindred spirit unlike any other. All its despair fanned the boy's own hopelessness and anger. With their combined voices, they cried out their need for vengeance to the multiverse. And Kal Arach, trapped within its prison, had answered. Using Calvin's emotions as its guide, the ruby bridged the unfathomable distance between worlds to connect the boy and the monster, and the Bargain was struck.

I'd seen enough.

Eight years ago, I had succumbed to the same soul-crushing experience the ruby had suffered. I had offered up my body willingly, because if I couldn't be with the woman I loved in life, then we'd be joined for eternity in death. Apparently, life and death both had a flair for the ironic. I knew what needed to be done. The node had languished, trapped in limbo for more than thirty years, unable to complete its natural life cycle.

Unable to die.

Make them whole.

"Kate," I whispered. "What you're asking me to do. I can't. I just can't."

A life for a life, the One had said.

"It'll be okay, Detective Holliday." Calvin's gentle voice floated to me from a great distance. My heart neared its breaking point. "You can help it. You can help us both. Please."

I set the Insight's fire aside, eschewing its protective sheath. I was now exposed, defenseless and vulnerable to the node's flagging essence swirling around me. The ruby sensed its opening and unleashed everything inside of it, all its pain and suffering, an unabated red torrent of despair that should have annihilated me.

But it didn't. I absorbed all of it. Every cell in my body shrieked, even the ones I thought I'd killed off from years of substance abuse. With the Insight as a guide, I used my connection with Calvin and the node's own energy transference to cauterize the wound, drawing on both mine, and the boy's dwindling life force to close it once and for all.

I opened my eyes.

"Detective Holliday?" Calvin asked weakly.

I stared ahead seeing nothing. The enormity of what I'd done resonated to the ends of my frayed and fractured soul. Silver fire laced with crimson flickered at the fringes of my vision.

"Yeah kid," I replied, my voice cracked and hoarse.

"Did you do it?"

"I think so."

I held my ground as the last vestiges of the ruby's despair ran its course, but its echoes would remain. Just more crazy shit to store in my overstuffed mental attic. I'd run out of space eventually, but today wouldn't be that day.

"Good," Calvin sighed. "I knew you could do it."

"That makes one of us."

"Is it time to leave now?"

"Yeah kid."

"What are you going to do about Kal?"

I fixed the boy with a determined stare.

"I'm sending Kal home."

46

Jarred to the present, I blinked rapidly to clear the disorientation. The SMART gun's tactical reappeared in my vision. EVI's familiar presence stuffed my sinuses. A light touch on my mind confirmed my restored link with Besim.

Get ready to sing, I projected to her.

What should I sing, Detective?

"You'll know," I said aloud.

The red haze was gone. So, too, were the spiders covering my body. Dozens quivered on the ground, locked in their final death throes. Calvin had collapsed behind the rocky pedestal. The fiery aura no longer surrounded him. The ruby lay inert atop the formation, just another unremarkable red stone. As I took it all in, powerful tremors rocked the underground chamber. Chunks of debris fell from the weakened ceiling, and from the looks of things, the rest would collapse at any moment.

Reality had returned to my familiar brand of normal.

The Insight blazed through my body, filling me with strength. Moving quickly, I grabbed the stone before gathering up the barely breathing boy in my arms. With the loss of the stone's protection, Calvin's body had returned to its former state. Every inch of him had been charred from the fire. Not a scrap of his clothing remained. Had I not known who he was, he would've been unrecognizable.

"WHAT HAVE YOU DONE?" boomed the monstrous spider clinging to its web, quivering with rage.

"It's okay, kid," I whispered in the wreckage that was Calvin's ear. One lidless eye turned to acknowledge me. "I'm getting you out of here." I felt his stick arms shift in mine, hugging me.

"You have meddled in affairs beyond your ken, Guardian," the One roared.

"Yeah, I hear that a lot," I shot back.

Mahoney was already leading a stumbling Flynn across a shimmering blue bridge spanning the crevasse. Colorless pockmarks along its side grew rapidly as the bridge degraded. The horde of spiders that had menaced Deacon's protective shield bubbled in gooey piles. Deacon, Besim and Charlie gathered on the other side. Besim held a hand to her head, unsteady on her feet.

More of the One's offspring poured down the web but when they reached its bulbous abdomen, they milled into one another, unable to cross. Enraged, the creatures tore into each other. Behind and above them, a swirl of stars had appeared, their counterclockwise movement accelerating by the second. Howling wind blasted through the chamber. The gale pulled at my body, dragging me closer to the web. I set my feet to steady myself. The Spider struggled against the strands, but it couldn't move. With the Bargain broken, the stable gateway the node had created was no more.

"Guardian, you cannot escape me!" it shrieked. "A

Bargain once struck cannot be unmade! Eight lives for one! That was the agreement! This boy owes a debt!"

I wheeled around to face it.

"Bullshit!" I shouted back in defiance. "Calvin owes you nothing! When you swapped another life in exchange for mine, you changed the terms."

"That matters not, Guardian!" the Spider chittered. "Our Ascension cannot be stopped! The boy must honor the contract!"

"Oh, but it does, Kal Arach," I countered, enunciating its name loud and clear. I sensed immediate understanding from Besim. "It's as old as time itself. A word given, wrought in blood. Calvin doesn't need to honor shit. Give my regards to the endless Void!"

"This is not over!" the One howled. "My children and I shall devour your world!"

The Denning thing rushed at me before I could reach the kobold cocoon. I raised the SMART gun and fired, but the creature was too quick. It pounced, striking my left shoulder while ripping the gun from my hand. I cradled Calvin, my arms shielding him as I tumbled heavily to the ground. I rolled to the side. A chunk of ceiling crashed two inches from my face. Bits of stone cut my cheek, and I tasted blood in my mouth. Before I could scramble to my feet, Denning loomed above me. Its mouth split wide as a pair of fangs dripping with venom burst through its skin.

"If the boy will not honor the Bargain, then you will both die!" the One declared.

I jerked my head to the side as Denning lunged forward to finish the job. Suddenly, the business end of a white-flaming truncheon shot between my face and certain death.

"*Defende nos in proelio!*" Deacon trumpeted. A halo of armor and pure white fire enshrouded him. "*Contra*

nequitiam et insidias diabolic esto praesidium!" With both
hands on the weapon, the former Protector bent his knees
and heaved with his arms, hurling the creature away.

Freed from Denning, I checked Calvin. The boy's
breathing was shallow. My heart raced.

"EVI," I shouted aloud, "call the Morris Plains peacekeepers. Have them send emergency response to the Darby
Psychiatric Hospital ASAP! Tell them ECPD officers are
under heavy fire, and need immediate medical assistance!"
If we could somehow reach the surface, the arriving EMTs
would get Calvin the care he so desperately needed.

Mahoney had crossed back to free the kobold from its
cocoon. Surrounded by a familiar silver nimbus, he used his
own SCU shield to hack through the thick web. Relief
flooded me as the kobold's fuzzy face appeared, dazed and
confused. I lurched to my feet, reclaimed the SMART gun,
then ran over to assist the captain.

"Tom!" Charlie yelled. "I can't hold the bridge for much
longer!"

Flynn was a statue beside her. He regarded the pitiful
ruin I held in my arms. No tears. No remorse. Nothing.

"Get the boy outta here, Holliday," Deacon growled over
his shoulder. "I'll deal with this."

Mahoney and I removed the last of the sticky webbing.
The kobold staggered, uttering unintelligible words. The
captain grabbed the kobold by the shoulder and led it
toward the bridge.

Meanwhile, the Confederate advanced toward the man-
spider. The monster hissed, and came at him, but Deacon
was ready. Brandishing the weapon horizontally across his
face, Deacon pivoted gracefully to the side at the last
moment, then drove the truncheon's point down and
through the back of what remained of Denning's head. Bril-

liant argent fire blasted the gaping wound, spreading rapidly across its torso and limbs to consume the foul creature. With a satisfied smirk, Deacon stalked toward us, leaving behind Denning's smoldering corpse.

Charlie aimed her sparkling gun at the crevasse. Fitful blue bursts splashed the fading bridge, strengthening whatever mystical adhesive held it together. Without hesitation, we all raced across.

Besim still hadn't moved. The wind gusts ruffled her clothing. I came up to her and placed my hand on her arm.

"Now," I said.

The Insight responded, rushing from me and into her. Her strange almond-shaped eyes met mine. A knowing half-smile dusted her lips. She straightened her back and raised her voice in song.

Besim's clarion voice rang out, enhanced by the Insight's power, a pure sound that reverberated throughout the failing chamber, overcoming the wailing wind and the crash of rock and stone. From nowhere and everywhere, echoes from the past converged, heeding Besim's magical summons. A choir of one hundred Vellan voices arose, their intricate harmony gathering in strength and purpose. Sung in their musical yet alien language, Besim wove the name *Kal Arach* into her song, reimagining the words into something far more intimate and profound. No longer a name, *Kal Arach* emerged as a symbol, tying it irrevocably to the creature trapped in the prison of its own design. The Spider, recognizing the melody, screamed to the swirling heavens above, its legs struggling futilely against the webbing holding it fast. Yet, with all its considerable might, the One couldn't escape.

"*Hell hath no limits, nor is circumscib'd in one self place,*" I said as Besim's song reached its crescendo. *"But where we are is hell, and where hell is, there must we ever be!"*

The spiraling galaxy of stars above the One burst apart, revealing a darkness so utterly black, no light could escape its hungry maw.

"NO!" the One wailed. "This cannot be! Eight lives, Guardian! Do you hear me? Eight lives! That is the price, and it shall be paid! IT SHALL BE PAID!"

"Time to go!" I said, releasing Besim. She nodded wearily, and we rushed to the spot where I'd first arrived. Charlie took my hand and pressed against me, fearful yet excited. Mahoney brought the kobold to the wall. It stared blankly ahead. Deacon held a dazed Flynn who stared wide-eyed at the crumbling chamber. Above, a resounding crack thundered as tons of broken rock, wood and concrete plummeted down.

"Get us out of here!" I urged the kobold, slapping the rough wall with the flat of my hand.

It looked at me, to my hand, then pressed its ass end against the rough wall. A foul stench set in, worse than the shitty alley next to my apartment. A half second later, the kobold's shimmering portal appeared. It chittered something before leaning forward to be swallowed by the black. We piled in behind it. The One's ululating lament echoed until it was devoured by the vastness of nothing.

One moment we were underground, and the next, we were arranged in a semi-circle surrounded by tall, thin oak trees. The ground trembled once, then subsided. Winter's silence echoed. Another dull gray sky bundled with clouds rode above while fitful, icy rain mixed with thin trailers of snow filtered down between the bare branches. I searched the area, but the kobold had disappeared.

"Is everyone all right?" Mahoney asked.

We all mumbled or nodded our assent, dazed by the magical translocation. Mahoney and Flynn both bore a sickly pallor in the pale daylight, although it appeared that the worst of it was behind them. Charlie studied the trees as if seeing them for the first time. Deacon and Besim were to my right, a rotten stump between them. The former Protector whispered something to her, his face betraying his concern. She didn't respond. A troubled frown creased her brow. She adjusted the colorful bandana around her head with shaking hands.

"EVI, please give me an aerial of my current position," I said aloud. The SMART gun's tactical was replaced by a contoured and colored map of the area. We were a quarter mile east of the hospital. Red and blue dots represented the local emergency services that had just arrived onsite. "Inform the Morris Plains EMTs of our location."

"Confirmed, Detective," she replied. "You also have a voice message from Father John Davis. Shall I play it for you?"

"No." Renewed anger dissolved my befuddled state. The Insight glowered. Argent waves made my vision swim.

"Detective Holliday?" Calvin stirred in my arms.

"I'm here, kid." I clutched him closer to my chest hoping my body heat would keep him warm.

"Calvin!" The banker rushed over, fear and apprehension mirrored in his eyes. "It's me! It's Daddy! Let me see him, Holliday!"

"Back off, pal," Deacon warned, stepping between us. He held his truncheon by his side, although its righteous fire had fled. Mahoney joined him.

"How dare you?" Flynn bristled. He stared down his nose at the two men blocking his path. "You have no right to keep me from him!"

"After all the shit you've pulled?" Deacon snapped. "You are out of your goddamn mind."

"I have no idea what you're talking about," Flynn sniffed haughtily. "Captain Mahoney, I demand to see my son."

"I don't think so," Mahoney shook his head, his countenance resolved and grim.

"You don't think?" Flynn scoffed. "You aren't paid to *think*, Mahoney. You only do. Now do as you're told."

"You know, I never thought this day would come," the captain said. "It's been thirty years since the kidnapping. Thirty years to think about your son and the killer who got away. Thirty years to blame myself for allowing politics to overrule my better judgment. Thirty years of never knowing the truth. Thirty horrible years because I failed to act. Well, not anymore. Not today. No, today, I make up for lost time. Today, I'm going to make things right again. Today, I'm going to do my goddamn job. Donald Flynn, you are under arrest for conspiracy and kidnapping. You have the right to remain silent. Anything you say can and will be held against you. You have the right—"

"Oh, how droll," Flynn sneered. "You have nothing. No concrete evidence. No credible witnesses. Nothing. I look forward to suing the ECPD for wrongful arrest. This will cost the taxpayers millions. And once Harold hears about this, Special Crimes will be disbanded, and all of you brought up on charges! Now, get out of my way!"

Deacon and Mahoney didn't move.

"I'm really cold and tired," Calvin whispered.

"I know, kid," I said. My pulse kicked into high gear as panic exploded in my heart. "Help's coming. You just stay with me, okay?"

"Damn you all!" Flynn glowered. "Holliday! Let me see him! Calvin! I'm right here, son!"

Charlie came up beside me. We exchanged a worried look. She laid a hand on my shoulder. The Insight shuddered at her touch. A ruby glaze suddenly stained its silver fire. The rain disappeared as the snowfall intensified. Thicker flakes fell, rimed in red, small blood drops encased in ice. I was about to speak up when something dark wriggled below the collar of Flynn's dress shirt.

"Charlotte," the businessman sniffed in indignation, unfazed by the crimson precipitation, or the thing crawling beneath his shirt. "Keeping secrets from me, I see. How long have you been working with the police?"

I glared at Flynn, my fury mounting. The SMART gun dragged in its holster. My trigger finger itched. Calvin's movement drew my attention.

"My mom used to sing me to sleep," the boy rasped. "Can you do that, Detective Holliday?"

"Yeah kid," I said as I stared into the soulful brown eyes that once belonged to an innocent eight year old boy. I bowed my head. Fresh tears froze on my stubbly cheeks. "I can do that."

Exhausted beyond measure by the effort hurling the One back to its prison, Besim picked her way carefully across the bloody snow. I raised my head at her approach, the request written on my face. She nodded once, offering me a soft, sad smile before sketching patterns along Calvin's forehead with her long, tapered fingers.

With an intake of breath, Besim's ethereal voice filled the air, silencing everyone. Soft at first, her lyrics spoke of hope and love, and the unbreakable bond that mothers shared with their children. Besim's melody soared, trembling with thoughtful impressions, summoning sweet memories of my mother when she had nurtured and encouraged me. Tempered by an enduring strength, Besim's voice fostered gentle devotion. But try as it might, her song couldn't lift the debilitating despair decimating my heart, the terrible revelations I'd discovered about Father Jack, or the terror and hopelessness engendered by the One and its foul offspring.

Calvin's face softened as Besim's song ended.

"Thanks for helping the magic rock, Detective Holliday," he whispered hoarsely. "It was so sad, but you made it better again, just like the voice said you would. You're a good person. Just like me."

"Nah, kid," I said, bending close so I could hear him. "You're better than me. Better than all of us."

"What are you doing, Holliday?" Flynn fumed. "What is happening to my son?"

Peace settled over the boy.

"Good night, Detective Holliday," Calvin breathed.

"When I see your Mom, I'll tell her how much you love her."

He sank into my chest and was no more.

I stared at him, seeing nothing.

I'd witnessed firsthand the darkness in people, their callous disregard for others on display every day. From shitty street corners in Brighton Beach and Bedford-Stuyvesant, to corporate board rooms along Fifth Avenue, I already knew that I lived in a fucked-up world.

I had sworn an oath to protect the lives and property of Empire City's citizens. To do that, I've made tough choices, hard decisions that often altered the course of more than one life. It was an ugly, difficult, and necessary part of the job.

But today was different. Today, to save an innocent boy thirty years gone, I had to let him die.

"*For in that sleep of death what dreams may come,*" I murmured, desolated by conflicting emotions I could barely contain.

Charlie caressed my cheek with the back of her hand. I leaned into it, wishing the warmth of her touch could shield me against the empty cold threatening to overwhelm me. I handed her Calvin's remains, then regarded the lifeless bundle of bones in her arms.

"You son of a bitch!" Flynn shrieked. "You murdered my son!"

Mahoney and Deacon stepped aside. The banker stormed over to Charlie who reluctantly passed the boy to him. I stared at Flynn in numb fascination as he cradled Calvin. His handsome face clouded dramatically as crocodile tears dribbled down his cheeks. Charlie moved from us, an inscrutable expression on her face. Her hand strayed to the glitter gun she kept inside her coat. She caught my glance, and for a moment, the glint of gold reflected in her irises. The Insight rumbled low in response, like the warning growl of an animal.

"You'll pay for this, Holliday!" Flynn pressed up to me, drawing my attention. "My son is dead thanks to you!"

"Can the act, Flynn," Deacon said. "You ain't foolin' nobody with this bullshit."

"You think this is an act?" he shrieked, wheeling on the former Protector. "How dare you! I loved my son, you son of a bitch! She promised me Darby would cure him! He was supposed to be safe here!"

"*You.*"

A cold fury settled in my gut, burying the yawning sadness threatening to drag me back to a place I thought I'd never return. I knew all of Donald Flynn's political and social connections along with whatever deals he'd brokered with the *bratva,* as well as everyone else drowning in his deep pockets would protect him. This whole fucked up thing would get swept under the proverbial rug, and Flynn would somehow capitalize on it all. Not only would he torpedo Special Crimes, but with his money, Flynn would bury the Sanarov murder investigation under a mountain of lawyers, e-media, and endless paperwork. Nothing would ever happen to him, and he knew it.

With my world tinged in red, I advanced on him, the SMART gun in my hand. When Flynn caught sight of me, he stumbled away, wilting beneath the pure hatred burning in my eyes.

"Control your man, Mahoney!" Flynn shouted in alarm.

"Tom," the captain warned.

"I'm not going to allow this goddamn piece of shit to walk, sir," I snarled. "He's mocked everything I stand for, and the promise I made to myself when the first gold shield was pinned to my chest. If I don't end him here and now, there will never be justice for Calvin or his mother, or the innumerable kids he's already shipped overseas to God knows where, never to be seen again. Besim said I'm supposed to be the Guardian of Empire City. Well, if it's my job to bring down scum like Donald Flynn by any means necessary, then that's exactly what I'm going to do."

"Detective!" the captain ordered.

I couldn't let Donald Flynn get away with murder. Calvin's vacant eyes stared back at me, and my heart broke.

"For Christ's sake, Flynn, he was your son!" I howled with despair.

Blood pounded in my ears. I grabbed Flynn and pinned him against a tree, then shoved the gun's barrel roughly beneath his chin. Liquid fear washed away his arrogance, the snow stained red and yellow at his feet.

I wanted to pull the trigger. I needed to pull the trigger.

"Detective," Besim said softly from behind me. "This is not your way."

"Well, maybe it should be," I snarled, my vision rimmed with ruby light. "I *saw* his memories when I went inside the ruby. Do you understand? I saw *everything*. This worthless sack of shit is a thief and a liar and a murderer, and he deserves to die."

"Perhaps," she replied. "However, you of all people know that justice without love, without compassion, without wisdom, is not justice at all. It offers nothing, leaving only emptiness and despair in its wake."

I leaned in close so that Flynn and I were separated by inches. His wild eyes blinked rapidly as oily, blood-red sweat ran down his face. I smelled his mint-flavored breath, and tightened my grip on the gun.

"Please let me go," Flynn whispered. White spittle coated the sides of his mouth. "I'll give you anything you want. Anything. Just let me go."

"Do not give in to your despair, Detective Holliday," Besim said not unkindly. "If you kill Donald Flynn now, you will become no better than the murderers you hunt."

I stared into Flynn's eyes, finding my feral reflection there. With all the fury and hurt I'd collected since well before this case began, I almost didn't recognize myself.

You're a good person. Just like me.

Calvin's words resonated inside me. I clung to them, drawing strength and purpose, and released my breath in a long, heavy sigh. The ruby light disappeared, consumed by the Insight's silver fire. I withdrew from Flynn, lowering the gun before returning it to my shoulder rig.

Flynn slumped in relief, but his haughty demeanor returned seconds later.

"Holliday, you'll pay for—"

A sudden crack split the air. Flynn's head snapped back as a hole appeared between his eyes. He slid lifeless to the ground. I whipped around to find Charlie holding her glitter gun, a thin trail of smoke rising from its barrel before fading into the cold.

"What have you done?" I asked, stunned.

"What you couldn't," she replied, and walked away.

47

I don't remember much after Charlie left. There'd been lights and sounds, familiar voices asking questions, hands touching me, a heavy blanket around my shoulders. Movement across snow-covered ground surrounded by thin, dead trees. More voices, these unfamiliar and authoritative. Eventually, I went from the frosty outdoors to a climate-controlled interior. Then, the soft lurch of electromagnetic propulsion transitioning to a smooth glide. Mostly, I felt a numbness centered around my chest. I might have had coffee. Correction, I'm sure I had coffee. *Lots* of coffee. EVI mentioned something about another message from Father Jack.

Only three things stood out from our ride back to Manhattan—Donald Flynn was dead, the Sanarov case was cleared, and Charlie was gone. Everything else was background noise. At some point, I passed through the elevator doors leading to Besim's penthouse apartments. I crashed on one of the leather couches and fell into a black, dreamless sleep.

A pot of coffee hearkened my return to the living. I was

alone, wearing the same clothes, in need of a shit and a shave, and smelling of graves and worms and lost hopes. Mamika arrived wearing her customary black slacks and violet top. She refilled the pot. Her sharp eyes betrayed nothing.

"Detective Holliday, you are welcome to remain here for as long as you require," she said. "There are clean clothes awaiting you in the bedroom down the hall. I have also asked our chef to prepare brunch."

"What time is it?" I asked, bleary-eyed.

"Nearly eleven o'clock," Mamika replied.

"I need to go."

I thanked Mamika, grabbed my blazer, and went to the elevator. EVI announced in my ear that I had messages from Mahoney, Abner, and Father Jack. Downstairs, I encountered no one on my walk to the silver bullet, yet I sensed Besim's eyes on me. The coordinates for where I wanted to go had already been programmed into the nav system. Once underway, I had EVI replay all the messages except for the one from Jack.

Mahoney simply said he'd take care of things. The apparent assassination of an Empire City citizen by a foreign operative created its own brand of headaches. Flynn's lawyers might try to pin something on us, but the captain believed all the heat generated by the trafficking operation at Caron Container coupled with the banker's offshore activities that had already been under British Intelligence scrutiny were enough to keep even Mayor Samson off our collective asses. I'd done my part, so Bill would do his. Other than authorizing a week of mandatory vacation, I was to check in with him periodically to remind him I was still alive, bless his crotchety soul.

An idea popped in my head. I rummaged in my pocket

until I found what I wanted, then fired off a quick holo-text. The return ping was immediate. It included ten smiley faces and twice that in exclamation points. At least I'd made someone's day.

I returned to the messages.

"Tom, it's Abner." The old man's voice was strained. "Adina told me you'd come by the hospital to see me. Thank you for that, my boy. I'm sorry I missed you...excuse me..."

There was a murmur, followed by the unmistakable sound of liquid poured into something. Abner gulped twice, then returned to his message.

"Thank you, Adina. Now, where was I? Oh, yes, I called Deacon. He said Besim's surgeon worked for hours. It was touch-and-go at first, but the important thing is, Leyla will be all right. However, she still hasn't woken up. Besim's people moved Leyla to a private room yesterday afternoon at a small boutique hotel with a nice view of the ice-skating rink in Central Park. Once she awakens, Leyla can look out at the winter wonderland which I am certain will cheer her right up. Adina and Deacon have been taking shifts watching her. You know, Tom, once you get past that gruff exterior of his, Deacon is a man of deep feelings. Now, I know what you'll say. I'm fine, really. Just a few bumps and bruises, nothing more. I've been in worse scrapes. So please stop worrying about me. I should be discharged from here soon, and then we can get together and talk all about, well, everything. Stay the course, my boy. All my hopes."

A touch of warmth crept into my heart, a welcome salve to the many wounds I'd suffered these past few days. I didn't know what I'd do without Abner and Leyla. I added Deacon to that short-list, just for good measure.

"EVI, please locate Father Jack," I instructed aloud.

The current traffic map on the windshield's HUD shifted

to the side, replaced by satellite imagery of the Holy
Redeemer Church. A blue dot representing Jack's ankle
monitor signal glimmered on the north side of the building,
in a small lot adjoining the property.

I recognized that place. It was the church cemetery.

He was waiting for me.

It didn't matter how he knew I was on my way. It only
mattered that he did. After a short ride, I found myself
outside the church's front steps. Gray and white blanketed
the world, fitful light cast by a pale sun lost to the brumal
heavens. Abner was right. Leyla adored this weather.

Thinking of her, I sent up a silent prayer to whoever was
on call.

Bad things happened. Good people got hurt. They just
did. Live or die, love or hate, condemn or be forgiven. I
didn't believe in miracles, but I trusted in the strength and
conviction of my friends. I didn't give a damn whether God
heard me. I only cared that he listened.

A thin dusting of light snow covered my head and shoulders. I worked my way around the side of the church and
away from the playground, following a cleared walking path
smeared with salt pellets. Despite the cover, black ice made
for precarious footing, slowing my progress. To my left ran
the wrought-iron fence separating the church from the
street. Few pedestrians had ventured out, kept home by the
bitter cold. As I passed around the broad girth of the
church, I was struck by its enormous size, the years etched
into its stonework, the intricacies of the stained-glass
windows, and the real promise of hope it offered for those
willing to listen.

I paused. The old garden by the small playground was
buried beneath snow. I glanced to my right, picking out the
small window to the little kitchen where I'd spent hours

sharing my innermost secrets with Father Jack. I'm not sure whether I was more angry than sad. Out of habit, I checked the SMART gun, then dug my hands in my pockets and resumed my trudge along the frozen track. Rounding the bend, the iron fence forked across my path while also continuing along the street. An open gate at the split granted access to the cemetery. As I stepped through, I closed the gate behind me, and set the latch.

The Insight hadn't been active since we departed Darby. I felt it stir when I crossed the threshold. I was glad of its presence, reminding me I wasn't in this alone. I paused to admire the regimented rows of silent memorials, faded hallmarks of the past. Thick clumps of snow capped the weathered stone and marble monuments of the church cemetery. Whoever had been buried here was long before my time, although the place had been well-maintained. I entered the hallowed grounds, sticking to a pathway of footprints that was being devoured by the falling white. My footfalls crunched loudly, almost an insult to the quiet sanctity of the graveyard.

Jack's back was to me, both hands inside his heavy coat. He stood before a tall headstone whose engraving had faded with weather and time. I stopped several paces behind him and waited.

"Christopher Elias Gurnisson." The pastor broke the silence, his hoarse voice as leaden as the sky above. "'Devoted husband and father. May his watch never end'. At least, that's what I think it reads. Hard to tell, after all these years. He died nearly a century before I was born, yet his message endures to this day. He'd been a police officer, like you. Had an unremarkable career, married and divorced, four children between two women. I hired a restoration company twenty years ago to salvage these plots. They did what they could, but a lot had already been lost."

He gestured to the other monuments with a tired wave of his ungloved hand.

"Ever vigilant are the dead, Tommy," he remarked, turning to face me. "Nowhere to run, and nowhere to hide."

"You lied to me," I spoke quietly.

Jack's sardonic laugh was wracked with phlegmy coughing. His ashen pallor belied the feverish heat burning in his eyes.

"I've lied to a lot of people," he said. "It's part of the job."

"Which job is that?" My body shook, but my hands stayed inside my pockets. "Is it the one where you helped Orlando Denning and Donald Flynn sell orphaned kids into slavery, the one where you took advantage of an innocent little boy, the one where your people lifted rare Spanish coins from museums, or the one where you're some high-level stooge for the *bratva*? Jesus Christ, Jack! I trusted you! Calvin trusted you, all those years ago! And all this time, you've fucked me. Fucked us both. Played with our lives. Pretended to be our *friend*. Is this the part where I'm supposed to ask you why? Because we're well past that. Right now, I'm trying to figure out whether I should drag you before your congregation so they can see the fraud you really are."

A melancholy smile crossed his face.

"I've watched your career with great pride, Tommy," he said. "Even after Kate and Wallingbrooke, I knew you would pull yourself together. Your convictions have always made you strong. Your will to do the right thing, even after nearly taking your own life. I admire that about you. It's what makes you who you are. But I never lied about being your friend. I was always there for you. I always made time for you. I swore on the day I—" Jack paused, grimacing from a pain born of the heart and not whatever sickness ailed him. "After Elaine died, I swore I would never let anything happen to you. And I meant it. I've kept you safe. Everyone in the neighborhood knew you were under my protection. So long as you never interfered with my business, nothing would ever happen to you."

Jack's countenance shifted. He stood taller, the sickness in his eyes replaced by a prophetic zeal that had fallen into madness.

"Then, on the night he murdered Gus, Calvin appeared to me, alive and whole, as if he'd been ripped from Scripture, like one of God's angels! I couldn't believe what I saw, yet I knew he acted as a holy instrument from a higher power, heralding the beginning of the end. He offered me a chance at salvation. He said he needed you, that it had to be you, and no one else. Then, I felt his righteous sting on my neck, and my eyes were opened. That's when I knew what had to be done because I was convinced you'd save me. I stayed out of your way so you and your team could solve the case and stop Calvin, or eight people would die. How ironic that I was both right and wrong."

"Save you?" I cried. "I would've *died* for you, Jack! You should've told me. I could have helped you!"

"Told you what, that I allowed a criminal organization to use the church as a front for their business longer than you've been alive?" Jack countered harshly. "Don't be naïve, Tommy. It's insulting. I'd spent decades cultivating and growing this segment of the Brotherhood. My arrangement with Flynn provided all the resources I needed to expand our interests far beyond Little Odessa. I wasn't about to let you or anyone else destroy my life's work."

I couldn't believe what I was hearing. Every moment I stood there drove another stake into my soul.

"My God, Tommy," he whispered. "You look just like her."

I stared at him, recalling the miserable life I had shared with Pop in a house devoid of love, growing up a half-Jewish kid in Little Odessa, running with Ivan and his crew, attending the parochial school at the Holy Redeemer, and all those quiet moments drinking hot chocolate with Father Jack in the kitchen. Then, more recently, my two confrontations with Pop. His jealousy and anger, and the things he left unsaid, plain for anyone else but me to see.

And my mother at the center of it all.

Suddenly, everything fell into place, and the little boy inside of me died.

"You murdered her," I said. My mind stumbled to form the words. "You murdered my mother."

Jack didn't move.

"Why, Jack?"

The old man bowed his head.

"*Tell me why?*"

"Because I learned the truth."

I knew the answer, but I had to hear him say it. "What truth?"

He lifted his eyes to meet mine.

"That you're my son."

A cold breeze whipped around us, sending sharp, frozen spray into my face. I never blinked.

"That's why the One needed me," I whispered as the horrible realization dawned on me. "I'm your own flesh and blood. You bartered my life to save your own. You goddamn miserable sack of shit."

"Tommy, please, you have to understand," Father Jack said. "I didn't know what to do!"

"Did you love her?" I managed, lost and afraid, channeling the ten-year old boy who'd returned from school one day to learn his mother was gone.

"Tommy, as God is my witness, I did," he replied fervently. "You and Elaine were the only two who ever mattered to me. But when she told me about you...about us...I couldn't..."

I didn't need a playbill. All five acts were written on his face, a face whose resemblance to mine I'd never noticed.

Until now.

I pulled the handcuffs from the hook on my belt. "It's over, Jack. You're telling me everything. An after that, I am going to tear down the Brotherhood, brick by fucking brick. Do you understand?"

"Tommy, I know you can never forgive me," the old pastor said. "Please understand that I loved you and your mother so very much."

I didn't see him pull the gun from his coat pocket until it was too late.

"*What are thou, Faustus, but a man condemned to die,*" I whispered into the winter wind as the final gunshot echo gave way to a deep silence.

EVI put in the call for me. The world arrived a short time later to clean up the aftermath at the Holy Redeemer. I sat with Bill in the church's little kitchen deep into the evening. It was easy to fall into the cop routine, to pretend Jack's death was just another homicide. The alternative was madness, although I wondered yet again if I was already there.

ECPD's Cyber Command began their investigation into the church's network, but I knew they wouldn't find much.

Jack had been part of the *bratva* network for decades, and he hadn't been careless. Between the combined efforts of Cyber and the Organized Crime Taskforce, ECPD would be busy for months trying to uncover the Brotherhood's operations. Mahoney promised he'd take care of things at the Redeemer and ordered me to head home. I didn't argue. During the ride, I had EVI ring Rena from the Daily Dose, following up on the text I had sent to her earlier.

"Russian mobsters, human trafficking, Brave New Beginnings, and corruption in the mayor's office?" Rena asked dubiously, although her growing excitement was evident. "And you're giving the Dose the exclusive?"

"Meet me tomorrow afternoon at Mortie's Kosher Deli in Brooklyn," I said. "And keep my name out of the piece, otherwise I'll deny everything."

"Of course. Discretion is my middle name." Rena paused. "Detective, you're about to make a lot of powerful people very angry. You sure about this?"

I closed my eyes. "Just meet me at Mortie's, okay?"

"I'll see you then."

We disconnected.

I had the silver bullet drop me off a block from my shitty apartment in Dyker Heights. The temperature had plummeted well below freezing, but I didn't care. No one bothered me on my slow trudge home. It was just too damn cold.

Once inside my apartment, I waved my hand over my holo-rig. Only one holo-window appeared—a saved audio file whose message I could recite by heart. My hand trembled before it. I stared at the far wall without seeing anything until the broken holo-frame on the end table caught my eye. I flicked the audio file away, then activated my music library. Picking up the holo-frame, I unwound my shoulder rig, laid it on the table and finally settled into a lawn chair. I studied the frozen image of a pretty brunette wearing a pink dress standing next to an old man in his brown suit, and a curly-haired boy of eight years with big blue eyes sitting on a stool between them.

I drew my finger across the holo. The movement disrupted the picture. I laid it face-down on my chest and leaned my head back. The frame's warmth, accompanied by Billy Joel's masterful live piano interludes describing a street singer from a bygone age, eventually lulled me to sleep.

The insistent vibration from my phone roused me awake. Stale coffee burned my lips. My body ached in places that had no names. Scratching my cheek, I cancelled the music before checking the phone. A call from Deacon, another from Abner, and a missed call from an unlisted number. According to the call history, that number had appeared six times over the span of ten hours. I stared at the phone's display.

Eight calls in total. Pieces of fucking eight. The One had been right.

I pushed myself off the couch and shuffled to the bathroom. After twenty minutes, I was clean-shaven and dressed, although by no means refreshed. My stomach gurgled, demanding to be fed. My appetite could wait. I still had a few hours before my meeting with Rena.

I was about to call Abner when I caught a light knock on my door.

I frowned. Nobody visited me, not even my landlady. You'd think working as a cop would be incentive enough for me to buy one of those wireless video doorbells. Nope. I may be cheap, but even the dumbest person spoke SMART gun. And I'd lived at Renaissance Apartments long enough for the locals to know not to fuck with me.

Another knock. My eyes strayed to my holo-phone and the unlisted number.

Had Charlie returned to offer me some comfort after all the shit this case had put me through? And, if so, what did it mean for us? Was there even an "us"?

I stood up, grabbed my shoulder rig, and stepped toward the door.

"Keep it together, Holliday," I muttered.

I peered through the peephole but saw nothing. Hefting the gun in my left hand, I drew the door open slowly, using its flimsy mass for cover.

No one there.

I sighed and shook my head, lowered the gun, then stepped into the hallway.

Suddenly, a small bundle hurtled into me. Startled, I stared down at my attacker.

"Home," Nine whispered, hugging me tight.

THE END

EPILOGUE

Alan Arthur Azyrim brooded in silence. His amber eye glinted dangerously, while the blue stared ahead, lost to introspection. Beyond the tinted window of his limousine, Morris Plains whipped past in a drab, muddy cloud. Light, airy music permeated the vehicle's interior cabin, some drippy romantic nod whose simple melody aggravated the rigid tension that had already set into Azyrim's posture.

"Is it done?" he asked, the question trembling with layers of meaning and intent.

Shadows danced around the figure seated across from him, twisting and bending the light so that its identity remained obscured. But Azyrim knew what lay beneath. He knew its true name, and from that knowledge came his power over it.

"It is done," the figure answered in an emasculated yet seductive voice. "Calvin Flynn is dead. Kal Arach languishes in the Void once more. And I have provided Truthseeker with the information you sought. My Lord, the calculations are complex. However, another Path is closed, and with it, one fewer piece on the Board."

Azyrim frowned. His blue eye regained focus to regard the figure. "Explain."

"How is it that Kal Arach was drawn to this boy?" it wheedled in plaintive tones, desperate to please its master. "Trapped beyond the material realm, the Spider was powerless. It was no accident the One chose Calvin Flynn. He was used as bait, to draw the Spider here. Surely not by your hand, my Lord, for Kal Arach was ever opposed to your will. I can only conclude your sister desired it and devised a means to connect the boy to the One for some fell purpose that I have yet to uncover."

Azyrim steepled his well-manicured fingers together across his broad nose.

"She gathers allies to her cause," he mused.

"How fortuitous, then, that the Guardian appeared," the figure answered slyly. A golden glint, like a firefly's light, sparkled once within the deep folds of the shadows enshrouding it. "At great personal cost to himself, he thwarted the Bargain and saved this world while protecting your plans from being laid waste."

Some external force tugged at Azyrim. He swatted the temptation aside, annoyed at the intrusion.

"You dare to curry my sympathy for the Guardian?" He turned the hungry glare of his amber eye on the figure. The shadows that surrounded it flinched in response before reasserting themselves.

"My Lord, I meant no disrespect," it said. "I merely wished to convey the Guardian fractures. His attention is scattered. He is no threat. He and his Sight are but pawns to be toyed with at your pleasure."

"As are all things," Azyrim agreed. "Yet, so long as Hope

and Harmony exist, the Guardian is protected."

"My Lord, if I may be so bold," the shadow offered. "Why not eradicate them, and free yourself of their troubling influence?"

The handsome man smirked.

"Because it amuses me to watch their desperate struggle," he said. "A prize is not worth winning without overcoming the challenges that are set before it."

"You are wise of course, my Lord."

Azyrim settled himself into his seat, his posture now relaxed.

"I have no more use of you." He waved a languid hand at the figure. "Return to wherever it is you dwell and await my summons."

"As you desire, my Lord."

The figure melted into the black leather seat and was gone.

Azyrim closed his eyes, allowing his mind to wander. The failure of Blakely's clones still rankled. Vanessa Mallery's stolen blood had lost its efficacy. Without Blakely's notes or the missing enzyme, any chance of replicating a body strong enough to withstand the transfer was remote. If Fatima, or Orpheus, or whatever she chose to call herself now sought allies, then her plight was as desperate as his own.

However, he had not been idle since Blakely's death. The Guardian's appearance merely complicated matters, but his plans would proceed despite Holliday's interference. Even now, the device was being assembled, and once complete, it would split the heavens to bring him what he wanted.

No, what he needed.

"The Guardian put Despair to rest," a silken voice purred. "The ruby is no more."

"Indeed," Azyrim responded without opening his eyes. "Holliday did not appear formidable, merely a mortal man who clings to a purpose he does not fully comprehend. I had hoped he would perish in his attempt to save the boy. Alas, that was not to be. I will not underestimate the Guardian or his companions again."

"And the Daughter of Night?" asked the voice.

"What of her?" Azyrim scoffed. "Yet another wrinkle to the Game."

"She holds no love for you."

"Of that, there is little doubt," he chuckled without mirth. "Most children often seek to overthrow their parents, do they not?"

"Or surpass them."

Azyrim frowned, then gave a slight nod, grudgingly conceding the point.

"And so now she stands with the Guardian?" the voice asked.

"That remains to be seen," Azyrim replied. "She protected Holliday from Blakely's creations, my synthetic, and the One, to be sure, and for reasons that are unclear. However, she has not revealed herself in full. It is likely she cannot. Regardless, it is no concern of mine."

There was a pause. Azyrim was content not to fill the silence.

"Be that as it may," the voice spoke after a moment. "I dispatched someone to remove her from the Board."

"And?"

"She failed."

Azyrim opened his eyes. He was alone. The soft scent of freshly cut roses filled his nostrils before fading like the evening tide.

"Well, then, sweet sister, how unfortunate for us both."

SAVE AN AUTHOR, WRITE A REVIEW

Now that you've finished PIECES OF EIGHT, what's next?

How about leaving a rating and/or write a review?

Independent authors like me live and die through aggregated Amazon and Goodreads ratings and reviews. The more we get, the greater the chance other readers looking for the right blend of science fiction, urban fantasy and crime thriller will find stories like PIECES OF EIGHT.

You, fearless reader, wield great power! And with great power...well, you know the rest. By leaving a rating or a review, you directly influence the story's exposure worldwide.

So what are you waiting for?

Thank you so much for taking the time to read and review my work!

(Kindle and Paperback) Amazon US: mybook.to/PiecesOfEight

(Kindle and Paperback) Amazon UK: mybook.to/PiecesOfEightUK

Goodreads: https://www.goodreads.com/author/show/18373280.Peter_Hartog

ACKNOWLEDGMENTS

No matter what anyone says, writing a sequel is just as hard, if not harder, than the debut. But none of it gets done without a massive amount of support from family, friends, co-workers, rabbis, and the occasional moments when you stare off into the horizon and ask yourself the BIG question: *Can I even do it?*

Sure you can. You just click your heels together three times and say, "There's no place like a sequel."

The truth is, this book wouldn't be possible without the incredible contributions from Christopher, Michelle, Wendy, Sean and Scott. You five make me a better writer, because you've always pushed my imagination further than it has ever gone. But, more importantly, you five make me a better person.

Thanks again to Lance Buckley Designs for capturing the essence of this story with the gorgeous and evocative cover art.

Thanks to Blake, whose helpful insights into Alabama idioms and the local lingo shaped Deacon's colorful dialogue far better than I could've done on my own.

So many thanks go to my dear friend Reverend Scott for your knowledge and friendship.

Thanks to Rabbi Alex, for your wisdom and willingness to help a poor soul of a writer out of a revenge-filled jam.

To my beta readers Lexi, Leigh, Abi, Arlen, Traci and Michelle, thank you for your critical feedback, without which this book would be sorely lacking.

Always extra thanks go to Traci and my two dudes. You are my three reasons for everything I do. I am nothing without you three by my side.

And to my dad, my one-man marketing army, and one of my greatest cheerleaders, thank you for being there for me, patiently listening to me babble every Sunday after football about my so-called writing career. Writing is a lonely business, but knowing you're in my corner, and have been from the get-go, is what family is all about.

ABOUT THE AUTHOR

A native son of Massachusetts, Peter has been living in the Deep South for over 25 years. By day, he's an insurance professional, saving the world one policy at a time. But at night, well, no one really wants to see him fighting crime in his Spider-Man onesie. Instead, Peter develops new worlds of adventure, influenced by his love for science fiction, mysteries, music and fantasy. Whether it's running role-playing games for his long-time friends, watching his beloved New England sporting teams, or just chilling with a movie, his wife, two boys, one puppy and three cats, Peter's imagination is always on the move. It's the reason why his stories are an eclectic blend of intrigue, excitement, humor and magic, all drawn from four decade's worth of television, film, novels, and comic books. You can learn more about Peter and his writing projects at peterhartog.com.

ALSO BY PETER HARTOG

Bloodlines

Printed in Great Britain
by Amazon